NOW SHOWING

Enough chatter now.

The lights are dimming.

The advertisements and slides are over.

The first credits are rolling.

Shhh.

Ron Elliott is a scriptwriter, director and academic, and author of the novel *Spinner*. His directorial credits include the feature film *Justice*, and episodes of ABC programs such as *Dancing Daze*, *Relative Merits* and *Studio 86*. Ron has written for *Home and Away*, *Minty*, *Wild Kat*, *Ship to Shore* and many more children's television series. In 2001 he wrote the AFI-nominated telemovie *Southern Cross*. Ron is currently a lecturer in Film and Television at Curtin University, Western Australia.

NOW SHOWING

BY

Ron Elliott

FREMANTLE PRESS
fine independent publishing

Special thanks (in order of appearance):

Ross Hutchens

Sue Taylor

CONTENTS

Norma Desmond: *You're a writer, you said.*

Joe Gillis: *Why?*

Norma Desmond: *Are you or aren't you?*

Joe Gillis: *That's what it says on my Guild card.*

Norma Desmond: *And you have written pictures, haven't you?*

Joe Gillis: *I sure have. Want a list of my credits?*

Norma Desmond: *I want to ask you something. Come in here.*

Joe Gillis: *Last one I wrote was about Okies in the Dust Bowl. You'd never know because when it reached the screen, the whole thing played on a torpedo boat.*

– *Sunset Blvd.*, Gloria Swanson and William Holden

INTRODUCTION – ADAPTING BACKWARDS

If you are reading this 'introduction' before the stories of *Now Showing,* as you have every right to do, then you are not like me. Me, I usually skip the introduction. I want to enter the work fairly untainted and unprimed, as much as anyone can. I want to let the story speak for itself. And mostly it does. However, occasionally, I have gone back to the introduction searching for some kind of clarification, context or justification. That is what this introduction is. I'm going to try to tell you 'how to read these stories'. As I've just said, this is not something I usually tolerate as a reader. So, let me extenuate ...

I believe these stories do not easily fit within the usual definition of the short story. While there are many forms to the short story and novella and they continue to be redefined, the pieces in this collection don't quite fit that mould. Something's not right. So, like a bite into that chicken and salad sandwich you bought from the Jiffy van, it might be timely to peel back the bread and sniff the meat. These stories don't taste entirely like short stories. They taste a little like films.

I have been writing original screenplays for the last twenty years, with the creative and financial support of producers, broadcasters and government screen agencies. These scripts have been rewritten, as markets and funding and ideas were sought in a process called 'development' in which 'drafts' are commissioned or requested. Some came very close to being made into films. *By the Light* was a television concept pipped at the post in 1998 by another new series called *Seachange.* On the other hand *Southern Cross* (adapted from the 1988 series *A Waltz through the Hills*) was made into a telemovie which was nominated for a Logie and an AFI award.

Some time after returning to Perth from the ABC in Sydney I began playing with an idea for a mini-series with the working title *Wonder Kid*, about a young orphan who was taken by his dodgy uncle to play cricket for Australia in the late 1920s. The view at the time was that it was too expensive for television and the mini-series was in one of its declines, so I put the project aside. I was busy writing a lot of episodes of television, mostly dramas for kids and directing a variety of film and television including the feature film *Justice*.

Around 2000, I looked again at the *Wonder Kid* material and started to turn it into a story called *Spinner*. *Spinner* was never written as a script. It was written as a novel and was published in 2010 by Fremantle Press.

Feedback for *Spinner* got me thinking about some of the scripts I had developed but which had not been made into films. I wondered if I might be able to turn some of my unproduced scripts into short stories or novellas. They were good stories with strong characters and I thought people might be interested in these short escapist dramas as read entertainments, especially given the suggested resurgent interest by readers in the short story form.

There are many elements of storytelling common to the short story, the novel and the film, which include notions of character, place and narrative. Even such seemingly film-specific notions as the close-up and editing rhythms can be created in prose.

The adaptation of prose fiction – both short stories and novels – into feature films has occurred since movies began. The baggage now associated with 'adaptation' is fraught and complex within academe, but often fruitful for the reader and film-goer as interesting sparks for note and discussion. There have been occasions of adaptation in the other direction, from film to prose, but they are rare and not many spring to mind. Apparently Graham Greene simultaneously wrote the script and the novel of *The Third Man*. Arthur C. Clarke did the same with *2001: A Space Odyssey*, although the scripting process was with Stanley Kubrick, based on the Clarke short story 'The Sentinel'.

And so I embarked with a simple general question. Could I create a collection of short stories based on my film scripts that would be akin to other collections of short stories? The answer, at the conclusion of the writing, is no. Well, yes and no.

Here are some of the things I have found. (In order to be concise, I will generalise often. Film, like other storytelling, has many conventions which are used or subverted.)

Structure. While there are a variety of structures that have been used around the world in writing screenplays, the dominant storytelling structure in Hollywood and Australia is the restorative three-act structure. Script readers and the film-going audience are attuned to this structure, which provides drive, character goals and turning points and a foreseeable conclusion within a ninety-minute to two-hour time frame.

Most of the stories in this collection were conceived and written with this film structure as the template. In structural terms 'Small Claims' has been most transformed by becoming a two-act structure, while the structure of 'Double or Nothing' has been most relaxed. I found that the turning points – absolutely crucial in feature films – could be made more subtle in the stories, even done away with in some cases. However, I discovered that trying to remove the structure of the stories, created as they were in this other form, was akin to removing the skeleton of a creature and then attempting to reinsert a different skeleton. An interesting exercise, but the poor critter was far from comfortable.

Scenes. Generally, film is constructed of many short scenes which accumulate. A good scene has a beginning, middle and end and propels the story into the next scene. While there are many prose works which use very short 'scenes' to build meaning and effect, I found intercutting or crosscutting short scenes to be less effective in the prose story writing. Staying with a character for longer rather than cutting away to another story builds tension. This may be true of all storytelling of course, but I suspect film is more amenable to crosscutting.

Immediacy. Film occurs in time and space, and unfolds before our eyes. Reflecting this notion of immediacy, film scripts are written in the present tense. Even when films are framed as something that happened once, such as in *Titanic*, the ago becomes the present and we are caught up in the moment-to-moment action. Momentum and pace are important (even within quieter films). A convention of scriptwriting is that the reading of the film script should feel like watching the finished film. Film scripts attempt to achieve one minute per page and attempt to keep the story moving. There are fewer departures than in prose. The writing is intentionally sparse, evocative, but almost terse in the descriptions. Film telling has strict economy, but often evokes rather than explores. I have consciously tried to keep things moving in these stories.

Point of view. The screenplay is a multipurpose document designed to be used by a variety of people to complete another, finished work. The script tells the story, but in a form that privileges who says what, much like a play. It is dramatic rather than reflective. It briefly notes where things occur and when, but also gives notes to various characters/actors and the director about what characters might be thinking. This is sometimes frowned upon, but a brief statement of intention or the pithy fragment of backstory can aid mood or motivation. The script thus flicks very naturally from a variety of points of view within the scene, sometimes line by line. It can address the art department, then cinematographer and always the actors, but obliquely. The diverse readership of the 'blueprint' is of course made up of creative professionals who don't like being told how to do their jobs, so screenwriters must suggest, allude and inspire.

Enter the director. The screenwriter knows that the director and cast and the crew will interpret the script. There is significant leeway to do as they will beyond interpretation. However, the writer also knows that each actor will make judgements about their character based on details beyond the dialogue and that each and every character must be provided with enough inner world to fulfil their life within each scene. The screenwriter also knows that the director will choose the moment-to-moment point of view from which to 'show' the audience the action. This is done through our attachment to character (whose story is this?) but also by staging, and is defined by where the director sets the camera. This point of view is further manipulated and refined during the editing process.

And yet, while film often sees what a character sees, it rarely sees into a character's mind, which prose often does. We only know what a character is thinking if she tells another character or, less satisfactorily, her cat. (Voice-over is another very interesting can of worms, but for now can I say, when it is used in modern films it is as unreliable as any human speech.) Film tells us through action. We are shown more and told less. Thus most films appear to adopt a third person objective point of view, but usually focus on a couple of individuals. Yet films will also show first person moments through 'the point of view shot', seeing what a character sees. Film does this through editing and convention. Film shifts the point of view every time there is an edit and every time we cut to a new shot or camera position.

A clear example occurs within the railway sequence in *The Bourne Ultimatum*. We set up the railway station, a variety of specific rooms, an overpass, an operations room and thus the general geography of the station, many of these shots seeming to be 'neutral' third person objective perspectives. Yet, in this sequence, we concentrate on three main characters, being Bourne, the journalist he's trying to contact, then save, and the chief official in charge of stopping the information transfer. There are various operatives whose point of view we momentarily share as they surveille and chase. Then we also follow an assassin as he enters the place and sets up a sniper vantage point. All within a crowded railway station full of, for the most part, oblivious commuters. Perhaps I'm merely pointing out the obvious. The audience need only see a wide shot of a place, then a close-up of a person before we can then slide within that point of view. We know who is seeing, but also seem to be able to juggle this variety of points of view most rapidly.

In the wonderful film adaption of *Atonement*, we spend some time moving from Briony's view of a wasp trapped at her window before she notices (and misinterprets) the actions down at the fountain. There is an earlier point of view transition that is less self-conscious. Briony and Cecilia are lying on the grass as Robbie pushes a wheelbarrow nearby. We simply cut to Robbie and he now takes our – the camera's – attention. Later Cecilia dives into the lake and we cut to Robbie in his bath. We switch to Robbie's point of view, but the water helps create the idea that they are thinking of each other. *Atonement*, of course, is about mistakes based on point of view. It needs to be quite strict, therefore, in showing who sees and when.

On the other hand, we might think about Martin Scorsese's visual creations in *Taxi Driver* and in *Raging Bull*. In both films the point of view shifts, seeming to adopt a third person stance, but becoming subjective without clear signal. The edges of point of view are blurred and we become implicated within a character's emotional world. Jane Campion also plays with point of view and subjectivity in *In the Cut*, jumping in and out of Frannie's view and constantly blurring the audience perception. I think it is interesting that the novel on which *In the Cut* was based was written in the first person and we are given an unreliable witness.

Choosing and exploring narrower points of view within these stories as they became prose has been one of the most challenging adjustments. Issues such as *who sees* also become *who tells* and *who knows*. The specific choices concerning which scenes and moments should be seen by which character have led to significant changes in the writing of these stories. 'Small Claims' was not Zac's first person point of view in the screenplay. 'Double or Nothing' evolved into one thousand and one nights where *who is being told the story* is as important as the storytelling.

At the same time, I wanted to preserve the inscrutability of some of my characters, much like characters in film. I think Simon in 'The Ring-In' derives some of his power through the reader not knowing. 'For the Birds' is possibly the closest to a third person stance with multiple characters and intersecting stories that nonetheless retains the sense of a third entity, observing if not telling. 'The Ring-In' and 'Random Malice' are more traditional in their telling perhaps as a consequence of their stronger genre ties.

Ultimately, point of view in prose, just as in film, is a strategy of storytelling and not a rule. As a writer, judgements are made leading to consequent discoveries. Point of view can and does shift within a paragraph in prose. But we need to be clear. There is always a frame through which we perceive the story and the frame needn't be the actual frame of the film camera or cinema screen.

Genre. None of these stories would be described as realism, much less social realism. They do not seek to change the world, though perhaps capture some of its realities. An awareness of the noir genre should enhance the reading of 'The Ring-In'. 'For the Birds' is romantic farce with a mix of social satire. 'Random Malice' is a thriller. 'Double or Nothing' is comedy heist. Unlike the other stories, it was originally conceived as the pilot for a TV series, rather than a feature film. 'Small Claims' is a road movie, but a pretty typical Oz subgenre which includes a journey into the past. It's also a love story.

After adapting these stories – adapting backwards – my conclusion is that they do indeed feel like longish short stories, but strange ones because there are so many residues of the kind of stories they once were and the thing they sought to become.

And so, these stories are movies. They are not even art films. They are entertainments. Just as when we take a couple of hours out to see a film and become distracted from our busier, more worthwhile lives, I hope these stories amuse, enthral and excite in equal measure. I hope they are like reading a movie in structure and in pace, but one created from words. That is my intention.

If you don't like movies, I'm not sure you will like these stories. And if you are the kind of person who does not like films, then hopefully you're the kind of person who reads the introduction first. It doesn't taste like chicken because it's pepperoni.

But enough chatter now. The lights are dimming. The advertisements and slides are over. The first credits are rolling. Shhh. Hope you've brought some popcorn.

SMALL CLAIMS

Forgive quickly, kiss slowly
Love truly, laugh uncontrollably
And never regret anything that makes you smile.
– James Dean (… and others)

It was after midnight and we were on our way home when there was a loud bang like a rifle shot. The car veered left and I hit the brakes. It jerked further left across the breakdown lane and into the cement freeway dividing wall. The car moaned and shuddered then stopped.

I looked over at Robin and said, 'That was fun. Wanna do it again?'

She didn't smile.

I got out and wandered around to the front left wheel. The tyre was shredded. It had been bald for a while, the accident waiting to happen finally had.

Robin looked out the open passenger window, at the twisted fender then up to me, faintly accusing but also just a little bored. 'Have we got any cigarettes?' she said.

'They're in your bag.'

I went to the boot and kicked it in the right spot which made it pop. I could see Robin in the front, head bent, rummaging. She found the cigarettes and lit one, blowing a long grey breath out the passenger window.

I rummaged too. There was a stained windcheater in the boot and some basketball boots and a lot of spoiling comic books and graphic novels that I had meant to find a good home for.

I waited for a car to go past then went back to the driver's window.

Robin said, 'No spare.'

'I got a spare. What makes you think I haven't got a spare?'

Silence. She knew.

'I haven't got a jack,' I said. I smiled and raised my eyebrows in a way I know cracks people up.

Not Robin, not tonight. She turned away from me and opened her door, thudding it on the cement retaining wall. She banged it again and one more time but the concrete wouldn't move.

'Want to have a picnic?' I said.

She pushed across the bench seat and out my door.

'I'll call Greg,' I said.

She got her handbag and got out the packet of Winnie Blues and pushed them into my hands. I looked at the packet and up to her, but she was walking away.

'Robin?'

'See you at home,' she yelled.

'Robin!'

She stuck out her thumb and a black BMW appeared out of nowhere, cut across three lanes and she got in.

I probably should have taken down the registration – popped it in my phone so if he was a deranged killer, the police could have traced him. I thought this as the car's rear lights turned into a spot of red and disappeared. I suppose I'm not such a good man to have in a crisis. Maybe I'm just not such a good man to have.

*

My car, a Valiant Regal, wagged its tail behind, its front wheels hitched up on Greg's tow truck as we drove through the burbs. I had my feet up on his dashboard, looking out the big windscreen. Greg is one of my Slav mates from way back before kindergarten even.

'I don't believe you haven't got a jack,' he said for about the tenth time. 'Everybody's got a jack.'

'You don't.'

'Oh I got a jack, Zac. I got the biggest jack in the world.' He pointed out the cab's back window.

'That's not what the girls say.'

Greg laughed, then said, 'Get stuffed,' then asked, 'Where's Robin?'

'At home.'

'She okay?'

'You ever see *The Misfits*? Old black and white movie. Marilyn Monroe. Clark Gable drives this pickup truck. Bit like yours I reckon.'

'You tell me every second time you get in. You know, they have made movies in colour.'

'Really? I bet they never catch on. Turn down that street.'

'Here?'

'Turn down here.'

'This isn't the way to your place.'

'No, a detour. You'll like it.'

Greg reluctantly turned down past Perry Lakes and back towards the ocean. I looked through his CD collection in the glove box. It was mostly Heavy Metal with a sprinkling of Death Metal.

'You know it's after three a.m.?' he said.

When we got to the padlocked gate at the end of the no through road, he said, 'What's this?'

But you could see what it was in the truck's headlights. It was a long-abandoned drive-in. There were the speaker-less cradles and tufts of yellow dead weeds that had come up through the broken waves of bitumen.

Greg threw the tow truck into neutral, but left the motor running. He looked around behind him making sure he could back somewhere before he relaxed.

I took out my plastic sandwich bag and started to roll us a joint.

'They closed this one down about twenty years ago. Before we were born, I reckon. Just left it.'

'To spite you. Land must be worth a bomb,' he said.

'Rob and I used to come here all the time. And I'd tell her a movie. She'd say a title, and I'd do it. You know, like in *Eternal Sunshine of the Spotless Mind*.'

'I haven't seen it.'

'It's in colour. By the guy who did the Smirnoff ad. Gondry. He does clips.'

'Which clips?'

I couldn't think of any. 'He slows stuff down and speeds it up in the same shot, like they do in *The Matrix*. Calls it bullet time.' I lit the joint and took a hit. Passed it to Greg. 'Put your high beam on.'

'What?'

'Put on your high beam.'

Greg switched to high beam. The light hit the white screen in the distance. A large sheet had come away, leaving a corner of black, but the rest of the screen was mostly intact, like it was hanging in the sky.

'See,' I said.

'Does this mean we're going steady?'

I got out of the cab. The air was cold and brittle and burnt my lungs with each breath. I looked at the screen in time to see it disappear as Greg dipped his lights again. I went round the front through the headlights watching half my shadow on the ground and the other half climbing up on the mesh of the gate. I went to Greg's window and took the joint.

Greg was watching me, waiting, patient.

'She can be quiet. You know. Sometimes, she's really quiet. Inside herself.'

'Ah,' said Greg. I gave him the joint.

'Other times you can't shut her up.'

'Yeah?'

'No, in the middle of the night, once she gets going. Lately ... It's just that lately – people get grumpy, you know. Normal, happy, together people sometimes get the shits, and it's okay. After a while. I mean, in the morning it's all okay again.'

'Sure,' said Greg.

I stood looking at the Valiant, red in the tow truck brakelights, hanging up like a caught fish. 'We don't need a jack.'

Greg didn't even look back. 'No.'

'It's already up. We can change the tyre, now.'

'Yep. Or back on the freeway.'

He's a good man, Greg.

'So how can you tell? When someone – when it starts to turn into something else, something bad? If no one says and it happens slowly, how do you know?'

Greg shook his head, looking at the decayed drive-in.

*

I stood in the doorway of our bedroom for a while until I could make out Robin in the bed. Then I turned the light on. She rolled onto her stomach.

'Greg came.'

She didn't say anything.

I stepped past her jeans and top and her small piles of dresses and underwear and went to the wardrobe and hung up my jacket. I looked at my rifle leaning against the back of the cupboard.

'We went to the old drive-in.'

Nothing.

The room smelt mouldy. It was a damp old house with creaking floorboards, especially upstairs.

'Haven't been there for a while.'

She didn't move.

I went back to the door and turned the light out and stood in the doorway again, waiting for my eyes to adjust to the light from her clock radio. The bed glowed green.

I took off my boots and then my shirt.

'Rob?'

No answer.

'Are we finished?'

She might have been asleep.

*

Robin wasn't in bed when I woke up. She sometimes wasn't, if she had an early lecture. I never started at the restaurant until just before lunchtime. I found her downstairs, arguing on her mobile.

'All I'm saying is, I don't remember reading it. I can't remember what it said. Okay?' She started to listen, her jaw grinding. She saw me watching her and turned to the wall.

I put the kettle on and tipped the coffee grounds down the sink.

She walked across to the other side of the kitchen, keeping her back to me. 'Oh well, if Terry said Jack said. Why would it be sent to me anyway? I'm not even in Kalgoorlie.'

Robin listened again. Then she staggered slightly like the bus setting off when she wasn't ready. She said, 'But, why would she do that? What possible reason? Look, Gail, this isn't getting us anywhere. You and Liz are there. I don't need to be dragged into it. Tell Jack to give you another invoice, for Christ's sake.'

I moved some wine bottles out of my way and got a bowl of muesli.

'Gail, I'll look. I know you don't ask much. I know I missed it. I'll look. I told you I'll look. Tell Terry, I'll look. Tell Liz. Tell Jack. Okay. I'll look. Byeeee.'

'Your sister?'

Robin grabbed her knapsack and started stuffing in the books that were on the table. 'What? Oh, some stupid invoice was sent here by mistake, and now the guy's hassling them about the bill, and they don't believe Jack, and Jack – stupid Kalgoorlie stuff. Kal-flamin'-goorlie.' Robin gave up trying to stuff a big dentistry book in with the rest, and pushed it up into her armpit.

'What was the bill for?'

'What?' She looked at me as though I'd insulted her.

'I can have a look for it. Before work.'

'It's got nothing to do with you,' she shouted.

I didn't say anything; didn't even know where to start.

She was already heading out of the kitchen, but she stopped. She came back a step and said, 'It's not lost. It's probably in a pair of jeans. I'll find it later. I'm late.' Tight smile, half a shrug. Gone.

The kettle whistled like a scream. It wasn't really like a scream, but it was shrill and I felt like screaming.

I started to clean up the kitchen. There were a lot of wine bottles on the table all with a bit of wine in them: booty/looty from the restaurants. I always took about six home and made a bit of a red blend. The white went in the fridge with the doggy bags. Free booze if you like average wine and free food if you like Mexican. The lunch restaurant has better, but with fewer leftovers.

Our house is old. The rent is cheap because they're going to bulldoze it anytime and build upmarket apartments like all the others around us. The kitchen is small and dark with hot and cold running cockroaches and those flat striped whistling crickets. There's a big casserole pot that is a Robin heirloom that we never use up on top of the cupboard which I suspect may be the cockroach condominium. There's nothing worse than seeing them pop out behind one of the movie posters we have up on the walls: *A Streetcar Named Desire*. Marlon Brando, Vivien Leigh and cockroach. Paul Newman IS *Hud*. Winner of three cockroaches. We could stick up a *WALL-E* poster and then it wouldn't matter.

I put the empty wine bottles in a crate next to the bin which is under our noticeboard. There are bills and Robin's class timetable and postcards and birthday cards with movie themes, but mostly there are photos people have printed off their mobiles. Lots of me at the restaurants. I do Scarlottas for lunch and Gringos for dinner. There's me at other restaurants I've worked at, but I'm happy with Scarlottas and

Gringos. Fun management, not hard arses. And tipping customers, of course. Me in a sombrero is a theme. I look a little bit like James Dean. Hey, I never said that. Other people say it. So lots of the cards are of James Dean. In the rain. With that puppet. In a cowboy hat.

Robin looks more like Audrey Tautou, but not in *Amélie*. All her other films, especially *Dirty Pretty Things*. It's the dark hair and the dark eyes. Her eyes are sometimes wary but every now and again in a photo, you can see them alight and burning. Most of the photos don't catch that. She pulls it back and smiles politely. It can make her look guarded.

Our whole history is up on the noticeboard. A photo of us in Margaret River. One of us at the top of Bluff Knoll. Us camping in Pemberton. Us camping in Kalbarri. Rotto. Lots in Rotto. She looks very good in a bikini. She looks good in a coat too, all black clothing and layers and the eyes. Someone even snapped a shot early on the night we met. She's with laughing girlfriends and I'm in the background carrying plates. It was a night they were going to forget men, and then they played a game of who could bag the cute waiter.

*

Later, when I was at Scarlottas, she texted me. *Going to Kal.*

I phoned her, but she wouldn't pick up.

I texted her: *What the?*

She texted: *Saturday.*

I texted: *Me too?*

No.

What the?

Then nothing. I tried to phone. She wouldn't pick up. I sent :(

She turned her mobile off.

I broke some plates. I yelled at Carlo, the chef, which is never a good idea. I broke a glass. They sent me home but I didn't want to go there.

*

Instead, I went to the movies and saw a shit rom-com which was perfect because it gave me the chance to think.

I drove to Greg's workshop and explained the car part of my plan. His workshop was dark inside and smelt of many kinds of car oil.

The acetylene hissed nicely, the oxygen adding a deeper rush. Greg had set the dials. He stood back and watched as I clicked the flint and set the big lazy yellow flame. More oxygen and the flame got pointed coming back to a tighter bluer thing with no soot.

'Behold, the neutral flame,' I said looking out at him through the dark safety glasses.

'Don't blow the place up,' said Greg.

'Oxygen off. Gas off. At the tanks. No smoking. Key in the Coke can when I leave.'

He opened the corrugated metal door that was cut into the roller. Sunlight washed in around him making him disappear in the burst of white for a moment, until he came back in as a phantomy silhouette. The Greg silhouette pointed at my car, which waited in the centre of the workshop.

'For a start, the chassis will probably fall in on itself. B – water will get into the panelling. And three – it's so rusted out to begin with, the roof's probably the only thing holding it together.'

I tried a horror voice as I went towards the car. 'That's what they said to Doctor Frankenstein *and* Furter. That's what they said to Tim Burton. *And* James Cameron, three times. Tonight, I make history!' I tried a maniacal laugh. It sounded good in the tin shed.

I punched Greg's boom box where I'd put a Coldplay CD. *Parachutes*.

My car is a 1969 Falcon Valiant Regal VF. It is a very dull green. I like that it's a car that is double my age. I like that it is battered enough for me not to worry about it in the city at night. I love the bench seat in the front and the two strip lights on either side of the hood. The new dent and scrape from the freeway add perhaps too much character, but that can be up for discussion.

I put the flame against the back strut until it glowed red, then hit the cutting lever. The paint flamed with thick black smoke as the metal sliced and melted and stank. Sparks poured out, scattering inside the car and dying on the workshop floor.

I flicked off one of the heavy gloves and got a smoke and held it into the tip of the flame. At one point the rear window exploded when it got too hot. After that I wound down the front windows before cutting through the other struts. A thousand pieces of broken glass reflected the blues and whites of the flame. I was careful around the front windscreen, cutting back about five or six centimetres into the roof. I crawled inside and teased out the ceiling light and wiring before I took the roof off completely.

Coldplay was the soundtrack as I worked. It had seemed perfect for how I felt. All those break-up songs. Sad bastard. But some pretty neat song titles too. 'Sparks'. 'Yellow'. 'High Speed'. I thrashed the one album all afternoon and evening as I cut up my car. The last song on the album is 'Everything's Not Lost'.

*

I turned on the bedroom light and went to the wardrobe and started stuffing clothes into my pack.

Robin sat up in bed. 'What are you doing?'

'Get up. Get dressed.'

I grabbed our sleeping bags and my pack and the rifle.

'What's happening?'

'Oh, and grab a jumper. It's colder than you think.'

I had a box of stuff ready on the kitchen table and I'd piled more stuff on the path ready to put in the boot. Food and toilet paper and two flagons of wine.

She came down the stairs in a jumper and skirt. 'It's two a.m.'

I grabbed a CD I'd chosen and raced out the front door so I could be ready when she came out. I jumped onto the back seat and over into the front and put the CD in the car stereo. I unlatched the passenger door, put on my Wayfarers and lounged back. That's how she found me, in my convertible.

She laughed, short but right. 'It's good,' she said. 'It's very, very good.'

The cutting was rough and there were bits of glass still on the back seat, but it did look like the real thing, not so much convertible as roofless.

I kicked my foot out so her door swung open towards her. 'Your pumpkin awaits.'

'Where's the ball?'

'Kal. Kal-flamin'-goorlie.'

She got it. She nodded. Then she looked doubtfully at the pile of provisions.

'Camping,' I said.

She kicked at the rifle.

I tried a southern accent, 'An' a huntin' an' a fishin'.'

'Yeah, well good luck with fishing. You know it's in the middle of the desert, right?' She was smiling.

I pushed the play on the car CD to clinch it. Bo Diddley's 'Tonight is Ours'. It wasn't one of his pared back blues numbers. It was lush, romantic and nostalgic. He had back-up singers. A crowd.

She was still smiling but started to shake her head. 'Tomorrow.'

With Robin, you can never tell which way she might go. 'You're not listening to the song.' I pushed my sunglasses up and worked my eyebrows, letting the car and Bo Diddley do the work.

'Okay,' she said.

'All right!'

'I'll get the invoice. That's the whole ... ' She finished the sentence with a shrug and went back inside the house.

I put the stuff in the boot and we drove out of town.

Robin didn't say anything until we stopped at some traffic lights in Midland. It is surprisingly hard to talk when the wind is ripping around you. She lit a cigarette and let the smoke trail out and put it in my mouth and said, '*Badlands* or *Thelma & Louise*?'

'*Badlands*? I never thought of *Badlands*. That's good. I was thinking *Something Wild*.'

Robin smiled, but then looked doubtful. She said, 'Am I the boring guy in need of the makeover or the psycho jealous ex-husband?'

Before I could answer, a Lancer pulled up next to us with three or four revheads leering out at my wheels. The driver gunned his motor.

I took my foot off the brake and touched the accelerator and eased off slowly through the red light, leaving them frozen at the line.

'Fresh air. Unobstructed view. The wind in our hair. An open road ahead,' I said. 'God, I love this country.'

'Which country?' she said, taking the cigarette out of my mouth.

Then she looked forward and yelled into the night, 'We're on a mission from God.'

'Which god?' I yelled back.

It was hard to hear Bo, even with the volume cranked up. I like the end of this one where he gets the crowd to yell back 'Have mercy' and 'Amen' while the guitar and drums go slower and slower, like it is late and couples are swaying on the dance floor without moving their feet in the 1950s or dancing in the church, maybe, and the band is going to keep playing.

*

It was a long drive. Longer in the night. Longer when your old car won't do more than eighty. I drove along with the silver pipeline that takes the water from Perth to Kalgoorlie. Sometimes it was on the left, then on the right. Sometimes it was way off on top of a paddock, then gone, then right up next to the car. Robin slept, curled up like a kitten on the seat out of the wind. I had a joint. At Southern Cross, the farms suddenly ran out and became scrub. I drank some wine. The pipeline crossed under the road. The petrol was getting low. The air was freezing as it scrambled around my throat.

The sky finally started to get lighter ahead as we came near Coolgardie, thirty K short of Kalgoorlie. Robin woke as both our mobiles chimed into range. She tapped me on the shoulder and pointed off to the side of the highway to the cemetery.

The earth was red. Red sand on red gravel on red rock with the occasional wink of white quartz. The scrubby gum trees were white like the stone of the graves. Plastic flowers. Ants. It looked like an abandoned cemetery, like it was halfway through being blown away.

The Valiant was the only car in the parking area and we were the only people in the cemetery.

The headstone said: *Rest in Eternal Peace. Wife of Bill. Loved mother of Robin, Elizabeth, Gail.*

Robin had the invoice out. She waved it at the grave. 'Well, old Jack does have a point,' she said brightly. 'One gravestone, delivered as ordered. No wriggling out of that. You pay your money, you can say what you want. Kind of difficult for old Jack to repossess the thing if we don't sort this out, mind you.'

There were real flowers, two limp bunches.

Robin must have seen me look at them because she said, 'The flowers would be Gail and Liz. Drive down from Kal to do the right thing. Busy, busy, busy. Two perfect girls.'

When I looked at her, she looked away. I said, 'You had an exam on and no money. How could you have got up? Remember, we ...'

'What are you talking about?'

'What I mean is that if you were feeling –'

'Feeling what? What "should" I have been feeling?'

I didn't have an answer.

She said, 'I was thinking about my mother and how she was sick and she died.'

'I didn't mean ...'

'Is that all right with you? If I was thinking what I was thinking, and not what you want me to be thinking?'

'I was just trying ... to make you feel better, I guess.'

She turned and walked back towards the car. Strode. She strode away.

*

We kept driving towards Kalgoorlie, in silence for a while. Then I said, 'Want to tell me?'

'What?'

'Anything ... about anything that you want.'

She pointed at the fuel gauge and then at a petrol station up ahead. 'We need petrol.'

The night she heard her mother had died, she was quiet. We drank a bottle of vodka and we fucked. With gusto. I'm pretty sure that was the last time.

The petrol station looked closed. One petrol pump; a large corrugated iron workshop; a wooden office, that doubled as a shop if the old metal Coke sign was still true.

The petrol pump had levers.

'I'll do that, mate.'

His skin was red and his big belly pushed out under his dirty t-shirt. The top half of his overalls hung down behind like a spare pair of monkey arms.

I said, 'I've seen these. I think it was in *The Postman Always Rings Twice.*'

'It's not new but it works.' Then he looked over at the car. He bent and looked at my rough cuts, his eyes narrowing like a wine snob. 'Up from Perth?'

'Sydney,' I said.

'Sydney!' he said, frozen in amazement with the nozzle halfway to the car.

'Yep. Drove from Sydney. Going back.'

I'd pushed it too far. He looked from Robin who wasn't being part of it and then to the car, weighing it all up for the bullshit it was.

That's when I said, 'Hawaii.'

'Huh?'

'Drove from Hawaii before that.'

'How much?' he asked.

'Fill 'er up thanks,' I said, with the biggest smile, then turned and went to the shop. I hate customers like me.

The shop was amazing. Old pie signs and basketball singlets mixed with car deodorant trees and bad hats. There were car parts including a muffler suspended from the ceiling. There were maps and prospecting pans. A sign said *You are in the Golden Mile.* Another said *Coolgardie Since 1892.*

I tried on some of the bad hats. I liked the canvas one with the big orange star pattern and the little mirrors in the middle of each star. Then I found the flowers. Maybe they weren't flowers. It could have been a feather duster. But it looked like a bunch of multicoloured flowers made out of feathers.

I was about to take them out to her, when I patted my back pocket for my wallet.

The petrol guy was hanging up the petrol nozzle. I watched him as he walked slowly from the pump and into the shop. It looked like he had a bad back. He said, 'Sixty-seven dollars forty-three cents. It's as full as it can be.'

I didn't doubt it.

'Anything else, sir,' he said in a way I do when I'm dealing with an arsehole.

'Yep. A packet of – not the Longbeach. B&H. And two Snickers. How much are these flowers, dude?'

'Twelve.'

'Yes.'

'Ninety-four dollars. Do you want the hat?'

'Oh. Um, but of course. I'll, um, get my wallet from the car.' Big smile. I went out of the door slowly, but not so slowly it wasn't casual.

Robin looked up at me and I pushed the hat forward over my eyes and said in my practised bad Mexican accent, 'Eese that you, Cisco?'

'Bad hat,' she said, not meaning it.

I lifted my sunglasses so she could see my eyes and pulled out the flowers from behind my back. 'And for the señorita.'

That got her. She looked at them and smiled and then I thought she was going to cry. 'Gracias, señor.' And I thought I was going to cry. Then she flicked her eyes over my shoulder.

I turned to see him standing outside the shop, two of his four arms folded. I waved. Turned back.

She saw something about it all and looked doubtful. Just a flash.

It was enough. I would do this. What a laugh. I readjusted my sunnies and went to the boot and kicked it in the spot. Up it came to reveal the rifle sitting on top of our stuff. I looked up and he was still waiting. I smiled again. Then reached in like it might be my wallet.

That's when the Ford Territory drove in. Mum, Dad and two kids. Holiday gear up to the roof.

The petrol guy went to them smiling, but it was as if he had two independent eyes, like an ant's antennas. He was watching me with his left eyeball.

One of the kids was watching me too. A chubby girl with big round glasses, straight out of *Little Miss Sunshine*.

I closed the boot before anyone could see and went to Robin. 'How much money you got?'

She looked at me. She knew.

I tried to make a smile but couldn't get it going.

She opened her purse, flicked past her savings card which I knew was empty and went into the money. A ten-dollar note. And coins. 'Ten. Um sixteen ... seventeen and about sixty cents. I didn't know we were doing this Zac, or I would have brought some.'

I looked up to where he was giving directions while he watched me.

'Fuck. Fuck. Fuck.'

I went into the back, pushing broken glass off the seat. I pulled it up. I said, 'Check in the glove box.'

There were coins under the seat. More two-dollar coins. Four dollars.

'How much do we need?' she asked, not looking at me.

'A hundred.'

She shook her head going through the glove box.

I checked in my jeans pockets. Bingo. Cash. Lots of it in my left pocket. Fives. Four scrunched up five-dollar notes. 'Fuck, fuck, shit.'

The Territory drove off.

I went round to the driver's side, feeling in my back pocket. More money. A lovely orange twenty.

'A dollar fifty,' said Robin holding it out to me.

'When I go inside, start the car,' I whispered.

'What?'

'Start the car.'

I turned and he was standing behind me, waiting.

'Ah, my man,' I said and stepped past him to go to the boot again. I shoved the money in my pocket. Robin didn't slide across the seat. She didn't start the car. She sat with her back to us, holding the feather flowers.

The petrol guy came a few more steps after me.

I tried to smile.

He smiled too. He smiled a bad smile that said you are so fucked, Zac. He came back to the boot letting his smile lick the air all around us.

I thought that I could still do it. Kick the boot and he thinks what the hell as it starts to come open and I dive in and bring up the rifle and say, cool and calm, 'So who's smiling now, monkey man?'

But he put his hand on the boot.

'All we've got's about sixty dollars.' I reached back into my pocket and brought out the twenty and ten and the fives and the coins. 'Sixty-two, something.'

'Is that right?'

I took off the hat and held it out to him.

He took it and said, 'Well what we gunna do then, *mate*?'

I grabbed the Snickers from the dash and pulled the cigarettes out of my pocket.

He took them but shook his head.

Robin was holding out the flowers. She still wasn't looking at me.

'Sorry Rob.' I grabbed them and held them out to him.

'For me? You shouldn't have. It's still not enough, is it?'

'Um, we could maybe siphon out some petrol.'

He shook his head slowly. 'I don't buy used petrol.'

'Comic books! You like comic books?'

'No, I'm a grown-up. I like your sunglasses.'

'They're Wayfarers!'

'Where'd you get them? Hawaii?'

'They're Wayfarers! They're worth over two hundred bucks.'

'No. I'd say they're worth about five dollars forty.'

'Excuse me. Do you know Bill Mays?' said Robin to the guy.

He turned and looked at her but still not friendly. 'Yeah, I know him.'

'He's my father.'

'So?'

'So I'm sure he'd be glad to hear he owes you five dollars forty.'

'Your father already owes everybody round here something or other.'

Robin's jaw tightened a moment, but she went on as tough as before. 'Then five dollars forty isn't going to make much difference, is it?'

The guy seemed like he was about to keep arguing, but then thought of something. He nodded to her and squeezed my shoulder. 'You're one lucky Hawaiian. Having someone big and strong to look after you.'

I shrugged off his hand and pushed past him to get in the driver's seat.

He said, 'Your mother was a good lady. I was sorry to hear about ... Sorry for your loss.'

Robin nodded. 'Yeah.' Then she said, 'Let's go, Zac.'

I took off but couldn't get any traction. There was no spray of gravel and no burning rubber.

*

I didn't say anything. I drove into the modern outskirts of Kalgoorlie, which resembled the outskirts of Midland leading out of Perth. It was a sprawl that lasted for only six long blocks. Then we were in the wide streets of the city centre. There was a Dome and Asian takeaway in amongst the big hundred-year-old hotels with *Skimpy Barmaid* signs. Lots of Thrifty hire utes were driven by men in orange or yellow shirts. And then we were out the other side where there was a hill of grey rock going off to the right and a small hill where the pipeline ended. Past that were giant metal poppet heads – the things that haul gold miners and their gold in and out of the ground.

'Down here,' said Robin, pointing to the left of the edge of town, where fibro houses sat on flat dusty blocks. 'That one.' She pointed at a red wooden house with red tin roof and red tin fence. I pulled up in front and turned off the engine and started to open my door.

'I'll be an hour,' she said as she got out.

'Is this about the petrol station?'

She looked at the house.

'The other car came. If it hadn't, I would have ...'

'I'll give them the invoice, and say hello. You should look around town. It's very historic.' She spoke like a computer. 'It has the largest open pit in the world, right on the edge of town. Three and a half kilometres long and one and a half kilometres wide. When I left school it was six hundred and fifty metres deep.' Her back was to me. 'There's a museum. The whole history of the gold rush and the continuing resources boom.' She started walking away.

A girl in her late teens and a floral dress opened the door and looked at Robin and then over her shoulder at me coming up the path behind.

Robin said, 'Liz.'

'Robin. What are you doing here?' It wasn't exactly a welcome. Then she looked at me and said, 'Hi.'

'How ya doing?' I smiled at Liz and ignored Robin.

'Come in,' said Liz, when Robin didn't make any introductions. 'You must have left early.'

'Last night,' I said.

She led us up the passageway to the lounge room where another teenage girl sat on the floor with two toddlers and two babies and piles of nappies in front of the TV.

'Robin,' said the other girl, excited. 'Oh,' she said seeing me. Then, 'You must have left early.'

'Last night,' said Robin, beating me to it.

'Hi everyone. My name is Zac. And I'm really, really glad to meet Robin's sisters.'

Robin dumped herself down on the lounge.

'I'm Gail,' said Gail.

'Liz,' said Liz.

'Zac again,' I said and they both smiled while all of us waited for Robin to jump in. An American evangelical talked on the TV. You couldn't quite hear the words but you could see the urging.

Gail said, 'Jade, say hello to Aunty Robin.'

One of the toddlers looked up at both of us and said, 'Hello Aunty Robin.'

I gave a secret wave to Jade and she waved back.

Robin was fishing in her bag.

Gail and Liz looked at each other, wary.

'I brought the invoice. That's why I came.'

'Oh,' said Gail, disappointed.

'It seemed important in your phone call.'

Liz turned suddenly to look at Gail who wouldn't meet her eyes.

Liz created a smile and said, 'You could have posted it.'

Robin said, 'I don't actually see why you need it. Couldn't Jack just show you a copy? I mean the stone's there.'

'Yes, you're right,' said Liz. 'I don't know why Gail bothered you.'

Gail said, 'You've been?'

Robin said, 'I went this morning.' She brought out the invoice. 'So he sent it to the wrong place. How he got my address I'll never know, but it's hardly ...'

Gail sat next to Robin, and said, 'She wasn't thinking. In the end, she ...'

Liz said, 'It's because you're the oldest. That's all. We'll take care of it, Robin.' There was an edge to it under the tight smile.

Liz and Gail didn't look or act younger than Robin. They seemed like mums – like my mum and my mother's friends. They were competent and kind of wise and not very interesting. They kept sharing looks with each other that said there was stuff being unsaid.

I sat on another chair. The walls were painted green. There is possibly no good green colour you can paint a wall. I had a bad case of the munchies.

Gail rescued us all again. 'Jack was saying round town that we hadn't paid him. And Doug and Terry ... Well, they want him to take it back. Admit that we didn't know. We can prove it was sent to the wrong place.'

Robin nodded. 'That you pay your bills.'

Gail said, 'We pay as we go.'

Liz saw me watching and I could see her getting ready to be mad with me because I was seeing things I had no right to.

'A cup of tea!' I said, standing. 'These damn Mayses girls don't even offer a man a cup of tea even though he's sawed the top off his car and driven the other Mayses all night to come here.'

Liz laughed.

Gail stood, socially aghast. 'I'm so sorry. Yes. Tea.'

'Or tequila would be good, and nachos. Too early?'

Robin sat looking at the invoice.

Liz said, 'Through here, Zac. So, are you a university student also?'

I followed them through to the kitchen ruffling the not-Jade toddler's head as we went past. 'No. Not me. I work for a living. I'm a full-time waiter. It's not a job, it's a career.'

'Oh,' said Liz in that disappointed way people do.

'You look like someone,' said Gail, like people also do. 'Someone famous.'

Sometimes I say, how do you know I'm not? But this time I held my face in the angle that's best for seeing it.

'Don't say it,' said Robin, coming into the kitchen. She was smiling, but before anyone could say Orlando Bloom or Paul Newman and finally google up James Dean and go, yes, you look like James Dean. Before they could do that, Robin asked, 'Are the men at work?'

'They're up north,' said Liz. She put the kettle on and went for cups, while Gail got cake out of an old round tin. It looked like carrot cake.

'Fly in,' said Gail.

'That's right,' said Robin.

'Back on Friday week.'

Robin sat at the kitchen table. I went over to Gail and let her see me steal the first piece of cake.

Gail said, 'With the way gold prices are they've been talking about getting their old jobs here at the mine. They're going back into the old mines and open cutting.'

Liz said, 'Doug says Dad could get a job.'

Gail said, 'He's not interested.'

Robin was. 'Is he prospecting?'

Gail said, 'You know Dad. The big strike.'

Liz said, 'Doug says, it never works, chasing that big strike. You can count on a wage and that's not too shabby.'

Gail said, 'Especially if you've got a family to think about.'

The kettle whistled. Liz poured the hot water over the tea bags. Gail gave me the plate of cut cake and I put it in the middle of the table.

I tried to catch Robin's eye, but was invisible to her. I sat down and took more cake. Very moist carrot cake.

Robin finally asked, 'When will he be back?'

'Doug?'

'Dad.'

'We don't see that much of him,' said Liz.

'Sometimes he pops in. When he's in town. You know Dad,' said Gail.

'No. Do you?'

Liz and Gail both blinked at Robin, then blinked at each other.

Gail said, 'I'll see if the kids are all right.' She went into the lounge.

Robin looked at me and I smiled at her. But she didn't smile back and kept looking at me, until I took my cup of tea and more cake and went into the lounge room.

Gail had picked up a baby and had her on her hip as she watched the toddlers make gouges of texta colour on a blank page. I smiled and nodded to her and pretended to be amazed at the glory that is children and watched the cartoons now on the big plasma screen. I was listening to Robin and Liz in the kitchen.

Robin said, 'Why wasn't this sent to him? Is he paying any of it?'

'Don't worry. We'll pay.'

'That's not what I meant.'

'Gail shouldn't have phoned you. We'll pay for it. You don't have to worry about anything. We'll keep doing it.'

'No, it's no trouble. I'm happy to help. Just a little drive. But Dad really should have. He should.'

'Anyway, not your problem.'

'Okay. Well, we better get going, I suppose.'

'Have some cake.'

'No, bit early.'

'For your friend.'

'No.'

'Well ...'

Chairs scraped on the floor. Then Liz said, 'You didn't even come to her funeral. For that, I will never forgive you.'

When Robin came out, Gail said stay for lunch but Liz shook her head and Gail gave Robin a kid's drawing. I said I loved their cake. Liz said lovely to meet me. Gail said I should be a male model or an actor. We all said goodbye at the door and went out into the glare of the sun and a pale blue sky that filled nine-tenths of everything.

When we were in the car, I said, 'Are you okay?'

'Drive.'

'Some things were said.'

'Drive, Zac.'

'Driving.' I put it into gear and drove in a wide arc of gravel dust.

Robin carefully folded up the texta drawing from her nieces and put it in the glove box.

I stopped at the crossroad, my flicker flicking right on the road that would lead all the way back to Perth.

Robin said, 'Stop.' She was looking the other way at a sign saying Leonora.

'Stopped,' I said.

She had a paper in her hand. It was the invoice. She must have scooped it up with or under the drawing. Maybe we needed to go back and deliver it, to either angry Liz or skittish Gail, her teenage middle-aged sisters. Robin turned the invoice.

'You still want to go camping?'

'Um,' I managed.

'I know a spot. A good spot.'

'Maybe.'

'Left.'

Sometimes she does that. 'Going to Kal.' Huh? 'Don't go back to Perth. Go left.' You what? I can never predict it. She suddenly jumps into another direction, without warning and without explanation. I think on Planet Robin she's part of a constant game of dodgem that I can't see or understand. Like conversations between sisters.

*

I drove up onto the highway leading out the other side of town. Our mobiles lost their range about five K out.

The country got flatter. The spindly trees had red-stained trunks. There were pale mounds of weathered dirt, one-person mines from one or a hundred years ago. Every now and then you'd see the body of a long-dead car, wheelless, glassless, paintless rusted shapes of the history of cars.

We were passed by huge mining trucks and we passed bullet-riddled signs pointing off right and left down gravel tracks.

'Ghost towns,' yelled Robin.

Then came big squarish hills near the road, like the ones in John Wayne westerns. 'Slag heaps,' yelled Robin. 'From big mine digs.'

The road was smooth and wide and well sealed, but even so, fine red dust settled on the windscreen and back seat.

'Stop,' Robin yelled as we came up to another turn-off.

I pulled off the road.

Robin peered at the withered strip of bitumen leading all the way to the horizon.

'Yep. That's it.'

The sign was unreadable because of all the bullet holes.

'Go down there,' she said.

'Where's it go?'

'Drive down it and find out.' She smiled, easy.

I smiled back, but then couldn't help asking, in the open moment, 'Did you work things out?'

'What?'

'With your sister. Liz. The invoice.'

'Not really,' she said, looking away. But she didn't close it down. 'Families. Can't live with 'em, can't ...'

I should have just nodded. But I wanted more. I always wanted more from her. More of her. 'You realise, in all the time we've been together, I've never met them before?'

'I've never met yours.'

'Ah, but I've invited you to meet mine. So many lunches you could have had.'

'You said there were about a million of them, so I've probably met half already, without even knowing it.'

Ha, see. She was too smart for me. She can weave words and win an argument, even when she's wrong. And have me laughing at another thing that wasn't what we were talking about.

'Turn down the road, Zac.' She said it slowly, like a hypnotist's voice. 'Turn down the road.'

I drove slowly, the big holes in the bitumen road making the Valiant shudder brutally. The red dirt edges kept biting in on each side like the road was a drying creek. Dust collected on the windscreen making it hard to see. It was hot and dry and my eyes were filling with grit. Then the car shuddered again, but not like hitting a pothole. It kind of clenched and died.

'Shit.'

'What?'

'Radiator, I think.'

The car stopped rolling. We were in sight of where the bitumen gave out altogether and turned into a gravel track. The mounds were all around us like miniature dirt igloos, with empty fishing holes in front.

Steam clouded up from under the front. 'Radiator for sure.'

We got out and I lifted the bonnet, but had to jump back as boiling water spurted.

Robin looked at the sizzling engine. 'Have we got any water?'

'It must be with the jack.'

She went and sat in the car.

I pretended to stagger around with my hands held out. 'Water. Water.' But then I stopped and looked at the washed-out un-greenness of everything around us. 'We could actually die, I guess.'

Robin said, 'Wanna smoke?'

'Good plan.'

She shuffled the glove box. 'Did you bring any other CDs?'

'Nope.'

'Your iPod?'

'Nope.'

She hit play in the car stereo.

Bo Diddley sang 'Somebody Beat Me'. It is bouncier than most of the other songs on the album and more pared back too. Just Bo and his guitar, banging it out, you imagine. He was stranded in Nevada. Someone was about to beat him up and steal his money. One line was all you needed for a song to fit your life.

I went to the boot thinking I might shoot a creature so we could drink its blood to slake our thirst, like Bear Grylls or that guy who sawed his own arm off with a teaspoon. Robin was rolling the joint when I went past with the flagon of white wines. I took a gulp. It was mostly chardonnays and very warm and possibly not life-sustaining.

Robin got out of the car lighting the joint and came to watch.

'Big drink now.' I poured most of the flagon into the radiator. 'You'll feel wonderful. Might I suggest the fish with the chef's orange and beetroot salad?' I explained to the car, 'Valiant means brave right. So, I need you to be brave car ... and work. We've all got jobs to do here, and yours is – to be a car that goes.'

'Emotionally tenacious.'

'Huh?'

Robin looked surprised. 'Did I say that?'

'Emotionally what? What?'

She smiled. Said, 'I think you're emotionally tenacious.'

The way Robin says things, you can never tell whether she means it or she means the opposite. And when you don't know what a word means either, you've got very little to go on. 'Is that good or bad?'

'I'm not sure.'

'Sounds like one of your dental conditions.' I turned back to the Valiant's engine. 'Oh, oh. Looks like you've got emotional tenaciousness to the ... um.'

'Frontal bicuspid,' she offered.

'If you'd only come sooner. Looks like root canal work.'

She leaned in. 'And a bridge. There's always a bridge. Dental upselling.'

'Oh yeah. A bridge for sure. Complete new swimming pool and patio area, I'd say, Dr Mays.'

'Yes Dr Pavlinovic. And now of course, the consultancy fee.'

'Yes! A spa. I always wanted a spa.'

'If you'd only come sooner.'

'If you'd only come sooner.'

She laughed and her face was like sunshine. I stood warming in it. She saw that and clouded. 'Shouldn't you keep the motor running?'

'Huh?'

'When you pour cold "wine" into a boiling radiator.'

'Yeah. I forgot.' I took the joint and had a toke.

Robin went away again.

I said, 'She's going to have a hangover in the morning anyway.' I went around Robin's side saying, 'Even if our phones worked, I can't see ringing that arsehole from the service station ...'

Robin had squatted in the dirt to take a piss. Her panties were around her knees. They were the ones with the tiny pink flowers around the top. Her thighs were open beyond as the stream hit the dirt.

She looked up, catching me and scowled.

I looked away, like I'd been caught perving, which I was, but caught perving on a stranger and not my girlfriend who I had looked at in ways far more open and sexual than having a wee. I went past and put the flagon back in the boot. But I turned back in time to see her stand with her back to me and watched as she hitched up her skirt and bent to lift her panties and saw her white gorgeous arse wriggling back in.

There was no one around. She could lay on the back seat and I could slide my hands up the outside of her thighs until my thumbs hooked under the thin sides of her tiny pink flowered panties. She would look into my eyes then and I'd look back. The smile. She could give me the special smile and then I'd start to pull down, and she'd raise up her bum to help me.

'Hey,' she said. Robin was standing in front of me, gesturing for the joint. She took it and went back to her car door and leaned against it, toking and looking out into the desert. It reminded me of a film.

I found one of Robin's scarves amongst her clothes in the boot. 'Put this on.'

'What?'

'Put in on your head, you know, as though you were going to keep the dust out of your hair.'

She looked at me suspiciously but started to tie it.

I went back to the boot and got my rifle. 'Now, kneel down.'

'What?'

I looked at the car and then off to an imaginary spot next to us and thought about how we'd look from there. 'Kneel down, here.'

It wasn't near the damp spot. It was behind her open front passenger door, like in the movie.

'No way. Not here, Zac. Not now.'

Her voice was sad. It was weak and sad and not even angry.

'I didn't mean that! Huh, I should be so lucky. Shit Rob! It was a fuckin' game. I meant, if you had kneeled down with that scarf you would have been like Elizabeth Taylor in front of the convertible, and I had stood like this.' I put the rifle across my shoulders, both hands hanging over. And then I moved my right leg so I bent it at the knee and my foot rested on the other, like him. 'I would have been James Dean like the poster for *East of Eden*, just before he struck oil.'

'Oh.'

'But seeing as you were so worried that I'd actually take a gun and force you to blow me, then let's forget it. Or maybe that's what it takes.'

I turned away from her and threw the rifle into the boot and slammed down the hood and walked out into the desert a couple of steps until I was at one of the mine holes. It was no more than two metres by half a metre wide. Old wood was laid along the sides lengthwise, to keep it from caving in, but the wood had broken in places and parts of the soil had fallen. I tried to see the bottom, but it was too dark to see far down. 'It was *Giant*,' she called from the road. 'The film about the oil was *Giant*. Rock Hudson.'

Oh fuck. Yeah. Damn.

She kept on, being right. '*East of Eden* was, um Cain and Abel and ice. There was an ice storage thing. If you're going to quote movies all the time at least get them right.'

I went back to the front of the car and screwed on the radiator cap. She might be smarter and always right, but where did it get her? So what if I made a little mistake like that? It doesn't mean I wasn't right on the bigger thing about how it looked from that photo I'd seen. I put down the hood, leaving eight fingerprints in the dust.

I got behind the wheel and turned the key. The engine spluttered but didn't catch. I tried again and it caught, the engine throaty and good to go.

I said, 'Ha, the Phantom never dies.' Water spatters were on the windscreen from when the radiator had boiled and I put on the wipers making the damp dust into a mud smear on the glass.

She got in her side.

I said, 'I'm pretty sure it was the Phantom.'

*

The gravel narrowed quickly and the dust got thicker on the windscreen. When I travelled at the right speed, most of it trailed behind us without coming into the car. Robin squatted up on her side of the seat, her legs under her skirt to keep them out of the sun. She squinted over the top of the windscreen as if she were searching for landfall.

After ten or so Ks, I said, 'This does lead somewhere, doesn't it? I mean there is a place somewhere that this is leading to?'

'Used to be.'

'Is there water?'

'Maybe. There used to be a river, I think. Or maybe a river every twenty years when it floods and nothing the rest of the time.'

She kept looking, trying to find the place on the horizon.

I said, 'Does it piss you off, me talking about films all the time?'

'No.'

'It never used to.'

'No, it's good.' She was yessing me.

'I wouldn't bring it up. I'm being emotionally tenuous again.'

'Tenacious.'

'That's it.'

'Well, actually, it can be fun. But then, sometimes, when you do it, it throws me out of the moment. Not every single thing we do or think has to be held up against the validating measure of a film from the 1960s.'

'It does piss you off.'

'That's probably too strong a word.'

'What else about me pisses you off?'

'How long have you got?' She didn't even turn around when she said it. It was casual and it was mean and it was empty of feeling. 'Here. This is it.'

We came in amongst the broken roofless ruins of an old town. I pulled off the track near a fallen veranda and the back wheel slid right and down. I gunned the motor and the back wheel spun itself deeper and deeper into the soft sand. 'Fuck.' I hit the steering wheel. 'Fuck, fuck, fuck.' I turned off the engine and got out to take a look. I'd bogged it up to the axle.

Robin was out of the car walking away.

'Robin.'

She kept walking towards a roofless, windowless wrecked house over the other side of the track.

'Robin, wait!'

She stopped and turned slowly. 'What?'

I started to walk to her.

She said, 'What do you want?'

The way she said it stopped me. 'What's going on?'

'We're camping. Like you wanted.'

'What's going on with us?'

'Can we talk about this later?'

'When?'

'Not now.'

'That's what I've been doing for the last couple of months, "not nowing". When is now?'

Robin closed her eyes and bowed her head. When she spoke it was like she was dead. 'I don't know.' She gave up on me then. It was clear. She didn't love me anymore. And still she stood with her head bowed like a nurse from the Second World War waiting for the Japanese to yell or execute or do whatever.

It was over.

I went back to the car and then, for something to do, I went and looked at the bogged wheel. When I turned back to Robin, she was gone.

Next to the car were the remains of what was once a row of shops. Front wooden posts still supported most of the sagging bullnose veranda roof. A piece had come all the way loose and lay on the ground like a metal person hugging their knees.

I saw Robin moving around in the house on the other side of the track. Some of the outer wall had collapsed into small hills of bricks. Robin was in a window frame, then wasn't.

I popped the boot and grabbed the rifle and a box of cartridges and I set off, away from her. The back of the shops was missing. A big roofless brick wall still stood. You could make out the faded white letters above the doorway, *Imperial Hotel*. There was a water tank on its side. Abandoned cactus had spread. A rusted Dodge truck, half buried and shot up. Bits of glass. A quarter of a plate. The handle of a cup. Then I was out of the remains of the town. Over on the left was another poppet head in the distance, its top barely visible against the sky, like a headless skeleton. I stood at the top of a one-person mine shaft, a metre by two, long and narrow like a grave. I kicked gravel at the edge of the mine and it spilled in and hit the bottom of the hole, clattering on tin and tinkling on glass deep in the darkness.

I knew. It was over. At least, I knew.

I got some cans and two mostly whole bottles and put them on top of a mound of dirt at the top of one of the little mine shafts. Then I went back about twenty metres to another mound of dirt and I lay down behind that, resting the rifle on my arm so I could sight easily at the line of cans and bottles. I proceeded to fire and to miss.

I should have held up the petrol guy as it had crossed my mind to do. So that when the family car drove off and he looked over, it would have been to see me by the open boot of the Valiant, holding the rifle. 'Okay, man. Wipe that stupid look off your face. Robin, start the car.' I'd be inside the petrol station shop. 'Okay, all the money in the till, thank you, fatso.' He would be blubbering a bit of course. 'Please don't hurt me. Please don't hurt me.' Yeah, yeah. 'And a carton of B&H.' No. 'Oh, look you've been hiding the Winnie Blues.' Two cartons of Winfield Blue. And I'd grab the box of Snickers. He's crying now. 'Please don't kill me.' Wrench out the phone. Take his mobile. Does he have a mobile? And I walk toward the car. She's behind the wheel waiting for me. I push the cash into my jeans and step into the back seat and over into the front. Step, step, sit. And she guns it, fishtailing the car in a spray of gravel onto the highway and into the sunset. Yaoow.

I lay on my back in the dirt where I really was and I aimed the rifle straight up in the air. If you could aim directly up at ninety degrees and you fired, the bullet would drop right back down on you and kill you.

*

She had never wanted me. Never. The night we met, she was not interested. The other girls were. It was a game tables of girls would sometimes play. Flirt with the cute waiter. See who can bag him. I have never minded. Fringe benefit with the tips and free food. I'd go home with the cuter ones, but it never really amounted to much except occasionally great sex, but mostly average sex and tears and all the girl's problems and past relationships and nothing else. I know. It's true. I was a bit of a tart before Robin.

Anyway, the night I met Robin, she was the only one at their table who wasn't hitting on me. She was quiet and a bit glum. She'd broken up with someone. I forget who. I forget why. I believe her friends were helping her cleanse herself of him and she had decided it was all men who were evil and she drank a lot of wine, which does not go with too many tacos, if I may say. And she argued with her friends. Loud and raucous is Gringos' kind of crowd, but they became loud and angry, Robin against the world.

They left late, and they left Robin. I found her in the back parking lot, puking up her guts near the Valiant. Small world if you look backwards. I couldn't get her to make sense. She was nearly unconscious. I opened her purse and found her mobile. I didn't find many numbers in it. I was going to try a few. Get one of her friends to come and get her. But I found her student card and an address. It was one of those university residential colleges on Stirling Highway near the river. There was a key with a room number. Her blouse was covered in vomit and I took it off and I put my jacket on her and buttoned it up, then I put her in the back of my car, with a windcheater under her head in case she was going to puke again. I put her over my shoulder when I got there and carried her up a flight of stairs. Two guys were in a small kitchen. 'Ah, you got her. Good one, dude.' The other one said, 'Can we have a go when you're finished?'

The room was small, like in the nurses' quarters but with a desk and books and a single bed. I laid her down. That's when I saw her movie posters. One was *Breathless* and the other was *To Kill a Mockingbird*. Gregory Peck. 'Ah, you like old movies,' I said.

There were three rag dolls on her windowsill and a Harry Potter wand. A big casserole dish was up on her bookshelf. The rest was books and papers and quite a few piles of clothes on the floor.

I took off her shoes. She had good legs and a beautiful face. I spread her top blanket over her and put her purse on the desk and her key next to that. I moved a litter bin to the floor next to her face. I clicked the lock in the door when I left, which I think was a good thing, because the arseholes were lurking. 'That was quick, man,' said one. 'Did you get any pictures?'

It was suddenly cold outside and when I got back to the car and smelled the bad smell and saw her blouse, I realised I'd lost a good coat. And that would have been it. Done, dusted and no Robin and Zac to break my heart.

Except that Robin came to Gringos the next night. I saw her come in with my coat.

'Hey, you brought it back.'

'So it is yours.'

I put a plate of refried beans down on the table next to me and reached for it.

'You admit it.' Her eyes were flashing.

'Sure. Do you want your top?'

'You fucking bastard,' she yelled. It was early, but the people in the restaurant went quiet. 'Do you see any reason why I shouldn't call the police on you, you fucking sleazebag.'

'Huh?'

'Hey, want to take it outside?' said Mike, the manager coming from the front.

'Is that how you get your kicks, is it?'

'I didn't get any kicks.' I included the customers. 'Honest. I ... I washed your blouse.'

'Exactly, and what are you doing with it and how did you get it off without my consent and what, arsehole, were you doing in my room for so long and why shouldn't I call the police?'

'I wasn't in there very long,' I said.

'In where!'

'No, your room. You passed out. I took you home. Left straight away.'

'You took my blouse off.'

'It was covered in puke. There was cheese. Mince. Pickles. Red wine.'

'Tequila,' she said, quiet, thinking fast.

'No carrots. That I could see. Contrary to folklore.'

'Some guys said ...'

'Not nice guys.'

She nodded, got it. She looked around the room. Someone laughed, but most had gone back to talking. She was embarrassed and blinking and blushing and she made me smile.

'I'll get your blouse,' I said and went out into the kitchen. When I got back my coat was folded on the table and she was walking out the front door. I went after her.

Someone yelled, 'Let her go, man. Too high maintenance.'

A girl yelled, 'I won't yell at you after.'

Outside I yelled, 'Hey. Your blouse.'

She turned. She was still embarrassed. She looked at her blouse in my hand and said, 'It's clean.'

'I washed it.'

'You washed it?'

'It was pretty pongy.'

'You washed my blouse?'

She looked up at me and smiled. It was delicate and hopeful and maybe a little scared, like I'd saved her puppy from drowning and given it the kiss of life.

'In the sink,' I said. 'I mean I didn't soak it in lavender and dry it on the French Riviera and iron it atop the Himalayas or anything.'

She laughed. The lines went away from around her eyes.

'Zac, if you don't leave your love-life at home and get in here and start serving the customers, I will fire your arse!' yelled Mike from the front door.

She stopped smiling.

'He won't fire me.'

'Anyway, sorry about the tirade.' Still not smiling.

'Wanna go see a movie?'

'I have to study.'

'They play old movies during the day at the Cygnet for half price.'

She looked at me, wondering how I knew she liked old movies, but then got distrustful again.

I gave my smile. I raised my eyebrows. I turned the smile up a bit.

'No. I don't want to be part of all your love-life, thank you.'

And she turned and walked away.

I like looking over at her at a party to find her looking back. I like hearing about her day. I like her jokes. The way she takes the piss out of me. I liked the way she made love. It had a concentrated intensity that became abandoned, like we were in a storm and she was the only one who could get us through, like she was the boat and the ocean both. Then we'd drown.

I lay on my back in the dirt and felt a chill. The sun was going down. The sky was turning orange and red, and the earth under that, from red to black, filling in with shades of grey. The deserted buildings were darkening too, into black lurking shapes.

It took me months of asking Robin to films before she said yes. *Doctor Zhivago* finally did it. I do not know why she suddenly said yes. I do not understand how Robin's brain works. And that, I suppose, is why it is over. I'm not up to it.

A fire was going at the house where Robin had gone. I went to the boot again before I went over to where she was sitting. She'd made a circle of rocks and stacked bits of wood. She was a good camper. Not always happy, but a first-rate woodsman.

I had the rifle in one hand and something hidden behind my back. She had changed into her jeans. When she looked up she said, 'What did you get?'

I brought out the can of soup I'd packed. 'Nothing out there. Just cans and bottles. And they all escaped.'

I put down the rifle and stood holding the can of soup.

'Can opener?' she said.

I went to the wall of the house where she'd built the fire and found a nail sticking out of a window frame. I tried to hit the nail at the right angle to puncture the can, but it only dented. When I stopped banging I heard Robin say, 'I'm sorry.'

I didn't say anything.

Robin said, 'I ...' and then after a while she said, 'Sorry.'

'Sorry about what? What are you sorry about?'

'For being mean. For being – a mess. For all the ...' She sighed and looked off into the dark. Then she said, 'I used to live here. In this house. We're sitting in the garage.' She stood and looked in through the glassless window where I'd been hammering the can. 'The kitchen was in here. Then our room. All three of us used to sleep there. Mum and Dad had the other bedroom. Us and nobody else. In 1899 there were six thousand people here. In 1907 there were fifteen. And then just us in the only viable house left. That's the history of this town.

Boom and bust. Mum wanted us to move out here to be closer to where – Dad was always out here. But we moved back into Coolgardie after a couple of years anyway. There wasn't any work here – for Mum.'

Then she turned her back on the house and walked to the other side of the fire and turned to face me, standing up straight, as though doing a speech at school assembly. 'My belief is this. History starts with us. The only history I care about is what happens between us. That's when it starts. That's why I've never talked about other things, because they don't matter.'

'Us?'

'Listen to me crap on. Yabber yabber.' She looked down at the fire with a scared smile.

I fell in love with her again. I couldn't not. I stepped out from the wall. I was going to hug her.

But she looked up at me as though I'd only just arrived. 'I'll get a flagon.'

'Rob.'

'I'll get the flagon of reds. Then we can talk. Okay?'

I nodded. I didn't want to frighten her off. She'd told me more in the last minute than she'd said in the last couple of months. Maybe more personal stuff than in all the time I'd known her. We had gone to a lot of parties and pubs and bands. We'd seen a lot of movies. We'd made a lot of love. But we had never talked that much about ourselves. It hadn't seemed necessary.

She was making the car light flash. I'd saved the interior light when I took the roof off. It was coiled on the back floor of the car and it still worked. Robin had found the point where the button in the door pops out enough to make the light come on. She was opening and closing the passenger door so the light winked on and off, showing her at the car and then gone. The shopfront behind would glow too and be gone. Town, no town; Robin, then no.

I heard a whine and turned to see a dusty blue heeler coming out of the desert behind the house. It stopped short of the fire and looked back. It was old with lots of nicks out of its grey coat.

'Here boy,' I called, but it didn't move. 'Yo, Rinnie? Lassie? Here Spot. Fang. Inspector Rex. Heel, Rex. Wolf?'

The dog wouldn't budge.

Robin said, 'Dog.' She had brought the flagon back.

The dog went to her, sniffing and then started to wag its tail.

'It likes you.'

Robin sat on a big rock by the fire, looking out at the desert, letting the dog lick her fingers.

'Here, boy, here.'

'Dog,' said Robin.

'Dog?'

'That's his name.'

The dog still wouldn't come to me. Robin took a big gulp of red wine as she kept looking into the darkness. She said, 'Did you hear about the insomniac, agnostic dyslexic?'

'The what?'

'He kept waking up worried about whether there was such a thing as a dog.'

I understood the word dog.

The dog suddenly turned and ran off.

A man appeared and walked towards us out of the dark with the dog by his side. His clothes were dusty, as dusty as the dog. He had a beard and a weathered brown face that made it hard to tell his age or his fearsomeness.

'Gidday. Saw your fire.'

He stepped into the light, looking at the fire and then the car and back to the rifle on the ground near Robin. He looked up at Robin and he smiled. 'Hello.'

'Hello,' she said.

The guy said, 'What you doing all the way out here?'

'Camping.'

He nodded and looked over to me.

'Pull up a piece of house and sit down,' I said.

'Bill,' he said, not offering his hand.

'Zac. Want a drink?'

He opened his eyes a fraction which I took for yes. I looked over to Robin, but she hadn't made a move. I got up and got the flagon from her. 'It's a red blend made to our own secret recipe.'

Bill took a sip, still standing, then a deep gulp.

I pointed at my soup can. 'You wouldn't have a can opener would you?'

He shook his head. Said to Robin, 'Been to Kal?'

Robin nodded. She wasn't actually looking at him, more his boots.

'How's everybody?'

Robin shrugged.

Bill shrugged too. He took another pull on the flagon, wiped it with his sleeve, passed it back to me with a nod.

'Well, better be heading back to camp.' He looked at Robin and said, 'Good to see you,' and said, 'Good meeting you,' to me and, 'Dog,' to the dog.

When he turned to leave, Robin said, 'Dad?'

Bill turned back.

Robin picked up the can of soup and held it up. 'Could you help us get the can open?'

Bill stood looking at the can for a couple of seconds before he nodded. He walked around the fire and took the can from her.

'Where's your camp?' I finally asked.

He took a huge knife out of his belt and used it to point into the desert. 'About a half a K or so that way. An old mine I'm reworking before the big boys come in with their front-end loaders.' He held up the can and he hacked off the top with one sweep of the knife. The lid hinged back and drops of soup hissed into the fire.

'Now that's a knife.'

Bill looked at the knife, then at me like I was a moron.

'It's from a film,' I said.

He handed the can to Robin and wiped the knife on his pants and put it back into the sheath on his belt.

'So, you're a prospector?'

'I scratch enough for food.'

Maybe he wasn't even forty. But weathered. He looked a lot like Indiana Jones without the whip. 'But you could strike it big?'

He shrugged and looked down into the fire. He was hard to read, like his daughter.

'Yeah, any day now,' answered Robin, flat, bitter.

Bill said, 'I'll let you get on with your soup.'

I said, 'You're welcome to some if you want, um, Mr Mays.'

'Bill. Used to my own company. Thanks for the drink.' He flicked his eyes to Robin. 'Say hello in Kal.'

'No worries. Nice to see you.'

Bill nodded and turned and strode back into the darkness with his dog who'd sat silent the whole while waiting. The dog and Bill walked out of the light but were visible for quite some time, dark shapes moving into the darkest black, hypnotically slow, like that scene from *Lawrence of Arabia* where the Arab comes out of the desert, only played backwards.

I put the can of soup at the corner of the fire to heat.

Robin lifted the flagon and gulped it down like water.

I said, 'Who was that masked man? "Oh that's my father. Haven't I ever mentioned him? Or my whole family." What's going on, Robin?'

'What?'

'We drive out to the middle of nowhere, and this guy comes out of the desert, and he's your father, and he chops the top off the soup and goes again.'

'Shit! I forgot to give it to him.' She stood and dug into her pocket and brought out the crumpled invoice again. 'He should be dealing with this. Really. Not Gail or Liz. Such a stupid plan. Send it to Perth, so that – on the off-chance we saw him. And I did. And I forgot.' She was talking too brightly.

'But he's gone.'

'Things didn't go according to plan. Mum's plans rarely ...' She ran out of energy looking into the fire.

'Did he? When you were little, your father didn't touch you or anything, did he?'

'What!' She looked at me in revulsion. 'Is that what you think?'

'Rob, you can tell me. You can tell me anything.' I took a step towards her.

'No he didn't.'

I stopped and she looked at me.

'He didn't.'

It was true.

She got mad again. 'Jesus, Zac. Is that my problem, huh?'

'It happens.'

'Yeah, something might be wrong. It has to be child abuse.'

'I was guessing, okay. He was weird. You were weird. I was guessing.'

'You guessed wrong.'

'Yeah, well if you gave me some little clues I wouldn't have to guess all the time.'

Robin stood glaring at me and I stood glaring at her. Finally she looked past me at the fire and she said, 'Soup's burning.'

The can was blackened and burned, the soup bubbling and sizzling down a side. I grabbed a stick and nudged the can back from the flames. I put wood on the fire.

I said, 'We should go and see him. We came all this way. We should go and see him about this invoice.'

'You're right.' She nodded. ' I'll go now.'

'No.'

She said, 'Maybe that's why I came. To sort this out with him. And I should ... do it.'

'Yeah, but you don't have to do everything alone. In fact, you can't. You're not allowed to under the rules of a relationship. It's the law.'

'Zac, the President's plane isn't missing. An asteroid isn't going to crash into the earth. It's stupid parent stuff.'

'Sure. Can we talk about it first? And we'll go and see him and get it sorted.'

She sighed and looked at me and nodded. 'Okay.' She stepped the four steps to me and she put her hand on my shoulder and she kissed me on the cheek. She stepped back again before I could hug her. 'You know, out on the road, when the radiator had overheated and you were doing James Dean with Liz Taylor?'

'Yeah. I know it was *Giant*, not *East of Eden*. It was a mental typo. No iPhone coverage. I couldn't google for a memory check.'

'When you were standing like that with your hands over the rifle and your leg bent over the other. I never realised it before. It's Jesus on the cross he was doing. You looked like Jesus.'

'Jesus, huh? I would rather look like James Dean.'

'That too. Zac doing James Dean doing Jesus. Whoow.' She took a big gulp of air and fanned her face with her hand. 'I need a smoke. I need a joint.'

'Okay. I'll get it,' I didn't want to see her walking away from me anymore. I thought if I went and got the deal and rolled us a smoke, we could keep talking it out.

I had to search the car even with the interior light in my hand. It was under the front seat. I had an idea about mood music. Like the night I'd put Bo Diddley on to get her to come. Track four. 'Little Girl'. It was old-time and spare. Guitar and drums. He wants her to go home with him. That's the song, over and over. I wound up the volume.

I went to the car boot and found a torch. I could tell she was gone as soon as I stood up.

I ran back, hoping she might have gone in the house. 'Rob?' I went to the empty window frame and called in quietly, 'Rob? Are you in there?'

I felt tired. I felt sagging, empty falling down tired. I closed my eyes and listened to the song. It's a happy up-tempo version. No piano. Bo gets them clapping. It sounded thin this far from the car. The sky was all stars maybe not beyond reach.

I looked at the ground by the fire and I saw that the rifle was gone.

*

I took the torch and went into the desert in the direction Robin's father had pointed with his knife. There were snake tracks in the fine sand and flickers of glass that caught in my torch beam. I found her footprints winding around one of the holes, like she had a sixth sense. Maybe she did. Maybe she was a vampire. Her old man too. I was being delivered, another victim. He'd take that big knife and slice the top off my skull. I have brought you a brain, father. I've driven the brain insane first. Gibbering. I know you like them that way. She could be a vampire. It would explain a lot.

There was a steady glow above a small, flat hill a hundred metres ahead, and part of an old wooden poppet lurking above. It was the one I had seen earlier. I found car tracks and boot prints on a dust road that cut through the hill.

Robin was standing near a ramshackle lean-to of corrugated iron and rocks and canvas. She was holding my rifle. I edged forward until

I could see Bill. He was standing about ten metres from her, holding a pair of pliers. I guess he had been working when Robin arrived. Now he was standing still in the middle of his camp.

'You've built it up,' she said, looking at Bill's hut. Her voice was clear in the stillness of the desert. I could hear the crackle of a fire. 'Four walls. Gettin' tickets on yourself.'

'Got a daughter who's a dentist. Have to put my best foot forward,' he said cautiously.

'I didn't know you knew that.'

'What?'

'That I was studying dentistry.'

'One of the girls musta told me. Or your –'

Robin swung around from the house, the rifle barrel going with her.

'I forgot to give you something. That's why I came.'

Before I had the chance to call out, Robin leaned the rifle against the table. It was a fold-out table next to a director's chair by a fire. She dug in her shirt pocket. 'An invoice.'

'A bill?' He walked to her.

'Yes. A bill for Bill. I'm the debt collector. Come all this way.'

She held the invoice out.

'You wouldn't be the first.'

'No. I heard that.'

He looked at her a moment but finally put the pliers on the table next to a half a bottle of Brandavino and took the paper.

Inside the dirt wall that surrounded Bill's camp was an old wheelless truck. I edged behind it, not wanting to interrupt what Robin needed to do. The dog looked over at me but lay down again.

Bill held the invoice towards a gas lamp that was on the table. Robin took the bottle of Brandavino and poured into a plastic cup, drinking while she waited.

'Why'd you bring a rifle?'

'It's Zac's. He stole it from his grandfather before he could hand it in. For hunting, he says.'

'I asked why you brought it.'

'Seemed like a good idea at the time.'

'They're not toys.'

'Yes, Daddy.'

'And you shoulda brought a torch. There are a lot of old mines around here.' He held out the invoice to her.

Robin didn't take it. She said, 'Liz and Gail said they'd pay it.' She took a drink from the cup.

Bill looked down at it. 'I don't understand.'

'I think you should pay.'

They stood looking at each other.

Robin said, 'Seeing as she was your wife. You should pay for her stone.'

'All right.'

'What?'

'All right. If you're all short. That sounds fair enough.' He folded the invoice and put it in his back pocket.

Robin started to laugh. It sounded happy for a moment but turned bitter and creepy.

Bill held a hand towards her like a claw ready to scratch out the laughter.

She pushed the bottle of Brandavino at him until he took it.

'But you won't pay it, will you? You're saying yeah to get rid of me.'

He turned to the table looking for his cup, then shrugged and sat in the director's chair by the fire, with his back to her, drinking from the bottle.

Robin sculled her own drink and pushed the cup in front of him. He poured.

A pulley up at the top of the poppet head began to clunk dully against the old wood in a breeze blowing somewhere above our crater.

Robin said, 'Do you ever get lonely?'

'No.'

'No. You don't care, do you? That's the way you like it.'

Bill stood. The dog growled.

'Fuck your wife, your family. Fuck everybody else. You know who'll be at your funeral?' She stopped talking. She looked bewildered. It was like she'd been slapped, but Bill's arms were down.

I stood and said, 'Rob?'

Bill looked over at me, annoyed, but straight back at Robin. 'Do you want an answer? Is that what you want?'

'Yeah, I do. Why you killed her.'

'Killed her? I didn't kill her. She died of cancer. I wasn't even there.'

'Exactly. You were never there. You left her to bring us up.'

'I gave her money when I had it.'

'Why did you hate us?'

'Hate you? Is that what your mother said?'

'No. She'd never say that. It's what I'm saying.'

He shook his head, like a boxer trying to clear away concussion.

Robin smiled.

Bill started around the table.

Robin reached for the rifle.

'No, Rob. No.'

She pointed the rifle at me then back at Bill as he walked up to her.

'I didn't love her. That what you want to hear?'

'It wasn't my fault,' Robin said.

'What?' Bill saw something and in that moment took the rifle out of her hands. He grabbed and twisted it in the one motion and held it up behind him. 'Who said anything was your fault?' He flicked his eyes to include me. 'It's no one's fault. Shit, I was twenty. Your mother was seventeen. We all do fucking stupid things when we're young.'

I came closer. 'Shall I take the rifle? Make it safe.'

Robin said, 'You know what work she did, Zac? She took in laundry.'

'Nothing wrong with that,' said Bill. 'We can't all be dentists.'

'There was everything wrong with it. She'd start working at five. Wouldn't stop. Piles and piles of dirty clothes. Slag heaps of dusty, sweaty, stinking miner's clothes. Underwear of people we didn't even know. Scrubbing the shit out.'

'Her choice,' he said.

'What choice did she have?

'Why didn't you help her?' he said.

'I did.' She looked at him, pleading. Then at me too. 'I tried. I couldn't do it all on my own.'

'So it is about you,' Bill said.

'It's about you. You and her.'

'Where were you?' he asked.

'Hey, that's enough,' I said. I stepped towards them and Bill pushed the rifle into my chest and reached into his pocket and pulled out the screwed-up invoice. 'Your name's on the bit of paper, not mine.'

'She should have put yours.'

'But she didn't. Here it is. Next of kin. Robin May.'

'I couldn't ...'

'Rob, you couldn't.' I stepped between them again and said to him, 'She's a student.'

He talked past me. 'Why did she put your name on the paper?' He pushed the invoice at Robin.

I grabbed it. 'That's enough.'

He said, 'You didn't even go to her funeral. It wasn't just me. You didn't go either.'

'Stop it.' I reached my hand forward to push him. He swatted it away.

'You know what I think?' he said. 'That's why she put your name on the paper. She knew you wouldn't come. Not when she got sick. Not when she was dead.'

'Leave her alone, you prick.' I chested him and made him take a step back.

'What did you say?'

'Leave her alone.' I tossed the rifle down and raised my fists.

The dog growled.

He moved the bottle into his left hand like it wasn't a weapon. Then he looked over my shoulder and said, 'She's getting away.'

I turned. She was. Robin was running out of the gap in the hill. Damn. I sighed and turned back in time for Bill to punch me. I fell on my arse in the dirt. Blood dripped onto my chest. 'You hit me.'

'It was a fight. You lost.'

'But I wasn't looking.'

'Yeah, that was the idea. Now fuck off and leave me alone.'

I tried to wipe my nose but it hurt. I got up and looked around for the torch. When I grabbed his gas lamp he didn't say anything. I got the rifle and went after Robin.

*

Her tracks were easy to follow. She was running straight, with deep steps, fleeing out across the desert.

Her footprints ended at one of the mine holes where they skidded in the dirt.

'Rob?'

The light from the lantern spread easily across the ground but not so well down into the old dig. I tipped the lamp and found her on a ledge, huddled in the corner. The ledge was only about half a metre wide before the shaft went down again beyond.

'Jesus fucking Christ, Rob.'

She had scrapes on her arms and a bruise rising on her cheek.

'Anything broken?'

She giggled. 'You said you wanted to meet my family. Careful what you wish for.' She sounded a little drunk.

'Can you stand up?'

'I thought he had all the answers. You know, living out here, away from – all the noise. My mysterious father.'

I took the light off her and looked around the top of the mine shaft for something to use to drag her out. There was a broken wooden winch but no rope. Only rocks poked from the mound of dirt.

'All this way and no answers to the meaning of life. What a rip-off.'

In the shaft were weathered poles of wood stacked lengthways along the sides, but they looked too smooth to climb.

'Can you stand up?'

Robin started to get up but saw the edge and she pushed back into the corner. 'You should leave me.'

'How about I get you out of this hole, and we'll see?'

'Ah, you're considering it.'

'Never.'

'I don't blame you. I'm a shit.'

'Can we talk about this later?'

'That's what I say.' She was looking into the darkness below her. 'I have no idea why I do shit. Why I do anything. Two days ago, I quit uni. I went in and I sold all my books.'

'Oh.' I tried to catch up. 'Yeah, I never saw you as a dentist.'

'What?'

'I can't imagine you being an actual dentist.'

'Yeah, well, snap. I need to see a shrink.'

I lay down on the ground with my arm reaching over the side. If she stood, I could almost reach her. 'I'm going to have to go back to his camp and get some rope.'

'No.'

'Rob, you're stuck.'

'Don't care.'

'You're being stupid.'

'Am not.'

'Are too.'

'You are.'

She smiled.

I said, 'We'll use the rifle. If you can hold on and kind of step up on those logs along the edge of the shaft.'

She squinted up at the light of the lamp in a studying kind of way and said, 'You should have held up that petrol station, you know.'

'Yeah. I really wanted to. But, you know.'

'The cops would have come. I'd have to take over driving while you held them off with the rifle.'

'I'd shoot out their tyres.' I moved the lamp onto a mound so it angled further into the shaft, then got the rifle and lowered the butt end towards her, but she wasn't moving. I said, 'Stand up, Rob.' When she didn't, I said, 'Of course, we would have to come out here because the cops would radio for all the police everywhere to get us. We'd have to hide out with your dad.'

'What? No.'

'Yeah. We'd be in his one-room rock house surrounded by hundreds of cops around the hill like in *Butch Cassidy*.'

'They die in *Butch Cassidy*.'

'Well, I don't want to have to correct you, but they don't die. The shot freezes. Before they are dead. Like *Thelma & Louise*. Anyway, we get away. There's this hidden mine shaft under his hut. But he tells you all the secrets first and says he'll hold them off and we get away.'

She nodded.

'Stand up.'

Robin stood, pushing back into the corner. 'Can he take a bullet?'

'He steps outside after we're gone, full of regrets. Gets riddled, especially by the Gatling gun on the chopper.' I pushed the butt at her again. 'Okay, now if you grab the stock, and I grab the barrel. Whatever you do, don't touch the trigger. Or let go.'

She had the stock.

'I'm not lifting you. You're stepping up on those bits of wood.'

She nodded.

The barrel was slippery. 'Just a sec.' I got up on one knee and I got one arm right along the barrel, kind of wound around. 'Okay.'

Robin pulled and I leaned back on my heels as she started to walk up the wall. I leaned further and further back as she found footholds between the wood logs shoring up the side. Her face appeared at the top. She was straining now but there didn't seem to be a way for her to take the last steps up onto level ground.

'Hold on,' I said.

And I held hard on the barrel and let myself fall back, dragging Robin up the last bit and over the edge and onto the ground, where she fell forward onto her knees. I lay looking up at the heavy stars, gasping for breath.

Robin stood, dusting herself like she'd simply tripped over.

'We did it,' I said.

'Yep, let's go.'

'Robin! Give me a sec.'

She picked up the rifle and her father's lantern while I got up and winkled my fingers to get the circulation back.

'Where's all the blood from?'

She held up the lantern, examining my bloody t-shirt.

'Your father. He sucker-punched me.'

She scowled. 'When we get back to Perth, I'll move out.'

'I just saved your life.'

'I know. I'm letting you go.' She gave me the rifle and started walking.

I followed. I didn't say anything. I had nothing left. Not after 'I saved your life'.

'You'll thank me,' she said after we'd gone a little way.

I could see a distant glow. Our fire had died down, but the car light was a presence in the darkness under the trillion stars. 'It's so quiet out here.'

We both stopped walking and listened.

'Your mum sounds like she was good. Working. Keeping you all together. Doing whatever she could for everyone.'

'Yeah.'

We started walking again.

After a while she said, 'When I left Kal, Mum and Gail and Liz came to the train station to see me off. The big success. So proud. "Off to university." "You're so smart." So excited. But, just as I was about to get on the train, she pushes this casserole dish at me. I mean, you've seen it. It's an oven pot, with a lid. "Still warm. For your first night." It was tuna casserole. What are you going to do, right? I've got a suitcase; I've got my pack, a handbag, sleeping bag. Now here's this giant tuna casserole – to cart through the city, while I find my way to the uni. Geek-girl from the country. No idea. "Bring the dish with you next time you're back up." Sure Mum. Next time – I'm back.' Robin stopped walking and gritted her teeth and battled not to cry. Instead, she growled, low and determined like a cough she wouldn't let finish.

'It's okay, Rob,' I said, reaching to pat her shoulder, but she shook me off.

'No it's not.'

We walked again. She walked. I walked with her. The fire embers were clear now, warm and orange on the earth near her old house.

'It wasn't the washing, it was the fucking people. The fucking customers. Strangers. When they'd give us the washing, they'd smile their smiles, "Here, this should help." Like they were giving us a fucking donation. "Here you go, lass." She'd have to kill herself every day to get their small change. And they wanted eternal fucking gratitude. Their squeaky Christian voices: "You should be very proud of your mum." "I hope you help her." My mother was a saint, Zac. Ask anyone. Everyone. In fact, the only two people in the whole world who didn't love my mother were my father and me.'

'No.'

She stopped and she pointed at me with a sneaky smile. 'He said she put my name on the invoice cos she knew I wouldn't come. He has no idea. She thought I caused the sunshine. The letters. Even near the end. I didn't hate him. I hated her, for making me feel bad every day of my life, and I ran away, like he said, as soon as I could. And I never came back. Even when she got sick. Even when she tried to call. Even when she ... she died.' Robin gasped but the gasp didn't stop. It was like a ruptured pipe in her chest. Her cry came from inside but like it was nothing to do with her.

I hugged her. She shook in my arms, her shoulders, her chest. The tremors kept breaking from her mouth in these awful moans. I hugged her until the gasps came back into shudders and pants for breath.

'It's okay. Shhh.'

'I'm cracking up.'

I hugged her so she wouldn't see that I was scared too.

Then she said, 'She loved me. She loved me, and I hated her, and I ran away, just like him. Even when she died, I didn't come back.'

'You're back now.'

'It's too late now.'

I needed something wise to say, something hopeful and true and useful. I needed to say something to help her and I had nothing. I had no idea. I wasn't smart enough.

'Are you crying?' she asked.

'I'm sorry, Rob. I'm so, so sorry.'

'I should be. Not you.'

'I know. I'm sorry.'

'Stop it.' She pushed herself away again. We were by the embers of the fire.

I said, 'No.'

'Leave me be.'

'You can trust me, Robin. You can trust me to know this stuff about you and still love you.'

'Haven't you been listening? I don't understand the word.'

'What?'

'I'm not sure I love you.'
'Oh.'

*

The dog fretting woke me. It was dawn and still cold. I eased out of my sleeping bag quietly so as not to wake Robin. She was asleep in her sleeping bag on the back seat, her cheeks smudged from tears and dust.

I patted the dog and got the rifle and used the butt end to scrape sand out from around the tyre. I went and got a piece of weatherboard from the house and slid that under.

One of the most beautiful songs on the Bo Diddley album that I can't name because I can't remember who burned the album for me is 'I'm Sorry'. It's got a slow musical intro with mournful guitar and piano and drums. Bo's voice is distant. The backup singers are girls. I should have played it before we'd gone to bed; so we could have swayed slowly together in the desert. It's a very sentimental song. Robin would have grabbed the rifle and shot me, if I'd done it. But it would have been neat.

The dog whimpered and Robin popped up looking down at me digging.

'Hi,' I said.

'Tell me I had a long bad dream.'

'It was all true and you promised me lots of sex.'

She looked at the rifle. 'It's kind of a Swiss Army rifle isn't it?'

The dog whined again and Robin slid across the back seat to look over at it. She scanned the remains of the town.

I stood. 'He must have come while we were asleep. He took his lamp back.'

She slithered out of her sleeping bag and climbed out of the car and patted the dog.

'I think he's a present,' I said.

Robin untied the rope where it was knotted at the dog's collar. It ran off into the desert towards Bill's camp.

I said, 'I guess he hadn't thought it through.'

'No idea.'

'He tried.'

Robin considered that. 'An empty gesture being better than none at all you mean?'

I shrugged.

She looked at me oddly. Said, 'Your nose is crooked.'

I turned to give her my left profile and turned again to show her my right.

'More Marlon Brando now. Maybe Montgomery Clift.'

'After the car accident.'

'Which is better than James Dean after the car accident.'

We both winced.

She said, 'I'm not magically fixed because I told you stuff.'

'I think we're out,' I said, tossing the rifle aside. 'You wanna start the engine? I'll push.'

She looked back out into the desert one more time, but got behind the wheel.

'You don't have to move out right away, you know. We could keep playing it by ear,' I said.

I couldn't hear Robin's reply because the engine caught and growled.

I kept pushing.

THE RING-IN

At last deliverance is almost here. Of course I was clumsy. I didn't know how to shoot; I almost missed myself. Of course it would have been better to have died at once, but after all, they were not able to extract the bullet and then heart complications set in.'
– 'A Young Girl's Confession', Marcel Proust

EXT. PINE PLANTATION. DAWN.

The taxi came into the pine plantation on two wheels. It wobbled a moment then went over onto the roof, wiping off the plastic taxi sign on the limestone track. It continued to slide on its roof, the driver upside down, belted to his seat, holding onto the steering wheel as though it were of some use. There was a dead guy on the roof next to him in the front, and another guy in the back screaming and scrambling amidst an assortment of firearms and blood. There was a beautiful woman in the back too, upside down with her seatbelt on. Her shirt was missing. The taxi continued to slide in slow motion between the trees like a boat sailing up a jungle river at dawn.

Simon and the Pieman

On a dark and lonely road at the frayed edge of the suburbs, Simon drove the same taxi, when it was new. It still had plastic on the trim. There was only three hundred kilometres on the clock. Simon flicked on the temporary dispatch radio.

A scratchy female voice came through. 'Simon?'

'I'm done. Lights out and going home.'

'See, you made it.'

'Yeah. Like falling off a horse.'

'I think that's getting back on the horse, sweetie.'

'Night, Cheryl.'

Simon turned off the two-way then flicked off the taxi sign on the top of the car. He tried to blink out a glitch but the thing in his eyes stayed there. Way out in the darkness beyond his headlights was a red dot. The dot got bigger and became two brakelights at a T-junction.

Simon pulled up, his headlights on the car in the ditch across the road. It had failed to turn right or left and was nose down in the drain, its back wheels still spinning in the air.

Simon sat at the junction, his taxi in gear, looking at the car. Its headlights were on, bouncing back off good dark river dirt. Dust or smoke formed a drifting haze around the car.

Simon looked left and right along the dark country road but there was no one else. He sighed and put the taxi in park. He took off his seatbelt and walked slowly to the other car, rolling his neck a little stiffly and settling his shoulders. The engine whined shrilly. He entered the brake-lit red of the exhaust smoke and looked down to the driver's side, but the windows were tinted.

'Hey, you'll burn out the motor. Hey.' Simon stepped off the bitumen and onto the gravel shoulder and carefully tapped on the boot. 'Hey.'

Simon looked down into the ditch, where the half-buried headlights kicked back some light. There was rubbish but the ditch had not seen rain for a year now. He stepped down and knocked on the driver's window. 'Hey.'

The engine stopped revving. After a moment the window came down. A middle-aged man in a shirt and tie blinked out at him. Then he peered at the other side of the ditch. 'I'm stuck.'

'You sure are.'

'I gotta get home. Late for dinner.'

Simon looked into the darkness. There wasn't even a farm light on this late. The engine began to tick as it cooled.

The man fumbled for his mobile, dropping it somewhere in the car. He bent forward, banging his head on the steering wheel. He waved a hand in the air, giving it up.

Simon said, 'You want me to call you a tow truck?'

'Hey, yeah. Great. I got a rope in the boot.'

'No, what I meant was ...'

The boot popped up.

'If you give me a tow out, then I can get home.'

Simon stepped back as the door swung open. The man swayed out of the car, hung for a moment on the door then sat down on the side of the ditch. 'Woaw, I'm fucked.'

'I'm Simon,' said Simon, not very loudly. He looked at the guy a moment then stepped up out of the ditch and looked back at his own taxi headlights across the road.

'Simon?'

'Yes.'

'My name's Frank.' He was standing now.

'Glad to meet you Frank.'

Frank reached his hand out and Simon took it, and Frank started pulling, so Simon got some purchase and hauled Frank up to the back of his car, where he stood looking into the ditch. 'Fuck, eh.'

Simon looked in the boot. There were lots of little cardboard signs. *Granny Jo's Pies.* There was some rope under the signs. 'You sell pies, Frank?'

'Fucken A. Sold more fucking pies than any other bastard last month is what I did. Shitload of commissions. King of the pies.' Frank looked up at the sky and howled at it like a wolf.

Simon had the rope, hefting it. It was nylon, and he doubted it would be strong enough. 'I'll give this a try, but I don't like our chances, Frank. My taxi's new, and I don't know whether the pistons ...'

Frank, who had been peering across the road, suddenly pushed himself up off his car and yelled, 'Taxi!' He stepped towards it. 'There's a taxi.'

'Yes, there is, Frank. Just over there.'

'I gotta go. Gotta get home for dinner.' Frank started across the deserted road towards the taxi.

'What about your car?'

Frank didn't turn. 'Fuck it.' He raised his hand and waved down Simon's taxi.

Simon tossed the rope into the boot and closed it. Then he went down into the ditch again and turned off the headlights and got Frank's keys from the ignition. He locked up and went to his taxi. As he got in the driver's seat and turned on the ignition, Frank said, 'Fifteen Royal Court, The Pines, mate.'

Simon started the meter. 'You got it.'

'Simon?'

'How ya doing, Frank?'

Simon drove back through Middle Swan where good flood plain country had turned from melons and pumpkins to vineyards, and then wineries with restaurants. On weekends you had to dodge 50cc scooters and tour buses, but some sagging stalls outside the old farmhouses still sold cheap oranges and table grapes.

Frank lived in a boutique housing estate wedged between the wine country and a huge pine plantation. Simon turned in to a cul-de-sac filled with McMansions in different shades of terracotta with big double garages and tiny neat lawns.

Simon pulled into number fifteen, and turned to find his passenger dozing. 'Frank. Frank. We're here.'

'Huh, oh, right.'

'That's twenty-eight forty.'

'What?'

Simon pointed at the meter. 'Call it twenty-eight. Well, you can call it more, too. That's up to you.'

'You stopped to help me.'

'Yes. That's probably why I was hoping it might be more.'

'You stopped to help me, as a ... as a ... Not as a taxi driver.'

'Ah. I see.'

'You gave me a lift, didn't you?'

'Well, the thing is, Frank, it's on my meter now. You know, if you don't pay, I'll have to.'

'You bastard. No. You're not ripping me off. No way.' Frank flung open the passenger door and staggered towards his house.

Simon got out and followed. Frank was leaning on the door and wrenching at the handle. Simon jangled Frank's keys next to his ear.

Frank turned. 'Simon. Good on ya.' He took the keys, unlocked the door and went inside.

Simon watched the door close. He stood a moment longer, rolling his neck again, teasing out the tightness. He went to the rear passenger door of the taxi and closed it gently, then to the driver's seat. He put his seatbelt on, backed out of Frank's driveway and drove out of the cul-de-sac.

We'll Always Have Paris

It was hot. Sweat beaded on Grace's temple and dampened under the arms of her dress. Grace was reading Jim Thompson's *The Rip-Off* at the tiny beer can–covered table of a small caravan. Her lips moved as she read.

A beer can popped. Johnny Johnston sat at the same table, bulging out of his slacks and an unbuttoned turquoise silk shirt. He took a gulp of the beer and looked over at Grace. 'What you reckon was the best place we went?'

Grace looked up from her paperback.

But before she could answer, JJ said, 'France was the best. That was the best place ever.'

JJ burped. He was looking at the empty beer cans on the table but thinking about France.

Grace started to think about France too. The Ibis Hotel in Paris. She was blonde back then, not dark-haired like now. And skinny. She remembered lounging in a bikini in the sun that hit the glass at one end of the indoor pool.

A cute young guy in tight black pants and a white shirt had two drinks on a tray. He put them down, smiling at Grace, not hiding that he liked what he saw. 'Mademoiselle.'

'It's madam. Merci,' said Grace trying to soften her Aussie accent. 'Monsieur.'

'Yeah, right garsonne. Beauty.' JJ took his drink and raised the glass towards the sun. 'How good is this, babe? How fuckin' good is this?' JJ was trim then, still fit and handsome and happy.

'It's good,' said Grace.

'Bet it's raining in Australia, now.'

Grace smiled at the pool as she sipped her vodka and tonic. Two days in the hotel and they hadn't yet set foot in the rest of Paris. 'What do you want to do JJ?'

JJ waved his drink at the pool and rooms somewhere above them. 'We can do whatever we want. Whatever we want.'

JJ was remembering the Ibis Hotel too.

Mostly he was remembering Grace's legs and her perfect little feet with bright red nail polish. He looked up to see her sparkling happy eyes catching him looking. She was a beauty no matter what country you were in. He said, 'I'll tell you what I want to do.'

Grace smiled back, dreamy like a cat.

JJ smiled in the cramped caravan far from France. He looked

at the green chipped walls. Sweat dribbled down his chest and slid sideways around his stomach. Grace was reading again. 'You wanna do something?'

'What?'

'I suppose a fuck's out of the question.'

Grace paused ever so slightly before looking up from her book. 'If you want.'

'You never used to read, when I first met you. Maybe a couple of magazines. That's normal. Now you always got your head stuck in some book. Like you caught Readingitus in all those Ramada Inns. Always reading. Can't stop.'

Grace put her book down. 'JJ, I said I would.'

'Yeah, like some favour. Like ...' JJ stood to pace, but there was only one step to the nearest wall. He banged his fist against the aluminium. 'This is fucked up.'

She picked her book up again.

JJ looked at his mobile amidst the empty beer cans. 'I'll see Mr Foster.'

'Don't.' She wasn't asking.

JJ looked away. 'Just to make sure it's still sorted out.'

'*You* decided that was the only safe move. *You* decided.'

'Things change.'

The Big Time

'Mr Foster, from Wooroloo?'

'What other Mr Foster do you know?' said Ellis.

Ellis and Ned were walking through a shopping car park, looking for a car that wasn't locked.

Ned stopped walking. 'I didn't know he was that ... um, heavy.'

'Maybe he learned a few things in prison.' Ellis smiled at Ned to remind him that they'd had something to do with the lessons.

'I only got a knife, Ellis.'

'George has a rifle. A twenty-two.'

'Oh.'

Ellis saw a woman with shopping. He nudged Ned and they headed towards her. She saw them, two unshaven men, one in shorts and a singlet, the other in filthy jeans and t-shirt. They were so obviously frightening, even in the middle of the afternoon in a shopping centre, that she ran the last steps to her car. Ellis and Ned stepped faster too. The shopper beeped the door unlocked and threw her plastic grocery bags into the front passenger seat, sending plums tumbling. She squeezed behind the steering wheel, pushed the key into the ignition and hit every button she could. The doors and windows locked and the hazard lights started blinking as Ellis reached her car door. Ned tried the back door anyway.

Ellis smiled one of his bad-toothed smiles. 'Hey, can you give me directions? It's to um, oh, um, Hungry Jacks, yeah.'

The woman started screaming. Then she hit the car horn. She leaned on it and kept it going.

Ellis slammed his hand on the roof, but backed off, looking around to see who was coming. Nobody. Nobody cared, but the car was locked and the horn was still going, so he and Ned drifted away like they'd never seen that lady before.

'Guess we can't go to George's,' said Ned.

'Taxi. We'll get a taxi.'

Ellis was pointing. Over near the shopping centre was a line of taxis.

Ned looked at the taxi and back to Ellis who was looking at him and getting angry.

'They'll be a witness. Is that what you think, Ned?'

'No. I didn't think anything, Ellis. Honest.'

Ellis reached up and grabbed Ned by his thick throat, rough but not quite choking. Ned let him. 'Maybe they won't be a witness cos maybe they'll be dead.'

The driver pulled some headphones off and tossed them into the glove box as Ellis and Ned got into the back.

'How's it going, guys?' he said as though he cared.

Ellis said, 'It's going good.'

Ned looked around the inside of the back of the taxi, touching the clear plastic.

The engine started. Ellis ordered, 'Midvale. We'll tell you where, when you get there.'

'You got it.'

'Yeah, I know.' Ellis turned to Ned and winked.

The Princess and the Frog

The dogs started barking and Grace went out to see.

Tim was out the front, bent over the engine of a partly rebuilt stock car, but looking next door.

Luke, his neighbour, was standing behind his ute in the driveway there, dressed in overalls, yelling at his dogs. 'Oi, stop that.' They did, like he'd flicked a switch. He looked up and saw Grace in front of the caravan and stood frozen, like some other switch had been flicked.

Grace smiled but he looked down and got busy with what he was getting from the back of the ute.

She heard her sister Lisa yell, 'You want a beer, Luke?'

Luke nodded and stepped over the low wooden fence into Tim and Lisa's front yard, carrying a dirty engine part.

Grace went out. 'Hi everyone.' Grace smiled, like she'd just arrived at a picnic. 'Sure is hot.'

'Just average,' said Tim. Grace guessed he was still generally simmering at the present 'situation'.

'Not like Europe, I bet,' said Luke.

'You heard about that? Secret's out now, it looks like.'

He nodded, but then looked away embarrassed.

Grace said, 'It was very cold in Switzerland. It snowed.' She shook herself in a demonstration of shivering but then felt stupid. 'I mean, of course. Derr. Switzerland and snow. Like saying it's hot in the desert.'

Lisa came down the steps with two cans of beer in stubby holders. When she saw Grace looking she gave her a tired smile.

'I was in Afghanistan,' said Luke. 'You want cold, you try those mountains. In winter. I mean you wouldn't want to try them.'

'Afghanistan!' said Grace. 'Are you a soldier?'

'Was,' said Luke.

Lisa gave the beers to the men.

Tim said, 'The captain here has a couple of medals.'

'I was just a corporal.'

'Nothing to be ashamed of.' JJ came from the caravan like a car salesman entering the yard. 'Army's the backbone of this country. There'd be no athletes if there was no army. And we know it. Good on ya, I say.'

JJ looked up at them. Tim was six and a half feet tall, and Luke nearly the same, only all muscle. Even Lisa was a head taller than JJ. Silence, like a hole in the ground.

Grace filled it. 'We stayed all over Europe. Spain. Rome. I went to the museums. I saw paintings of Impressionists in Paris and they were real, not prints. There were statues in Rome. In Madrid, there's statues everywhere outside and they're really old, with fountains. I saw a concert in one of the hotels that they had in the grounds.'

'Fancy,' said Lisa. 'Living in hotels for two years.'

'Biggest shitload of free food and grog you ever saw,' said JJ.

'Looks like you got most of it,' said Tim.

Grace said, 'And in France I started learning French. "Excusez-moi l'étranger, est cela la voie au musée?"'

Luke laughed, delighted. Even Lisa and Tim were smiling at Grace's performance.

'Yeah,' interrupted JJ, 'I got a lot of French over the last couple of years.'

Grace stood, trying to keep her smile going in the new silence.

Finally, Tim said, 'If you're hiding out from the police and everybody, is it smart to be hanging around out the front of the house?'

JJ suddenly looked up and down the street. There was a narrow strip of bush and a freeway over the road. 'Yeah, good point.' JJ went back around the side of the house.

Tim said, 'The athlete has left the building.'

Lisa said, 'Well, I better get dinner started.'

'I'll help,' said Grace.

Grace peeled potatoes while her sister sprinkled spice on the meat.

Grace said, 'Sorry, Lisa.'

'What are you gunna do?'

'Well, I've seen the world.'

Lisa looked over and saw that her sister was being ironic. 'On the run!'

'It wasn't like that. Not like how the papers said. We mostly just stayed in Ramada Inns. Like a holiday. Then it was a bit like prison anyway, I guess.'

'You don't love him. I can see that.'

'I try to.'

'He's a pig.'

'He's my husband.'

Grace sat by the pool of the Four Seasons in London, reading Pride and Prejudice *with furrowed brow. It was a hard book. She looked up and saw herself in one of the huge glass walls that surrounded the pool. She was in a white hotel robe over her bathing suit on account of the cold, but not just that. Grace had been worried about her looks, about how all the eating and sitting and doing nothing was making her face round and her body plump. It had taken a while, but she felt like she'd turned from Calista Flockhart into Britney Spears. The waiters still gave her the look, but JJ had gotten a little unseeing around her.*

She looked up at the underneath of the pool roof where thousands of droplets of water quivered. The steam from the pool condensed and every now and then a drop would get big enough or cold enough and would fall. If one got you, it was quite a shock. The swimming pool was in its own room attached to the hotel. All the walls were clear glass between columns. It reminded Grace of the picture of the coffin where Snow White lay after biting the apple. She sniffed at the warm, oversweet smell of chlorine.

JJ came from the hotel, his burgeoning body spilling out of tiny speedos and his robe flowing out behind, like an angry midget wrestler on his way to the ring. 'He's in jail,' he yelled.

'Foster?'

JJ sat on his pool chair, facing her and nodding. 'Wooroloo.'

'Not for the ring-in?'

'Naw. Something else. Some business shit. He's fucking up lots of things.'

Grace watched JJ clench and unclench his hands. 'So are the bills still getting paid?'

'I don't think so. I think maybe we dropped down the list of priorities.'

Grace looked back to the hotel and then to JJ. 'So what did you tell them?'

'Nothin'. I haven't thought of anything yet.'

'Let's go home.'

'What?'

'Let's go back to Australia.'

'We're on holidays.'

'JJ, I'm bored.'

'Well don't read all the time. Do something. I'm showing you the world here.'

Grace got up and went around behind JJ and started to knead his shoulders. 'I'm sorry, baby. It's all good. It's been amazing. Just amazing.'

He grunted, but was leaning back into the massage. 'It's not easy being on the run, you know.'

'I know, JJ. And all the pressure is on you.'

'Puttin' my career on hold.'

'You'll get that back.' She looked doubtfully down past his shoulders at the watermelon that had replaced JJ's once flat stomach. 'What are we going to do about the hotel concierge?'

'Yeah, I s'pose I can try to get through to someone who does some shady stuff for Foster. Bobby, maybe.' He looked up suddenly with a smile. 'Or we can do a runner?'

Of All the Gin Joints

Simon waited in the taxi outside a block of flats in Midvale. He'd been left with the bigger one. Simon watched him in the rear-view mirror as he teased at a piece of the plastic on his door, managing to get a little bit loose by the window trim.

Simon said, 'Be another warm night, I reckon.'

Simon watched him look out at the world with little interest and no comment. Simon turned towards a movement over at the flats. The smaller one was coming back. Then Simon saw who he was and turned away, perhaps too quickly, pretending to fiddle with the GPS.

Ellis got in the taxi. He said, 'Wasn't there.'

'Oh.'

'That guy in the pub. In Guildford.'

'In Guildford? That pub burnt down.'

'Not the pub. The guy. The one from the caravan park.'

'Gary. Near the river.'

'Gary, yeah. He said he had ... one. Was hiding it for a bikie. Yeah, Gary. Hey, taxi guy, drive us to Guildford Caravan Park.'

'You got it.' Simon pulled out, trying not to give Ellis a look at his face.

After a while Ellis said it. 'Say, do I know you?'

Simon said, 'I don't think so, mate.'

'Hm, let's see this little plastic picture here. It says Simon Carter. Simon? Hmm. Now I think I know that name. Simon.' Ellis was playing with him now. 'You ever played football?'

'No sir.'

'Sir! I'm pretty sure it wasn't prison. You know this guy from prison, Ned?'

Ned shook his head.

'Hey, I knew a Simon at school. Was that you Simon?'

'Yes, it was. Hello, Ellis.'

That stopped Ellis a moment. But then he said, 'Yeah. It's me.' Like a judge's sentence.

Simon didn't say anything, waiting for Ellis.

Ellis started giggling. 'A taxi. He's driving a taxi. Ned, you don't recognise Simon?'

'No.'

'I thought everyone knew Simon. He was famous. At school, he was always up there on the stage at assembly, where we could all, um just admire him, I s'pose. I think those teachers used to put him up there for us to try to be like him. Was that the plan, Simon?'

'I don't know, Ellis. I was a kid too. Long time ago.' Simon drove. His left hand sat on his knee, but not too far from the temporary two-way radio.

'You still got those two crazy eyes, Simon?'

'Yep, still there.'

'Guy's got two different colour eyes, Ned. When he stops, get a look.'

Simon could still only see Ned in the rear-view mirror. Ned looked at Simon a moment but quickly back to Ellis, uneasy. It seemed that he didn't know which way this was going to go either.

'Like yesterday to me – all that school shit. Sports captain. Cricket and basketball. All the kiddie brown-nose committees. Oh, and top of the class. Not my class. I was in criminal class. He always had clean shirts. Only the honeyest, cutest, cleanest girls – lining up for old Simon to pop their cherry. Like a rock star. Ned, you better bow down to this guy. This is Simon Carter ... and he's driving a fucking taxi.'

Ned said, 'I didn't go to your school, Ellis.'

'It's a very clean taxi, Simon.'

'I think it's brand new,' offered Ned.

'Is that what you do, Simon? Are you like a test pilot for the new taxis?'

'Ha, no Ellis, I just drive it. Here we are.'

Simon pulled off the road into the Guildford Caravan Park. It was not a family holiday destination, but a neglected long-term accommodation spot, half a star from being condemned.

Simon stopped by the front gate and turned with a smile. 'Here you go Ellis. Ned. Good to meet you. Tell you what, for old times' sake, let's say this ride is on the house.'

Ellis went cold. 'Let's say not. I don't need your charity.'

'Not charity. Just a present.'

'No!' shouted Ellis.

Ned reached for a plastic bag in his lap.

Simon wished he'd turned the other way, so he could reach his doorhandle.

'See his eyes,' said Ellis, suddenly not angry.

'Weird,' said Ned, looking from Simon's blue eye to his grey eye and back.

Ellis said, 'We got lots of money. I'm a very successful guy now. And we haven't finished our ride yet. This is just a stop. Places to go. And I need the ride.'

Simon looked at Ellis and then nodded. 'You got it.' He turned back to the wheel, casually waiting.

'Sure is a new taxi you got here, Simon.'

'Yeah. The owner just got it.'

'Told you,' said Ned.

'You got the old kind of radio there.'

'Yes. Just until they put the dispatch computer in.'

Ellis looked around the inside of the taxi, too carefully, then got out of the car. He leaned back in as Ned started to open his door. 'You stay here.'

'But I want to ...'

'I said stay.'

Simon had a good position on the side mirror now. He saw Ellis glare and indicate that Ned was to watch Simon. He looked to the rear-view mirror to catch Ned touching the top of a knife handle he had in the plastic bag. Simon looked back to the other mirror to find Ellis, but he was by the driver's window. Simon wound it down.

'Sure is some coincidence, eh?' said Ellis.

'It's a small town.'

Ellis suddenly adopted a gun fighter stance and put on a bad American accent. 'This town ain't big enough for the both of us.' He mimed drawing a gun, his finger pointed at Simon. 'Pow,' he said without much volume. 'See you guys in a minute.'

Simon watched Ellis walk towards a wheelless motor home that had a motorbike out the front. Ellis stretched his arms out and wriggled his fingers, loosening for the quick draw.

Simon dropped his hand back to his knee and let it sit there a moment before it started to crawl towards the radio.

'No,' said Ned from the back.

'I got to let them know I'm stopped, but still on the job.'

Ned looked to the meter. It was already up to fifty-six dollars.

Ned said, 'No radio till Ellis gets back.'

Simon turned back to him but then shrugged, easy.

Ned looked at him for a while, flicking from eye to eye, before settling on his nose and saying, 'If you're so smart, how come you're driving a taxi?'

Simon nodded at the good question. 'I kind of drifted into it. I like it fine. Well, I don't not like it. As my ex-wife explained, I have a problem with ambition. Anyway, I don't like it less than other things I've done, which I disliked more. So here I am.'

Ned was looking at the motor home where Ellis was knocking on the door.

Simon said, 'You gotta pay the rent.'

'Why?'

Gary, Get Your Gun

Gary opened the door to peer at a ratty little guy in an AC/DC t-shirt.

'Gary.'

Gary finished tying his sarong.

'How you doin', mate?'

'What do you want?'

'Business. Can't do it standing out here.' He held up his mobile phone like it meant something and began a quarter smile working, but gave it up and started inside.

Gary tried to step across, but too late. He looked at the taxi waiting before closing the door.

AC/DC fiddled with his phone as he sat in the middle of the couch, making himself at home. He nodded at the bong in the middle of Gary's huge jarrah coffee table. 'Made out of a science tube, right?'

Gary gave his ponytail a little tug to shift the elastic up firm at his head but didn't say anything.

The guy looked at Gary's samurai sword mounted on the wall. 'Man, that sword! What a beauty. That's a *Pulp Fiction* sword. A *Kill Bill* fuckin' sword.' Ellis put on a voice. 'Are you okay? No. I'm not okay. I'm very not okay. I'm fucked up.'

Gary crossed his big biceps over his tight pecs. 'What kind of business?'

'Aren't ya going to offer me a beer?'

'I'm out.'

The guy blinked a couple of times trying to shake off the insult, but still not taking any hints. 'Oh. I shoulda bought something. I'm sorry. Been rushed off my feet. Lotta business to take care of.'

'Look mate, I know we've met somewhere but I can't remember where and I don't want to be your friend, so, you wanna tell me what you want?'

He went empty. It was like he'd gone somewhere for a moment. When he came back there was a sparkle, like a little charge of electricity filling all of him. 'I want your gun.'

'My gun!'

'See we got to remembering you bragging about having a revolver. I think it was some old revolver that a bikie asked you to mind.'

'I haven't got it anymore.'

'I just want to borrow it.'

'Sorry man. I gave it back. You know, to all those bikie friends of mine.'

'You never had a gun. You're a bullshit artist. You never had a gun.'

'Yeah, right. Let me show you my gun to prove I'm telling the truth. Nyah nyah.'

'You being mean to me, Gary?' He stood again. 'I came here in friendship. With respect. To offer you a deal. And you're throwing it in my face.'

The guy was little, but not that little. He was skinny, but maybe it was all bone. He was working himself up. Gary said, 'Now that's not what I meant, man. I just don't have a gun. What can I say?'

'You're spitting in my face.' He started to come around the coffee table. 'You're a fucking liar. You're lying to me.'

Gary stepped back against the kitchen bench, and grabbed up a steak knife from a dirty plate on the counter. 'Enough now.'

The guy looked at the knife held out toward him like it was unjustified criticism. He looked at the mobile in his hand as if he might call someone to complain. 'Oh man. This is uncalled for, Gary.'

He started to turn away, but suddenly slammed his mobile phone into Gary's forehead. It shattered, diodes clinging in a little trickle of blood. Gary wasn't hurt, but paused to blink it all back into focus. The guy was at the coffee table. He had the bong. He raised it like a club, spurting dirty water as he turned back. Gary raised the knife towards the descending bong, but missed. The bong crashed into his shoulder, numbing his arm, and sending the steak knife to the floor. Gary tried to see the knife, which was a mistake because the guy kicked him in the balls, dropping him amongst the mobile phone bits and old bong water.

The guy kicked Gary in the shoulder. Gary was trying to hold his balls. Another kick glanced off his head. He had to save his head and he twisted around on the floor so his legs were all the guy could kick at which made him stop kicking.

He stood looking down trying to figure how he could get at Gary's head.

Gary rolled quickly and then crawled up under the coffee table. It was a big varnished slice of jarrah tree, put onto four legs. It was solid. Unbreachable.

The guy said, 'You look like a big turtle there, Gary, hiding in your shell.' He heard the guy moving around.

Gary just needed to catch his breath. He needed to give himself some time for his balls to stop electrocuting him.

'I wonder where Gary's hiding?'

There was a stab in his thigh. Gary gasped as his leg convulsed, banging his knee into the table. The guy had the steak knife. Gary tried to roll over a little but he was stuck under the table. He felt another stab, deep into his calf muscle.

'Ahhhh. Enough man. I'm cut.' Gary reached his hand out to try to hold his leg. Stab, stab, stab. The guy stabbed quickly up his arm, like pecks from some bird.

'Where's the gun, Gary?'

'In the cupboard. The cupboard in the kitchen. And there's some bullets too.'

'You insulted me, Gary.'

'Sorry. I'm sorry.'

'One in the bum.'

'Ahhhh, orrr.' Gary tried to push himself further under the table, making it rise a little.

The guy stepped up onto the table, yelling, 'Whoooa, ride 'em cowboy. Earthquake.'

Gary could feel blood dribbling out of his anus. He had some deep stabs. His shoulders were wedged under now so he couldn't move. Couldn't breathe, even though his face was now out the other side of the coffee table.

'Gary! Here you are.' The guy crouched over Gary's head, squatting on the coffee table edge like an eagle looking down at its dinner.

'Take the gun. It's yours. Take it. You've beaten me man. I lose. Just stop.'

'Hey, you're crying aren't you?' He slowly reached down. Gary couldn't move. Couldn't do anything. His finger touched Gary's face. He dabbed at Gary's tears.

'I need to go to a hospital.'

The guy shook his head. 'Can't go there. Bad idea. Witnesses.'

'I won't tell. I won't tell anyone, ever man. I won't tell. Please.' Gary was having trouble breathing. He could hear gasps and whimpers and all kinds of bad noises coming from himself. He was hyperventilating and knew this was a bad time to not be able to talk. But he couldn't think of any words.

The guy wasn't doing anything. Maybe he'd had enough. Maybe he was gone. Gary got his breathing a little slower and looked up at the demented bird guy crouched above him. He wasn't looking at Gary. He was smiling up at the wall at Gary's samurai sword.

Ned was out of the taxi looking over it towards the motor home.

Simon said, 'Now that was definitely screaming. You think Ellis is okay?'

Ned had his hand resting on the door, still unsure. 'You'll stay here and wait for us?'

'You got it.'

Ned nodded, as he shook the knife until it came free of the plastic bag. He trotted heavily towards the motor home, in shorts and singlet, his thongs thwacking on the bitumen.

Simon started his engine, put it in gear and gunned it. He headed straight up, hitting a speed bump, but not slowing as he looked for a way off the main caravan road. Old caravans and the occasional motor home flicked past. The road started to turn. It kept turning into a big loop until Simon was headed back the way he came, the only way in and out.

'Shit.'

The taxi took the bend and he was on the way back now, the road looping behind the caravan where he'd left Ellis and Ned. He could see the main road up ahead. The taxi shuddered as he hit another speed bump.

Ellis came out from between some caravans twenty metres ahead.

Simon kept his foot on the accelerator.

Ellis extended his arm, a gun in his hand.

Simon thought about swerving, weaving, soaring. The gun. Ten metres, five.

Simon braked. The taxi skidded left a little but came to rest next to Ellis where the gun was aimed at Simon's head. Ellis went around the front of the car, keeping the gun pointed at Simon. He tried the passenger door but it was locked. He tapped the barrel on the glass, and Simon unlocked the passenger door. Ellis got in front with Simon. There were great gouts of blood splashed across Ellis's jeans and t-shirt.

Simon said, 'Hi Ellis.'

Ned hurried up to the car.

Ellis said to Ned, 'Get in fuckwit.' And then to Simon, 'Plant it. Go.'

Ned scrambled into the back just as Simon drove. Smoke was coming from Gary's mobile home.

'I said stay with Simon.'

'We thought you was in trouble.'

'Ned?' Ellis signalled for Ned to lean forward a little. When he did, Ellis cracked him on the side of the head with the pistol. It made a woody clunk.

'Oww.'

Ellis pointed the gun at Simon's chest. 'Where were you off to?'

'Turning around, while Ned checked on you.'

Ellis looked at Simon and Simon looked back.

Ellis smiled a complicated smile. It started like an angry kind of smile, but then it got nasty deep down before it bubbled back out as happy. It was a smile that did a lot of twists and turns. 'See Ned. When you got brains, you can make anything sound like it's okay.'

Ellis looked out the window at a pink sky.

The sun was setting at the coast where there was probably a breeze. But not here.

'No need to worry about me boys. Whoooa. Will you look at all this fucking blood.'

Simon looked over at Ellis's lap where the pistol rested, still pointing at Simon's stomach. He looked up to see Ellis looking at him, flicking looks from one eye to the other and back.

Ellis settled on the blue one and said, 'You do anything like that again, I'll kill you.'

The Party's Over

Grace had changed out of her dress into a skirt and cool blouse. She sat in the caravan looking at two plates of grilled lamb chops and overcooked vegetables. JJ wasn't there. Nor was his mobile phone.

The door opened and he stepped up, making the caravan tilt a moment.

'Where have you been?'

'Out. For a walk.'

'JJ,' she said with a mixture of pleading and impatience.

'I know. It's dark. No one saw me.' He looked down at the food. 'This looks like a marriage doesn't it? Where have you been and dinner cold on the table. We still don't get to eat in the big house huh?'

Grace let it go. She took up her knife and fork and started eating, but looked to the table where his mobile wasn't. Finally, she said, 'I'll try and get a job tomorrow. Lisa said there's lots of salons looking for people. It's a boom. People like to look nice.'

'You think I like hanging here like a shag on a rock?'

'Sitting.'

'What?'

'A shag doesn't hang. It sits or stands. Kind of alone and feeling stupid.'

JJ studied her in a way he'd got when he thought she was being sarcastic but couldn't quite be sure. 'Did you know what I meant?'

'It doesn't hang?'

'Sitting, hanging, doing headstands for all I fucking care. Did you know what I meant when I said it?'

Grace didn't answer. Didn't look up.

'You think I like hiding in a caravan in your sister's backyard while you have to go back to hairdressing? You think I deserve all this after what I've been? Done?'

'No, I don't, but ...'

'Well maybe I'm not going to hang around on the rock anymore. How about that?'

'You called him, didn't you?'

'Maybe I flew off the rock? Shags fly don't they? Is it all right if a shag flies?'

'JJ, we decided.'

'Maybe I changed my mind.' JJ thumped his left breast. 'Maybe I'm back in charge.'

Grace was reading What Darwin Meant. *She'd found a stack of old books in the shelves either side of the window in the front room of the boarding house overlooking the coast in the south of England. There was also* What Freud Really Said *and* The Great Ideas of the Great Minds. *Each idea was a chapter of about two pages which meant it was easy to read and think about. She wore a thick jumper and sipped her cup of tea as she looked out the window at the wonder of snow falling on the beach. Her hair was still red, but she'd lost some weight since the Four Seasons Hotel London through some sobriety and solitary walks along the stony shore. She thought she might be evolving, changing into something new and better. She hoped that maybe she might be in a kind of pupa stage, gathering her energies for when she would come out a butterfly.*

JJ came in, talking before he arrived. 'He's changed phones again.'

Grace didn't look at him, even when he tossed his mobile at a lounge chair in the corner and it bounced off and clattered under the table.

'He's fucking dodging me.' JJ was in a tracksuit, rounder than ever. He waved a glass of scotch and coke and slurred his words. 'He's out of jail

and he has to take care of business or I'll take care of him. Or he'll be right back in there.'

'And.'

'And what?'

Grace still didn't look up from her book. 'And he'll be right back in there. You want to make him mad?'

'Who's fucking mad here? Me. I'm mad. What we supposed to do?'

'Let's go back to Australia. Move over East somewhere. Start again.'

'How would we get back – swim?'

Grace put her book down, thinking this might be a good time.

JJ stared out at the snow, or possibly at his own reflection in the big window.

'I could ask my sister. She'd lend us some money for plane tickets.'

And now here they were in a caravan outside her sister's house having the same conversation, déjà vu forever. Éternité. Perpétuité?

JJ spoke through some half-chewed chop. 'I can't ride. My name is shit. The only thing I'm any good for now is star witness for the cops.'

'You didn't ring the police. JJ, you didn't ring the police.'

'Don't be fucking stupid. Of course not. Fucking death sentence.'

'Okay. But you were never going to be a jockey forever.'

JJ smiled, pushing away his plate. 'That's exactly what I was thinking. New start. Become a horse trainer. Owner. Mr Foster is a businessman. He knows I need a little something in the swag. And he knows he's already invested in me. He understands that if he doesn't look after me ...'

'You didn't put it like that?'

'Course I put it like that. So he understands.'

'You didn't tell him where we are, did you?'

'Course not.'

Grace sat staring, trying to see into JJ's brain to see if there was a light in there, flashing red for LIE. It was usually easy to tell, but this time she couldn't be sure. She gave up. 'I'm going to the shop. You want anything?'

'Yeah, some beer.'

America

Simon sat back behind the steering wheel while he watched Ellis at a telephone box. Glass glittered at Ellis's feet where it had been smashed, perhaps by the kids who rode their skateboards and bikes under a single light in the skate park beyond. Ned had one hand on Simon's shoulder and the other under his chin holding a large hunting knife.

'They'll wonder why I've had the radio switched off for so long, Ned.'

Ned didn't say anything.

'I could just call in and say I was going to have the night off or something like that. Say I'm getting a cold. Then I could leave it off and no one would worry.'

'If you touch it, I'll cut your throat.'

'Plenty of time for that,' said Ellis, as he opened the front passenger door. He sat in the front again, the revolver casual on his lap. 'Give me your mobile, Simon.'

'I don't have one, Ellis.'

'Bullshit.' Ellis pulled open the glove box then rifled through the centre console and cash box. He looked at Simon and raised the gun. 'Give me your phone.'

Simon said, 'I don't have a mobile phone. You can look.'

Ellis stared at Simon, gauging, wondering. 'I might just do that.'

Simon shrugged.

Ellis smiled. 'Drive to High Wycombe.'

Simon put the car in gear.

Ellis said, 'Say "You got it" in that happy voice you got Simon.'

'You got it.'

Ellis leaned forward and ran his hand over the smooth new vinyl of the front dash. He said, 'Why haven't you got a GPS?

'I know the streets.'

Ellis snorted. 'I bet. Ha. Take the highway. Why haven't you got a phone?'

Simon shrugged.

'You travelling off the grid, are you Simon?'

When Simon didn't answer Ellis started nodding to himself. Then he said, 'You ever see that film *Collateral*?'

'No.'

'It was about this taxi driver and he got this killer in his taxi.'

Simon said nothing.

'See this kind of thing is much harder here. Just getting a weapon is harder, even if you do know people. I mean we're like connected, to other heavy dudes. But in America, you can just ...'

'We don't need this guy,' said Ned.

'I'm talking.'

'I can drive.'

'I'm talking to Simon. He understands this stuff.'

'I understand. I saw that movie.'

'See in America you just go to the shop. I'll have a bag full of guns, ta. Machine guns. A fucking bazooka, if you want.'

'A tank,' said Ned.

'I don't think you can buy a tank, Ned.'

'In Russia.'

'What are you going to do with a tank? "Oh honey, what's that noise in the street?" "Why, let me see, sugar. Hey, it's a tank coming towards the house." Don't you think they might notice a tank? Or were you thinking of painting it. Maybe paint it pink and play the ice-cream music. Jesus. What's that ice-cream music, Simon?'

'Greensleeves.'

'See Ned. He understands all this shit because he's a Mensa guy.'

Simon kept driving, like a taxi driver not listening to the conversation.

'A what guy?' asked Ned, suspiciously.

'It was at the school assembly. They made a big presentation to him. We were always doing that. Simon was always getting up on the stage for us to clap and cheer at the latest thing he'd done. They did speeches thanking him for being in our lives.'

Ellis seemed to get lost in his thoughts for a while as Simon got onto Roe Highway.

'Like knowing all the streets without a GPS. See, Mensa guys are like geniuses. They do these special tests and have a club, just for geniuses. Then you can drive a brand new taxi.'

Ellis looked to Simon, waiting. He was forced to say, 'What you think about that, Simon?'

'I should report in, Ellis. On the radio.'

'Or they might wonder where he is,' said Ned.

'Is that right?'

'It's been a while, since I turned the radio off. They'll think it's a worry.'

'You haven't even got one of those security cameras.'

'Haven't fitted it yet.'

'See, this taxi's not right. No GPS. No ... you know, that job computer. Just some old-style radio. You don't have a panic button, do you?'

Simon had been hoping they wouldn't notice his lack of driver safety features. 'Part of a backlog. So they gave me the radio.'

'So you think they'll be sending people, if they don't hear from you? Where's Simon and our brand new taxi? Quick, send a SWAT team.'

Simon could feel Ellis looking at him.

'See, I'm not so dumb, am I, Simon?'

'No, not at all, Ellis.'

Ellis wasn't quiet for long. 'Why do you have such a new taxi, Simon?'

'I had a crash.'

'You fucked up.'

Simon didn't reply.

'Simon fucked up. We're taking a big chance riding around with such a bad driver, Ned.'

'I can drive.'

'Give me your knife, Ned.'

Ned handed it forward, fast.

Ellis said, 'I really want to thank you for drawing my attention to your radio.'

Simon held the steering wheel loosely, looking at the speedometer. He'd edged it up to a hundred and thirty kilometres an hour.

Ellis suddenly lunged forward and stabbed the taxi radio, popping out some buttons, then dug the knife behind it, gouging it from under the dash. It fell near Simon's feet and he swerved a little, trying to kick it out from under the brake pedal.

'Whoa, there Simon. Watch the road. Don't want another little accident. Now there's no radio. All alone. Slow down. What's this street?'

Simon slowed, as Ellis checked the exit sign.

'Yeah, turn here. Nice and slow.'

Ellis gave the knife back to Ned.

Ned said, 'We don't need this guy just because of that movie.'

'Hear that Simon? Don't need you.' Ellis was peering at the houses.

'I'll kill him. Let me kill him for you.'

'Can't do that, Ned. Matter of honour, dude. See, Simon once saved my life. So I can't just up and kill him can I? Not without a good reason. Wouldn't be Busheedow.'

'Saved your life?' said Ned in wonder.

Simon wondered a little himself.

Ellis touched Simon's arm with the revolver. 'Stop here.'

The Hit

It was the address he'd been given. There were lights on inside the house, but the front yard was dark. A car body there, maybe. A dog barked, just once, not sure. There was a caravan down the back with a light on inside.

Ellis saw Simon look from the house to him, then back to the house.

Ned looked at the house, scared.

Ellis felt good, ready to do it.

A moth smacked into the windscreen and it was like they all woke up.

'Time to kill the jockey,' said Ellis.

Simon turned to him only to find the gun already pointed at his stomach.

'Out of the car. Everyone out.'

Simon got out the driver's side and looked towards some bushes nearby, but he saw Ellis watching as he came round the car.

Ellis whispered, 'I'm going to shoot this guy in the head. Bang. Then, when he's down, I'll put one in the back, at the top of the neck. Pop. Let them know it was a professional job.'

'Don't do it,' said Simon.

'What?'

'Don't do the job.'

'I'll do it,' said Ned.

'Take the cash box. There's a hundred in there. Take the taxi.'

'A hundred bucks?'

'I'll do it,' said Ned again.

Ellis ignored him, only talking to Simon. 'I'd *pay* a hundred to do this.'

'Don't do it, Ellis.' He was pleading.

'Are you trying to be a fucking hero?'

'I'll do it. Ellis, let me do it,' said Ned.

'You said I saved your life. Pay me back. Don't kill this guy.'

While Ellis was trying to sort out all the little edgy things Simon had just said, Ned stepped between them, poking Simon. 'I'll cut this guy and I'll go down there and shoot the jockey, for you Ellis. I'll blow him away as a present for you.'

'Shut up,' said Ellis.

'Don't do it, Ned. I've killed someone. It never leaves you.'

'Shut up,' said Ned.

Ellis reached past Ned and rammed the gun hard into Simon's throat. He fell to the side of the road, coughing and gasping.

'Shut up,' said Ellis. Dogs were barking.

'Let me do it, Ellis,' said Ned.

'Shut up, Ned. Let me think.' There were things firing around and Ned was just noise, getting in the way of the real things. He stepped past Ned to see Simon.

He was sitting back against the taxi, clutching his throat, trying to breathe.

'We can't be arguing like this outside the hit, Ned.' Ellis looked at Simon, suspiciously. Then the something that was bothering him clicked in his head and he said, 'When did you kill someone?'

Simon didn't say anything.

Ellis looked at Simon again, then to the house. The dogs had stopped. Ellis smiled. 'Lying. Getting us to fight. Trying to get us to make some noise and – they'd hear. Always thinking, but not so you can catch him. See.' Ellis punched down on Simon's face, sending him down onto the road.

Ned stepped forward, drawing his knife back to stab Simon while he was down, but Ellis got the pistol in Ned's face before he could go all the way. Ned looked into the pistol and stood up slowly.

Ellis waited till he saw Ned get it and go soft and obedient. Then he turned back to Simon, 'Come on hero. Shout out. Shout out and I'll shoot you and the gun will make a big noise and you'll save this guy. Do it.'

Simon pushed himself back up to sitting. There was blood on his cheek from the pistol blow.

Ellis watched, ready, his feet moving up and down, keeping the balance, ready, his finger straining on the trigger, ready.

Simon swallowed, but then he reached a hand to his throat and gave a little cough, spitting up some blood. He let out a big long sigh, giving it up, and turned to look at Ellis. Not at Ellis. At the end of the gun barrel in front.

Ellis smiled. He wasn't going to shout. He had nothing. Ellis nearly pulled the trigger, right then, just to do it. He only just stopped at the last fraction of a moment by pulling the gun away and holding it out behind to Ned. 'Here.'

Ned took it but stayed and Ellis turned around to see him looking at the gun, confused.

Ellis said, 'Go for his face. The jockey. You let him get close and you shoot him in the face. So he'll go down for sure. But then you got to do that last shot in the head, Ned. That's the kill shot. The make sure you done your business.'

Ned turned the gun from one side to the other. 'I got this Ellis. I got it.'

Ellis took Ned's knife. 'You fuck this up, I'll fuck you up, Ned. You know I will.' He turned away from Ned, not even watching him go.

He dragged Simon up by his shirt. 'Simon and me, we'll be watching. Two expert killers. Giving you a score maybe.'

Ellis took Simon by the hair and steered him around to the passenger side where he pushed him in and made him get to the driver's seat over the gearstick. Simon was being a lamb, but Ellis didn't trust him. Not since the caravan park. Once they were settled, Ellis said, 'Don't do it? To pay you back? Like it was nothing important. Like saving my life all those years ago was nothing to you. Like I'm ten cents?'

Ellis suddenly jabbed Simon's bicep with the tip of the knife.

Simon flinched away but didn't cry out.

'You being brave, Simon? I like when people try that. It makes it last a bit longer.'

Ellis looked at the dot of blood growing on Simon's arm.

Simon wouldn't look at him, not even out of the corner of his grey eye like he had been doing when he was driving.

Ellis said, 'I thought you'd do better though. I thought you'd save this guy.'

Nothing from Simon. He seemed to be looking out to the darkness ahead, trying to see past the edge of the headlights.

'You could still call out. I'd kill you, but you'd save this person's life. Like you saved mine.'

Simon turned and said in a hoarse whisper, 'You hit me in the throat, Ellis. Yelling out is not something I can actually do. Even if I was brave enough. Which I'm not.'

'Yeah, that's right. Ha. I must admit you have a point with that, Simon. That was necessary, that first punch. Too much noise. But the sucker punch, the pistol whip, while you were down. Maybe that wasn't right. You hurt my feelings. Which I admit was kind of a good move. Trying to mess with my head there, about you're a killer too.'

Ellis sat, looking at the side of Simon's head. He looked at the knife and then back at Simon's head. He wondered about stabbing the knife in there, like he did with the taxi radio and maybe dig out Simon's secrets – see how it all worked.

'I got it. You can't yell, sure. But you could beep your horn. You could hit that horn and keep leaning on it and those dogs would start up again, for sure. Look, I'll give you an even better chance.'

Ellis made a slow-motion show of carefully placing the knife in his bloody lap. 'Simon, look. I haven't even got the knife anymore. Look.' Ellis raised them a foot above his lap. 'Go for it, dude.'

Ned was having trouble negotiating the front yard in his thongs. It was dark and he kept banging his toes into scattered engine parts. He rested just past the car body near a big bush and looked back out to the road. The taxi headlights could be seen easily, and Ned wondered if he should go back and tell Ellis to make Simon turn them off. Simon wouldn't bother him after he killed the jockey. It would be back to just Ellis.

Ned eased up the steps onto the veranda and to the front door. He tried the screen but it was locked. He started to twist the handle harder but it wouldn't give. He peered through the flywire at the closed door just beyond. He knocked on the frame of the flywire. Then he stepped back a full step and aimed the pistol, waiting.

Simon sat looking at the car horn. Although his hands remained on his legs, his fingers were flexing.

He knew Ellis was watching. He also knew he was cheating. Although he left his nearest hand up waving where Simon could see it, his left hand had drifted down. Wherever it was, it must be close to the knife.

Then Simon saw something ahead. He peered out along the headlights beam at a girl walking towards them along the road. She was carrying a plastic bag.

Simon turned to smile at Ellis. 'I'm not going to hit the horn. But I am going to do something with my hands.'

Ellis tensed.

'Even if I hit the horn, it's too late now. They'll just come to the door to see who's ordered a taxi. What I am going to do is bring up my hand, but keep it forward of the steering wheel. That way, even if I try to make a fast move for the horn, the steering wheel will be in the way.'

Ellis watched, then suddenly grabbed up the knife and looked at Simon's left arm, as though it might lash out. 'What you trying to do, Simon?'

Outside the girl stepped into the headlights.

It was quite important that Ellis watched every gesture Simon made, waiting for the final magic trick move.

'See, I'm bringing my hand up behind the steering wheel. I'm leaning forward to get it up there, so I'm easy to stab. I can't defend myself.'

'What?' asked Ellis, impatient now.

'The headlights, see.'

Simon flicked the headlight switch from high beam to street. The girl disappeared into the new stretch of darkness.

'I'd left them on.'

Ellis suddenly looked out the front window into the dark.

'They're still on.'

'Right. Turning them all the way off. You going to let me do that.'

'Do it.'

Simon reached around again, using his right hand in slow motion up under the steering column to get to the lights. 'I was sitting here thinking about the horn, I have to admit, Ellis, and then I knew I couldn't.'

Simon was looking at Ellis as he flicked the lights up to high beam for a flash before turning them all the way off.

'What did you do?' Ellis had seen the flash out of the corner of his eye.

'Turned the lights off.'

'What did you do?'

'I saw we'd left the lights on, Ellis. I didn't want you to blame me for leaving them on. Thinking I was pulling something on you. But I also thought, if I just said I've left the lights on, you'd think that was a trick to make you look so my hand could get close to the horn.' Simon looked out into the darkness. He couldn't see anyone.

'You did something. I'm going to take this knife and I'm going to push it in slowly, Simon. It's going to hurt. Tell me what you did.'

Suddenly Ned was in a lot of light. No one had answered his first knock and he'd had to do it again, and still no one had come. He finally found a button that sent a sound inside. And then the porch light came on with Ned standing right under it, holding the pistol pointed.

The door opened before Ned was set.

The man looked out through the flywire. 'Yeah?'

Ned stood, embarrassed to not be ready.

The man looked down to what Ned was holding out to him. He stood looking at it.

The gun fired.

He fell back into the hallway, clutching his stomach. He started screaming.

Grace dropped the bag of beers where she stood in the garden and started running for the house.

In the taxi, Simon had a good view of the front veranda in all the white light.

Ellis urged, 'Finish it, Ned. Finish it.'

Simon closed his eyes.

The shot man lay in a growing puddle of blood in his hallway trying to push his hands at his stomach.

Ned turned towards the taxi and took a step to run but made himself go back. He edged up towards the hole in the flywire and aimed the pistol at his head. A woman in a green dressing-gown came out of a door at the other end of the hall. She had white cream on her face. Ned looked at her, trying to work out why Ellis hadn't told him about the woman.

She was running towards him. Ned lifted the gun and fired, but the shot went into a picture on the wall. She was still coming, yelling, 'Tim!' Ned tilted the gun and fired at the man, then ran.

Grace was coming round the side when the big man came down the steps and knocked her over. He ran off towards the taxi on the road, its lights back on showing two other men waiting.

She got to the first step but turned to see Luke come over the fence with a rifle. 'The taxi!' she yelled, pointing.

She didn't wait to see what he did but heard the rifle shot as she reached the front door. Lisa wailed as she tried to prop Tim up and keep him out of all the blood. Grace stood outside the locked flywire with the three holes in it unable to reach them.

Luke pushed Grace out of the way and wrenched the flywire door open with one quick pull. 'We need an ambulance. Grace, right now.' He spoke calmly, as if describing how to cook meat on a barbecue.

She fumbled out her mobile, dialling 911, before remembering it was triple 0.

Luke leaned down to look at Tim. 'Grace, I need something to stop the bleeding. Sheets.'

Grace pushed past him and ran up the hall tracking footsteps of blood to the nearest bedroom. 'Emergency. There's been a shooting.'

She heard Luke still being calm. 'Lisa, I need you to stop crying darling. Tim, can you hear me? Tim, you old beanpole, wake up. Wake up. Lisa, he can't go to sleep, okay.'

Grace ran back with floral sheets, 'Here. They're on their way.'

Luke took one and just balled it at the wound, pushing. 'Lisa, can you keep the pressure on here.'

She did, then saw Grace as if for the first time. 'They shot Tim. With a gun.'

Luke said, 'Grace, can you ask JJ to come here?'

Grace said, 'Oh.'

She handed Luke her mobile with the ambulance people still talking and stepped over Tim's legs again and went to the caravan. She felt like falling but kept from doing that – like there was a wind pushing her towards the top of a cliff. He wasn't in the caravan, but the cupboard door was open, his side empty, but his mobile phone was still on the table.

She went outside again to see him coming from the back door of Lisa's house with some car keys.

'Got to get going, doll. Can't let the cops find me here. No way.' He went to Lisa's Camry. His bag was already in the back.

Grace stepped between him and the open driver's door. 'No. You have to come and see them.'

'What if they're waiting out there? What if they come back?'

'Luke needs you.'

'We have to get out of here.'

'No. It's my sister. They've been helping.'

JJ pushed her. She fell back, cracking her head on the car roof as she kept falling across both front seats, her back catching the gearstick, sending all the air out of her. She felt JJ grab her feet and lift and push and twist her until her head went down into the passenger's foot-well.

Then JJ lifted her legs again and pushed them out of his way as he got into the driver's side and started the car.

Grace yelled, 'Stop. JJ. Stop now.'

But JJ didn't stop. He didn't even change out of second gear until they were two streets away and even he noticed the screaming engine.

Excess Baggage

The wind was making a weird moaning at the back where the rear window had been blown to bits. The bullet must have just missed Ned's head as he'd dived in the back when Simon hauled arse. There was an interesting hole in the back strut where it went out again.

'I got him. He came to the door and blam. Got 'im.'

Ned was pumped from the thing, but Ellis had that warm, dreamy feeling, like he'd just had some good soup with a big shot of rum. 'Yeah. Pop, pop. Not so hard really, is it.'

'Squeeze and blam.'

'There's not so many hitmen in Australia, you know. Well, maybe Mr Rent-A-Kill or whatever, in Sydney.'

'And Chopper Read.'

'No, I'm talking about professionals. Not a bunch of Melbourne guys just killing each other. That's gang stuff. I mean men who you come to when you need it done.'

'Yeah. Us.'

Ellis had been watching Simon, but getting nothing. 'You're riding with the genuine article, Simon.'

'We don't need him anymore. Job's done now.'

'Give us the gun.'

Ned handed it over the seat.

'You dipped the lights back there to attract attention,' said Ellis.

'I told you what I was doing, and why.' Simon only rasped a little.

'Should I kill you?'

Simon seemed to have some problem thinking about it for a while before he said, 'No.'

Ellis said, 'Beg.'

Simon turned to look at him mostly with the grey eye and said, 'No.' He turned back to the highway. Cars were passing.

'You're not like I thought.'

'No, I've been a pretty big disappointment to everyone, Ellis. And I promised so much.'

'Ha,' laughed Ellis, that Simon could keep surprising him. 'This guy.'

Ned said, 'We gotta shoot him, Ellis. Like you said, no witnesses.'

'Except the woman, you mean,' said Simon.

'The one who ran down the side?' Ellis shook his head. 'She didn't see anything.'

'The other one,' said Simon.

'What other one?'

'The one who was screaming. The tall guy screamed, then the woman screamed.'

'That's right,' said Ellis, turning around to Ned. 'I heard her too. Did you shoot her?'

Ned looked away. 'I got the guy.'

'The tall guy?' asked Simon.

'What? Why do you keep going "the tall guy"?' asked Ellis mocking Simon's gravelly way of saying it.

'How tall's Ned?'

'What are you trying to do now?'

Ned said, 'He's trying to mix us up.'

'I couldn't see much but the guy looked a foot taller than Ned.'

'I wasn't scared,' yelled Ned. He lashed out, punching Simon behind the ear.

Simon fell forward, going for the brake. The car pulled to the left as it lost speed, spilling Ellis back into the dash. He scrambled up onto the seat and turned the pistol to Simon, who was busy getting the taxi under control and looking out at the passing traffic.

Ellis turned in his seat again, 'Ned, I swear to god, if you say another word, or touch anyone without my saying, I'll fucking shoot you.'

Ned started to open his mouth.

Ellis thrust the gun over the back seat. 'Go on. Do it. One word.' When he could be sure Ned was going to behave he said, 'Spit it out Simon.'

'What?'

'The tall guy?'

'Yeah, well he looked pretty skinny, but he was the tallest jockey I ever saw.'

'Fuck,' said Ellis. 'Fuck, fuck, fuck, fuck.' He turned the gun back at Ned, reaching it out as far as his arm would go.

Ned closed his eyes, scrunched up his face and waited to die.

'You dumb prick. That wasn't the jockey. Fuck.'

Ellis took a moment, centring himself. 'A setback. I should have gone. Doing a hit is a bit more complicated than just "Go to this address. Get my bag." Little more to it. Okay, turn around and we'll go back.'

'You got it,' said Simon. He put the indicator on, getting ready for the next exit.

'Wait. There'll be cops.' Ellis stared at Simon, distrustful again. 'Quiet now, kids. Daddy needs to think.'

Simon drove. Some plastic in the back rattled in the wind from the missing rear window.

Ellis said, 'Pull off the freeway. Find a phone. We'll call Foster.'

Educating Grace

Grace was in a hot tub in Switzerland. Her long dark hair floated over her breasts, tickling a little, as she read Sophie's World, *through the steam.*

She stopped when JJ came out of the hillside apartment, muscular and naked, carrying two drinks. He stood a moment blinking at the distant snow-topped mountains then shivered. 'It's cold.'

'Do you think God is in everything?'

'If you mean Foster, then yes I do. And I praise him for it.' He put down the drinks, staggering a little.

Grace looked out past the wooden decking to fields below where cows munched in the thin sunshine. 'Spinoza says we're all part of everything, and everything is part of nature. So we can feel our little part of the whole universe and all eternity all at once.'

'My little part is trying to crawl up inside me.' JJ jumped into the tub, sending a wave of water rushing out the sides of the hot tub.

Grace stood as quickly as she could, holding the book high above the splash.

'Hot,' said JJ with a laugh, as he stood up out of the water.

Grace bent over to put the book safely up on a box of plants. She turned back to find JJ nodding appreciatively at her bare arse. She dropped back into the pool. 'Have you heard of pantheism?'

JJ lowered himself back down into the tub, searching the edges for where he'd put the drinks. 'I never heard of any of the things you're coming out with, baby. It's all like those French tapes you're practising on – fuckin' Greek to me.'

Grace smiled and when JJ reached his foot out and up to fit between her legs under the water, she giggled, going with the good feeling until she focused on something out in the world and asked, 'Do you think animals have feelings?'

He followed her eyes to the cows in the meadow below. 'Cows? Maybe. Sheep, no.' JJ took his foot away and drifted himself over to his drink. 'Horses sure got moods.' He took a sip, admiring his mixing.

Grace stared at him, intent. 'Would you ever not hurt a horse to not win a race?'

'Do you know what that sentence means?'

Grace laughed, and glided herself to JJ. She leaned on his shoulder while she got her own drink. 'Would you say, I'm not going to hurt this horse – I'm not going to use a battery or the whip or nothing that will hurt it. It's just not right. Just some race and I'm not hurting this ... um ...'

'Horse?'

'Living creature.' She leaned in and kissed JJ.

He sucked the top of her lip. 'Chlorine.'

'Would you?'

'If you asked me not to, then I wouldn't do it, baby.'

Grace smiled, her face glowing from the warm water and her eyes darting from JJ's left eye to his right and back, like a movie star in a close-up. Her lips moved towards JJ's, opening slightly in anticipation.

Grace grimaced as she looked out the motel room window. There was an empty pool outside. It was above ground, empty and sagging next to some builder's rubble. The round version of JJ pulled the thick curtains closed.

She punched him as hard as she could in the arm. 'You hurt me.'

'Accident. There were guns going off, baby.'

'You ever hit me again ...'

'It wasn't a hit. A little push. Anyway, they might have still been around. If they were, we had to lead them away. Not let anyone else get hurt.'

Grace looked at him.

JJ stared back, unblinking, rehearsed.

She sat on one of the single beds, near the telephone on the table between. She felt for her phone, but remembered she'd given it to Luke on Lisa's veranda. 'I better ring and see how Tim is.'

'Not now Grace. They might not understand ... call the cops or something.'

'Tim looked bad. Really bad.'

'I'll call Foster.' JJ patted his pockets looking for his phone.

'No!' Grace stood.

'If there's a misunderstanding.'

'JJ, what do you think just happened?'

'Why I have to promise him my lips are sealed. Make him understand.'

'Promise me you won't phone.'

JJ nodded. 'I promise.' He sat in a chair by the motel room door.

Grace sat back on the bed.

JJ said, 'We don't phone. Nobody phones nobody.'

Mr Foster

The taxi pulled into a parking bay in Kings Park, a big hill that overlooked the city and river. It was a good place for romantic couples and other assignations.

'Turn off the engine and give me the keys.'

He did.

'Ned. If either of you gets out of the car for any reason at all, I'll kill you. Not even for a piss. You got it?'

Ned nodded, picking up his knife and waving it like a sword so Ellis knew he was on this.

Ellis nodded and got out and headed a couple of cars along towards a black Statesman.

Simon said, 'Ellis saying not even for a piss reminds me of something.'

'Don't talk.'

'It's about Ellis. Can I tell you, if it's about Ellis?'

Ned looked at Simon's ear where he'd whacked him. Simon didn't turn around. Just sat, working his one hand at his throat, waiting.

Ned tensed a little with the knife, ready. Then he said, 'Okay.'

'This is about when he was at school. I'm just trying to explain to you Ned, why maybe Ellis doesn't want to kill me. Because we go way back, you know. Ellis had another mate at school. Tall guy. Simmo. Had bets about fights. If they had a fight with someone and won, the one who didn't fight had to give the other guy a dollar. Not so much a money-making venture as icing on the cake, I suppose.'

'We did that. In prison. Packet of cigarettes. But then Ellis started not fighting them for a carton.'

'Anyway, so the story went that Ellis fought this one kid, after school, in the sports change rooms I think it was. But that wasn't the end of it. The kid apparently was begging him to stop hitting him and Ellis made him open his mouth and he shit in the guy's mouth. Very disturbing ... full of all kinds of power and fear and also a primal disgust, but what always stuck in my mind was, if it was true, Ellis had some pretty amazing bowel control. I don't think I could just poop on demand like that.'

'I know,' said Ned. 'Ellis told me about that already. Ellis isn't afraid to do anything.'

Ellis sat in the back seat of the Statesman. There was a guy with a ponytail and suit behind the driver's wheel who never turned around but kept watching Ellis through the rear-vision mirror. It was this guy that was putting Ellis off a little, rather than Mr Foster talking disrespectfully.

Foster was dressed in a checked shirt and bathers, like he'd just come from the beach. He was turned around in the front passenger seat so he could look at Ellis and at the driver. 'You said you could handle it.'

'No one told me he'd be guarded.'

'Guarded?'

'There were at least two other men there, with guns. I took one of them down, but I'll have to go back for the jockey.'

'Only we don't know where he is now, do we? All that shooting.'

'Just a hiccup. You gotta understand that in my line of work, things don't always go ...'

'Your line of work!' interrupted Foster. 'You're a petty criminal who keeps being sent to prison because you're a violent psychopath who gets caught. Don't pretend you're a CIA agent, for Christ's sake.'

Ellis flicked his eyes to the man in the suit. He was still looking back. No smile, just watching. Ellis said, 'You shouldn't talk to me that way, Mr Foster. You wouldn't have said that in prison.'

'No. You would have hurt me in prison. And I wouldn't talk that way if Bobby wasn't here either. You're a nasty bit of work, Ellis. And I have a very nasty job for you to do. This is killing a man. I have never killed a man. Never wanted to. Jesus, I paid him to have a holiday for two years so I wouldn't have to.' Foster panted, then looked up to Bobby and shrugged before refocusing on Ellis. 'But I don't want to go back to prison and be prey to the likes of you, and so I'll do anything not to let that happen. But don't be mistaken, Ellis. We're out here in my world now.'

'It's my world too, Mr Foster. I just gotta work harder making it mine, that's all.'

Ellis looked out the car window at the city lights down below. He never went in the city much. Finally he realised that no one was saying anything. 'So what do you want me to do?'

'We wait for JJ to call us.'

'Call you?'

Mr Foster turned away, 'Oh, yeah. He'll do that. I'd say it was a sure thing.'

Bobby turned around in his seat to look at Ellis full on. 'Then I'll come with you and give you a hand.'

Simon was getting Ned to open up.

'Do you know the story about Ellis's mum in the sack?' sneered Ned.

'No,' said Simon.

'See, you don't know everything.'

'What kind of sack?'

'Ha,' said Ned, pushing the edge of the knife just a little further into Simon's throat. He wasn't cutting, but he had his left hand on Simon's left shoulder, and his right over and around Simon's other shoulder, with the knife under his chin.

'The knife, Ned. It's starting to cut.'

Ned eased if off a little.

Simon looked to the car doorhandle and to the bush beyond.

'You don't know what kind of sack it was, do you, Ned?'

Ned's hand tightened again but then eased. 'It was hessian. A big potato sack. Big enough to get their mother in.'

'Ellis?'

'And his brothers. She'd get drunk and nag them. They grabbed her one day and pushed her in the hessian sack.'

'They drowned her?'

'No. See, you don't know nothing about Ellis. Anyway, it's a funny story, the way Ellis tells it.'

'Right.'

'They took the manhole cover into the roof off and they got a rope and tied it around a rafter and they hauled her up in the sack a metre and told her they wouldn't let her down unless she stopped nagging. And they pushed the sack a bit and smacked her on the arse a few times because she started yelling and screaming a fair bit. I think one of the brothers got a stick or something.'

'Would you do that to your mum?'

'No,' said Ned quickly. Then he said, 'I don't know. I was fostered.' They were quiet a while, then Ned said, 'They left her in the sack for a few days. She pissed herself and that and their dad made them take her down cos of the smell and he wanted some dinner. But after that any time she started nagging the boys they'd say, "Shut up, or we'll give you the sack." See. That's the funniest part. They'd give her the sack.'

'You're right, Ned. I didn't know that one.'

Ned loosened his grip on the knife for a moment.

Grace put the bedside phone down.

A key turned in the lock of the motel room door.

Grace sat on the end of the bed, facing away from the phone.

JJ came in carrying a couple of cans of Coke. 'You want a drink?' he asked, brightly, closing the door on the courtyard of other motel rooms and cars.

Grace went to the minibar and opened it, revealing little spirit bottles, beers and soft drinks.

'Oh, I didn't see the fridge.'

'Why did you lock me in?'

'Did I? Force of habit from all the hotels we been living in.'

Grace went to the little bathroom and got two glasses.

JJ opened the minibar again and took out a little bottle of scotch and a little bottle of Jim Beam.

When Grace put the glasses on top of the fridge next to the kettle, she asked, 'Was there a phone? Near the soft drink machine?'

'What? How would I know? I wasn't looking.' JJ pulled the top off the Coke and poured.

Simon's hand rested on the door hand. There were a lot of trees and bush outside the car, lots of dark garden to jump into. Ned still had the knife under his chin, but loose.

Simon said, 'You wondering why Ellis has been so long?'

'No.'

'I don't think he's in trouble. Not like with that guy in the caravan park. I was thinking he might be trying to protect you. Trying to explain to Mr Foster that how it happened was like an accident, or something.'

Ned started to ease back a little more as he turned to try to see to the Statesman. Then he tightened his grip again. 'They're coming.'

'Oh.'

Ellis opened the back door of the taxi and said to Ned, 'Get in the front.'

Simon caught a glimpse of a guy in a suit. Could hear him brushing broken bits of glass off the back seat before he sat down.

Ellis got in the other side and tossed the keys onto Simon's lap. 'Middle Swan Motor Inn.'

Simon said, 'I'm going to have to get some petrol.' He started the car.

The new guy said, 'We need to ditch this and get something less conspicuous. Something with a back window.'

'Bobby doesn't like your taxi, Simon.'

Bobby leaned forward and looked at the taxi meter. It showed six hundred and seventy-three dollars. 'This guy is the actual driver?'

Simon backed out and turned into the tree-lined road leading down the hill and out of Kings Park.

Ned said, 'Ellis and Simon went to school together.'

'Our very own driver, Bobby,' said Ellis.

Bobby looked at the bruise on Simon's head and the spot of blood on his arm. He said, 'Simon, this bush track up here. Can you pull in? I need a leak.'

Simon nodded, sadly. He pulled off the road and into one of the fire tracks that crisscrossed the bush park, stopping at a gate.

Bobby said, 'Yeah, this is good. Come for the walk, mate. Stretch your legs.'

Simon got out and looked up and down. It was as deserted as a country road.

Bobby got out of the taxi, patting something underneath his Armani coat.

'Quiet for such a hot night,' said Bobby.

'Yeah,' said Simon, 'it's pretty late though and you never can tell on a weeknight.'

Bobby looked at Simon a moment but then turned him by the shoulder and pushed him gently up the bush track.

'I suppose if I explained that I didn't care about any of this, and I promised not to say anything ...'

'Sorry, mate. Wrong place, wrong time.' Bobby took his handgun from his shoulder holster, pointing off the track and out of the taxi headlights. 'Businessmen get into dodgy stuff and then panic. These fuckwits don't know what they're doing. Lots of fuck-ups.'

'No consolation at all,' said Simon.

They stepped off the sandy road and into thicker bush. 'Here,' said Bobby.

Bobby pushed Simon down to kneel. When Simon heard the shot he fell.

The leaves were rough and scratchy. Tough Australian plants not given to offering free lunches to the wildlife. The soil smelled dry but there was a whiff of thin fecundity. Desperate fecundity? Simon became aware of feet moving behind him.

He opened one eye and saw Bobby on the ground. Ellis stepped up to put his gun behind Bobby's ear and fired again. Then Ellis kicked Bobby in the leg. 'Fuckwits eh? Well, we know what we're doing, and fuck you.' Ellis kicked Bobby's body again and turned to Ned. 'Look at this fag's ponytail.'

'What a girl,' said Ned.

Ellis picked up Bobby's pistol, and stepped around the body to prod Simon with his foot.

Simon sat up in the bush, unshot. He brushed sand and dead leaves from his cheek.

Ellis said, 'Get the guy's wallet and stuff. We got another gun now.'

Ned started going through Bobby's pockets. Said, 'Can I have his watch?'

'Sure Ned. See if he's got a phone. And get that shoulder holster. No! I got a better idea. Leave it on him. Simon, help Ned carry this guy back to the taxi. New plan.'

Simon stood up and into the dim light from the taxi and then looked down expecting blood.

Ned pointed, 'He's pissed himself.'

Ellis looked. 'He did. Looks like ya sprang a leak down there, Simon.' Ellis patted his own groin. 'Get you a nappy, boy.'

Ned laughed. 'That's a good one.'

'You get his feet, Simon. We'll leave Bob at the motel. The cops will think he shot the jockey, and tell Foster the jockey got him. And we collect. It's perfect.'

The ute coasted into the Middle Swan Motor Inn with its headlights off. It stopped at a metal fence where a sign read, *Pool Closed due to refurbishments.* Luke Balder looked over to the Camry parked in front of room twelve. He flicked the interior light so it wouldn't come on and checked around the court. Only four other cars were parked in front of rooms and only number twelve had lights on.

Luke took his .22 from the front seat and eased out of his car. He closed the door with a gentle click and walked to number twelve with the rifle down along his leg. At the door he looked around once more, before moving a pistol that was stuck in his belt a little further around so it was hidden beneath his jacket. He took a half step back and balanced to kick in the door, but then thought better of it. He tried the doorhandle. It wasn't locked. He opened it and stepped inside.

JJ, who was sitting on one of the beds, yelped and threw himself down between them.

Grace sat on the other bed and looked a little relieved to see Luke standing inside the motel room door with the .22 up and ready to rescue her. She said, 'Lisa told you.'

'She thought it best.'

'You phoned!' JJ knelt up between the beds. He took in Luke standing in front of the door holding the rifle. 'I want you to understand I had no idea that anyone was trying to kill me.'

Luke fought the desire to punch JJ. He said, 'You caused it.'

Grace stood up, almost between the men. 'I said we should come back. It was me who said we should come back to Perth.'

JJ said, 'I never wanted to live in a caravan behind her sister's house.'

Grace nodded. 'I shouldn't have asked her.'

JJ said, 'It wasn't my fault. I got caught in the middle of all this.'

'I don't want you,' said Luke, silencing them both.

JJ blinked, still kneeling between the two single beds.

Luke said, 'I want those three guys in the taxi. I want the shooters.'

'For Tim,' said Grace. She got it. Understood what was right. She looked at Luke and nodded at what needed to be done.

He met her eyes and nodded back.

'So,' said JJ standing up, 'you haven't actually called the police yet.'

The Showdown

Simon's taxi was parked at a petrol bowser in a twenty-four-hour petrol station. Simon sat, leaning slightly out of the driver's window, looking at one of the petrol station's security cameras. Ned was inside, paying.

Ellis had his head down so the cameras couldn't catch him as he went through the glove box again looking for treasures. He pulled out some paperbacks and tossed them down at his feet. *The Waste Land*. *The Power and the Glory*. 'Your pants drying all right, are they? Pretty stinky.'

Simon looked down at his lap. There was blood there too and some on his hands from helping to put Bobby in the boot.

Ned headed back from the shop, his arms full with cigarettes, soft drinks and microwaved chicken rolls.

Ellis took out Simon's MP3 player. 'Still, could have been worse. If you'd shat yourself, that would have been a problem. That would have been curtains for ol' Simon.'

'You've got a bit of a thing about poop, don't you Ellis?'

Ellis looked up, blinking, hurt.

Simon undid his seatbelt and got out of the car.

Ellis grabbed for the two guns on his lap, spilling one to the floor but getting the other in his hand, to point at Simon. 'Get back in the car.'

Ned arrived a couple of kicks behind the play.

Simon turned back towards Ellis as though he were just stretching. 'If you shoot me Ellis, the security cameras will catch it all. Take them no time to track you down. They would take an interest in that.'

Ellis put on his wounded look. 'Don't you want to play with us anymore, Simon? Ned, put that stuff in the back. If I have to shoot Simon, we'll have to go in there and kill the petrol attendant and all the witnesses and get the security camera tape, or DVD or whatever it's on. Be a bloodbath, I reckon. Crazed taxi driver. You know. That's another film with a taxi they done already.' Ellis smiled up at Simon, lazy, happy to still hold all the cards.

Simon got back in and did up his seatbelt.

Ned got in the back.

Ellis put on Simon's MP3 player and started to hum to the classical music.

Simon drove out through the deserted streets of Midland to the start of the Great Northern Highway, a road that led three thousand miles to the top of the country.

Ellis opened the passenger window and dropped the player out the window, looking at Simon as he did so. 'Classical shit.'

'Bach.'

'Bark?'

'Johann Sebastian. I think I was listening to the Brandenburg concertos.'

'This is our old stomping ground, Ned. Near where we went to school. Sure has changed, but. You still live Upper Swan? That's where he lived, I swear. Up a swan. I guess a guy would have a lot of trouble with swan poop, if you lived up one. You still live there, Simon?'

'Yes, I do.'

'You're kind of stuck, aren't you, Simon?'

Simon turned, smiling at the triple joke. 'You got that right.'

Ellis snorted like a joyous sneeze. He nodded a few times to hug the feeling to himself.

Simon drove.

Ellis reached behind and his hand came back with a chicken roll. Ellis pulled down the foil and chomped on the soft mayonnaisey thing, chewing loudly. 'You know, I saved your life back there. I mean I kind of saved it in the petrol station just now, but the one I'm talking about is Kings Park. Bobby Ponytail was going to cap you. Had his gun coming up. I got there just in time. I stepped in and – pop. Just in time. Saved your life.'

Simon said nothing.

'You got nothing to say about that?'

Simon thought a moment, then said, 'Thank you.'

Ellis laughed, but didn't sound like he meant it. Then he got the end of his chicken roll and dabbed it on Simon's cheek, leaving a dribble of mayonnaise. 'Now we're even.'

'There's a debt here,' said Luke Balder. Luke sat on the chair by the motel room door, his rifle leaning up against the wall nearby, his eyes intent on JJ. 'He got shot because of you and now you need to help him.'

'We have to, JJ. We have to now.' Grace sat on the bed next to her husband.

'What if I ring Foster, but like make a truce? I say we'll stop everything if he gives us the guys who shot Tim?'

Luke shook his head, wearily.

Grace said, 'You've got to stop trusting Foster, for a start.'

'Says who?'

'Who do you think tried to kill you?'

JJ looked at the empty glass in his hand. He stood and went to the bar fridge. 'Crossed wires, that's all. He's been good to us.'

Luke said, 'This is not negotiable.'

The two men looked at each other.

Grace said, 'I think it's time we called the police.'

'What?'

Grace turned to Luke and he shook his head.

She said, 'Let them take care of it. Tell them everything. Let them catch these guys. Put them in jail. Foster too.'

JJ had a new drink. He wandered over to her. 'And me too? Why we been hiding for two years?'

'Tell the truth and take the time and we can move on.'

Luke seemed to be thinking about this, studying it carefully, wondering if it were possible.

JJ turned to look at him, a dopey smile forming. 'You getting ready to move up again, Grace? While I'm in prison, who'd look after you?'

Grace stepped towards JJ, putting a hand on his shoulder. 'I'll wait for you.'

JJ stepped back as though from her touch. What he was really doing was stepping to the rifle. He let his drink fall as he grabbed up the rifle and pointed it at Luke.

'Admit it, you were thinking about her, just a little, with me in a prison.'

Luke looked up, guilty.

JJ said, 'Distracting, isn't she. I know.'

'No, JJ, no,' she said again.

'I'm not a dog, Grace. Don't talk to me like one.' JJ backed away from Luke, towards the bathroom door with room to swing the rifle at each of them. 'You'll wait for me, will you? Let's have a new plan. How about we wait for Foster's travelling money? How about that for a better plan?'

'Money?'

'Foster's sending someone with some money. No killing. No prisons.'

'You promised you wouldn't phone.'

'You know, Grace, you're getting very whiny.'

The taxi drove in and parked in front of number nine.

Ellis said, 'This is a Glock.' He pointed it at Simon's side.

'A police gun,' said Ned from the back.

'We know,' said Ellis. 'So Simon, same deal. Call out and save him. Maybe he'll have time to scramble out a window or something and you can be a dead hero. Not that anyone would know. They'll think you're a dead nobody. Or ... maybe if he gets away, he'll say, I heard a gunshot. Papers will track it back to you. Say, hey isn't that Simon, with his bright blue eye? It just had to be him. That's exactly the kind of thing he'd do.'

Ned said, 'Are we going to do this or not, Ellis?'

Ellis looked over, but not annoyed. He nodded. 'Simon, help Ned get Bobby out of the boot.'

Ellis fished around at his feet and got the other gun.

Grace and Luke tried to reason with JJ who stood inside motel room number twelve pointing the .22 at Luke.

Luke said, 'When they get here, they'll kill me. You know that, don't you?'

Grace said, 'JJ, they tried to kill Tim. They shot at Lisa. They'll kill us.'

'Shut up,' said JJ, not looking at her.

She said, 'I'm trying to save your life, you dickhead.'

JJ turned. 'Shut the fuck up.' He raised his hand to hit her.

Bang.

Grace looked at JJ with his right hand up and the rifle barrel dropping.

She looked over to Luke sitting in the chair with a pistol in his hand.

She looked back to JJ who dropped the rifle and walked to the bed. 'JJ?' she said. 'John?'

JJ sat on the bed and looked down to where blood was oozing from his liver.

Luke stood quickly and picked up the .22. He said, 'I'm sorry. I had to.'

Grace turned and slapped Luke hard in the face. She raised her hand to strike again, but Luke grabbed her by the wrist. 'I'm sorry.'

The door opened.

Someone yelled, 'Look out!'

Luke turned.

There were three men in the doorway. One sat down and the two behind held up guns and stepped inside, shooting.

Luke shoved Grace towards the bathroom door, and stepped back into the middle of the room firing the .22 from his hip. He hit the big man, the one who'd shoved Grace at Lisa's house, in the thigh. The man fell back against the wall near the door. The first man, without a gun, rolled back out of the door. The smaller man, with blood all over his jeans and t-shirt, kept shooting.

Grace turned to see JJ hit in the arm. Luke stepped in front of her and pushed her all the way into the bathroom where she fell on the tiles. They kept shooting. They shot a lamp, the telephone, a window. And they shot JJ again in the leg. He kept sitting on the bed in the middle of all the shooting like he wasn't hurt, but trying to remember something. Or maybe it was the jockey in him, staying on the horse, no matter what.

Ellis couldn't get a clear shot at the big guy with the rifle. He kept moving around the room behind the bed and jumping up and firing and rolling away again. Finally, he just put his head up into where

Ellis was randomly shooting and took a bullet in the middle of his forehead. Splat.

Ellis pulled the trigger again, for no particular reason, but the Glock was empty. 'Fuck,' said Ellis looking around the smoke-filled room in awe.

Ned lay on the floor, moaning. He'd taken another bullet somewhere in the chest.

Ellis went around the bed to the rifleman and prodded him with his foot. He picked up the rifle and turned to look at the guy sitting on the bed. 'This guy has to be the jockey. I mean he's pretty fat, but he's short, right?' When no one answered, Ellis shot him in the head.

Simon had rolled up to a sitting position just outside the motel room door. Lights were coming on in a couple of other motel rooms. He looked at his taxi, and started to get up. That was when he heard a girl giggle. It was an inappropriate sound, like the reaction to someone burping at a dinner table.

Simon leaned in to see the woman from the headlights, sitting cross-legged in the bathroom, looking at the bullet-riddled body of the jockey.

Ellis looked at her too. He stepped around the bed, pointing the rifle.

'Ned's been shot,' called Simon. He started to step into the room.

'What?' Ellis continued to advance towards her.

'We need to get him out of here. Ellis, before the police come.'

Ellis looked over to Simon. 'Police?'

'There was a fair bit of noise,' said Simon, apologetic.

Ellis woke. 'Yeah. Fuckin' yeah, eh.' Ellis grinned then looked to Ned, who was struggling to get up. 'Dumb fuck. All right.' Ellis turned to shoot the woman.

'I'll need her to help carry him.'

Ellis stopped.

Simon crossed in front of the rifle. 'You need to have your hands free. There could be others.' Simon grabbed her by the shoulder. It seemed impossible for her blouse to be so white and untouched by all the blood. 'Help me carry him. Now.'

Ellis stepped back, then bent to grab Ned's pistol.

She wouldn't stand. She was pretty and she was young. She sat in her white blouse and dark skirt, staring at the bathroom tiles. Simon said, 'Help me, or you'll die.'

Ellis said, 'See, Simon. I knew you'd get the hang of it.'

Simon got under one of Ned's arms and the woman under the other and they walked him towards the taxi.

Ellis stopped when he got to Bobby's body which lay on the ground where it had been dropped when they'd heard the gunshot inside. He fumbled amongst his weaponry until he found the empty Glock, which he carefully wiped for prints before pushing it into Bobby's hand.

At the taxi, Simon whispered, 'If there's even the briefest moment to get away, run. Run and keep running. Okay.'

She didn't seem to hear.

Ned did. He said, 'I don't know if I can. My leg hurts.'

Ellis opened the front passenger door. 'Put Ned in here.'

Simon helped Ned sit and lifted his legs in.

Ellis turned to the court where all the room lights were out and fired a couple of shots with a vague wave of the gun. 'Bang, bang,' he said. He saw the girl and stood looking at her. He smiled and grabbed her by the neck, squeezing. 'You're in the back with me, sugar.'

The Horror

Ellis put the pistol in his lap then checked the .22 to see how many bullets were left. He felt a little flat. It was quiet in the taxi apart from the wind at the back. The meter showed nine hundred and forty-three dollars owing. It was four in the morning and still dark outside.

The girl was doing nothing interesting.

Simon said, 'Ned needs a hospital.'

Ned bounced on the passenger door.

'No hospitals.'

'He's in a pretty bad way.'

'You go to a hospital, you'll end up back inside. Ned, you don't want to go back to prison, do you?'

'Okay,' mumbled Ned.

Ellis lifted the .22 and rested the barrel on the back of Simon's seat so the tip nuzzled Simon's left ear. 'Head for the Gnangara pine plantation.'

'You're a taxi driver?' gasped the girl.

Ellis said, 'Yep. Simon's my taxi driver. Say "You got it".' Ellis tapped the back of Simon's head gently with the end of the barrel.

'You got it.'

She started sobbing then, in tremulous big breaths that broke in her throat like burst bubbles of hope.

Ellis smiled at the sound and moved forward a little in his seat to see her tears. They glistened every now and then in the passing streetlights. Ellis saw that she was more than good-looking. She was beautiful like all the unreal ones that you only ever see in films or *Hustler*. And here she was, and she was sobbing. He looked at her chest. Her breasts quivered below her blouse like whimpering puppies.

Ellis kicked her leg. 'Cheer up, girlie. At least he died like a man. More'n ol' Simon here.'

'No he didn't. He just sat there.'

'The fat guy! You were with the fat guy?'

She stopped crying, went distant. 'They both died because of me.'

'No, they died because of me,' said Ellis. 'Me.' When she didn't look at him, he kicked her leg again and said, 'What's your name?'

'Grace.'

'Like what you say when you're about to eat at the convent, huh?' Ellis actually licked his lips looking at her. He wanted to hear her sob again, to be touching her when she did it.

Simon said, 'How you doing, Ned?'

Ned didn't say anything.

'He's okay,' said Ellis.

'I can just pull off here by the river. Let me bandage him up.'

Ellis yelled, 'Ned, ya cockhead.'

Ned said, 'Ellis,' like he was calling from under water.

Ellis punched the back of Ned's seat, but not very hard. 'Okay. Pull over.' He looked over at Grace, nodding at the idea of her too. Then he suddenly looked up to find Simon watching him with his two different eyes in the rear-view mirror. Ellis raised the rifle barrel into the mirror line, aiming at the grey one. 'You going to mount a rescue are you, Simon?'

'Just going to bandage up Ned.'

Simon, the taxi driver, pulled off the highway. Ned was the big guy. Ellis was the psycho.

Ellis said, 'Ol' Simon here likes to try to rescue folks. He don't say much – just flashes his lights.'

Grace remembered the taxi doing something with its headlights outside Lisa's. It had made her move off the road and go slow.

'Only he's no good at it. Can't rescue shit. Not the jockey. Not even himself. I think the only one who can rescue you is me.' Ellis changed hands on the rifle and put his free right hand high on Grace's left thigh.

She made herself sit still.

'I'll just turn in here, Ellis.'

Ellis gave her thigh a twist through her skirt, hurting.

She bit the inside of her lip, determined not to cry out.

Simon drove down a hard mud track to a cleared area near a jetty.

Ellis took up one of the pistols and pointed it at her.

The taxi pulled up on some grass and the engine went off.

Ellis said, 'I notice you still have your headlights on, Simon.'

Simon turned them off. There were lights across the river. It looked like some kind of factory. A lone light on the end of the jetty had a halo like a Van Gogh painting. It put a wash of faint blue over the taxi.

'I also noticed you keep interrupting me every time it starts getting interesting back here. Aren't I paying you enough attention now we got the pretty girl?'

Grace watched Simon sit, doing nothing in a way that was like he was pretending not to be there, but somehow not rude either, just waiting for Ellis.

'I noticed you slipped out the door back at the motel too, Simon. And I noticed you yelled "Watch out" when we were going in.'

'How do you know I wasn't yelling "Watch out" to you and Ned?'

It stopped Ellis a moment. He seemed to struggle with the idea before he said, 'I know that's not what.'

Grace watched a little war go on inside Ellis. She wondered about it.

Simon said, 'I'm going to get out of the car, Ellis, and go around and open Ned's door and bandage him up.'

'Go right ahead, Simon. Me and her can get to know each other better.'

'What about Ned?'

'He can watch. He likes to watch.'

'I meant I could use Grace's help with Ned.'

'Who gives a fucking shit what you want? Every bloody time I fucking start to think, you're in the fucking way, pushing into my head. Shut the fuck up, Simon, you hear me?'

Ellis looked at Simon, half turned but with his head down, waiting. Ellis had screamed it, he knew. He looked at the girl and caught a trace of fear before she tried to hide it. Ellis wanted to bite her. He wanted to bite out a big hunk of her flesh and swallow it.

Simon was still waiting. She had her head down waiting too. Ned was just sitting there. It was all on Ellis to keep it together and get it going again.

He felt the guns. He felt the pistol's weight and aimed it at her cheek. He tapped the barrel of the rifle on Simon's shoulder. He got up a smile bouncing a little to some music – Metallica. He sniffed the cold river air and thought there was some perfume on her. He changed the music in his head; switched it down, kicked it back – The Black Keys. They sat waiting and quiet until Ellis got it back together.

'Simon, stay where you are. Good dog, stay. I've got you covered. Got everything covered.'

Ellis opened his door and backed out a couple of paces with the rifle pointed at them. 'You, girl. Slide out this way.'

She slid across the back seat feet first while Ellis watched her legs slithering and squirming around in her skirt as she came towards him. When she tried to stand, Ellis grabbed her shoulder and pushed her face down on the grass. He put his foot on her back with the pistol in his left hand aimed down at her while he kept the rifle aimed at Simon. 'Okay Simon, come on down.'

Simon rolled his neck a little, loosening the tightness as he went around the car to Ned's door and opened it. Ned fell sideways before Simon got him by the shoulder. One of Ned's thongs was floating in the blood in the foot-well. 'Cold,' said Ned.

Simon said, 'I need someone to hold him up.'

Ellis took his foot off Grace.

She scrambled up and went to Ned, holding him by the shoulder while Simon took off his shirt and wrapped it around Ned's chest.

Simon whispered, 'If you get the chance, run and don't stop.'

Grace said, 'You too.'

Simon said, 'What?'

Grace looked at him. 'You've got David Bowie's eyes.'

'No talking,' said Ellis. He grabbed Grace with his pistol hand and pushed her back against the car, forcing the back passenger door shut with her weight. He tried to grab at her blouse, but didn't have enough empty hands. He tossed the rifle and used his right hand to rip her blouse away.

Simon stood and Ellis pointed the pistol at him then held out her torn blouse until he took it. Grace tried to cover herself while she glared defiantly at Ellis.

'You're so great. See with Simon, it's all way back hidden, so you never know what the fuck he's thinking. That's his edge. But you ... everything you think just lights up like some big TV screen at the cricket.' Ellis grabbed Grace's arm and turned her to him. 'A red bra. You got a lacy red bra on.'

Grace stood tall, pushing her chest out, still glaring, building to something irretrievable perhaps.

Simon said, 'Ned needs a hospital.'

Ellis called, 'Ned, ya dumb sack of shit. Ned.'

Grace said, 'He's dying, you moron. It's what bullets do.'

Ellis stood stunned, blinking at the ground between him and Grace.

He heard Simon say, 'She didn't mean it. She's upset.'

Ellis jammed the pistol into her cheek and leaned into her anger. Her eyes opened in pain then panic and fear. A surge went through Ellis. He grabbed her shoulders and spun her onto the boot of the taxi and felt for the hem of her skirt to lift it so he could get at her panties and rip them away. He heard a noise.

Simon was behind him.

Ellis turned to see Simon bending towards the rifle. He raised his pistol but got pushed from behind as he pulled the trigger, sending the shot somewhere towards the river. Ellis elbowed back, catching her in the guts and dropping her. He stepped back along the car away from her and brought the pistol up to fire at Simon, but Simon was standing with his arms folded like he was waiting for a bus. Ellis relaxed then turned and pointed the pistol at Grace on the ground.

'No,' yelled Simon as he pushed himself between them.

Ellis pushed the gun at Simon's chest. The girl yelled, 'No!'

Then Ellis saw it, in Simon's face. Fear. Finally. There it was for Ellis to see –into Simon's mind.

Sirens started somewhere. Lights were flashing white somewhere.

'Beg,' said Ellis, 'beg for *her* life.'

Simon said, 'Ellis, please don't kill her.' He got down on his knees and looked up at Ellis and said, 'Please, Ellis. I know you have the power to let her live. Don't do it. Ellis, don't do it. Please.'

It was like a perfect echo of the past. Word perfect. Ellis felt a rush and some kind of thing tumbling down around the rush, like fire and vomit coming over a waterfall together. That would have been the time to shoot the girl; shoot her but keep looking into Simon's eyes – but lights swept them brightly and Ellis recognised the siren sound. He'd heard those sirens during lockdowns. He said, 'Simon, go and get the rifle for me.'

Simon went to where the rifle was lying. He said, 'I don't know how to use this, so ...'

Ellis knew he was saying it to her. He stepped to the girl and grabbed her hair and dragged her up to standing with the pistol barrel stabbing her cheek again. Her breasts shook like jelly over the red bra.

Simon picked up the rifle by its barrel and held it out towards Ellis.

'Smart robot. Toss the rifle in the back, Simon. Simon says.' Ellis patted her cheek. 'My remote control.'

Simon pulled open the door and placed it on the back seat.

Ellis said, 'Get Ned's door closed and drive us out of here.' Ellis finally looked across the river to where searchlights were dancing and sirens were blaring and shadows were moving frantically from when they'd heard the gunshot. Simon had parked them across the river from the women's prison. Ellis laughed like a backward burp strangled halfway out.

The Petrified Forest

Simon drove up onto the road and headed back towards the highway and the grey light of imminent dawn.

Ellis said, 'The pine plantation. If you say "You got it", I'll dig out one of your eyes with Ned's knife.'

The taxi meter showed one thousand and thirty-seven dollars.

It was cold in the taxi, shirtless with no back window.

Simon moved his rear-view mirror so he could see her.

She saw the movement and looked back at him. He nodded to her and she sent out the thought to him that she was ready.

Simon said, 'Ellis, Ned is dead.'

Ellis was quiet. He finally said, 'Yeah, well we can find a good spot for him in Gnangara. We can bury him like a real citizen.' He looked over to Grace and added, 'Then you two and I can play some games in Ned's honour, now I got you both a little bit trained. Don't think I don't know that you two owe me for the shit you tried to pull back there.'

Simon said, 'Grace means elegance and beauty.'

'Who gives a fuck?'

'It can also mean the free and unmerited gift of love from God. A divine piece of forgiveness.'

Grace looked at Simon in the mirror, trying to figure out what he was doing. There was something about him having two different-coloured eyes that was distracting about his meanings.

'Mensa shit. I'm not forgiving anyone,' said Ellis.

'Maybe she's here for you and me, Ellis.'

Grace saw Ellis flickering a moment, his brain computer glitching before getting back on the program.

'She's here for me,' said Ellis.

'No, I think you're here for me, Ellis,' said Simon.

Grace found herself able to watch them and watch herself at the same time without the fear, like Simon clearing some space somehow. He was working it, but it was like a different language.

'What?' asked Ellis.

'I did kill a man. A stranger.'

'See. I knew you knew.'

'He went to sleep on the road. I came round a bend and I ran over him and did squash him flat like a bug.'

Grace tried not to think of the story, which might be true or might not, but to think about what Simon was trying to do.

'That's it? That's not killing.'

'I skidded and ran into a tree afterwards. Smashed up the taxi. That's why I got the new one, Ellis.'

'An accident, that's all?'

'Yes. I don't think there was anything I could have done, except maybe not be on the earth so I wasn't there at the time to do it. Not my fault, said the judge. And my wife. But then she changed her mind I guess. Anyway she left.'

'Why you suddenly talking so much?'

'Only he wasn't a bug. He was a cabinet maker. Wife and three kids. The youngest is four. A Jack Russell named Scruff.'

'Time to shut up, Simon.'

'Thing was, Grace, I just wished I could have jumped out of the taxi, before that bend coming up, before it all happened.'

'What?' said Ellis.

'No,' said Grace.

Ellis had let the pistol rest loose on his lap. He swung the rifle round to Grace, pushing the barrel at her bra. 'Put your seatbelt on. No one's jumping. Just me. Jumping on you pretty soon.'

Grace put her seatbelt on.

Ellis swung the rifle back to Simon's head. Simon already had his seatbelt on. Always.

'Simon, you're a prick. Now you're trying to fucking hypnotise me or some shit.'

Grace said, 'If you crashed now, I guess we'd all die together.'

Simon flicked his eyes to Grace's in the mirror to see whether they were on the same page. She smiled. It was an encouraging smile, but perhaps too serene like Grace Kelly in *Rear Window*, only this Grace winked.

Simon reached up and turned the rear-view mirror so he could see Ellis. He looked back, smiling like Robert Mitchum in *Cape Fear*. 'Yeah, you watch me, Simon. You better be watching me.'

The taxi drove past the villas it had driven into only twenty-eight hours before. The tops of pine trees could be seen beyond. The sky was lightening still.

'Nearly there,' said Simon.

A truck passed going the other way.

Grace said, 'Are you gay, Simon?'

'Huh,' said Simon looking to find Grace's face but not.

'The way you keep helping Ellis, like you like it.'

Ellis wasn't looking over to her. He was watching Simon.

'It's like you just keep waiting for Ellis to tell you what to do, like you're his wife.'

Simon drove.

Ellis was holding his breath, his mouth starting to twist slowly, like he was sounding out some difficult word.

'I saw the way you bandaged Ned. How you were trying to look after him. You are very tender, Simon.'

'Ned,' said Ellis.

'Ned's dead,' said Grace.

Ellis looked towards Ned, his head shuddering on the window.

Simon nodded once.

The Gnangara pine plantation was on their right, the tops of the pine trees catching the first rays of the new sun.

'Poor Ned,' said Simon. 'I couldn't save his life. I saved yours, Ellis.'

'I saved yours.'

Grace said, 'You never answered me, Simon. Are you a poof?'

'Maybe you're right. Denial. Maybe that's why I haven't found love yet. I'm ready. I want it, but I don't know the way.'

Grace looked out at the pine trees as they came over a rise. She looked at the pistol just resting on Ellis's lap and the rifle pointed at Simon before she went on. 'It's just that Ellis keeps telling me how he's going to hurt me and fuck me. Only I don't think he knows how to fuck a woman.'

Ellis was having trouble following. They were jumping around on too many important points.

A limestone road at the bottom of the hill went off to the right and into the heart of the pine forest.

Grace felt the taxi slow a little, and hoped Simon was in on her plan, because if he wasn't she would die. 'Simon, he's been keeping you around. Hanging on every word. Watching, listening. I'm the one in the way. I think he wants to fuck you. Ellis wants you so bad Simon, I'm amazed he hasn't bought you flowers, and dropped down on his knees so he can put you in his mouth and love you till –'

'Agggggggh,' growled Ellis as he swung the rifle towards Grace.

Simon braked hard, sending Ellis forward. The rifle went off, putting a hole in the roof and filling the car with noise.

The taxi veered right across some dirt towards the limestone track. It clipped a tree stump, went up on two wheels, sending Ellis crashing into the rear passenger window. The taxi held there a moment, up on two wheels, driving along the pine plantation road, with Ned and Ellis down against their windows and Grace and Simon hanging against their seatbelts.

The taxi tipped all the way over onto its roof, squashing the plastic taxi sign. Windows exploded. Ellis screamed.

The taxi slid along the road of the pine plantation in a constant scrape of crumpling, tearing metal roof. Simon sat, upside down, grimly holding the useless steering wheel.

Grace hung upside down in the back. With her red bra and the way her arms waved around, she looked like she might be dancing at a beach party.

Ned and Ellis were on the roof which was now the floor in a tangle of guns and glass and blood.

The car finally stopped sliding and did a little half turn, slowly rotating around on some point of the roof until it stopped.

Simon pushed the release on his seatbelt and fell past the steering wheel to the car roof. He crawled out through the missing driver's window and leaned into the back and released Grace's seatbelt. She dropped on top of Ellis, making him squeal.

'Come on,' said Simon. He dragged Grace out through her missing window.

Ellis was half under Ned. He kicked him off then slithered around on his elbows until he saw the pistol laying in front of him. He reached for it, but instead of his hand there was scraped skin and shattered bone. He growled and grabbed for the pistol with his left hand.

Simon tried to lead Grace off, but his leg was hurt. He pushed her towards the trees. 'Go.'

She paused a moment, then ran awkwardly through the pine trees. Simon noticed she was wearing only one shoe.

Ellis crawled out of the car. Simon moved away from Grace, stopping at the nearest tree.

Ellis got up and leaned back against the car. He looked at his mashed wrist where a hand should have been, then to Simon.

Simon staggered between the trees towards the rising sun.

Ellis yelled, 'You're a dead man, Simon. A fucking dead man.' Ellis coughed a gob of blood. He felt his chest and was sure there was a broken rib poking into something important. He pushed himself up off the car and trudged after Simon like a half blown-up Terminator working on its last battery pulses.

Simon limped up the rise but paused to try to figure out where he should go.

Ellis found the gap between that row of trees, saw Simon some ten trees up, raised the pistol and fired.

Simon staggered and fell. He grabbed at his calf then jumped up and tried to hop. He made it past a couple of lines of trees before the pain in his knee from the crash dragged him down again. There was a fallen pine tree nearby and Simon started to crawl for it.

Ellis came along the line of trees, bubbles of blood popping on his lips. He stopped when he saw some spots of blood on the ground, bright red against the yellow of the fallen pine needles.

Simon dragged himself behind the tree, pulled off his belt and tied it above his calf as a tourniquet. He got ready to get up, but Ellis's face appeared over the log.

Ellis limped around the cut end of the tree, his gun hanging.

The sun was starting to hit the ground in places, golden and hopeful.

Ellis flopped down next to Simon and squealed in pain. He raised himself back up to rest his back against the rough pine bark and aimed the gun again, left-handed.

'Ellis.'

'Yeah, it's me.'

Simon laid back on the sharp pine needles and closed his eyes. 'I got the girl away.'

'She got herself away.'

'Yeah, I think you're right.'

Ellis was trying to raise the pistol and sight along the barrel. He couldn't focus.

Simon stayed down, feeling the pine needles prick him all over his back. It was a good smell, pine, first thing in the day.

'You didn't save those others.'

'No.'

'Your guy who you ran over doesn't count.'

'He does.'

'Want to know how many I've killed?'

'No.'

'Now I'm going to kill you.'

Simon didn't open his eyes. He just lay there. He could hear a bird somewhere. A willie wagtail, he thought, chirping angrily. Then he said, 'When did I save your life?'

'You know.'

'School? When that kid had the stranglehold on you?'

'Yeah. I knew you knew. Jiujitsu guy had me.'

'You took to cornering guys in the change rooms after sport.'

'Ha. Yeah, that way they couldn't get away. I shit in one guy's mouth after, too.'

Simon looked at Ellis. The gun was still aimed at him, but Ellis was leaning back on the tree with his eyes closed, blood dripping between his grin. 'I was nearly passing out and there you were, Simon Carter standing in your ironed shirt talking to him like a psychiatrist. "No Steve. Steve don't do it. Steve." I watched you looking at him and talking to him and he stopped. He stopped strangling me. And you took him away. You were showing me, weren't you? I think you're nothing, Ellis, but I'm going to save your life and then not even ask for anything back.'

'Is that what you think?'

'Foster's got his money and that girl has got her tits and you got your brains. But see, I did pay you back.' Ellis's words trailed into a weak cough. The gun rested on his lap. His eyes stayed closed. He was smiling like a stoned idiot.

Simon propped himself up on one elbow. 'That's not why I did it. I didn't stop Steve for you. I stopped him for him. He was going too far and would have regretted it later. My saving you was ... there was no plan. Just coincidences, and a jumble of things meaning nothing. My saving you was collateral kindness.'

Ellis sat not smiling. The gun was still pointed but Ellis was dead.

There was a footstep. Simon looked to see Grace coming from behind a tree. She had the .22. She aimed it at Ellis as she came forward. She pulled the trigger, but nothing happened. She kept coming and kept pulling the trigger but it was out of bullets.

Out of the Past

Simon and Grace limped out of the edge of the pine plantation into a tiny suburb of fake Tuscan homes with roll-on lawns. The retic was going in front of one of the houses. Others had newspapers waiting for folks to wake.

Simon smiled when he saw that it was The Pines. He led Grace into the cul-de-sac where he had delivered Frank, the drunk pie-seller.

She'd gotten rid of her one shoe and she was barefoot. Her toenails were painted a bright purple colour.

Simon knocked on Frank's front door.

Frank's wife was dressed in tight-fitting tracksuit pants and a green blouse, ready for some power walking after she dropped the kids off to school. She opened the door to find two half naked people covered in blood. 'Oh.'

Simon said, 'Hi, is Frank home?'

Grace, her blood-smeared arms folded over her bra, nodded an encouraging smile through a swollen lip.

Frank, already in his white shirt and suit pants, came up behind his wife.

Simon said, 'Frank, great. Listen, can you call the police?'

'Do I know you?' Frank stepped to the door, taking it from his wife. He was getting ready to close it.

'I drove you home. Your car was stuck in a ditch.'

'Oh, yeah. No worries mate. Got it back.' Frank closed the door.

Simon reached quickly for the handle and opened it again before Frank had time to push the lock.

Frank straightened as Simon pulled Bobby/Ellis's gun from his belt. 'Frank, this isn't acceptable.'

'What's going on?' said Frank's wife from the edge of the kitchen as Frank retreated, his hands raised like he'd seen on television.

Simon and Grace followed. Two kids dressed for school were sitting on the other side of a table eating their breakfast. There were eight different kinds of cereal boxes on the table. In an alcove near some glasses was a little television emitting animated kid-show noises. There were lots of boings and skids, no English required.

'Hi kids,' said Grace.

No one was looking at her or the TV or Simon. They were completely focused on the gun with a collection of expressions ranging from fear to wonder. Frank's wife let her eyes follow Simon's leg down to where blood was staining her carpet.

Simon said, 'This is not acceptable, Frank. Just common courtesy. Politeness. Dealing with another human being in a civilised manner. I mean, Ellis ... Ellis was just always Ellis. A seriously damaged, hurting, animal kind of thing. But surely we haven't all devolved back into jungle behaviour. We know there are deranged evil things, but don't the rest of us have to be better, then? Make some effort?'

Frank, his wife and one of the kids stood or sat transfixed trying to look like they agreed with what Simon was saying. The other kid had gone back to watching the cartoon.

Grace touched Simon's shoulder. She rubbed the skin gently then patted him.

Simon looked down at the pistol in his hand. 'I'm sorry. I can do better than this.' He stepped to the freezer and put it on a packet of frozen crinkle-cut chips. He closed the freezer door firmly. 'Right, let's forget the gun. Frank, let's forget that I helped you a couple of nights ago. Let's say, I'm a complete stranger, who is in need. I'm asking you for kindness, sir. Let's say, I've asked you for a lift into town and you say, hey, sure.'

Frank never took his eyes off the freezer. He said, 'Hey, sure.'

The automatic door of Frank's garage wound up and Frank's car, from that first night, eased out into the bright sunshine. Grace was driving. She wore a green tracksuit top. Simon wore Frank's shirt. It was clean and ironed.

Grace turned the car out of the driveway and down the cul-de-sac and out onto the road.

FOR THE BIRDS

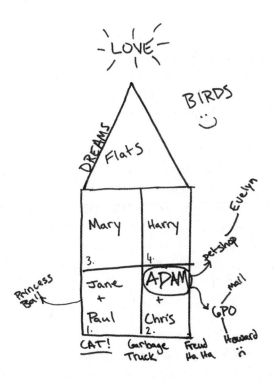

Connectivity: the extent to which components of a network are connected to one another and the speed with which they can converse.
– ABC Definitions On line

Convergence: the tendency for different technological systems to evolve towards performing similar tasks.
– Diction fairies

The taxi pulled into the quiet tree-lined cul-de-sac observed by a *Ninox connivens connivens*, commonly known as the barking owl. A dog barked somewhere, but not the owl. It watched Adam emerge from the back of the taxi and go to the popped boot to get out a slightly fire-singed suitcase. Adam was dressed in jeans, a checked shirt and cowboy boots, a little bit too country even for 1991.

'Wanna shut the boot there, mate?' called the taxi driver.

Adam did, then put the suitcase on the curb next to a neat row of metal rubbish bins. He went to the back seat and got out a covered birdcage and set that down next to the suitcase before going to the driver's window.

'Forty-four thirty. Make it an even forty-five.'

Adam looked up from his wallet. 'That's a lot.'

'There was that detour I explained about and the live animal transporting fee, and you know, now you've seen the city – even went past the museum. Lot bigger than ... where did you say you was from?'

'Mukinbudin.'

The taxi driver said, 'Welcome to the big smoke,' as he plucked the fifty from Adam's hand and drove away.

Adam turned to look at the maisonette-style flats. Four flats, two above the two below. There was an ornate entrance way in the middle. 'Number two, Chris,' he said to the birdcage before picking it up. 'The key is hidden under the mat. Lovely garden.'

The owl sniffed the air. She thought she smelled canary. She liked canaries. They tasted like chicken. Most things tasted like chicken. Even mice. She barked hopefully.

*

During the meandering taxi journey through the streets of the city Adam had indeed passed the impressive sandstone museum. Twice. The taxi driver had noted the age of the building and the night lighting of the façade. It had been dark within and still was now, long closed for the day.

Inside, two figures flitted from shadow to shadow. An imposing polished jarrah staircase led up. A threadbare polar bear stood near a toilet door. In a huge room off the other way the plastic replica of a pterodactyl skeleton shone white in the darkness. The likeness of an *Archaeopteryx* fossil, urvogel, glowed in a cabinet beyond.

Paul crept from beneath the stairs to a computer set on a black velvet–covered stand. He pushed the green plastic button which activated the multimedia program. A poorly lit photograph of the museum appeared on the screen with a superimposed title: *Your Museum*. Music played, neither driving nor particularly inspiring, filling the gaps in the commentary, like instrumental putty. The voice of a local newsreader spoke in a friendly tone. 'Welcome to your museum.'

'Can you turn the sound down?' Jane whispered, stepping up behind Paul.

Paul fiddled with a dial but it didn't seem to change anything. He used the arrows on the keyboard to bring up the floor plans of different levels of the museum.

'You were supposed to have done this already, Paul!'

'I'm just checking,' he lied.

'Antiquities – third floor,' she pointed. 'Come on.'

A photograph of a metal ball came up. It nestled on blue satin. Regal trumpets, muted. 'One of your museum's most prized possessions is on loan from St Petersburg. The Princess's Ball is a perfect sphere fashioned entirely from gold.'

'Turn the bloody thing off and let's go,' hissed Jane.

Paul pushed the red plastic stop button but there seemed to still be a few bugs to iron out in the cutting-edge technology of the museum's multimedia display. Drawings of a Wiccan goddess holding a triple moon replaced graphs of the world's rarest metals. The voice kept explaining as Paul put on his balaclava and picked up his very heavy canvas bag and shuffled after Jane.

'The triple moon of maiden, mother and crone, waxing, full and waning moon, is associated with feminine energy, mystery and psychic abilities.'

Upstairs a guard walked past a large glass cabinet depicting an avian-themed bush scene. There were dead trees full of stuffed birds and a fake waterway with stuffed ducks. A swan sat atop a nest. A dugite lurked. There were eggs everywhere. The guard shone his torch across the dusty little glass eyes until he found his favourite, a pink cockatoo.

'Polly want a cracker,' he said. 'Bwark, bwark.' He listened. Somewhere downstairs there was someone talking.

'With a circumference of seventy centimetres, the Princess's Ball is hollow at its core, but scientists suggest the gold crust to be of two hundred and fifty millimetres in thickness.'

The guard moved carefully down the stairs, his torch at the ready.

Jane and Paul slipped into the Antiquities room as soon as he passed. There were cabinets of special crockery, some weathered clay soldiers, many large vases and urns. In the centre of the room, spotlit, in a protective glass case, surrounded by red alarm beams, lay the golden ball. It was smooth and unadorned. It glowed on the blue satin bed.

Paul opened the canvas bag and picked through intricate cutting devices and complicated electronic measurers.

Downstairs the guard went to the multimedia computer. It was on again, droning its endless trivia. 'The orb contains seventy ounces of eighteen-carat gold. At today's gold prices, this makes the ball extremely valuable. However, as an artefact, the Princess's Ball is of inestimable value.'

Jane stood by the door, keeping lookout.

Paul examined the electronic beams and the intricate wires leading to the base of the cabinet thoughtfully before taking a sledgehammer out of his bag. He took a deep breath then a full swing. Glass smashed and the cabinet tumbled. The ball fell to the floor with a crack and stuck. It sat there in the dent of broken floorboards like an egg in a wooden nest.

Alarms began to howl. Lights flashed and swept.

*

Adam woke, panting, to orange light pulsing in the darkness. His first thought was bushfire. He jumped up ready to get water to the hay shed, but he wasn't on the farm anymore. He could hear bangs and clatters outside. There was a metallic grinding noise. A motor.

He went to the window. A huge blue truck with a rotating orange light on top idled and revved in the street as men with big metal rubbish bins on their shoulders ran to the bins behind a shopping centre, throwing down their lids with more clatters and up-ending them. They wore blue singlets and bandanas but their sweat glistened in the orange light. They wrestled and dragged the metal bins back to the growling truck, its back open and mashing. They hurled abuse at each other and laughed aggressively.

Then Adam saw they weren't all men. One was a woman, although she had the same short army-style haircut, wore the same shorts and sweat-dripping biceps. She emptied a small bin near the flats and tossed it into the brick letterbox next door. She spat from between perfect white teeth.

The truck rumbled on down the hill, its rear closing and squashing with the faintest gurgle somewhere in its guts. The garbos fell in behind, chanting like army grunts in training, 'Boom chugga lug, boom chugga lug.'

Adam woke, sweating, at dawn, wondering if he had heard more banging noises upstairs. He looked at the ceiling. There were many cracks, like a map of country roads. This was not his room. That was gone. Adam's suitcase lay open on a dressing table. He thought he could hear sawing.

He went to his window and looked out. There were empty bins lying behind the shopping centre, lids scattered. Some paper blew, caught by an easterly. It hovered then drifted towards a tree in the garden.

Adam was dressed for work in a blue short-sleeved shirt and a blue tie. He opened and closed empty cupboards as he explored the furnished but unstocked flat. 'Did those garbage collectors wake you up last night? The city sure is noisy.'

'There's a cat! A real brute of a thing. Sat outside the window most of the night, watching me.'

Adam left the kitchen and investigated the adjacent lounge room. There was a couch, chairs and a little desk in the corner. 'I thought I might get one of those personal computers. You can get CD-ROMS full of information. A whole encyclopedia. Anything you want to know.'

'I'm pretty sure I heard an owl too. I was hoping he'd get the cat. Adam, we gotta get outta here.'

On a table in front of the lounge window sat the birdcage. Inside a canary jigged up and down on his perch, agitated.

Adam looked into the canary's plastic feeder box. 'Chris, you've eaten all your food.'

'Comfort food. I ate to reduce stress. It didn't work. I'm going through a lot right now.'

'I'll have to buy some seed on the way home from work.'

'Hey, not to worry. I'll hunt. Maybe head for the river – plummet out of the sun, and catch some salmon.'

Adam turned around in front of the cage. 'Well, how do I look? Gotta make a good impression on my first day.'

'You look like mallee fowl. The female.'

The sawing sound came again from above. Something heavy hit the floor up there, sending a fine spray of plaster down on Adam as he looked up. There were more cracks on the lounge ceiling, some quite big. Adam shook away his feelings of foreboding. 'I'm going to be late.' He grabbed his keys and his wallet and hurried out.

Chris contemplated the door. 'Look, I know what you're thinking. Sad, lonely guy who talks to his canary. He wasn't always like this. The fact is I'm all he's got now. By the way, he can't hear me. Sometimes I think he can when I focus hard on food, but mostly we have parallel conversations. It's a species thing, I guess. Anyway, he was happy once.' Chris raised his tail delicately and pooped. 'Shit happens.'

Adam caught a bus into the city, noting the bright colours the girls wore and their full hair. Young men had full hair too, often dented in the middle by the headphones of their Sony Walkmans. He was about to cross the road to his new workplace when he saw the pet shop. The shop had lots of fish in tanks but also some cages of birds at the back.

There was a girl. She moved through the birdcages, filling each water cup from a little blue watering can with a long curved neck. She had a slender neck too. And long dark hair. She had a small nose and large dark eyes. She moved to another cage and tipped the watering can, like a dark feathered crane dipping towards a river, completely intent on the end of the water spout.

Adam was about to go in, but caught the reflection of the GPO in the window. He turned and hurried across the road to his new job, his new life, perhaps to be reborn.

*

As Adam went into the General Post Office, a uniformed postman entered the front door of Adam's flats. He went straight up the internal stairs to the landing, where he knocked on the door of flat three.

The hammering in flat four stopped, but then started again more vigorously.

The door to flat three opened with a flourish. Mary's full figure was barely held by her red underwear and black suspender belt. She wore stockings and high-heeled shoes and held a whip. She was panting.

'Oh,' said the postman. 'I'm sorry, Mary. Are you busy?'

'Practising my swing, Toby.'

'Ah,' said Toby, looking down at her shoes and losing himself in their angry sharp heels.

'Toby,' said Mary, firmly. 'You didn't ring.'

'I've got a letter, for you. I thought I'd bring it ... straight up.'

Mary softened. 'Bring it in. We can steam it open together.'

She held open the door and the postman shuffled in. She looked towards the hammering noise.

*

Underneath flat three was flat number one.

At a small table in the corner of flat one, Jane sat at Paul's personal computer waiting for dial-up to connect her to the stock market. She had recently discovered *Gopher*, an application layer protocol that aided in finding documents from around the world.

Paul sat at the kitchen table, the golden sphere nestling in the canvas bag open at his feet. Paul was taking his long-playing records out of a cardboard box to make room for the Princess's Ball. 'Are you sure we're doing the right thing, Jane?'

'Yep.'

'I know this is an artificially fetishised object arbitrarily designated art by those in power and being owned by the oppressive monarchy lauding its wealth ...'

'Gouged from the oppressed.' Jane was a university student, studying anthropology, sociology and social work.

'Yeah. But ...' Paul was a university student too. He was studying occupational therapy. 'Isn't it also a symbol of, you know, the power of wimminhood. Like it's the moon god and the tides and cycles.'

'And it's made of a shitload of gold.' Jane scanned world gold prices on a special site on the internet devoted to stock prices. It was updated every day.

'For setting up the wimmin's refuge,' said Paul, nodding at the ball. 'We're doing good here.'

'Yep. Sell this baby and we'll use that money to ... once I've moved it around a little, you know on the currency markets and global trading shit. The best wimmin's refuge we can buy.'

A knock on the door stopped them. The floor was covered with their burglar gear. There were two balaclavas on the sofa.

Jane put her finger to her lips to signal for quiet.

A woman's voice called from outside, 'Paul? Are you home?'

Jane glared.

Paul grabbed the golden ball, straining to lift it as a key went into their front door lock. 'Paul, are you decent?

Jane had her embroidered, patchwork shoulder bag up and over her shoulder. She strode towards and out the door as it opened.

'Oh, it's you Jane. Hello. Paul?'

'Muuuuuum,' said Paul, frantically sticky-taping the top of the box.

*

Adam stood on a walkway above the biggest mail-sorting room he had ever seen. Letters raced along conveyor belts where girls grabbed them and read the postcodes in an instant, flicking them to the correct suburb, where they bounced into large canvas bags ready to go out to the suburban branches. Other letters and packages continued on to International, where more girls grabbed and checked and tossed them into other canvas bags with countries written on them. The bags would be trucked out to a loading bay and taken by vans to the suburbs and airport where they'd be sorted again and put in smaller bags and given to posties who'd cycle along streets and put each letter, each package, each important communication in the letterbox of the person it was meant for. It was fast and efficient and moved like clockwork. It was the postal service and it connected everyone to everywhere in the world.

'Wow,' said Adam.

'Yeah, whoop de do,' said Howard coming along the walkway to grab the rail next to Adam. 'And it will all be gone soon. So don't get too settled.'

'Why, what's happening?'

'I know you're from the country, mate, but you gotta have heard about fax machines.'

'Yes?'

'Well, think about it. If all you have to do is push a button to send your stuff, you don't need a stamp and you don't need a postbox. Everyone's gunna have a fax machine, so goodbye mail. Don't even start me on barcodes. That's why we gotta make hay, mate.'

'Hay?'

'The chicks, mate.'

Adam looked to see Howard winking at him and wondered if he was missing some reference to his country background. 'Chicks, right.'

'Look at all these chicks.' Howard waved his hand down across the sorting room below. 'Some of those girls in sorting get so ripe during their shift, they're ready to pop. She's new.'

Howard leaned forward peering down at a blonde girl, battling to keep up with her pile of letters. Howard looked back to Adam and gave a leer. 'Wouldn't mind bending her over the counter and playing post the parcel, eh?'

'Sure is a big place.'

'What?' Howard sounded like he'd been insulted. He glared at Adam, then demanded, 'You tellin' me you don't want to fuck her brains out?'

'I don't even know her.'

'What's to know? Look. Nice arse. Good tits.'

Howard was staring at Adam, waiting.

Adam said, 'Right.'

Howard scowled.

Adam said, 'She seems nice. Yum.'

Howard shook his head. 'I know where I'll put you.'

He led Adam through sorting and down past the loading bays and further down some wooden stairs, past cleaners' rooms and further along a concrete corridor where plumbing ran. He talked about a new television show called *Baywatch* and about an actor called David Hasselhoff who had been in another television show before with a car. It was clear that Howard wanted to be this actor and to be with the actresses especially one named Erika Eleniak. Howard confided, 'I got two *Playboy* spreads of her. Hope they do some more.'

Howard stopped at a small desk which was covered in packages. A desk lamp with a very strong globe illuminated piles of loose letters in trays.

'This'll be you, hot shot. Lotta people can't write their own name, let alone anyone else's. You work out where they meant them to go.'

There was a magnifying glass on the desk. Some black paper and white. Dusty bottles of fluid.

Howard pointed to a bookcase filled with street directories from around Australia, including the country towns. 'You look up addresses. Me, I like looking up dresses. You can wear 'em if you like.'

Adam sat down at the desk. The left arm of the chair was loose.

Howard said, 'The last guy did this job is now in a psychiatric ward. Keeps saying, Station Street. Station Street. So many Station Streets.' He grinned at Adam before he walked back along the corridor whistling.

Adam looked at metal shelving behind his desk. There was dust on some of the packages and frayed string around bundles of yellowed letters. On the wall at the end was a metal sign with painted letters. It said *Lost Mail Department*.

Adam picked up the top letter on his desk and read, 'Gardiner Street? Gardenier?' He brought up the magnifying glass. 'Gandieve? Gandierri. Gardair Street.' He reached for the local street directory.

By 4.30 that afternoon Adam had deciphered three letters, one parcel and had found out the GPO's policy on mail addressed to Father

Christmas and Not Known At This Address, which Adam had correctly surmised was more a lost person rather than a lost address. He hoped he had done a fair day's work.

*

Outside the GPO Jane and Paul sat in a battered white Rover 2000 TC.

'It was an honest mistake,' said Paul again.

Jane didn't even turn to him.

'She wasn't to know,' Paul continued to explain. 'I had to keep wrapping it. As soon as you left, she said, what's in the box and I grabbed the paper and started wrapping it. And I had to think of something heavy and I said paperweight, then she got more sticky tape to help. I had to write a fake address or it would have looked suspicious.'

'I don't blame her, Paul. You and your father have so terrorised her, she has no role left in life but cleaner.'

'She likes cleaning. Last time I told her she couldn't clean the flat anymore, she cried.'

'You and the dominant male patriarchy have stripped her of any other identity. Now you spit out her husk, empty and used. She only knows slavery.'

'Yeah, if men didn't subjugate and torture wimmin we wouldn't have lost the package. Sorry, Jane.'

Jane turned from watching the GPO to examine Paul. His eyes showed no trace of piss-taking whatsoever. 'Okay,' she said finally. She turned back to the GPO. 'So if the address you put on the package is false, it must be here. They'd have some lost property part. Let's go.'

Paul checked for a break in the end-of-day traffic. 'She must have needed a wheelbarrow to get it to the post office.'

'And now we're going to have to steal the bloody thing again.'

Paul looked at Jane in alarm, which is why he didn't see the office guy coming across the road.

*

Adam didn't see the Rover either, partly because it didn't indicate but mostly because he was focused on the pet shop and the girl he'd seen in there. The car lurched out suddenly making Adam push both hands at the bonnet before it stopped. He looked up to see two hippies inside, the girl glaring and the guy looking fearful.

'Sorry,' yelled Adam as the car continued out into the afternoon rush hour.

She was at some fish tanks wiping the front glass. An older man sat at a computer on the counter. 'The budgies aren't moving this year. Who would have thought budgies would go out of fashion?'

She didn't seem to be listening. She was looking at a large cod. 'Fish are so cold, aren't they?'

They hadn't noticed Adam drift into the shop.

'They're cold-blooded,' said the man.

'Not like birds,' she said. 'Birds feel everything, I'm sure.' She smiled.

Her smile looked a little sad, but optimistic too. Adam thought her smile was full of hope.

The man said, 'They feel hungry and thirsty, that's for sure. I better finish the aviaries before we knock off.' He headed out the back, leaving Adam to watch the girl wiping another tank, until she sensed him and looked up.

'Hi. Quiet day?'

She thought a moment then said, 'Peaceful.'

He smiled. It was warm in the pet shop. She was looking at him, so he said, 'Ha,' and when she kept looking, 'I wish.'

She nodded but started to get impatient.

'Oh, um, I'm here for birdseed. Do you sell birdseed?'

She glided behind the counter where there were shelves stacked high with birdseed packets. 'What kind of bird?'

'A canary. Named Chris. I guess that's an advantage working in here. The peace?'

She put a packet of birdseed on the counter. 'Anything else?'

'Um, look. Maybe you better make it four packets. No five, to be sure,' he added, taking control.

'That's a lot!'

'Yes, it is isn't it? I've moved. Need to stock up. Don't want my bird running out. My name's Adam. What's your name? Chris was out of food this morning, so he'll be hungry.'

'Evelyn?' she said it like a question, as though she wasn't sure. Then she looked at the five packets of seed on the counter, perhaps suspicious.

'Not sure whether maybe he's got worms or something. You know if canaries get anorexia or anything?'

'Let me check,' said Evelyn doing something with the computer. 'We've got a new thingie, *Know Your Pet Bird*, and it's got lots of bird information on it. There might be something under feeding.'

A bright American lady's voice came up saying, 'Feeding problems and your canary,' but Evelyn turned down the sound and read the written information silently.

Adam hoped he hadn't said the wrong thing about anorexia. He'd meant it as a joke really, but Evelyn was serious as she looked through the computer. And thin. Not that she looked unhealthy. Simply thin. 'I'm going to get a computer,' he said. He noticed the computer had a little picture of an envelope which meant it could receive e-mails.

'No. Nothing like that mentioned here. Maybe he's lonely.'

Adam felt a little jolt at that idea, but before he could decide whether to change the subject or pursue it, Howard walked in.

'Adam! You getting a pet rock or something?' He grabbed a huge bag of dried dog food.

Adam hurriedly paid for the seed.

'Buying your dinner, huh?' He winked at Evelyn. 'This explains a lot, you know. You gotta eat more meat, mate.'

Adam took his change and the packets, looking only at Evelyn. 'Thank you, Evelyn,' he said, but she was attending to Howard.

*

A scarf was draped over the lamp in the bedroom of flat one. Neil Young's *Harvest* whined on the cassette deck in the lounge. Jane lay on her back on the bed completely naked with Paul's face between her legs. Her eyes were closed, relaxed, but her concentration was mounting.

Paul looked up at her from where he was kneeling fully dressed on the floor. 'How much do you think we can get for the ball?'

'Don't stop, I'm nearly there.'

'I was thinking about the wimmin's refuge.'

'Think about licking. Go!'

Paul waggled his jaw from side to side, and ducked his tongue back to lap more vigorously.

Jane shuddered a little. 'Fuck the women's refuge,' she whispered. 'I want to be rich.'

'Whaw id oo ay?' mumbled Paul.

That did the trick. Jane's back arched. She gasped loudly, bucked and wheezed in a long groan as her stomach kicked and kicked and her climax ran on, until she had to sit up and push Paul's head away. She lay back again, limp.

Paul sat back on his haunches, grinning like a puppy. He looked up her legs to where she was pink and wet and open. He stood and started to undo his jeans.

Jane's eyes sprang open. 'What are you doing?'

'Love?' said Paul, confused. 'We're making love.'

'We've talked about this, Paul.' She rolled away from him and sat up, her feet on the floor on the other side of the bed. 'You're being selfish again.' Her back glistened with sweat.

'But ... You initiated it. I think it's wonderful – that we decided not to make love unless you initiated it. To break down the male-dominated, woman as sex object, power thing. But you initiated it.' Paul had become whiny.

'Now you're being every bit as demanding. I've had some pleasure, which I thought was a gift from you. Wimmin always make those sorts of gifts, without expecting anything in return. But you, being male, have to try to turn it into a transaction. You cheapen it. You spoil the gift.'

Paul's pulsating cock shrank back until it became just a penis in his undies. 'I never, ah, thought of it like that.'

Jane stood. 'Maybe we're making progress in our relationship. I'm going to take a shower.' She headed to the bathroom, calling back, 'What's for dinner?'

'Mum left some pasta. Fettucine in pesto.'

Paul sat on the bed. When the shower started, he considered begging. He hadn't had sex with Jane in twenty-four days and was starting to become distracted. He grabbed a tissue and was starting to work on taking the edge off, when Jane called, 'After dinner we'll go and get some dynamite.'

*

Adam entered the vestibule to the flats with a lot of boxes. Most of them were large and held the various components which would make up his Commodore personal computer. There were other boxes holding software and others of complimentary software such as *Microsoft Excel for Windows 3.0*, *Compton's MultiMedia Encyclopedia* and a game called *Civilization*. He hadn't been able to find *A Compact Disc Compendium of Useful Information for the Owner of Pet Birds*. There were also the boxes of birdseed. The bus driver had been reluctant to let him load so many items onto the peak hour bus, but there had been so much interest, and as it worked out, considerable combined wisdom, from the other passengers about their operation that folks shared out the packages and also came out at Adam's stop and helped load him up with it all before they went on their journey again. A couple of people suggested Adam should probably buy a car, which was very good advice, he thought.

Adam stacked the boxes by his front door and was putting his key into the lock, when a voice called from upstairs. 'Hey.' Adam looked up to see a hairy man in boxer shorts standing on the upstairs landing.

'Could you give us a hand with something, neighbour?'

Adam looked to the stack of valuables outside his front door, but then shrugged and headed up.

'That's the shot,' said the hairy man.

As Adam reached the top landing, the door to flat three opened. A chubby lady in a very frilly red dressing-gown came out. Adam tried to avert his eyes from her ample bosoms which seemed about to break free over the top of her nightie, like surging waters breaching a dam.

'Thought I heard you,' she said to the man. 'You busy tonight?'

He looked towards his own door and grunted. There were wood shavings caught in the thick hair of his chest and ample stomach.

The lady said, 'I've got Sergeant Crean until nine, but ...'

The man smiled in a not unfriendly way, but then said, 'I'll see how I'm going.'

'Well, the kettle will be on.' She leaned forward and allowed him to give her a gentle kiss on the cheek. The man had a wild beard and an unruly tangle of unwashed hair. He could have recently emerged from a cave.

They both turned to Adam and the man said, 'And this is our new neighbour. I'm Harry, but you can call me Jake. This is Mary.'

'Adam. Pleased to meet you, um ... both.'

Mary said, 'If you ever get ... hungry, Adam, you come straight to me.' In spite of the fact that she seemed older than his recently departed mother, Adam was sure she gave her breasts an extra jiggle.

'Now Mary, he needs his strength – so he can help me.' At that he clamped a large hand on Adam's shoulder and steered him into flat four, where Adam discovered the source of the sawing and hammering. Harry was building a boat.

It sat like a giant rowboat with its stern near the front door and its bow nudging the single bed in the bedroom. Most of the wall to the bathroom had been removed with two metal poles propping up the ceiling joist. Half of the wall leading to the bedroom had also been removed. The bricks were stacked along other walls where they supported tools, papers and a dusty personal computer screen. A record was spinning on a turntable – Elvis. The floor was covered with wood shavings, chunks of plaster and fair depth of saw and plaster dust. A couple of empty rum bottles floated on the mixture.

Harry held his arms open. 'Ain't she a beaut? Well, she will be. Here.' Harry lifted the plans from a stack of bricks, dislodging a couple of pieces of old spaghetti noodles. 'Had the deck braced using the ceiling joists as my framework seeing as they was already there.'

Adam looked up to see where Harry had punched a huge hole in the ceiling and attached his woodwork frame to the jarrah beams below the tiles of the flat's roof.

'Better not tell Mrs McGready about this. Sure there's some goddamn rule somewhere against hobbies.'

'The landlady? No, I won't tell.'

'Good lad.'

'How have you kept her from finding out?'

Harry fished under some tools and brought out half a bottle of brown rum, wiping the top on his boxer shorts. 'She got you psyched out, huh? What I do is I complain first.' He gulped some rum. 'About everything. Her damned cat. The plumbing. My plumbing. You start in on your ability or inability or overability to take a crap, most people back off pretty quick. Got her so she doesn't want to come near me to get more complaints. Or maybe she thinks taking a good, cleansing shit in the woods might be catching.'

Adam smiled, but shook his head at the offered bottle of rum.

Harry went to a very long wooden beam. 'Grab the other end.'

Adam went into the bedroom and got the other end of the pole. It was heavy. 'Is this the mast?' asked Adam.

'Yep. Got to get it up there on the deck. I was going to use a hoist, but I don't think the joists'll take it.'

They began to manoeuvre Harry's end of the beam up over the deck. 'Where you from?'

'A place called Mukinbudin.'

Harry nodded as though he knew the town. 'Wheat and drought?'

'Yes, sir. And floods once a century.'

Harry had his end up on the boat and came down to help Adam lift his.

'So how you finding the city?'

'I'm not sure. I feel a bit disconnected right now.'

They heaved and the mast thumped onto the wood of the deck.

'Disconnected huh? That's a good word. Fella your age should be disconnected. Stay loose. And wild!'

Adam worked his shoulder a little, easing a twinge from the lifting. 'Yeah, well I'm loose all right.'

Harry began to study Adam. 'If you don't mind me saying it – you are anything but loose, Adam. Relax. You got a girl yet? You have,' laughed Harry. 'I can tell.'

'I've only been here a day.'

'Gotta move faster in the city, Adam. If there's anything that will relax you, it's getting ...'

'What are you going to do with the boat when you finish it?' interrupted Adam.

'Yacht. A sloop actually. Thirty-eight-foot monohull. All wood. Boats are for bathtubs. What I'm going to do with this baby is I'm going to sail it around the world.'

Adam looked at Harry's ceiling and the remaining walls. 'But how are you going to get it out of here?'

'Cross that bridge when I come to it. You think of all the problems, you'd never do anything.'

Adam nodded, considering this philosophy.

Harry patted Adam on the shoulder. 'You see, my belief is this – dreams are only the blueprint for building reality.'

Adam smiled. 'That's good.'

'You like it huh? Well, if you want you can use it any time you like, but you gotta give me five bucks every time you do.'

'Five dollars, huh? You got any cheaper philosophies, Harry?'

Harry chuckled. 'Nope, that's my cheapest one.'

Adam became aware that Elvis was singing, 'It's now or never'. He realised he had the rum bottle. He noticed that the hairy man dressed only in his underpants was smiling at him a little too tenderly.

'Gotta get going, um Harry.' Adam gave back the bottle and headed for the door.

Harry called, 'Don't be a stranger now.'

Adam left flat four to see a boy and girl of about his age coming out of the other flat at the bottom of the stairs. They were dressed in black. The boy stopped to look at the boxes outside Adam's door, but when he saw Adam, he turned and said something to the girl.

She looked up. 'What do you want?'

'I live here. Well there, in flat two,' said Adam going down the stairs. 'I've just moved in.'

'Hi,' said the boy, now looking at Adam as if he were trying to place him, but the girl grabbed his arm and hustled him out the front door.

Adam opened his door and began dragging in the boxes.

Chris looked up as the light came on. 'Where the fuck have you been? No phone call. No message.'

Adam stacked the birdseed on the table next to Chris's cage.

'I thought you'd been run over or something. Is that my dinner?'

Adam started to open the boxes and unpack his new personal computer on the other little table in the corner of the lounge room. 'What a day. I've made an enemy, and a friend, and I've met the woman of my dreams. Things sure happen fast in the city.'

'Yeah, well maybe I should get out more too.'

'You can send e-mails with this. On a computer, all you have to do is type in the number and you can contact the person.'

'Like a telephone you mean. Or like meeting them? Anyway, I wouldn't get too excited. We're not staying. You've clearly recovered from all your post-traumatic stresses, so we can go home.'

Adam pulled out the monitor and put it on the desk. 'What do I say?'

'Adam, there's a cat here. It wants to kill me.'

Adam started to pull plastic from the heavy keyboard. 'I don't want to come on too strong, you know. Harass her or something. I only want to get to know her.'

'You're asking a canary for advice on your love-life? You listen to me you'll end up dry-rooting her armpit or something. Not that my knowledge is anything other than theoretical, you understand. Thinking of which, can we get a television again?'

Adam pulled out a number of cables. 'Why is it all so complicated?'

Chris looked out at the five unopened packets of birdseed. 'Hey, I'm starving here.'

Adam spent the evening setting up his Commodore Amiga 500 personal computer, running floppy start-ups, attaching the special modem cable and contacting a dial-up service to connect him to the rest of the world. After two hours he remembered he'd bought birdseed and fed Chris. Soon after that he realised he'd forgotten to get some food for himself and started snacking on Chris's seed. It was surprisingly tasty.

Adam marvelled that e-mails could flit across the world in moments; could speed across the city like a rocket-propelled carrier pigeon. If Adam were able to work out what he might say to Evelyn, and if he had her e-mail address, the e-mail would reach her in an instant.

*

Only, Evelyn, who did live on the other side of town, in some much taller flats than Adam's, did not have a personal computer. All her e-mails went to her work computer. And she was asleep, her bedroom blind open to the stars. She slept under a white frilly doona glowing in the moonlight. There was a poster of white swans gliding on a tranquil pond. Some peacock feathers poked out of a grandmother's vase. There was another poster, of a curly haired girl, in pinafore, clutching a battered teddy. Evelyn slept and dreamed.

Looking down from above on a nineteenth-century bell-like cage as wide as it is high in the centre of an ordered park. Passing through the steel ribs into the palms and ferns and fully grown trees within. Colour splashes soaring flitting, floating bright. Birds. Scarlet parrots. Emerald rosellas. Multicoloured toucans. A snow-white ibis lifts its velvety wings, stretching, then settles. Looking up at a high branch, nestling together, a pair of red-faced lovebirds. Going there to gaze at their red faces, the yellow on the breast and blue in the tail. A contented sigh, from the dreamer, blows gently at their feathers. The lovebirds nuzzle in a patch of golden sunlight.

*

Jane and the Rover 2000 TC were under a bright patch of arc light on the docks. The hood was up and a security guard from the nearby mining company warehouse was looking at the engine judiciously. 'Bad place to break down.'

Jane, who was now dressed in a Che Guevara t-shirt and what could best be described as skimpy sleeping shorts, giggled and said, 'I thought I was off to Captain Munchies for some Choc Bots, and I must have turned the wrong way. I always get mixed up with my directions.'

'Choc Bots?' It was hard to tell which of the words he was most interested in.

'The yummiest biscuit in the whole world. Chocolate on the bottom, of course. And a kind of cookie on top with more choc chip bits in that.'

The security guard smiled, indulgent and a little besotted.

'I'm really glad you came along,' said Jane. 'This is a very lonely and desolate spot.'

He looked down at the car's engine again hoping something about its operation would come to him. 'Are you a member of the RAC?' he finally asked.

Jane fought to keep her eyes bright and empty. 'What's that?' She pointed to the distributor cap.

'Oh, it's the ah ... manifold carb.'

Jane allowed herself a derisive eyebrow raise before saying, 'Is that little squiggly piece supposed to be on or off?'

'Hey, it does look loose. Let's give it a try.'

Before the guard could reattach the distributor, an alarm started in the mine stores he was supposed to be guarding.

'Oh my goodness. What's that?' yelled Jane as loudly as she could.

The guard was already heading for the padlocked gate which led into his workplace, fumbling for keys, torch and radio all at once.

Jane scowled towards an orange flashing light somewhere in the yard beyond. She leaned in and reattached the distributor and threw down the hood. 'I might try the engine,' she called as she ran to the driver's side. She started the Rover and wheeled around in the wide deserted dock, driving to the end of the fence where Paul was squeezing from the opening he'd cut earlier. He grabbed the back door of the car and tumbled in as Jane accelerated, sending seagulls scattering near the grain terminal.

*

In the Lost Mail Department, Adam's desk is empty. The shelves, sagging with stacks of lost letters and packages, stretch off into a dim distance. Down the end, far away, there is movement. Something bright, floating. It is Evelyn coming out of the dark in a white, flowing dress. It should be diaphanous, but the light coming from her skin is too strong. She's wearing red lipstick. A smile? No. A secret look. She glides to a shelf. Chooses. A bundle of letters, tied with a red ribbon.

She turns. She looks straight at him. Mischievous now. Plucks the red ribbon, the letters cascading down. Flit, flit, flit. Now up. The letters turn to white doves. They fly. Behind her other letters pour from the shelves then float, feathers filling the aisle, all around her. She stands facing him, amidst the fluttery blizzard, her hands coming up. She has the red ribbon still. She tosses it forward and it becomes a rosella that flies slowly forward. She is smiling. She is reaching for the buttons at the front of her dress. She is looking at him. The rosella smashes into his brain.

Adam woke sweating. There had been a noise that wasn't his brain smashing. He listened upwards but Harry wasn't working. He went to the window.

A rubbish bin rolled in the street. Mrs McGready's cat made off into the darkness.

*

In the Lost Mail Department the actual light of day meant the green yellow of hanging fluorescents. Adam worked under the brighter white of his desk lamp.

'Grandilla! Yes.' Adam gave a little punch to the air and flipped the found mail into the out-tray, where it sat alone. He swung on the recently fixed and now firm arm of his chair and contemplated the rows of lost mail. He peered down to the wall at the end of the rows, lit now and covered by a huge grey filing cabinet and the sign: *Lost Mail Department*. No rosellas.

Adam shook off the unsettling half memory and went to a large box that had arrived that morning. The *Lost Mail Procedure Journal* had suggested that working the most recent cases first was the best approach and only after clearing most or all of those to work chronologically back through the older, more difficult or dead losses later. *After all, your predecessors had trouble there, didn't they?*

Adam suspected his immediate predecessor was the writer of 'the journal'. It had started in an orderly fashion suggesting the logging and categorising of incoming items and hints for approaches to common street names. Then it got more and more philosophical. It soon interrupted itself with printed scrawls like *WHO ARE ALL THESE PEOPLE?* And *Communication. What does that mean? Is it possible?* Soon there were little messages down the bottom of the page, like footnotes, such as *Don't tell your supervisor if you break an item of lost mail. It gives him too much power over your life.* This theme, Adam thought, was picked up near the last entries, where it was written *Howard is a brute.*

Kill him. Kill him. The last two pages seemed to be a long letter or poem which started *To My Dearest Wuffles.*

The diarist's sense of loss reminded Adam of his parents. He could not help drawing a link between their death by fire and Amber-Lee being taken by water, the latter as retribution for his former negligence in losing Amber-Lee to the flood. But now he wondered if the drowning might also not have been another punishment, almost immediate, for wantonness in the car. They had been trapped by rising waters in what was usually a salt flat. They had decided to wait. There was giggling. Black cockatoos screamed excitedly. Adam remembered the windows of the car getting fogged. He remembered being in the back seat. He remembered flesh, Amber-Lee's and his, and the abrupt loss of both their virginities. Then the water came up. And she was washed away and then his parents were incinerated.

Adam caught himself staring at the barely lit stained concrete wall across the corridor in front of his desk. He knew this was not a good thing to do. He closed the journal and put it in the bottom drawer of his desk and reminded himself to do what that doctor had suggested. He would keep busy.

The large box was new. It might be easy and would clear a whole shelf. Adam pulled it forward with difficulty to read the label. It was heavy. He had to tilt it forward.

'Joan Arc. 1 Dolphin Street. Oceania? Not even a postcode!'

The box began to tip further towards him and Adam tried to push it back, but a pin supporting the front right of the shelf snapped, swinging the shelf and box forward. Adam jumped back as it crashed onto the floor with a woody crack. The corner of the box was crushed. The floorboard under looked broken too.

*

Jane sat at Paul's computer using Gopher to go through lists of topics like-minded people around the world wanted to share. She was delving into a category called *Terrorism Made Easy.*

Paul sat at the kitchen table nibbling a Big Mac and looking in agony at the ten sticks of dynamite sitting on the coffee table. 'Can't we burgle the post office, like we did the museum?'

Jane ignored him, selecting *Bombs*, but scrolling past *Do it Yourself Thermonuclear Devices,* and options for *The Controlled Explosion.*

Paul said, 'I'd hate, you know, to see someone get hurt.'

Jane had found something that looked about right. *How to Make a Bomb when You Don't Own a Shed.*

There was a knock on the door.

Paul jumped up and leapt in a couple of directions while not leaving the table.

A key was inserted in their front door.

Jane scowled and killed the computer screen.

Paul lunged towards the dynamite, cracking his thigh into the table edge on the way through. He grabbed it and thrust it into his takeaway McDonald's bag, turning to smile as his mother came through the door carrying a washing basket.

'Paul! Oh, I didn't know you were home. Takeaway food, really!'

'Mum. I didn't get a chance to answer the door.' Paul limped to Jane and gave her the McDonald's bag. She put it carefully in the bin under the computer desk.

Paul's mum put down the washing basket, took out a casserole dish and headed for the fridge. 'I thought you'd be at the university. Studying occupational therapy can't be easy. I'm still not sure what an occupational therapist does, but now you're studying it, I've begun to notice that they're everywhere. It's not going to be overcrowded by the time you finish is it?'

Jane folded her arms in Paul's direction.

'Ah, Mum?'

She turned from the fridge with a patient exasperation, and went to him. 'Don't I get a kiss. You too old to kiss your old mother now you're at university?'

Paul pecked her on the cheek and she patted him on the head before grabbing the washing basket and humming her way to the bedroom.

Paul turned to Jane. 'I've asked her not to come.'

'Get the key.'

*

Paul's mother was stacking Paul's ironed t-shirts and jeans in the wardrobe, trying to avert her eyes from the tousled bed.

'Mum, I don't think it's a good idea for you to have a key to the flat.'

'How would I get in?'

'I'd let you in.'

'No. This way is better, Paul. I can make sure you're all right, without being a bother.' She began picking up dirty washing, careful not to come in contact with any of Jane's things. 'That's why I got the extra key from Mrs McGready in the first place.'

'But Mum ... can't you check with me first?'

'I can't. Your phone line is always busy. Oh, you're still grumpy about that package aren't you?'

'I ... was going to take it there myself.'

'I wish you'd wear more shirts with collars. They make you look more grown-up. When they weighed it at the post office, they nearly had a fit, I can tell you. It was forty-five dollars in postage. But I don't mind. A paperweight to a charity can be important.' She paused. 'Where is Oceania, anyway?

Paul winced as the front door slammed.

His mother dusted her hands with satisfaction. 'That's the chores done. Let's have a lovely cup of Milo, shall we? I've bought gingernuts.'

*

Mary was on the upstairs landing, dressed in a floral housecoat. She watched the girl from downstairs storm out of the flats. She knocked on the door of flat four. The sawing stopped but then started again. Mary knocked again.

When Harry opened the door, Mary tried to see past a dust-covered shoulder, but he stepped outside, closing the door behind him.

Mary held up an empty cup. 'I wondered if you had any sugar, Jake?'

He shook his head. 'You could try Adam. He might have a sweet tooth.'

'Is he your next project, is he?'

'What do you mean?'

'As I recall, you convinced the last fellow who rented flat two to go into the woods and face the bear.'

'Yes?' said Harry, folding his arms across his chest.

'You ever hear from him after he went to Canada?'

'Maybe he faced the bear and felt no need to revisit childish counsel. Do you ever hear from him?'

'Maybe the bear ate him.'

'Maybe, that's one of the risks, when a man has to do what a man has to do.'

'And maybe you should take a bath.' Mary stomped back into her flat.

*

It took Adam a surprising amount of time to find a spare box capable of holding the post package he had damaged. The mysterious object inside was heavy with at least one rounded edge. It might have been a vital component of an immense factory machine, or a digger that sat un-digging waiting on the mail. He eventually found a large enough box outside the stationery storeroom and carried it with great purpose back down to his dungeon where he'd managed to drag and push the heavy lost mail item under his desk. He put the empty box on his desk and turned to see if the coast was clear.

It wasn't. Howard had followed him. 'What you doing with that box, Adam?'

'Thought I'd get things organised down here.'

'They are organised. Been organised for about a hundred years.' Howard looked at the shelves then back to Adam with suspicion. 'Could be a lot of valuable items amongst these shelves. Tell me why you left the country post office.'

Adam looked away. 'Personal reasons.'

'You wouldn't be the first problem that got transferred to somewhere else with a glowing testimonial.'

'I give up, Howard. We got off on the wrong foot. Cheryl up in sorting ...'

'Sharon.'

'Sharon. You're right. Her boobs – unbelievable. Her arse – I'd like to grab it and hold it forever. I'd like to screw her until the skin peels off my dick. Okay? Will you get off my back?'

'Have you ever heard of sexual harassment, Adam?'

'What?'

'I've started going out with Sharon.'

'Oh.'

'Tampering with Her Majesty's mail is an offence. I'm watching you, Adam.'

'I know, Howard.'

*

The Rover cruised past Milton's Pet Shop and turned down a laneway behind the GPO. Jane stopped the car twenty feet before a huge, closed roller door. Paul sat next to her clutching the bomb in the McDonald's bag on his lap, the sweat from his hands starting to make the paper soft and thin in places.

'We'll blow this wall here.'

Paul looked at the sign on the wall. *No Parking Anytime Ever.*

Jane opened her door and reached in for the bag of dynamite, but was interrupted by the noise of a car horn behind.

At the street end of the laneway a red mail van was waiting.

'Shit.'

The mail van beeped twice and in response the huge roller door clanked and rattled upwards.

Jane started reversing out of the laneway. 'Shit.' As their car backed out into the street, Jane realised there were four more red vans, all waiting behind the first, to go into the post office. 'I thought you cased this place! Shit.'

'I did. But not at five o'clock. I thought they'd be going home.'

Jane backed across the street slowly, forcing her way through two lanes of honking, brake-squealing traffic.

Paul watched the vans go in, joined by more arriving behind. 'You'd think with computers and this electro-stuff that people wouldn't be sending so many real letters anymore. It's quite encouraging really – people still wanting the personal touch. With real paper from real trees.'

Then Paul saw the geeky-looking guy from their flats. The one they'd nearly run over outside the post office the day before. He was coming from the GPO.

Jane said, 'Okay. New plan. We hijack one of the mail vans. Drive right in and demand the package. Force the driver to show us the lost property room or whatever. We'll need guns. Machine guns would be best.'

Paul said, 'That's the guy from our flats. I'm pretty sure he works in the post office.'

Jane said, 'It'll take too long to get machine guns. We could get some gaffer tape and tape the dynamite to your chest, like a plane hijacker. Do exactly what we say you arseholes or Paul blows everything up.'

'That guy works there. He might have a key.'

Jane looked over in time to see the pet shop door close.

*

The balding man was at the counter when Adam entered. Adam guessed he must be the boss. He looked up and said, 'Can I help you?'

'I was after Evelyn. I mean looking for ... um, there was a thing about my canary, that I wanted to know.'

'I know a lot about canaries,' said the man.

Evelyn came from the back and said, 'Not more birdseed!'

'Oh, no. Got lots of that. Ha. More birdseed. I um wanted to ask your advice about what we were discussing, about Chris, my canary.'

Evelyn nodded and the boss went away.

'I was wondering about what you said about Chris's eating problem.' Adam took a breath. 'Do you think he could be lonely?'

Evelyn nodded seriously and looked to the computer. 'Yes. It's very likely. Birds like company. They shouldn't be left alone. It's cruel really, unless you're home a lot with them.'

'I don't think it's fair on him. You know, if you enter into a relationship, even with a pet, you have ... enormous responsibilities.'

Evelyn got the CD-ROM of *A Compact Disc Compendium of Useful Information for the Owner of Pet Birds*. It had a cluster of zebra finches on the cover. She studied the computer screen.

So did Adam. He was trying to find her e-mail address. He couldn't see it in all the clutter of writing and pictures on the screen.

'Do you want a companion or do you want to breed?'

'Me or the canary?'

She blinked at the screen then swivelled her long neck to look up at him. 'The canary.'

'Yes, silly joke. Of course.'

She read from the computer, 'The hen should be in her breeding cage some time before she is introduced to the cock.'

Adam gently bit the side of his cheek. He found it helped him concentrate.

Evelyn read, 'He should on no account be placed in the breeding cage without preliminaries.'

'Oh no. That wouldn't be right.'

'You should get two cages, so they can view each other, so she can "gradually get used to his advances".'

'So you really let them fall in love?' asked Adam.

'Of course. For life.' She looked at Adam with a radiant smile.

He smiled back and she became more businesslike. 'Although, for birds and animals, of course, love isn't really correct. It's instinct. They get in season and they mate, in season.'

Adam tried, 'Whereas people?'

Evelyn smiled an ethereal smile then and Adam thought his heart had seized, but she shook it off and headed towards the birds at the back of the shop, 'We've only got one young hen. A bit highly strung.'

Adam followed.

The hen, the only one in the store, leapt and fluttered about her cage. She flapped her wings wildly, leaping at the side of the bars, sending feathers and a light dust everywhere.

'Shh shh shh. Settle down. Ooh, she doesn't like you,' said Evelyn.

'No. Well, she doesn't have to like me. She has to like Chris.'

'Shh now, shh,' whispered Evelyn trying to comfort the canary, which had now leapt to the bars at the back of the cage where she hung on with her claws, while her head rocked wildly trying to see them behind her.

'Is she all right?' asked Adam.

'Look, why don't you buy her, and if she doesn't settle down, you can bring her back.'

'Oh. Um, okay. And can I keep asking your advice?'

'Of course.'

'You're good with animals, but birds are your favourite aren't they?'

'Yes. I dream about them.'

'Dream?'

'Oh,' said Evelyn, as though wakening. She seemed embarrassed to have shared too much. 'So, will you take her?' She headed back to the other side of the counter, all business again.

'Yes,' said Adam. He pointed to the computer. 'Could I have your e-mail address, in case ...'

*

Jane had parked the Rover in the No Standing Zone outside the pet shop. She called instructions to Paul through the open driver's window. 'See if he's got keys to the place.'

Paul stood on the footpath, still trying to calm her. 'Let's just meet him and you know, gain his trust. He might let us in.'

'Be much quicker to put a gun to his head and make him.'

'Can we try it my way first? For once.'

Jane looked past him urgently.

Paul swung around to see him coming from the pet shop with a birdcage under a hood. 'Hey, don't I know you?'

*

Adam looked at the guy and then the girl in the car.

'We're neighbours! I thought it was you,' said the guy.

'Flat one?' said Adam.

'Hey, what a small world, huh?'

The girl called, 'Hey, want a ride, man?' She was doing something strange with her eyebrows, sitting behind the wheel of a car that looked familiar.

Adam looked at the birdcage and then to the guy who was opening the back door of the Rover as though it was a limousine. 'So, um a bird, huh? Wow.'

'Thanks, um, people,' said Adam, getting in the back with the birdcage. 'Lucky for me I bumped into you.'

'I'm Paul, this is Jane,' said Paul.

'Adam.'

Paul swivelled around and looked at the hooded cage and then to Adam. 'You like whales?'

'Not in a cage,' said Adam.

Paul didn't smile. He became more focused. 'How about dolphins? Don't tell me you hate dolphins.'

'I don't hate whales. Or dolphins. I've got nothing against fish.'

'How about baby seals?'

'I thought we were talking about fish.'

'We're talking about all kinds of creatures, I guess.'

'Well, I must admit, I haven't really thought about them, but I have a pretty positive feeling about baby seals.'

Paul turned to the driver, 'See, didn't I tell you Jane? I had a feeling we'd have a lot in common with this guy and we do.'

'Yeah, and we live right next door to each other.'

Paul said, 'Jane and I met on a protest against live sheep exports. I was organising the picket line. I look up, and there she is – chained to the gangway. And I thought what a … caring person. What courage. You know what – Jane's action alone forced them to unload that ship and send the sheep right back to the abattoir. Their suffering ended.'

'I come from a farm,' said Adam.

'What?' said Paul.

'From the country. Where the sheep come from.'

'Oh,' said Jane, looking at him with narrowed eyes in the rear-vision mirror.

'Hey,' said Paul, 'maybe they were your sheep we saved.'

'Anyway,' said Jane, 'So, do you work at the post office?'

'Yeah, how did you …?'

Paul said, 'I saw you come out, um when we were, um … um …'

'Eating our burgers,' said Jane.

'Oh, yeah. See.' Paul lifted an old-looking McDonald's bag delicately between thumb and forefinger and then carefully returned it to his lap.

The Rover turned into their little street.

'The post office,' Jane said.

'Yes,' said Adam.

Paul asked, 'Are they real bastards? Do they try to grind you down, as though you're a little cog in the giant machine?'

'It's clerical work, so … it's the post office.'

They pulled up outside the flats.

'Take the food in, Paul,' she said and turned to look at Adam.

Paul stayed.

'Thanks for the ride,' said Adam. 'Sure beats the bus.'

'Paul, get out.'

Adam started to open his door.

'Wait,' she ordered Adam. 'Wait, Adam. I'll be right in, Paul.'

Paul got out of the car, carefully carrying their dinner.

Jane said, 'It must be exciting.'

'Sorry?'

'It must be exciting where you work.'

Adam looked at her to see if she was teasing. She didn't look like she was. It looked like she was trying to crack onto him.

She said, 'Being at the hub of all that communication. The holder of so many people's … important things.'

'It's the post office!'

'To think you live right next door.' She leaned over the seat and touched Adam on the arm.

Paul was outside, hovering.

She said, 'Listen, do you think you could show me round one night? I'd love to see how such a huge thing works.' She licked her lips and looked down at Adam's crotch.

'I'm sorry. There's a lot of security and stuff. People send cheques and valuables. A civilian – no.' Adam scrambled out of the car.

Jane turned to Paul who was standing by her window. She said, 'That's what I thought.'

Adam leaned in and grabbed the covered birdcage and dragged it out.

Paul said, 'What about wrongly addressed mail?'

Adam looked at him.

'Another time,' said Jane.

'What do you mean?' Adam asked Paul.

'Nothing,' said Paul. 'See you round, dude.' Paul went back to the car.

Adam got a couple of steps up the path carrying the birdcage when he turned and said, 'Did Howard send you?'

They didn't hear. They seemed to be arguing.

*

'This will be your new home,' said Adam, unlocking the door to flat two. 'I hope you like living with us. Chris,' he called, turning on lights. 'I've got a surprise for you.'

'Please, no more bells.'

Adam took the birdcage over to Chris's table. 'Must be lonely here all day. I thought you'd like a little company.' Adam whisked the cover from the new bird's cage with a flourish like a conjuring trick.

The two birds looked at each other without moving.

Adam said, 'This is Chris. Chris, um, what shall we call her? She?'

'The cat's mother?' offered Chris.

Adam watched the two birds looking at each other. 'Love takes time, I guess.' He went to his computer and turned it on.

*

Chris walked along his wooden perch towards the other cage.

'Let's get one thing straight from the beginning, fella,' said Antigone. 'You bring your little vent anywhere near my wing and I'll peck it off. You got that?'

'Excuse me. Did I miss something? You assume way too much about your personal charms there, honey.'

'Don't call me honey.'

'I'm not calling you at all.'

'Fine.'

'Fine.' Chris started to move back toward the centre of the cage, but then stopped. 'And I'll move anywhere in my cage I feel like, thank you very much.'

*

Adam's computer monitor glowed. He clicked on e-mails, and typed in the e-mail address Evelyn had given him. Then his face dropped. 'Dreams,' he said finally, but the keyboard remained untapped.

There was a knock on the door. Adam went reluctantly, hoping it wasn't Paul and Jane. He looked through the little eyehole and saw that it was Harry, wet and in a dirty towel. He opened the door.

'Adam. Need your help again.' Harry looked past Adam and then walked in, forcing Adam to retreat as he came. 'You got a cleaner or something?'

'No?' Adam looked around his flat. It was perhaps time to get some pictures or knickknacks. Now he thought about it, it was time to buy some food.

Harry said, 'Two canaries, huh?'

'Yes. Company.'

Harry turned to look at Adam, shaking his head, sadly.

'For the other canary,' said Adam quickly.

'And how you doing on that front?'

'Well, if you have to know ... well to be fair, that talk we had the other night helped. I've taken the plunge.'

'Good for you.'

'I've actualised my dreams. Nearly.'

Harry leaned into Adam, shoulder to shoulder, and nudged him like a friendly ram. 'I knew you had it in you. Or in her.'

'Harry, it's not like that.'

'Call me Jake.'

'She's not some piece of meat. She's not a computer game. I'm interested in her as a person. It's got nothing to do with sex.'

'Everything's to do with sex. Everything. No. You're right. Gently, gently, catchee monkey. Then when she's lulled, you jump her and go for it.'

'I'm not an animal!' Adam walked away from Harry for some steps. He looked down at his hands, and noticed he was clenching and unclenching his fists.

He felt Harry pat him on the shoulder. 'You need to get laid, Adam. You're gunna implode. Come on and help me with my yacht. I want to get my mast up.'

Adam turned to see Harry heading for the door. There was a puddle where he'd been standing.

'No. I'm not going to unless you apologise.'

'I'm sorry.'

'You don't mean it.'

'Oh, I gotta mean it now. You want me to bring flowers? You know what? You're starting to sound like a bloody woman.'

'I'm not helping you.'

Harry looked hurt, but then stood tall. 'And fuck you too, you little pussy.' He left, slamming the door behind him.

Adam looked at the door then looked at his computer. Then he sighed and went to bed.

*

A mail sorter on the night shift wheeled a canvas trolley to the conveyor belt. He tossed some letters and then leant down to grab another package.

'Jesus H. Christ!' he wheezed as he struggled to get the very heavy box onto the conveyor belt. It ground its wheels and cogs struggling before whirring back into life. 'Oughta be a law against it,' said the sorter.

*

In a clearing in the bush, a large bower has been built from postal items. Envelopes. Ribbons. Stamps. Postal packs. Official stickers. Lacky bands.

Adam stumbles into the clearing, and stands looking at this intricate construction.

Evelyn steps out from behind the bower. She is dressed in the bright colours of a Spanish dancer, black and flowing red. She strides, her arms bent out behind her like wings. A guitar plays. Her arms swirl. Her back arches. Her legs open and flex. It is flamenco, and she dances her arms around him.

Adam stands before her, his shirt now gone, his nipples hardening in a new breeze. Drums join the guitar. Jungle drums.

Evelyn begins to swirl her whole body, her arms spinning and swaying and turning, but her head always returning to gaze fiercely at

Adam. She lifts the red of her skirt, swooshing it back and forward showing her knees. And higher. And still the stare fixing Adam where he stands, frozen.

She comes forward, her face flushed and beaded, inches from his face. She is panting. The guitar stops. The drums grow louder, faster. She bends, her tongue out, bending still, slowly, towards his nipple. The drums stop. Evelyn stops there centimetres from his nipple. She looks up at him, wounded. She says, 'I don't want to.'

Adam sits up in bed. He's panting, sweating, shirtless. He looks towards the ceiling. Drums, but not above.

The crash of a rubbish bin turns him towards the window where an orange light sweeps across the sill and curtains. There is a whoosh of truck air brakes.

Adam looks out to see the garbage truck coming up the hill. The garbos troop from behind. The butch girl is there, dressed in her usual blue singlet and shorts. The other garbos are women too, in overalls, or black leather jackets. They march forward, swinging clenched fists. Piano joins the drums, lyrical. The women garbos sing 'There is Nothin' Like a Dame' from *South Pacific*. The butch garbo girl sings about letters and packages as she dances with each of the other women, mirroring movement, caressing a cheek. Letters begin to shoot up from the back of the garbage truck like paper tracer bullets.

The top of the truck lifts now and velvet carpeted stairs descend. Skinny men in white suits and white top hats wave canes as they dance down the sides of the stairs in full Busby Berkeley, as the butch girl dances up, between the lines. Violins begin. The male voices are replaced by female vocals, singing the next verse of 'There's Nothin' Like a Dame'.

Something is rising out of the top of the garbage truck. A circular dais on a pole.

The men line the edges of the stairs, pointing up with their canes. The women in overalls and leather jackets down on their knees, hands raised toward the dais like a Mississippi church chorus.

Evelyn is tethered to the pole on the dais, a chain going to a studded choker. Her flimsy dress is torn. The butch girl reaches her.

The violins cease. Drums speed to frenzy.

Adam stands transfixed in his flat, lit orange in the glow from outside.

The butch girl raises a sacrificial knife.

Adam sat up in bed once again, panting, terrified. He ran to the window. They were not there. There was only the Rover parked in the street with a cat sleeping on the bonnet.

Adam went to the lounge and turned on his computer again determined to do something about his dreams, especially the unsettling ones. He sat and looked at the bluish blank screen.

Both birds blinked in the strange light. Chris looked through the bars of the two cages and found Antigone. 'Do you dream?'

She turned and looked at him for a little while. 'Yes.'

'Are your dreams scary?'

'I often dream about my father's death, which is very strange because I was incubated.'

'There is a cat. I don't mean cats. I mean a specific cat. Out there. It's got my number. I can't explain. I just know, like a dream. Like there's no difference between the present and the future. Our paths are … indivisible. It is.'

'Could be Jungian. Maybe Freudian. Are you afraid of women?'

Chris looked towards the window. 'I'm afraid of cats.'

*

In flat number one, it was dark. The bed was squeaking quietly but rhythmically. Suddenly the bedside light was turned on and Jane sat up looking at Paul who lay frozen in a somewhat awkward position.

After a moment, he said, 'Huh?'

'What were you doing?'

Paul's eyes stayed closed. 'Huh?'

'You were masturbating, weren't you?'

Paul stayed silent, still.

'If you must do that, can you do it in the bathroom? I'm trying to sleep.' Jane turned over and switched off her bedside lamp.

'Sorry. Bit inconsiderate,' mumbled Paul in the darkness.

A bad silence like green leaves burning.

Jane said, 'Well, are you going into the bathroom or not?'

'Oh. No. I don't really feel like it now. You know.'

Jane switched the lamp back on and turned to him. 'Don't you start laying all that guilt on me. It's not fair. Have you thought how you're making me feel right now? As if I've ruined it for you. Like I'm taking away your pleasure. When you are the one who woke me up.'

'I never thought about it that way.'

'That's why it's important we keep communicating. Now go in the bathroom and have your wank. Not for me, but because you want to.'

Paul sighed. He got out of bed and was halfway to the bathroom before Jane asked, 'Who were you fantasising about?'

'You. It was you.'

Paul went into the bathroom while Jane lay on the bed, her light still on. She said, 'That post office guy isn't going to let us into the post office.'

'No,' called Paul. 'As soon as I saw he kept caged birds, I knew.'

'We're going to have to kidnap him.'

'But we won't hurt him, will we?'

'Haven't you learned anything about Urban Revolution? You think that anti-vivisection group would have freed those poor animals if they weren't willing to torture that security guard? It's war, Paul. There are casualties.' Jane turned off her lamp. Then she called, 'Hurry up and finish, so I can get back to sleep.'

Paul leaned back against the cold tiles of the bathroom wall, his penis lying in his hand like a sausage that had fallen off the barbecue and been retrieved from the sand.

*

Adam woke to sunshine dappled and dancing on his bedroom wall. The traffic had begun its buzz somewhere down the hill and for the first time he found it comforting. He lay looking at the open suitcase sitting on top of the chest of drawers and thought he might unpack it.

He got up and headed for the bathroom, whistling.

'Oh, good morning Chris, ol' buddy. How was your night? Not a word!'

Antigone gently fluffed the feathers at the top of her back then let them settle. 'He's in love. Listen to his song.'

'No. He's been traumatised. The dance has been beaten out of him by events beyond his control. He's a string bag of neuroses and they're about to tumble through his gaps.'

'Are you sure this isn't a little bit of reverse anthropomorphism? Are you projecting?'

'Don't start on me, lady. I've seen things ... the flames of Orion, not to mention a once in a millennium flood in Mukinbudin – you can't even begin to comprehend.'

'It is about you. You don't know the dance!'

'I know the dance. Don't you worry about me. Collective unconscious is like riding a bike – you never forget, even if you never have.'

'Deny, don't deny. You can or you can't.'

'You're right. I'm over-intellectualising my dislike of you. No more denial. It is what it is – hatred.' Chris ruffled his feathers and shook his neck, sending out a scatter of tiny feather bits.

There was a knock on the door which became louder. The shower went off. Mary from flat three came in dressed in a cheesecloth caftan dress and carried a plastic bag to the kitchen counter.

Adam came out of the bathroom, starting to wrap the towel around his hips. 'Ahh,' he screamed, dropping the towel and then frantically grabbing at it again.

'The door wasn't locked,' said Mary as she started to bring fruit out of the plastic bag. 'You have a very nice body, Adam. Don't be ashamed of it.'

Mary brought out a banana, strawberries, a pomegranate and two peaches.

Adam stood, transfixed and dripping.

She produced a large tub of yogurt. 'This should get you going,' she said. She took the banana delicately between her thumb and forefinger and lifted it.

'I don't want this,' Adam pleaded.

'Ah, but there's a difference between what you want and what you need.'

She started to slowly peel the banana. 'By the way, I think Harry is wrong about this, but ...'

'Harry?'

'Yes, he's worried about you. I said I'd help.'

Adam grabbed the top of his towel tightly in one fist and marched out of his flat.

Mary looked over to the canaries and said, 'I knew this wouldn't work but you can't tell Harry anything.' She looked at the cages sitting near each other in front of the window and went to them. She opened Chris's cage door, then opened Antigone's and pushed the open doors up against each other. 'Enjoy.'

Chris blinked at the opening. Antigone was blinking too.

*

Jane peeked through the eyehole of the door of flat one and watched Adam stomp upstairs and hammer on the door to flat four. 'I think he's going to complain about the sawing noises. Won't get much change from Jake.'

'Who's Jake?' said Paul.

'We'll surprise him when he gets back.' Jane opened the door and moved swiftly across to the open door of flat two. She was carrying a balaclava and a vicious-looking steak knife.

Paul followed less swiftly, also carrying his balaclava.

'Oh, hello,' said Mary, looking up from the kitchen bench.

'Oh,' said Jane. 'Um, is Adam home?'

'He can't be far. He's only wearing a towel. Hi, Paul.'

'Oh, hi there. Neighbour.'

Jane dragged Paul back across the hall. The door to flat one slammed as Toby, the local postman, backed in dragging a very heavy cardboard box. Mary came to the door of flat two and said, 'Shall I tell him you called?'

'Mary!' said the postman. 'This is so heavy.'

'I'm not expecting anything.'

'No, it's for flat two.'

'Oh, you poor thing. Bring it in.'

Toby dragged the package into Adam's flat. He said, 'I don't suppose, um, you'd have time to take a look at my back?'

*

'Harry, please get her out of there.'

'Hand me those six-foot planks, man. And you said you'd call me Jake.'

'No, you told me to. I never said I would. There's a difference.'

'That's the spirit.'

Harry was working on the deck. Sections of ceiling were stacked against one wall. Electrical wiring hung. On the record Elvis sang 'Don't'.

Adam held his ground and his towel. 'Harry, I have to go to work. Can you get her out of my flat?'

'You still look very tense, Adam.'

'I'm tense because all these things keep ... keep rushing at me. No, wait. That's not true. I didn't wake up tense. I woke up happy. I woke up happy because I had a dream.'

Harry crouched and nodded to him, interested.

'And I woke up this morning with a decision. I'm going to ask Evelyn out. On a date. I'm ready and I think I can do it. I've sent her an e-mail.'

Harry stood up and started beating his chest like King Kong. It made a fat-slappy sound.

Adam said, 'So, you know, I don't want to have fruit tipped all over me, and have it licked off by the local prostitute.'

'I won't have you running down my wife, especially when she was probably making you breakfast.'

Adam stood very still. He finally whispered, 'Your wife?'

Harry nodded, serenely proud. 'Can't live with 'em, can't live without 'em. You know that saying. That's a ten-dollar piece of philosophy if ever there was.'

Adam looked around the gutted flat and then up to Harry standing on his boat. He looked to the door and out across the top landing in time to see a postman going into flat three with Mary. 'She pays for all this, doesn't she? The boat materials. Your time.'

'And the rent on two flats. Food, rum. You wouldn't believe the power bills.'

'You are the most selfish man I have ever met.'

'I try to be, Adam. I try.' Harry rubbed his hairy stomach with affection. 'On the other hand she does have sexual needs that one man cannot possibly satisfy.'

Adam was distracted as he dressed for work, failing to get his happy whistling feeling back. He found a plate of fruit salad and yogurt in his fridge and decided to eat it. He turned on his computer to check if he'd received a reply to the anonymous e-mail he'd sent the night before. There was nothing. He didn't notice that the two birdcages had been pushed together. Nor could he notice their silence. He didn't notice that there was a large cardboard box under the bird table.

He looked out the eyehole of his door. The door of flat one was closed. The sound of hammering immediately above him was underscored by an occasional whipping noise drifting down from flat three. He went out, softly shutting his door before hastening out of the vestibule door.

*

Paul raised the curtain a little. 'He's going to work.'

'Good,' said Jane at the computer. 'Gives us time to build this.' She had found an interesting site: *Hand Guns Using the Spare Parts of a Rover*. There were helpful diagrams. 'I need you to break off the radio aerial. Oh, and get the wheel brace.' She looked around the room. 'I guess we'll also need to saw off a bit of the leg of the kitchen table. Coffee table might be easier.'

'But he's gone.'

'We can't do it here. Too many people have seen us. By the way, how did that woman know your name, Paul?'

'We say hello. On the stairs.'

'Really.'

'You said you admired her. Her defiance. Her willingness to use men's craven desires against them.'

'I was trying to support a sister. She's a receptacle used and discarded by men. At least, unlike your mother, she gets paid for it. You don't get any of this, do you?'

It was true. Paul didn't. And he was getting it less every day. He looked at the plans for the zip gun on the computer screen glumly.

'And you're sure,' said Jane, 'your dad has bullets? None of this is going to work without those bullets.'

Paul nodded. He regretted that he had mentioned his father's bullets. At the time, it had excited Jane in a way that Paul had mistaken for something else. His eyes dropped to the waste bin under the computer desk where seven sticks of mining grade dynamite still lurked in a crumpled McDonald's bag. He was starting to hear a ticking sound somewhere in his own head.

*

Adam went straight to the pet shop but found the front door locked. He peered in the window but there was no sign of Evelyn, even though the lights were on and the birdcages uncovered. Adam wanted to ask Evelyn out and he had wanted to ask that morning before work, while the e-mail was fresh, while his resolve was strong.

He wondered whether his poem had somehow affected the previously smooth running of Milton's Pet Shop. He'd been worrying about his e-mail since leaving the flat. He'd spent some time on the first line the previous night. The problem had become finding a term of friendly endearment for Evelyn. He'd originally typed, *To the girl of my dreams*, but it somehow seemed patronising, suggesting an imaginary age difference based on an implicit gender superiority of maturity. Whereas, *to the woman of my dreams* sounded a little tribal and implied ownership. Yet Adam could not bring himself to adopt the recent spelling he'd seen. Besides how did you turn *wimmin* into a singular, or was this the intent, a kind of indivisible army of sisterhood? Adam tried *To the person of my dreams* but knew he may as well be writing *Dear Householder*. He loaded the CD-ROM *Thesaurus* and found *human being, spinster, matron, mistress* and *consort*. He gave up after *squaw*, and finally settled on *To the one of my dreams* as the least offensive, if not the most passionate.

He wondered if there was a reply waiting in his computer right now. He wondered if he'd offended her so much with his advance that he'd made her ill and unable to go to work. He went to the post office wondering and worrying.

*

When Evelyn's boss, John Tagliatelli, had turned on his computer that morning after opening up the pet shop, he too whistled. Business was good and the ability to look for things and order them via his computer was proving to be one of the most satisfying parts of his day. The computer made him feel as if he was linked, almost instantly, with every component of his business. It gave him, as the sales blurb on his *Complete Stocktake and Ordering Interface for Small Business* CD-ROMs had suggested, 'the power to stay on top'. The shop and everything in it was part of John and now he felt even more in touch with it than ever before.

When the computer powered up, he found an e-mail and when he clicked on the e-mail he found a poem.

> *To the one of my dreams.*
> *I see you every day*
> *But haven't found a way*
> *To tell you how I feel.*
> *If dreams can come true*
> *Then I have to tell you*
> *My love is very real.*

The e-mail declaration had caused him a deal of confusion. He had not considered himself and others in a romantic way for some years now. He had certainly never regarded himself as having any power over his young employee, nor had he ever done anything which approached flirtation even of an innocent kind. On the other hand, and probably more to do with having loving parents and brothers and sisters and nephews and nieces, rather than any particular gifts, John liked himself. He assumed others did too. So John took the shy little missive seriously. He also took the timidity of the person who had sent it in such a way with great delicacy.

John did not wish to embarrass or confront Evelyn with her brave attempt to reach out to him using the Milton Pet Shop e-mail address, so he decided to delete the e-mail instead of pressing reply. He also needed time to think of what and how that reply should be conducted. He tried to think of a way to return such a fey approach without scaring her away. When Evelyn arrived for work he greeted her with, 'And I see you every day too.'

Her quick rejoinder of 'Except Sundays and Mondays' hadn't left much of an opening. However, he thought on that too and began to form the view that this might be another hint. Perhaps she wanted to see him outside of working hours.

He walked along the fish tanks ostensibly to check that all the water filters were in good working order and to retrieve any floaters. It was at this point that John had wished he had not deleted the poem. He wanted to study it for further clues. He couldn't recall whether 'dreams' had a rhyme in the poem.

He decided it was now up to him and not Evelyn. She had shown her interest and was waiting for him, the male, to make the next move. The move probably needed to be decisive and somewhat unequivocal. And so, John closed the front of the shop before nine and followed Evelyn out the back to talk to her while she watered the outside aviaries.

He ambled up to Evelyn's cage, where she was watering the budgies, and feigned interest in two birds he had been worrying over for some months. 'I might breed those two.'

'Goodness no. Never waste a superior cock on a mediocre hen. Anyway, they're both too old, I think.'

Old. There it was. 'You're right. I'm being stupid.'

Evelyn came out of the cage and latched it. 'I'm sure I've seen something in one of the pamphlets you printed out for the customers.'

John had spent some weekends exploring *The Art of Printing* CD-ROM on the computer and come up with a variety of colourful pictures and jaunty fact summaries for potential customers. He'd stopped when the costs of the coloured inks for the printer had outstripped customer interest, but he liked that Evelyn had noticed his creative side.

'Here.' Evelyn began to read aloud from the pamphlet. 'While some cocks remain potent and can fertilise eggs over a period of years, hens quite often become unreliable after their third season. Ageing budgerigars should not be paired with each other but each should be provided with young mates.' Evelyn looked up with a particularly meaningful raise of her eyebrows.

'So the old cock won't be rejected by the young hen?'

'Not once they get used to each other.'

John smiled at her, trying to show he understood her message.

Evelyn looked at him oddly, then said, 'Well, as you always say, these birds aren't going to water themselves.'

John realised that he did say that often. He wondered if he was funny. Women liked funny. Evelyn went about her watering as she did most mornings, but for the first time, John found himself looking at the way her small bum moved in her tight skirt.

*

Adam tried to concentrate on his work. He reminded himself of the promise of the humble postage stamp and how that little sticky square represented not only the Queen but also the interconnected apparatus that was the postal service and its web of other postal services across the whole world as it had done for hundreds of years. He was part of a giant net thrown across every human on earth. He thought of the ships, sails unfurled, decks awash, carrying the mail across the oceans. He recalled the tales of men on horses pursued by Indians, trying to get those satchels of letters through. He imagined a pith-helmeted postman in Afghanistan, leading camels up rocky trails evading bandits. He saw snow and sleet and rain and nameless trudging sack-bearing posties. He saw one swim a swollen river – only the river became the river in Mukinbudin, in full flood, frothing as it surged and broiled, tearing Amber-Lee's partly clad body away from him forever.

Adam stood at his desk, panting. He had not delivered Amber-Lee safely. He had not delivered her at all. He looked at the grey concrete wall across the corridor. The lamplight barely illuminated the stains and cracks there. Sometimes Adam imagined mountains and once an eagle, half-stretched. Now Adam thought he saw a wolf's face, eyes blazing, but then it was gone. He needed to get out of the dark of the Lost Mail Department and find some air and light. He had a couple of letters, the addresses of which he had deciphered that morning. He wrote them into his dispatch book and hurried them up to the bright and noisy mail sorting department full of its ordered clatter and happily shared industry.

*

Paul crept in through the back door of his parents' house using the key that was kept on a hook behind the camellia bush. He'd been waiting over the road with Jane until they saw his mother leave. His father was at work.

Jane had stayed with the stolen Holden Commodore VN with the motor running. They had hot-wired it using instructions Jane had found through the computer, and they weren't sure whether they could turn the motor off and restart it using the same method. It was a shame computers weren't portable. Jane had chosen the car model by accessing government reports in which the police stated that the Holden Commodore VN was the most stolen vehicle of 1988. She hoped it might still be the easiest in 1991. She had also used other studies which suggested the statistical clustering of car theft at large suburban shopping centres to select their hunting ground.

Paul stopped at the fridge and found some cold chicken. Then he went to his childhood bedroom and was pleased to see that it remained clean, tidy and with his bed made. It was all as he'd left it a year before. He made his way to his parents' bedroom, comforted that the room still smelled of a very specific combination of his parents' various skin creams, complex yet dominated by vanilla.

At the bottom of his father's side of the built-in robes, he opened one of his father's boxes of bullets and took three out. He had promised Jane three. He hadn't mentioned that there were boxes of bullets. Nor had he mentioned that there was a .22 rifle in the cupboard that used the bullets. He hadn't told her about the shotgun. He wished he'd never said anything about the bullets. Now he was simply trying to minimise the damage. He also knew that he couldn't mention the shotgun because it was used for his father's hunting trips. His father would be criticised. Paul would be implicated. Jane would discover that he had participated in the duck slaughter, albeit when he was twelve. Paul recalled the smell of cordite and men's sweat. He remembered finding pellets in the flesh of the duck they'd roasted by the water and spitting them with little tinkles into a metal plate for that purpose and the good-humoured teasing laughter of the other hunters. Even now he couldn't manage to feel fully ashamed. He put the three bullets in his pocket, put the chicken bones in the kitchen tidy and washed his hands in the bathroom, locking the back door before returning the key to its secret hook.

*

Howard was at Adam's desk reading the dispatch journal. Adam stepped back into an alcove where the plumbing pipes went into the floor and watched Howard look from the journal to the shelves. 'Got you,' he said, straightening with a triumphant smile. Adam edged back further under the darkness of piping as Howard strode past. At his desk, the dispatch book was open under Adam's lamplight. The dispatch book listed the lost mail that the Lost Mail clerk had found. It listed where it had now been correctly sent. The large box which Howard had seen him acting suspiciously around was not listed. And yet it was no longer on the shelf. Howard had indeed got him.

The idea of posting the item to himself, so that he could fix the box at home and then mail it back to the Lost Mail Department, had seemed like a good one at the time. Perhaps he would have been better trying to fix it at work. But Howard kept lurking. And the journal by his predecessor had been quite adamant in warning about telling. Now the explanation of Adam's honourable intentions sounded flimsy even to Adam. Theft? Fraud?

All Adam could think of was running away. Had he done this from the flood-swept car? Had he done this from the ashes of the farm? Would he run from Howard now? Yes. Well no. He would leave work now, early it was true, but it was not to run away. It was to run to. He would go to Evelyn and he would ask her for a date and possibly later marriage and a lifetime of happiness.

At four p.m., exactly one hour early, Adam defiantly crept out of the GPO.

It was four p.m. when Paul's mother came out of the flats carrying the rubbish. Living near the rear of the supermarket had many advantages, one being a biweekly rubbish pick-up. She was pleased to be rid of the prawn shells that she and Paul's father had eaten the night before and had been surprised by the extra tidying needed in Paul's flat. Paul had never been an untidy boy. She emptied the rubbish into the bin for flat one, affixing the metal lid firmly.

The Rover that Paul's father had helped him 'do up' and 'get going' was still parked outside, yet Paul wasn't home. He'd probably caught the bus to the university. Someone had snapped off the car's aerial. She went to inspect the car for any other signs of damage. 'This place is full of vandals, Baby.'

Baby was the name of Mrs McGready's cat. It wound itself around Paul's mother's legs, luxuriating in the self-administered caress and faint aroma of prawns.

*

When Adam entered Milton's Pet Shop, Evelyn ran up to him. 'Adam!' she said. 'Not more birdseed!' Her face was flushed.

'No, um, I'm good for seed.'

'Those two birds. Are they getting on?'

'Yes.'

She blinked a number of times, and smiled eagerly.

Adam said, 'I want to ask you out on a date.'

'A date?'

'Not a date. Terrible word. Um, a meeting. Outing? The movies. Um, Friday and we'd just be watching the same film, sitting next to each other.'

'Evelyn, can you come here please.' It was Evelyn's boss, standing at the back door.

'I'm serving a customer, Mr Tagliatelli.'

'You! What are you always doing here?'

'This is Adam, Mr Tagliatelli. We're going out. On a date. Tonight. Now.'

Adam said, 'Now?'

The boss said, 'You can't go now. It's not even half past four.'

'I'm leaving early. With Adam. To see a film.' She went around the counter to get her black cardigan.

'Now,' said Adam, quietly.

Mr Tagliatelli said, 'But you can't. I was going to do a stocktake. Tonight.'

He had been pursuing Evelyn all day, asking her to feel his muscles when he lifted things needlessly and made weak puns about feather ruffling and counting eggs before they hatched. She'd been trying to evade him all day, but he had only then managed to corner her between cages. He told her about his wife dying and never daring to dream. He panted and tried to push himself against her. But she'd heard someone come into the shop and now she could get away from him.

Mr Tagliatelli said, 'I was going to get some Chinese takeaway.'

Evelyn took Adam's elbow and steered him out of the shop.

They crossed behind a green Commodore and walked away from the GPO.

'What film shall we see?' asked Adam as he walked with Evelyn towards where he thought he'd seen a cinema from the bus.

'Um. I don't know. I don't see many films. They seem to start well and then someone has to spoil things.'

'Oh, well, we'll see what's on. I'm sure there's something. I hadn't checked, you see. I would have been ready for eight p.m. Friday, but I wasn't thinking about four p.m. on a Thursday. I've only been in the city for four days.' Adam clamped his hand over his mouth to stop himself telling her his life story.

A whoosh of air brakes made Adam turn before he could say more. It was a blue garbage truck. A man jumped down at them. Only it wasn't a man. It was the butch girl with her breasts pushing her singlet. She grabbed up the public litter bin out of its metal cage right by them and hoisted it to a man on the back of the truck. He emptied the papers and crusts and cool drink cans and handed it back down. The girl crashed the bin back into the cage and yelled, 'Slam dunk!' She looked at Adam and smiled, her teeth bright white in her grime-smudged face. The truck moved off and she turned and chased it yelling, 'Frank, you bastard. You're a fucking bastard.'

Adam turned to Evelyn who must have been watching too, for she was standing still, breathing shallowly, with her fists up over her ears.

'Are you okay?' Adam asked.

She opened her eyes. Shook herself. 'The street. It's so ...'

'There's a park. With a seat.' Across the road was a tiny park of grass between two office towers, stretching from this street to the next. It had a path leading to a bench seat in the middle and another path leading out to the other street.

'There's pigeons,' she said.

'We need to run,' said Adam, holding her hand tightly as they stepped onto the city street and ran across a break in the traffic and into the park.

A green Commodore indicated and tried to cross the three lanes of traffic, but car horns beeped and two taxis neatly closed up and blocked the attempt.

The pigeons were milling around the seat.

'I'm sorry,' Evelyn said brightly, 'we haven't got anything for you.'

They ignored her, continuing to work on the grass seeds.

'How are your birds getting on?' she asked as she settled on the bench.

'I think they're a bit wary of each other.'

Evelyn nodded seriously.

'So, apart from loving birds, tell me something about you and your life,' Adam said.

She nodded and thought and finally said, 'Birds can fly. I mean, isn't that so ... exquisite? But that is why they're so delicate. Their feathers are also pretty.'

She looked at Adam and smiled.

Adam tried to think of something insightful to say about birds. His mind veered from Chris, reasoning that Chris led to too many of the traumatic events of his life. This made him think of the magpie. Adam found himself needing to confess. 'When I was little, on the farm, I saw this magpie flying toward me, low, with what I thought was a golf ball in its beak. I grabbed a rock. There were lots of them in our paddocks. I threw it at the magpie and it dropped the ball. Only it wasn't a ball. It was an egg. When I went to look, there was this little body with big black eyes dead in the broken shell. And the mother magpie was on the branch of a tree making this awful cawing.'

'You killed its baby,' she said.

'I was only little.'

'That's terrible,' she said, standing and backing from him.

'I didn't know. I felt awful. I feel awful. I'm an orphan.'

Adam saw Howard coming into the park with Sharon from sorting. He grabbed Evelyn's hand and said, 'Let's go down here.'

He led her along the path towards the street at the other end of the park where a green Commodore was illegally parked up on the grass.

Howard caught them near the other side of the park. 'I see it but I don't believe it.' Howard dragged Sharon towards them. 'You've snuck off with the pet shop girl.'

Adam turned to them. 'Hi, Howard. Hi, Sharon. This is Evelyn. We're going to the movies. Running a bit late.'

Adam turned as the side door of the green Commodore swung open to reveal a girl in a balaclava holding a weird contraption towards Adam. 'You. You will get in zee car.' It was a bad Russian accent.

Sharon gasped. Evelyn stood frozen. Adam looked at the driver who was still scrambling to get his balaclava on as he sat behind the wheel. Paul from flat one.

'It's all right folks, I'll handle this,' said Howard as he flashed a confident smile towards Evelyn and stepped towards the girl with the zip gun. 'That isn't even a real gun, is it darling?'

She looked at the object in her hand and then lifted it slightly and shot Howard.

He staggered back, grabbing at Adam for support. 'Owww.'

Sharon looked at blood spreading on Howard's crotch and screamed.

The un-Russian grabbed Adam by the arm, pointing the zip gun at his chest. 'Come on.'

But Adam couldn't come on because Howard had his other arm and was dragging him down.

'Let go,' she ordered Howard.

Evelyn stepped towards the street. She called, 'Help!'

'She shot me. She bloody shot me,' yelled Howard.

Sharon kept screaming.

'We gotta go,' called Paul from the car. 'Jane, we gotta go.'

Jane straightened, looked at her gun, then grabbed Evelyn and pushed her into the back of the Commodore.

'Evelyn!' yelled Adam, managing to break Howard's grasp.

The green Commodore VN spun its rear wheels on the grass before they gripped on the bitumen and howled away amidst the peak hour traffic.

*

Inside Adam's flat, Chris stood on his perch near the abutted open cage doors. Antigone was pecking at her feeder box. Chris tried to concentrate on the evening developing outside the window.

The sky filled with colour as the few clouds refracted the rays of the setting sun. The lower clouds were white and grey with golden underbellies, while the upper ones remained dark but orange. The sky went from blue to red and then purple. It was as though an enormous bird were breaking from its egg and fluffing out its soft plumage for the first time.

Chris turned to watch Antigone again. 'You like the little black ones don't you?'

Antigone looked up from the plastic tray that held the assortment of seeds. 'They're my favourite.'

'I noticed. You always eat the little black ones first and leave the sesame. Whereas I eat the sesame and leave the poppy.' Chris touched the little talons of his left foot on the metal where the two doors touched.

'Hey, I said don't cross that line.'

'I was stretching.' Chris raised both wings, stretching them to full width before retracting them. 'You look beautiful when you're alarmed.'

Antigone stretched her own wings and gave some gentle flaps. 'Only when I'm alarmed?'

The throaty roar of a Commodore approaching startled both birds. Antigone fluttered up to grasp the high back of her cage and Chris stepped back along his own perch.

The sky was beginning to darken, causing deep shadows every-where in the garden. It was hunting time and they were not in a high place.

Jane pushed a blindfolded Evelyn towards the flats, Paul running ahead to get the doors.

'I'm really sorry about this,' said Paul. 'It's pretty ideologically unsound, I know. Taking a woman by force. But, seeing as it was another woman who did the taking, I suppose it's … equitable. I'll get the door. I mean, only because you both can't. I mean, are busy.' He held the door to the vestibule open, making sure there was no one inside.

Then he went for the door of flat one, fishing for the key. 'You know, like that woman investment adviser who ripped off all those women. The chauvinists got down on her, but as Jane explained – that's genuine equality.'

Jane pushed Evelyn into the flat.

'Wimmin have as much right to be a good criminal as any man,' Paul said. 'Better.'

'Will you shut the fuck up?' said Jane. She hustled Evelyn to the chair at the computer desk, and removed her own balaclava. 'Don't move or I'll kill you.' As if prompted by her own statement, Jane fumbled in her jacket for the zip gun and the two remaining bullets.

'We're really sorry about all this,' said Paul.

'You used my name, you moron.'

Paul whispered, 'I was in shock. You shot that guy.'

'Yeah. Bang. God that was a buzz.'

Paul looked at her, aghast. 'What are we going to do now?'

Jane thought. 'We drop him a ransom note. Get the package. Give it to us. Or your girlfriend dies.'

'He's just a friend,' said Evelyn.

'You better hope he's a bloody good friend,' said Jane.

Sharon was giving a statement to the police. 'They seemed to want Adam. But Howard tried to save everyone.'

A sergeant with a notebook asked, 'But they took the girl?'

'From a pet shop.'

Howard sat up in the ambulance and grabbed a paramedic by the arm. 'Have you found it? Have you found it yet? You can sew it back on, can't you?'

The sergeant asked, 'So this Adam guy, where's he?'

'He ran off, chasing the Commodore.'

'Stolen most likely. Most stolen vehicle of 1988. It's the ignition system,' said the sergeant.

'Found it!' yelled a paramedic with a torch, shooing away some pigeons and an insistent seagull.

Everyone went quiet, including the sergeant. The onlookers edged forward as the piece of flesh was carefully put into a small medical eski. The barking owl sat atop her favourite tree and watched Adam creep past the green Commodore, the white Rover and the neatly stacked rubbish bins and into the garden in front of the flats. The sunset had been glorious and the air began to flicker with the promise of excellent hunting.

Adam crept to his door and silently inserted the key. There was a piece of paper inside. A ransom note.

'Adam! Great. Listen, mate – you wanna shut these cage doors. Antigone is starting to, you know, lose it.'

'If you need bars to give you self-control, you have none.'

'I think it's her legs. Have you seen her legs? Adam, you gotta help me.'

> You don't know us. If you want to see your girlfriend or partner or even just a good friend ever again, go to the post office and find the package addressed to Joan Arc, 1 Dolphin Street, Oceania. Bring it to this [crossed out]. Place it in the public bin halfway up ...

Adam stopped reading the note. Under the bird's table he saw the large cardboard box with forty-five dollars worth of postage and Adam's writing and Adam's address. He tore off the outer box and then the crushed box underneath until he found what appeared to be a gold bowling ball.

Adam looked at his front door then went to the window in front of the birds' cages and opened it.

'Good idea Adam. Set her free. Can't live with them; can't shoot 'em. Well, if they were twenty-eights or crows, sure. Starlings, of course.'

Adam turned from the window and left his flat, slamming the front door loudly enough for flat one to hear.

Paul turned from the window of flat one. 'Should take him a couple of hours.'

'I think your mother has been.' Jane was looking at the clean kitchen table.

Paul asked Evelyn, 'So, what do you think about dolphins?'

Evelyn didn't know he was talking to her because of the blindfold.

Jane came over to the computer table and looked into the empty litter bin. 'What night is it?'

'Thursday.'

'It's one of the bin nights.'

'So.'

'You asked him to put the package in the rubbish bin down the street,' said Evelyn.

When Adam got to the cars he ducked down and then crept back into the garden where he stopped behind a tree. He went down on all fours to crawl to the window of his flat.

Baby the cat sat in the garden. She ignored Adam going in. Her eyes were fixed on the window he'd left open.

In flat two a gentle breeze flicked and lifted the lighter feathers of both canaries as they sat very still and very quiet in their respective cages.

Nearby, Adam's computer was on and on the desk in front of the computer was the leg of a chair, a thimble, cleaning chemicals, the bolt from a cupboard door and the lead of a pencil.

The computer was still parked at the site Adam had found: *How to Make a High Velocity Weapon out of Kitchen Utensils and a Beach Umbrella.*

Adam had discovered some of the neophyte features that were way beyond e-mail and CD-ROMs. He'd found ISP and UUNET/AlterNet and also CIX. He'd found a thing called the internet and it led to all kinds of knowledge around the world and not only from universities. It was for everybody, although a lot of people appeared to be offering free kittens.

Adam scrambled back in through his window, this time dragging in a red and white beach umbrella he'd found next to Mrs McGready's swimming pool. He rested it on the computer chair, and looked at the diagram again. His shoulders sagged.

On cue, a sawing noise started above.

Adam headed out of the window once more. He climbed up the drainpipe that went past Harry's balcony. He knocked on the glass.

Harry came to the dusty French doors as though this were a perfectly natural point of entry.

'Adam! Not still mad with me then?'

'I need to borrow a hacksaw.'

'No problem,' said Harry, moving plans and wood while he looked for one. 'How'd your date go?'

'They shot Howard and took Evelyn hostage. If I don't get the stolen golden ball from the post office where it isn't, they'll kill her.'

Harry looked up from his search for only a blink before he said, 'Sounds like she won't forget this date in a hurry. Where does the hacksaw, which I can't seem to find, come into it?'

'They're holding her in flat one, I think.'

'Hmm,' said Harry, 'that Jane's got father issues, I suspect.'

'I'm going to build a rifle, drop the package off in the rubbish bin down the road, and go up onto the roof. When they pick up the package I'll shoot them and rescue Evelyn.'

Harry stood and looked into Adam's steady gaze. 'When you discover the warrior in yourself, you don't just sit around a campfire hugging blokes, do you?'

'She's innocent. I ... I can't run away and leave her.'

'Good for you,' said Harry, wandering off into the bedroom.

Adam looked at the mast, now fixed to the yacht, going up through a new hole in the roof. There were stars in the sky.

'This might be better for accuracy.' Harry came back with a .303 rifle. 'Got it to keep the pirates away.'

Adam grabbed the rifle and turned towards the French doors.

'You might want to make sure she's there.'

Adam turned to see Harry grabbing a toolbox and motioning him to follow.

They went out the door of number four and crept over to the door to flat three. Harry produced a door key and unlocked Mary's door.

In Mary's lounge room a man was in his underwear and tied to a rack of leather. His eyes opened with fear but he could only gurgle his alarm because of a black rubber ball tied into his mouth.

'I thought I had one,' Mary was saying triumphantly as she came from the bedroom with a ping-pong paddle. She was dressed in a leather corset, suspender belt and straining fishnet stockings.

Then she saw them. 'Oh? Jake. Adam.'

'Don't mind us, love. How ya doing, Mr McGready?'

The tied up man grunted wetly.

Harry bent to the floor and took out a drill.

'How was your fruit salad, Adam?'

'Very tasty,' said Adam as he watched Harry drill a hole in Mary's floor.

In the flat below, Jane stood looking out the lounge window with binoculars.

Paul was sitting on the very low coffee table, talking urgently to Evelyn. 'The Princess's Ball symbolises the moon and wholeness and a kind of uterine symmetry that encompasses, like Gaia, the earth itself.'

A tiny drizzle of white plaster dust spread from the ceiling and drifted down into flat one.

Jane turned from the window. 'What was that noise?'

'Was it a whipping kind of noise or a hammering kind of noise?'

Jane listened, then shrugged.

Paul said, 'On the other hand, it was also fashioned by the czars, who were evil patriarchs and it was kept in St Petersburg. Which reminds me, did you know, it was renamed Petrograd in 1914 and then renamed

Leningrad in 1924 and only this year renamed back to its original St Petersburg. Weird, huh?'

Jane counted her bullets again. Two.

Mary and Harry watched Adam looking through the hole in the floor.

Mary said, 'Why don't you call the police? I've got a couple of numbers.'

Mr McGready whimpered.

Harry said, 'No, police mean loudhailers and sirens and ... a whole siege.'

Adam stood up. 'I better deliver the package.'

'A man's gotta do what he's gotta do, Mary,' said Harry proudly as they both followed Adam back towards flat four.

Mrs McGready's cat sprang onto the windowsill of Adam's flat. She stood, her tail waving, as she waited for her eyes to adjust to the light.

Baby watched the two birds flutter in an exciting panic until they were both in the same cage. She looked at the table where it was butted right up to the windowsill. She wouldn't even have to jump.

Adam took the rifle towards the French doors once more.

Harry said, 'I got an idea might make your various moves easier.' He grabbed a sledgehammer and swung at the floor.

Baby was on the table flicking a playful paw at Antigone's empty cage, shifting it slightly, as though she completely understood the principles of peeling, when the bang from upstairs made her look up.

The second huge blow sent a large piece of ceiling swinging down into Adam's flat where it landed near the table. Baby screeched in a pissed-off cat way and leapt out the window before the dust had a chance to rise up into the room.

Another crash sent splinters of old wood and more plaster crashing into flat two.

A ladder was lowered through the new hole in the ceiling and Adam climbed down, carrying a rifle.

'Adam, I've never been so glad to see someone in my life.' Chris and

Antigone sat next to each other on the perch in Chris's cage.

Adam propped the rifle on the birds' table, then dusted himself off and hoisted up the box containing the golden ball.

Antigone coughed. 'My whole life passed before my eyes, and it was very short.'

Adam moved the cages to the side of the table, shaking the birds, but resealing the gap that had been pushed open by Baby. They clung to the perch, watching the open window.

Then Adam pushed the package out the window with a dull thwock and clambered over the table and out.

'Surviving death has made me feel so small.'

'Yeah, and a bit horny.'

Upstairs Mary stood looking at Harry's yacht. 'Jake, it's beautiful.'

'Yep, nearly finished.' He turned and looked towards the new hole in his floor. 'I hope there're some bullets in that rifle.'

Mary looked from the yacht to Harry. 'When it's finished, will you take me with you?'

Harry smiled and went to stand behind Mary with his arms around her. 'If you'll come. I can't live without you.'

'You haven't ever invited me in to see it. I thought ...'

He took a deep breath and said, 'Probably only big enough for two, though.'

She settled back into him. 'Perfect.'

'Am I enough?'

'Jake, everything I've ever done has been for you.'

'But your desires. All those men?'

'They pay me to talk to them or torture them. I have remained faithful, my Odysseus, waiting.'

'Huh,' grunted Harry in a guttural pleased wonder.

'All he's doing is standing there, by the bin.' Jane was looking through her binoculars. 'Oh, shit. Quick, get out there.'

'What?' asked Paul from the kitchen where he was reheating the chickpea curry his mother had left some time that day.

Down the street, Adam had put the heavy box at his feet by the public rubbish bin. He too was looking further down the hill as the orange flashing lights of a garbage truck approached.

'Get down there and get the package before it gets taken to the dump.'

Paul raced to the apartment door, but turned back, yelling, 'Make sure you stir that curry. It'll burn at the base if you don't.'

Evelyn finally said, 'You shot that guy in the park.'

'I shot him in the groin actually. On the groin? Lovborg, in *Hedda Gabler*, shoots himself in the bar. We always liked that at school. Got all us girls tittering. He was shot in the bar.'

'He was trying to protect us.'

Adam stood in the street watching the garbage truck coming up out of the darkness yet again. He thought it had been only a few days ago. He recalled a dream of it too. He wondered if rubbish trucks came every night in the city. It whooshed and clanked towards him like his grunting metal nemesis. Its orange light whirled. Its rear crushed and ground and stank. As it reached him a diesel cloud spurted, blinding him with black smoke.

'I can and I will,' yelled Adam at the thing.

'Good for you.' The smoke cleared. The garbage girl stood in front of Adam smiling. 'Is that for the bin, then?'

Adam looked down to the battered box at his feet. 'No. No,' he managed to say.

'Cool,' she said and looked in the litter bin which was empty. 'Way cool.'

Adam put his foot on the box, thinking she might try to take it from him.

She said, 'Did you see the sky tonight? What a motherfuckin' pumpin' sunset.' She turned to the departing garbage truck and chased the red glow of its tail-lights, yelling, 'Frank, wait, you bastard.'

Paul, the guy from next door, was standing on the pavement a couple of metres away, looking at Adam. He started walking. 'Oh, neighbour guy. Just getting some milk. Want any?' He kept walking past Adam and down the street. Adam watched him. He turned a few houses down, made a show of waving and pointing further down the road before he kept walking.

Adam lifted the heavy package and rammed it into the empty litter bin. Then he ran. He ran past the garbage truck and the garbos. He ran past the bins waiting outside the flats. He ran past the cat and leapt through his open window.

Inside, he grabbed the .303 and climbed up through the ceiling. There was no sign of Harry, so he climbed up onto the yacht. Harry and Mary were in the unfinished cabin, naked and fucking. Adam climbed onto the cabin roof and from there up into the rafters where he slithered through the gap in the tiles and so up and on top of the roof of the flats, dragging the rifle with him.

Way downstairs Jane watched Paul through her binoculars. He had the box open and he was stroking the golden ball. He dragged it out of the bin and started to carry it up the hill.

Jane turned from the window and picked up the zip gun from the couch. She began to insert a bullet. 'We've got the package now.'

'So you'll let me go?' asked Evelyn.

Down in the street the garbage girl emptied the bin from flat one. There were a lot of leftovers and sawn bits of furniture and a McDonald's bag. She noticed that flat two's bin had lots of computer packaging and no food refuse. It was one of the things she liked doing, besides ragging on the truck drivers – reconstructing the people whose rubbish she collected. For instance, she knew that in flat three there lived a couple of prostitutes. Flat four was unoccupied. Elementary, my dear whatsaname.

Baby was in the garden outside the open window, coiling, ready to spring once more.

Chris wasn't aware of that. He only had eyes for Antigone whose glorious neck feathers he was busy nuzzling. 'You are the most beautiful bird I have ever seen in my life.'

She pecked him on the chest a couple of times, but then looked up. 'And after? Will you say that after ... this?'

'There is no after. There is only this.'

The garbage girl emptied her bin into the back of the garbage truck. The McDonald's bag slithered into the chute towards the grinders.

Adam lay in the prone position on the up slope of the roof, tracking Paul with the sights of the .303. He was from a farm. He'd grown up with guns. His finger was on the trigger. All he had to do was pull. Pull the trigger and finally act, taking control of his life and with one great act of power and violence, wipe away all the grovelling and fear and failure. All he had to do was kill Paul and become a hero and make whole his fractured psyche.

Ego. Ergo. Time slowed. Adam's id made his finger squeeze the trigger. At a fraction of a millisecond before that, his superego pulled the rifle forward and down.

There *was* a bullet in the chamber and the shell detonation sent a nearby owl flapping into the air.

The bullet hit the pavement at Paul's feet, making him drop the box, which sent the golden ball rolling down the hill.

The bullet flew up off the street and might have sailed safely into the sky, but for a quaint rooster-shaped weathervane atop a nearby house. Ping. The metal rooster spun wildly. It also sent the bullet ricocheting at an eighty-four degree angle onto the back metal of the garbage truck. Ping, the bullet sounded as garbage collectors dived for cover.

Shatter went the lounge window of flat one as the slightly slowing .303 bullet entered Paul and Jane's lounge room where it hit the side of the zip gun, which was pointed at Evelyn. Ping. Jane screamed in pain as her gun catapulted from her hand and into the screen of her computer. Thunk.

It was from this moment that circumstance and coincidence combined with the hitherto rudimentary mathematics of projectile trajectory to affect the bullet's path and life force.

In Paul's haste to abandon cooking and fetch the package he had left the fridge door a little ajar. The bullet hit the fridge door in the kitchen. Ping. The bullet bounced off the fridge door at such an improbable angle as to go exactly through the eyehole of flat one's door and into the eyehole of the door to flat two. Phht. Phht.

Which was a stroke of luck for the two canaries who were obliviously mating in one of the cages on the table. The bullet entered one end of a beach umbrella pole negligently lying on the table, exiting the other end as if it were a makeshift rifle barrel. Baby the cat had only then leapt at the cage of birds. She found the bullet, midair. Wwwaaa. Although a large number of calculable angles and losses of velocity and power would have suggested the heavily dented bullet might be about to simply drop, it still had sufficient force to carry Baby out the window and into the garden. Thud. Baby and the bullet were dead.

Adam lay on the roof. He had failed again. It was as though he were cursed. He rolled over on his back and looked up at the sky. 'Why, why?' he yelled, not seeing an owl circling there.

The garbage truck exploded in a white conflagration. The surrounding letterboxes were pulverised. Windows shattered and walls crumbled as blast force and giant chunks of hot metal sprayed.

Harry and Mary fell away from each other in the cabin of the yacht in awe as Adam clambered past.

Chris and Antigone disengaged. 'Holy fuck.'

Antigone's cage knocked over in the concussion. 'Yes, it was.'

Adam slid down the ladder and raced for his smashed front door and the fire beyond.

Paul chased the golden ball all the way down the street and halfway across the intersection, where he skidded to a halt when he saw it come to rest at the feet of a policeman who had come out of the McDonald's there.

The cop wasn't paying any attention to the ball or to Paul. He was looking up the street where various bonfires were punching holes into the night. 'It looks like Mary's place,' he called.

To the policeman behind Paul, who had just grabbed him by the windcheater. 'So, son, looks like the ball from the museum robbery. Got anything to say about that?'

Adam waded through a torrent of water pouring from upstairs where Mary's and Harry's pipes must have burst. Once he'd fought through the deluge, he pushed through shattered wood and fallen bricks into what was once Paul and Jane's flat.

'Evelyn! Evelyn!'

'I'm here,' came a weak voice.

Adam pushed through the smoke and the growing flames, the dampness of his clothes protecting him. He found her under the computer desk, diving down next to her. She was smouldering. 'Evelyn,' he coughed. 'I found you.'

*

The next day, the garbage truck still lay like a big burst tin can in the street metres from the burnt out Commodore and Rover.

Adam stood watching a giant crane hoisting Harry's nearly finished yacht up above the missing roof. Harry must have been standing on some surviving joists. He directed the operation with one arm around Mary's shoulder.

Adam went into what was left of the vestibule. He was covered in soot and dirt and plaster dust and something that smelled like chickpea curry. He found an eviction notice nailed to the doorjamb of his flat, citing theft of private property, being one garden umbrella as the reason. It was Friday. Adam had been in the city for five days and already he had been evicted. He thought he had probably lost his job too.

He didn't go into flat two or up to flat four. Instead, he went to the hospital to see Evelyn. If he had gone in, he might have seen Chris going to the open door of his cage to peer out at the world.

'Are you going?'

Chris turned around and went back to Antigone, running his beak along the back of her neck. 'Are you kiddin'? I'm a cage bird. I'd die out there.'

At the hospital, Adam found Evelyn's bed empty. He eventually found her in Howard's room. She was sitting in the visitor's chair by Howard's bed.

'Evelyn,' he said from the door.

She looked pleased to see him. 'Adam! Have the police found Jane?'

'No. Escaped, or atomised.'

She turned and patted Howard's leg. 'Look at my hero here. He took a bullet for me.'

'Oh.'

Evelyn whispered loudly, 'They've sown it back on but his penis might never get hard again.'

'Well, you know, they might be wrong,' said Howard forlornly.

'Oh, you.' Evelyn reached out and tweaked Howard's nose.

Adam turned away and nearly bumped into a girl in a wheelchair.

'I got burned,' said the garbage collector girl.

'Me too,' said Adam.

She sat in the wheelchair with both her arms completely straight out and bandaged in a kind of ready but empty hug.

DOUBLE OR NOTHING

For the first time in our history we are located in the right part of the world at the right time.
– Wayne Swan, Australian Treasurer, 2011, post-GFC1.

Dave Kelly was not in the middle of nowhere. He was somewhere; somewhere between Newman and Marble Bar in the far north of Western Australia. Marble Bar is the hottest town on the planet. The earth is red and black and so filled with minerals that working there is like standing on the hotplate of a barbecue.

Dave crouched on top of a bullet hole–riddled wire mesh telephone cage repairing the antenna next to the solar panel. It was midday and the solar panel thrived. So did the litter of flies on Dave's sweaty shirt. They gathered and bit through the fabric and then fought to get to his mouth and eyes. The husk of a dead kangaroo lay across the road, ignored by the flies now that Dave had come along, like a godsend.

Dave felt the screwdriver start to slip through his sweat-slick fingers and leaned to catch it but missed and it dropped and disappeared in the soft red dust below. 'Shit,' he said as he stood. That's when he saw the jeep coming towards the T-junction where he was working. It was going like the clappers, trailing dust and heading straight at Dave. Dave looked at his Telstra van parked by the solar telephone, then up at the approaching jeep which showed no signs of slowing. If Dave was a betting man he might have tried to calculate the odds of a vehicle collision between the only two cars within a three hundred kilometre radius.

The jeep tried to turn right without braking, and began to slide sideways. Dave felt a little surge of excitement as he looked to where he could jump to avoid being skittled, but the front wheels of the jeep caught as it cut across the corner and growled away, showering Dave in a wave of thick, choking dust. So he didn't see the crash. He just heard the unmistakeable thump and the sad, empty clatters.

*

Dave's van skidded in its own slew of dust coming to rest a hundred metres up the highway.

The jeep lay on its back, one wheel still spinning. A mobile phone was ringing amidst the bits of luggage and food and broken glass. Dave found the driver, his legs pinned under the jeep. There was a lot of blood and no pulse. The flies were already gorging. The mobile phone stopped ringing, so the only sound was the slow gurgle of liquid escaping from some ruptured engine part.

Dave looked along the debris trail that led from the jeep to a shattered tree stump near the road. The unlucky bastard had hit the only tree in a thousand kilometres. Dave dialled on his Telstra sat phone.

Something flashed in the sun. Dave walked towards it.

'Newman Police Station.'

'Yeah mate. Car accident. About a hundred and fifty K north of you.'

'Near the phone box?'

'Yeah, very near the phone box. Anyway, the driver's dead.'

'Oh. Okey-doke. No rush then, eh. Be up in a few hours. Don't touch anything.'

'Wouldn't dream of it.'

Dave looked down at an aluminium case. He looked back to the man lying under the jeep and to the desultory scatter of his personal effects. He looked out at a stretch of temporarily unmined emptiness of the North-West. Maybe it was the heat and its dry crushing weight. Maybe it was that the dead man looked vaguely like Dave himself. Maybe it was the lazy backhanded bad luck of the tree stump. Whatever the cause, Dave was given to an uncharacteristic moment of soul searching.

*

'You know,' said Dave to Terry on the phone later, 'I thought of Maverick.'

'The film Maverick?'

'Yeah. He's sitting on a horse with a noose around his neck in the middle of the desert with the rattlers slithering out of the sack towards the horse's feet, and he thinks the first lines he says in the film ...'

'He thinks he should give up gambling?'

'Not at all. No. His voiceover says, "It had been just a shitty week for me from the beginning."'

*

Dave was installing a wall phone in a perfectly air-conditioned executive apartment kitchen.

The owner stood talking on her mobile in the living room. The curtains were open and she looked out at sailboats on Perth's Swan River as though they were all hers. 'I don't care, Richard. Sell everything European. Yes and German. Even German. They may get dragged down into this. I want to lay low until this new meltdown finishes ... melting.'

Dave checked the dial tone and gently replaced the landline telephone in its new cradle on the wall. He looked over to the lady, ignoring him as she listened to her mobile. She was dressed in a business skirt and blouse. Diamonds sparkled from her ears. More diamonds winked and twinkled from around her neck. The 'at home' jewellery.

She was in her mid-forties and in pretty good shape, but she had one of those small mouths which seem best shaped to indicate angry disappointment. 'And dump Asia. No, Richard. Not the Chinese. They don't count as Asian. I know the Japanese never used to be considered Asian either, but have you seen their GDP to national debt ratio?!'

Dave headed for the bathroom. It was a palace designed for an Ancient Greek. There was slate with gold trim and a wall-sized mirror. Dave lifted the phone and heard the dial tone purring again.

He went into the bedroom, frightening himself as he confronted two Daves stepping towards him. The lady sure liked her mirrors. And her telephones.

The bed was unmade and strewn with light filmy lingerie. Dave picked up the telephone on the bedside table, checking the dial tone there. She liked her diamonds too. There was a chunky diamond bracelet on the bedside table. Dave picked up his tools from the table and two pieces of snipped wire he'd missed from the installation.

'Richard, am I going to have to spell everything out to you every step of the way this morning? I don't care whether it's night there. It's morning here. Don't be pedantic. The Indians are usually Asian but just might be a little Chinese right now.'

Dave closed the bedroom door, silencing Richard's dimness about economic racial profiling.

He picked up the bedside telephone and dialled. Daryl answered at the other end, saying the company name, 'Sure Thing, You Betcha.'

'Daryl, can I talk to Mungo?' asked Dave, keeping his voice down.

Daryl was one of Mungo's enforcers. He made up for his lack of physical power with hard work. 'If you haven't got it, Dave, Mungo's not gunna be happy.'

'Yeah, well I want everybody to be happy. So, can I talk to him?'

Dave picked up the bracelet and twirled it around his index finger watching the pretty sparkles while he waited for Mungo. There was a book on the table. Ellora's Cave. *Beg*. There was a huge-chested black man kneeling before a woman's shoulder.

'Is this good news, Dave?' asked Mungo at the other end of the phone.

'It's going to be excellent news, Mungo. Five hundred on Denmark Prince. That's today at Flemington.'

'How is this good news, Dave?'

'That's five thousand right there, only hours away.' Dave watched himself in one of the mirrors. Saw his face bright and happy and convincing.

'Which, even if it comes in, Dave, isn't enough, is it?'

'No, but I get to keep my legs for a few more weeks while I work on the rest, don't I?'

'See, there you go doing it again, Dave. You think you're making a joke, but what you're really doing is describing exactly what's going to happen.'

Dave heard a noise and turned to find the woman in the bedroom, her little mouth crumpling smaller.

Dave turned back to the phone and said, 'No Terry, it's still feeding back with the echo. I'll try calling you back from one of the other lines.'

'Kelly!' yelled the phone as Dave hung it up and then stood to smile at the owner.

'Looks like I still got a couple of glitches to iron out.' Dave smiled again and then politely smoothed the sheets where he'd been sitting.

'You were placing bets.'

'What? Oh that. No, we use certain key words to check the frequency modulation. You know, like the roadies do for a band. Check, check. L-l-l-l-l-egs. Leg-gs breaker breaker.'

'You were placing bets on my phone.' Her eyes were fixed on the phone as if his act of defilement were visible. She started around the bed towards the phone.

Dave didn't panic so much as make a split second strategic decision which, in hindsight, proved tactically poor. He grabbed the phone and cradle with both hands and pulled hard, ripping the socket out of the wall and upending the bedside table.

The woman stood, looking in horror at the wall and then the table and finally at Dave holding her telephone.

'Sorry. I had to do that. For your own protection. Couldn't risk feedback shock from the digital pulse through an unalloyed signal.' Dave tried to meet her eyes.

She raised the mobile telephone that was still in her hand and poked buttons.

Dave righted the table and set the broken phone back on it. He picked up the book which had fallen.

She said, 'Yes, Complaints Department please.' She stood waiting, looking at him.

Dave's pulse quickened. His breathing got faster. His brain clicked into an extra gear. It was the feeling he got when he'd put everything from the whole meet on the last race. The longer the odds, the greater the rush.

'Okay. You're probably the richest, most powerful woman I've ever met. Right now, this very second, I've got to tell you, you look like one of the sexiest. And most powerful.'

Her eyes widened.

'I can tell you work too hard. All these phones. All those calls. Work work work. And for what? What about you in all this. You have needs. I can see from these mirrors, the bathroom, these soft, delicate nightclothes – that you're a sensuous woman.'

She looked down at her bed, possibly aghast. But maybe, just maybe – not aghast.

Dave said, 'Let's not leave this room wondering all our lives what might have been. Say "no" to the rest of the world. Say, "Yes. Let's go a bit crazy, and both make wild, passionate love together, right now."'

Dave was panting, just a little. He smiled. Knew he had the shy thing going in the smile that women had said made him look like a cute, naughty boy.

She was looking. She had looked at him and then to the bed,

calculating the potential profit/loss perhaps. For that frozen moment, Dave knew, she was starting to think about it.

Then her mobile, still at her ear, said, 'Telstra, Complaints.'

Dave said, 'What do you say? Want to take a chance?' He tossed the book on the bed.

'Yes,' she said to the telephone. 'I'd like to make a complaint about one of your workers.'

Dave sighed. Throwing the book on the bed had probably been a touch too much.

'Actually, it's a large number of complaints that include malicious damage and sexual harassment.'

She smiled at Dave, her mouth like a paper cut.

'You used to be a lawyer, didn't you?' he said.

'That was the job I came back from.'

'I know.'

'You were on the phone when I got back from it.'

'I remember.'

*

Dave's desk abutted Terry's in their workshop/office area. There was one piece of paper on Dave's desk and nothing else.

On Terry's desk were two computers, two blotters, two staplers, two paper punches and two telephones, one of which was at Terry's ear.

'Keep the Telstra shares and the Commonwealth, for sure, but I want to get into insurance. Any big company. Right.'

Dave looked at the paper on his desk, then back up to Terry as Terry put down the phone.

Dave said, 'Can I use one of your phones?'

'Nope.'

Dave looked over his empty desk. 'My chair?'

'What are you going to sit on?'

'Who says I'm going to lose?'

'You always lose. Ray's looking for you, by the way.'

Dave looked down at the piece of paper in the middle of his desk.

'Yeah, well maybe I'll get my reprimand a bit later.'

Terry smiled in the smug way he had.

'Get stuffed.'

Terry smiled and said, 'Okay. Your chair against one of my phones.' He took the well-worn deck of cards from his drawer. The cards had once been Dave's. 'Why don't you use your mobile?'

'No credit.'

Terry shuffled, looking up at Dave. 'Don't take this the wrong way, mate.'

'I'm pretty sure I will, but get it out of your system.'

'You sure you're not spinning out of control?'

'Is this a roulette wheel image, Terry, or a crashing plane image?'

Terry put the cards down on the desk, face down. 'Hmmm,' he said. 'Maybe I'm thinking of a ferris wheel. More your style. At the fair. Next to the bearded lady.'

'Maybe I like spinning.' Dave cut the deck, holding up the face card. It was a five, not good when high card wins.

'But the ground is rushing up to slap you on the face.'

'That's beautiful, Terry. That's a beautiful turn of phrase. You were at the fair, I could tell and the thing *was* a ferris wheel and it spun me off, didn't it?'

Terry nodded.

Dave said, 'Now are you going to cut the fucking cards?'

Terry cut the deck. Kept his hand face down a moment for dramatic effect, then showed Dave and watched Dave's face to see, but Dave gave him absolutely nothing, forcing him to look at his three of diamonds.

'Get stuffed.'

Dave said, 'My luck's turning,' as he dragged one of the phones back onto his desk.

'Watch out for the ground.'

Smug. Very smug.

Dave's flat was nearly empty. There was one black vinyl armchair, a phone and an answering machine in the living room. Dave believed that message bank was a rip-off. Some racing formguides were scattered across the floor.

Dave switched on the answering machine, and headed for the kitchen.

'Hi. Dave Kelly. Speak to me nicely.' Beep.

In the fridge alcove was an eski. Dave opened the eski and took out a can of beer and a pizza box.

Kevin came on the answering machine. 'Um hi, Dave. Um. Sally asked me to call. Um. It's about your maintenance payments. Um. Sorry mate.' Kevin lowered his voice and said, 'You could try Excalibur tonight. I'm riding, and I reckon it's got the nod.' Beep.

Dave sat in the chair with his beer wondering about Kevin pimping his ride so his wife's ex-husband could make the back maintenance payments.

There was another call. Mungo. 'Denmark Prince is still running. Which is extremely bad news, Dave. Come and see me. Now!' Beep. Click. Whirr.

*

Trish Fong ran a thriving Cash Converters franchise very close to Dave's house. Trish said it had picked up considerably during the two-speed economy era of rampant mining profits for some and soaring unmanageable prices for everyone else.

Dave took his eski into the shop.

'Dave. What you doing here so late?'

'Missing the home comforts.'

There was a couch and another armchair that matched the one in Dave's lounge room. There were other bits of furniture that would probably kit out Dave's flat rather nicely, including a newish refrigerator.

'I had to shift your TV, Dave. Sorry.'

Dave shrugged, then reached into his pocket and pulled out the diamond bracelet.

Trish jumped back from it with a squeal, 'Agggeee.'

Dave twirled the thing, making the diamonds flicker.

Trish came forward. 'Dave. This is no good.'

'Thought you'd be interested.'

'A present? For my daughter?'

'Trish, you never let me near her. No, I mean business. Big sentimental value mind. My dear grandmother's. But I need to sell it. For her operation.'

Trish didn't smile. She was looking at the bracelet like it was a blue-ringed octopus. 'Are you crazy? With agreements and police checks and waiting periods, unless you've got an actual sales docket, and twenty years worth of provenance and chain of custody. And a stat dec – even with all that this'll take about four weeks to clear.'

Dave shrugged, returning the bracelet to his pocket. He picked up the eski from the floor and took out his passport and his telephone answering machine.

'I'm not buying your passport.'

'I could Chinese up the photo.'

Trish shook her head. She pointed at the answering machine. 'Nobody uses those things anymore. It's all on your mobile.'

Dave looked glum.

Trish sucked her front tooth as she did and then said, 'I'll give you ten for the eski and the thing.' She meant the answering machine.

*

Dave came out of Trish's Cash Converters and was punched in the nose.

He fell back to find himself sitting on the pavement looking up at Mungo's enforcers. Daryl was smiling. But Tiny, who wasn't, looked concerned.

Dave touched his nose experimentally. 'I was coming to see you guys.'

'What a coincidence,' said Daryl. 'And here we are.'

Dave looked at his fingers and saw there was no blood. 'Are you losing your touch, Tiny? It's not broken. I'm not even bleeding.'

Tiny said, 'Yeah, I pulled it a bit, Dave.' Tiny demonstrated his gentler punch in the air above Dave's head.

'Thanks, mate. I appreciate that.'

Tiny nodded.

'When you two girls have finished catching up, Mungo says you're to give us $20,000.'

'Quite right,' nodded Dave, remaining down on the pavement.

Daryl said, 'It's broken legs time. On account.'

'That's fair.'

Dave reached into his jacket pocket and pulled out the diamond bracelet, holding it up towards them like garlic to vampires. Or was that raw meat to wolves?

Daryl took it and stepped close to the light of the shop window where he pretended to have jeweller skills. Finally, he said, 'Twenty-four hours.'

'Forty-eight.'

'Thirty-six.'

'Done.'

Daryl started walking towards a dark Lancer, but Tiny shuffled forward and bent down. 'You didn't steal it, did you Dave?'

Dave didn't want to lie to Tiny. He liked him. He nodded.

Tiny said, 'Don't take this the wrong way, but I've always respected you, Dave.'

'Thanks, Tiny.'

'But now I don't.'

*

Dave stood near the monitor in the sparsely populated TAB listening to Kevin's race. The buzz had been mild as he'd placed the bet. True, it was his last ten dollars, but it was only ten. A bald punter stood in a corner, red, sweating and grunting, as if he were in the middle of a solo sexual act. Dave waited for his own rush of anticipation or adrenaline or dread. He waited as the race neared the end. Another punter, a lady in very stretched trackie daks, looked like she might cry. Dave took his ticket to the window, feeling nothing.

Geraldine fed it in. She brightened. 'Good call, Dave. Nice odds.'

'Winners are grinners, Geraldine.'

She started counting out money. Hundred dollar bills.

'Let's put it all on the next, eh?'

Dave sat in the visitor's seat across the desk from his supervisor. Ray raised his finger like a conductor about to start the orchestra up. Looking at Dave he moved the finger over to the mini-recorder on the desk between them and pressed the record button.

'I am giving you a verbal warning concerning dissatisfaction with your performance. Do you acknowledge you understand this?'

Dave leaned forward and talked into the recorder as slowly as Ray had. 'Yes, Raymond Beam, I, David Kelly, understand your verbal.'

'This is the third verbal warning of poor performance.'

'Yes, three.'

'Have you received written material concerning your rights and the nature of your performance management?'

'Yes. Received and read.'

'Is there anything you do not understand about these verbal warnings concerning poor performance?'

'I, David Orlando Kelly, understand, Raymond Beam. What's your middle name, Ray?'

Ray pressed stop. 'When you get back from up north, I'll have something in writing.'

'North?'

'Yeah, Dave. As far away from other humans as we can find. Middle of nowhere. You can pick up a van in Port Hedland. Now fuck off.'

'Ah, so he'd turned the recorder off by then?'

'Ray is less polite when he's not "on".'

'You do have a way with authority figures.'

'Yeah, well. It has been a shitty week.'

'That's why I've called you. You're not still up north are you?'

'I'm coming to that.'

'It's not nowhere, Ken,' said Dave to the dead man. Dave had covered him up with a jacket. He'd found his wallet and was looking at Ken's driver's licence.

The driver's phone started ringing again. The ringtone was 'Journey'. Dave tracked it to an Iridium 9555 lying in the dirt behind the jeep. He'd always thought 'Journey' should have been called 'Marrakesh' or 'Kasbah'. Something Middle Eastern. 'Hash Salesman' would have worked.

He buttoned on the phone and a Scotsman started yelling, 'Aboot bloody time. I don't like being messed aboot, Ken, and ye're messing me aboot. I've set things up fir Perth. Yir ticket and travelling money are at airport. Getting t'stones through is up tae ye.'

'Um,' said Dave, when there was a gap. 'Bit of bad news on that.'

'Don't ye start haggling wi' me, laddie. Twenty thousand. Do it or I'll huv bad news fir ye,' yelled the Scotsman. 'Doon't fook me aboot.' Click.

The aluminium case flashed in the sun again like a wink. It was the kind used by geologists to carry samples. Dave opened the case. Inside were small brown and white rocks. They didn't look so much like stones as bits of muesli. One of the bits of muesli sparkled.

'Gold?'

'Diamonds, Terry.'

'Diamonds!'

'Diamonds.'

'Cos you were working a mere two hundred kilometres from Argyle? Dave, you are so full of it.'

'Am not.'

'You can barely fix a fucking phone. How come you know you've got a case of diamonds?'

Dave left the scene of the accident and he flew back to Perth. When he opened the aluminium case at the Cash Converters, Trish Fong leapt back and screamed like a fifty year old Chinese-Australian woman jumping into the cold surf.

When she recovered she said, 'Have you suddenly got a direct line into the diamond industry?'

'Things are starting to fall my way.'

Trish took a metal pen and used it to turn a couple of the rocks. 'Diamonds, but uncut. They look industrial.'

'Industrial?'

'Not for jewellery. For making cutting tools and drills and shit.' She shrugged.

'So worth anything? Curio value?'

'Are you crazy? Ever hear of Triads? Tongs? These have got to be hot. You heard of the Spider Boys? Africans. There's Africans here, you know. Everywhere you look. Are these blood diamonds?'

'I don't think they're blood diamonds. I was working up north a few hundred K away from the Argyle Diamond Mine.'

'And you thought you'd dig in the ground, huh? They aren't very pink.'

'Pink?'

'They have these pink diamonds. No. No good. You're trying to get me killed. No more diamonds please, Dave.' She nudged the case closed using her elbow. 'Household goods and electronics.'

'You already have most of my household goods, Trish.'

'I'll give you twenty for the case.'

*

Dave stood near the check-in of the Perth International Airport counting the money in the envelope for the third time. One thousand English pounds.

Dave had shown Ken's driver's licence at a pick-up counter in the airport, deciding the photo on that looked a little more like him than the one in Ken's passport. They gave him a manila envelope. Inside was an airline ticket to Amsterdam and an address. A typed note said *Go by the name of Angus MacFergus, rest of payment COD.* There was a smaller envelope containing the money.

Dave was calculating how many Aussie dollars that would be and how quickly he could build that stake into a dream run at the track when a couple of businessmen hovered a little too close and he felt he should not flash his roll. That was when Terry phoned.

Terry said, 'Where are you?'

'Mate. Um, trying not to spin out of control.'

'Well, I think you're seconds from impact.'

'You're such a pessimist, Terry.'

'That solar panel you were supposed to fix. You didn't. And there are certain enquiries from the cops up north that you might be the person leaving the scene of an accident.'

'Ah.'

'And they'd like to ask you if you took any personal effects, like money and identification, from the deceased.'

'Hmm.'

'Daryl and Mungo have been calling the office.'

'Yes, of course.'

'And more police down here in Perth would also like to talk to you as a person of interest.'

'Oh? What's that about?'

'A missing diamond bracelet.'

'Is that everything, Terry?'

'I think that brings us both up to date with the events of this week. Maybe you should head for Darwin.'

Dave looked past hundreds of waiting or wandering passengers to a beautiful woman standing near the newsagent's. She smiled at him.

Terry said, 'So, what are you gunna do?'

'I think I'm going to keep spinning, Terry. But not to the ground. I'm going to spin faster and faster and go up – like a helicopter.'

Dave buttoned off and looked for the beautiful woman who'd smiled and made him feel like good things could happen in his future, but she was gone. Instead, the businessmen were there again. Their suits were cheap and ill-fitting and slightly out of fashion. The younger one winked at Dave.

'You shouldn't have winked, Bruce.'

'Then you punched me in the arm, Mal.'

'Thank you, officers. Let's back up a little, Ken.'

'My name's Dave, Inspector Compton.'

'No, let's not do that again please. Ken, why are you going by the name of Angus MacFergus?'

'It was at the airport. At a counter.'

'From Dewar?'

Dave bought a carry-on bag for nineteen dollars and ninety-five cents and used his ticket and Ken's passport to get a boarding pass. As he was walking towards the security person who checked boarding passes and passports he recalled his few international travelling experiences. He'd been to Bali twice and to New Zealand once. Each time had involved questions and X-ray machines. He began to doubt the wisdom of trying to get on the plane with diamonds stuffed in every pocket. So, just before the door of no return, he patted his top pocket, as though searching for cigarettes and turned around and went out of the terminal.

'Mal thought you'd bailed, Ken. Gutsed out on us.'
   'Yes, thank you, officer. Your version, Ken. For the record.'
   'Call me Dave.'

Dave got his Telstra van from the parking lot and drove to one of the service gates around the side. He beeped his horn until a security guy came. He didn't get out of the van. The guard waved and yelled. Dave waved his hand impatiently. The guard finally opened the gate. And Dave drove past him.

Dave parked his van near the baggage handlers shed and wandered in, yelling at the first guy he saw, 'You got a problem with the phones?' It was a safe question. Everyone had problems with their phones. But the guy shook his head and raised his hands and indicated a hearing impairment or too little English and pointed back to an office.

Dave nodded and waved, but as soon as the worker turned, he joined a luggage trolley heading out towards a Qantas jumbo connected to the departure gate number printed on his boarding pass. 'Is this the plane to Amsterdam?' he yelled.

'Man, you can't come out here,' yelled the baggage driver.

Dave pointed to the emblem on his shirt. 'Telstra.'

The guy was already driving away towards the open stomach of the plane. The engines were warming, whining painfully.

Dave went under the back of the plane near the wheels and up the rear steps where they were loading sealed containers of food and drink.

A hostess blocked his way, just inside the rear door. 'Hey.'

'Telstra.' He tapped his chest insignia as though it was a police badge. 'Your inboard communication system has problems?'

'You'd have to see the captain,' she said, pointing forward.

Dave stepped past her into an aisle where early passengers were getting seated. Another hostess stepped out, her smile on hard.

The first one said, 'Doesn't it get fixed by engineers?'

Dave reached into his envelope and produced his boarding pass and waved it at both of them. When they looked confused, he said to the hostess who'd met him, 'Just professional interest.' Then he turned to the hostess in the aisle and said, 'I wandered back here for a look. I'll come back later, when you're not so busy.'

Dave wandered down the aisle, with his boarding pass out and a studied expression of seat-searching, fighting the tide of passengers coming the other way.

He found his window seat but someone was in the way. In the aisle seat sat the beautiful woman who had smiled at him from the airport newsagents. Serendipity is a glorious thing when the converging items aren't jeeps and Telstra vans. He put his empty carry-on in the overhead locker, then gave the woman his winningest smile. 'I can hoist myself over, or we can shuffle?'

She stood and stepped out into the aisle and Dave slid and sat too heavily on one of the mounds of rocks in his back pockets. He gasped.

The beautiful woman moved back into her seat with a swish of knees from her ruffling skirt, looking at him oddly.

Dave said, 'So, flying eh?'

'Yes. That's what my ticket suggests.' She reached for a magazine.

Dave considered this first rebuff as no more than part of the process like, say, the haka before a good rugby game. He offered his hand, smiling. 'Angus MacFergus.' He thought that next time he said it he might try to put a bit more Scots spittle in 'Fer'.

She said, 'And don't tell me. You work for Telstra.'

Dave looked down at his shirt in shock. 'How did you guess?'

Dave saw her supress a smile. There was hope. She had dark brown eyes and dark hair and a kind of perfect Italian nose.

'And you are?'

'Not looking to make a new friend.' She opened her magazine and started reading. She hadn't said it that rudely. It wasn't irrevocable.

Dave adjusted a couple of the rock bulges in his back pockets. 'I'm betting that by around the thirteen hour mark, I'll have worn you down.'

'Given that this flight goes to Singapore and that's only five and a half hours, those will be very long odds.'

'My favourite kind.'

*

Her name was Margaret St James. Dave had shaved and showered as she'd instructed and stepped out of the bathroom and into the main room of the houseboat in Amsterdam wearing nothing but his best smile. Margaret was waiting for him.

'You're a legend, Ken.'

'Cheers, Bruce. Unfortunately, also waiting were Campbell and Karushi, although I didn't know that was their names. Not then.'

'Oh,' said Dave on seeing the men in the dim kerosene lamplight. They looked as displeased as Dave felt.

'Angus,' said the tough-looking one in a thick Scottish accent. He stood blocking the stairs leading up to the deck. Campbell.

'Ah,' said Dave.

The Indian man held a briefcase and looked from Dave to Margaret. Karushi. 'What the ...' he said in a London accent.

Margaret got up from the table. 'Angus, you've obviously got things to do. How about we take a raincheck. I can see this isn't a good time.'

'Wait,' said Campbell. He had scars crisscrossing both cheeks. 'Whit's she daein' here?'

Her name was Margaret St James and he did wear her down but somehow she got ahead coming off the plane from Singapore to the Netherlands and Dave couldn't seem to push through all the other passengers to catch up to her as they filed into Schiphol airport. Then he saw the two dodgy business guys up ahead. They were scanning the passengers. The younger one was tall and tanned and fit-looking.

The older one was in his mid-fifties, with an angry red face and rumpled body. They stood with a new thin man in a much better suit. The thin man talked into a walkie-talkie, also examining the incoming passengers. Dave finally felt the prod of alarm and ducked away to the toilets.

He went into a toilet stall and considered a new plan. Every pocket of his pants was stuffed with the uncut diamonds, the delivery of which would bring him twenty thousand somethings, which it was not unreasonable to assume was cash. Twenty thousand was a very good number to be dealing with, given the debt to Mungo. It was seriously worth the punt.

Dave figured he might as well get comfortable. He emptied the stones from his pocket into the carry-on bag and joined the dazed and addled line of passengers trudging to customs. He had his passport ready. He felt his breathing go shallow, his pulse begin to get up towards the happy level. He recalled that in many airports today, apart from having men in dark uniforms carrying machine guns, there were also cameras pointing at the incoming. Trained professionals, possibly mothers and priests, scanned the faces of passengers looking for signs of guilt. Dave wondered if the mounting excitement he felt as he approached his customs official would be mistaken for guilt and unleash the machine guns.

'Hello,' said Dave to the customs man as he handed him his passport.

'Good morning, sir,' he said. 'Anything to declare?' Before Dave had time to manufacture his lie, or make up a really good joke, the customs man looked over Dave's shoulder.

Dave turned. The thin man in the good suit stood examining Dave, his left hand cupping his chin, his index finger tapping on his pursed lips. He looked past Dave, and nodded, precisely.

'Thank you sir,' said the customs man. 'Have a nice stay in the Netherlands.' He put Dave's passport on the counter and looked up for the next passenger.

A more circumspect man, given to cosmic questioning, might have taken a moment at this point. Dave, on the other hand, believed in gift horses and never looking them in the mouth. He picked up his passport and walked through.

Dave stood in the freezing wind looking down at the houseboat. It was sagging and badly in need of paint and possibly a bilge pump. It was dark inside.

Dave looked back at the row of well-preserved three-storey brick buildings squeezed along Amstel, Centrum. They had shiny brass number plaques and warm yellowish glows from upstairs windows. Across the canal were other houseboats and street lamps and pretty trees. Dave barely had time to note its olde-worlde charm before a cruising police car sent him scurrying onto the deck of T.0.59.

He hurried to the door of the upper cabin, pushing it open to reveal wooden steps leading below. 'Hello. Um, Angus, here,' Dave called.

He moved slowly down the steps searching the wall for a light switch. There was one at the bottom of the steps, but it clicked uselessly. Dave bumped into a table and then a chair before he found a curtained window. He pulled them open allowing in some dim yellow light from across the canal. The cabin was threadbare and dusty. There was a kitchenette and a dining room table with a kerosene lamp. He put his bag of diamonds on the table and got a thin blanket from the bunk bed built under the stairs.

Dave went to a door at the end. 'Hello. Angus MacThingie here.' He opened the door to a little toilet and shower. He went back to the bag of diamonds and put it under the pillow of the bed. He sat on the bench seat under the window shivering in his thin Telstra shirt. He was cold and hungry and tired. He could use a beer. He looked at the bag poking out from under the pillow under the stairs. He got the bag and emptied the stones into the drawer in the kitchenette. He stood, shivering, and looked out the window. Across the canal, on the wall of a big building, the sign said Amstel Diamonds. 'The glamorous world of international diamond smuggling,' said Dave, a little ungraciously.

*

There were many bridges and many women sitting in windows in their underwear. There were blonde women and dark women, fat women, gaunt women, African women, Thai women, Japanese women. There were women who may not have been women. Men window-shopped, occasionally being let in the front door.

Dave roamed, freezing and hungry. He passed 'video cabins' with X-rated signs in neon pink, Live Shows, Live Girls, sexual memorabilia shops, marijuana cafes amidst the Heineken signs. And there seemed to be drunken youths from every country in the world stumbling and staggering with forced laughter amidst the red and occasionally green lights.

However, Dave could not find a real shop. He needed warm clothes. He asked some young guys who replied in American accents. 'You can get sex and drugs twenty-four seven, but try buying toothpaste.' 'Or a decent hamburger.' 'All the shops shut at six.'

A man in a black leather jacket stopped next to them to light a cigarette.

Before Dave could approach him a youth appeared in front of him. 'Hey, how you going? Havin' a nice time?'

Dave doubted he was the diamond contact, but said, 'I'm Angus MacFergus and I'm cold.'

'Cool. Cool man,' said the Moroccan. 'You want anything? I got ecstasy. Really good gear.'

'How much for your jacket?

The Moroccan wore a denim jacket with a fleecy collar. 'Jacket? What's that? I can get anything, man. Not sure we call it that here.'

'Your jacket. I'll buy your jacket. And some warm pants.'

'Fuck you, man. You want that, then go to the flower district. I'm selling drugs.'

The offended youth pointed his finger at Dave then lost tension and floated away with the other pedestrians. The guy in the black leather jacket was talking to his cigarette packet but caught Dave watching and turned away before Dave could make an offer on his jacket.

Dave saw a bright blue and red parka ahead. It was on a young guy outside a shop window where fat African women were gyrating in their underwear to no discernible common rhythm. The parka looked waterproof. It looked like it was full of some eiderdown or equally Nordically-tested warm material.

Dave tapped the youth on the shoulder. 'How much for your jacket, mate?'

He said, 'Fifty euros for the fuck and suck,' in a French accent.

'How about fifty pounds?' Dave peeled off a fifty from his envelope.

The youth in the parka stepped back and abused Dave in seemingly unpunctuated French. The youth's two mates slapped the French youth on the back and pushed him in the chest, laughing and obviously urging him to accept Dave's unintended offer.

'The girls, not me,' the youth finally said in English.

Dave raised his arms in apology. 'Sorry, mate. I want to buy your jacket. I'm freezing.' Dave took out a hundred pounds and waved them.

One of the African prostitutes banged on the window and gestured for them to move off.

'Why should *I* freeze?' said the French guy.

'Two hundred pounds.'

More French. His friends were urging him on. 'Get his shirt. It's cool,' said one of them pointing to the Telstra shirt.

'Okay,' said Dave, 'jacket, pants and shirt. Two hundred pounds for the lot.'

Dave looked around for a place to change then dug another fifty-pound note out of his magic envelope and waved it towards the African prostitutes behind the window. The door opened and Dave and the French guy and his mates all piled in. The African ladies started yelling in Dutch. The French guys started assuring in French. The African women smiled and started speaking French to the boys.

There was now no room to change in the window area so Dave grabbed the parka youth by the elbow and started up the stairs.

A big Maori stepped out on the landing above. 'What's going on down here?'

'Just a bit of a fashion parade, mate. Hands across the ditch?'

'Not bloody likely.' The Maori looked past Dave and yelled, 'Hey, what are you lot all doing in here and not buying?'

'They're making sure this man doesn't try things,' said the Frenchman.

'How about ten pounds for the use of the room? To change. Mate, I need some warm clothes. You can chaperone. Two minutes.'

'Chaperone, yes,' nodded the French guy.

'Twenty,' said the Maori.

'The All Blacks are losing it.'

'Thirty.'

'Fair call.'

The Maori opened a door to a tiny, windowless room. There was a single bed, washstand and tiny dresser. The ceiling globe cast a smoky blue light.

'Very classy,' Dave said to the Maori bouncer as he went in.

'I'll thump you,' offered the Maori, mildly.

Dave took out thirty pounds and gave it to the Maori, and then another two hundred pounds and handed it to the young guy. He peeled off his Telstra shirt and his pants. The French kid was doing the same but watching Dave very warily.

As they swapped clothes Dave became aware of a slightly different tenor to the general commotion downstairs. He could hear a loud Aussie voice. 'Let's go darlin'. I like 'em big and meaty, like me. Up this way? Fifty euros eh? Only place in the world where the prices haven't gone up. You know, I reckon I've been in here before. Hope they've changed the sheets.' The Aussie swayed into the doorway. It was the older businessman from Perth, from Schiphol. He was puffing from the stairs, his face bright red and sweaty.

'You,' said Dave in alarm.

'Oh, sorry. Room's full huh?' He winked at Dave then fixed his eyes on the French kid now dressed in Dave's Telstra shirt.

One of the African prostitutes had pushed up onto the landing outside the room, and the Australian bumped into her as he turned away. 'Changed my mind.'

'Hey,' said the Maori looking from Dave to the other Australian. 'What's going on?'

The Aussie pulled a mobile phone from his pocket and said, 'Contact. Go, go, go.'

The Maori slammed him to the wall. The African prostitute screamed, her bright red bra and the landing wobbling dangerously.

Dave grabbed the red and blue parka and started out of the tiny room, squeezing upstairs through the threesome of large people on the landing.

The front door was being pounded. The French guys and the other

African prostitutes howled and pushed back against the door. 'Descente de police!'

Dave clambered up another flight of stairs, turning to see the Maori and the Aussie grappling on the landing. The French youth ran down the stairs. The front door gave way and uniformed policemen pushed through the screaming Africans and yelling French. They rugby-tackled the Telstra shirt. Then the Australian and the Maori fell, tumbling down onto all of them amidst the screams and yells of a pretty good scrum pack.

Dave raced around the bend and found an open window. There was a fire escape and he slithered down it into a series of alleys filled with garbage and the smell of urine and the sound of many scurrying things, smaller than Dave.

Dave came out further up the street. The flashing blue mixed prettily with the red lights coming from the brothel window and the yellow from the street lamps. It was the light. It was frozen in balls in the night like … like …

Dave nearly crashed into Margaret, who was berating a man in staccato Dutch. She turned to see Dave in surprise. 'Angus!'

'You speak Dutch,' Dave said.

'I shouldn't come along here at night,' she said, indicating the departing man. 'Nice jacket.'

'I'm trying to blend in, like a native.'

'I'm never going to get rid of you, am I?'

'Can't fight good luck.'

She raised an eyebrow, but then took in the commotion down the street. 'Actually, if you wouldn't mind, you can escort me out of here. I'm getting sick of the attention.'

'Okay. Can we eat?'

They went away from the police action, Margaret switching into tour guide mode. She'd explained on the plane that as part of her travel agency she regularly saw the sights so she could tell her clients first-hand where to go. She'd already told Dave where to go a few times by that stage. As they walked Margaret pointed out historic areas, listed the seafaring history of the Dutch and explained why the cyclists might be getting angry with him – because he kept blundering across the dedicated cycle lanes.

And then they were back by another canal and standing in the middle of a high stone bridge looking at the yellow lights flickering in the dark water. She pointed across the canal. 'There's a wonderful restaurant up there next to Amstel Diamonds.'

The sign looked familiar. Dave looked to the other side of the canal. 'You're not going to believe this, but I live up that way.'

'You're kidding! You don't. In one of those gorgeous houses?'

'A little closer to the waterline.'

'What does that mean?'

'I'm in a houseboat.'

'How wonderful. That's not a bad idea for tours. You know. Fly to Amsterdam and stay on a canal.'

'Well, I don't think they'd be keen staying on mine. More your hovel boat.'

'Oh? Why are you staying there?'

'Ah, that's a long story.'

'You seem to be good at those.' She stood smiling at him, some lamplights gleaming from her eyes.

'Enough about me. Let's talk about you and me.'

'Is this hovel boat one of your compulsions?'

'Huh?'

'On the plane. You said you were the impulsive type. Compulsive impulsive I think you said.'

'And you remembered. Told you I'd wear you down.'

'I think it was somewhere after Singapore. Not that you wore me down. But I must have been listening at some point.'

'Ah, good, I think.' There was a small boat coming along the canal with its lights on. Dave looked towards the Amstel Diamonds sign and where he supposed food was cooking. Margaret didn't seem in any hurry to leave the bridge.

He said, 'I was listening to everything you said. I believe you told me you were married.'

'Yes?'

'But there's no ring.'

'Maybe I'm simply not wearing it.'

'And maybe you were lying.'

'Why would I do that?' She smiled. She was enjoying herself.

'Maybe you thought it would put me off.'

'Whereas it made no difference whatsoever.'

'Maybe.'

'You are right. I am a liar.' She was flirting and she was good at it.

'Are you?'

'What?'

She studied him a moment, then looked towards the Diamonds sign. 'It looks too busy.' There were some Volvos and a dark van all manoeuvring for parking spots nearby.

She suddenly squeezed Dave's arm and said, 'Let's go to your houseboat.'

Dave could not quite believe his luck. He managed to gasp, 'Yes.'

She took back her hand and looked down, a little shy, but then she looked up and said, 'See, I can be impulsive too.'

Dave leant to kiss her, but she stepped past and he missed.

*

He lit the lamp and turned it down. Margaret stood examining the inside of the houseboat.

'So you reckon it might not make your tour list, huh?'

'It did look better before you lit the lamp. Authentic would be the real estate word.' She went to the window and looked out on the water. 'Must be a policeman's birthday.'

Dave went to the window and looked out. 'What do you mean?'

'At the restaurant.' She looked at him.

'What?'

'The police Volvos. The vans with tinted windows.'

Dave looked across the water. 'Are they?'

She drew the curtains and they both straightened together and she kissed him. It was gentle and she tasted like white wine, but as he tried to kiss her more fully she stepped back, crinkling her nose.

'Hold that thought, lover. I believe you smell.'

'Testosterone?'

'Possibly. Or twenty hours on a plane with a hint of three different kinds of very cheap Middle Eastern perfume.'

'Ah. I stink huh?'

She nodded, still smiling. 'Nothing a shower and shave and clean teeth and nakedness won't fix.'

Dave's mind went blank, like he'd put everything on the last race and was waiting for the start.

She was speaking again. 'What say I meet you in there?' She pointed to the bunk under the stairs.

'You bet.'

*

Campbell looked from the bunk bed to Margaret to Dave and then down to Dave's shrunken aspiration. 'Ye just met her?' He didn't look like he believed any of it.

'On the plane,' said Dave.

'And the brothel?' asked the Indian.

'Getting a jacket. It was cold. Speaking of which.' Dave gestured towards the pile of clothes by the bathroom door.

'Well, whatever was going to happen won't now,' said Margaret with what Dave was sure was regret. A lot of regret. 'If you'll excuse me gentlemen?' She took a step to get past Campbell, but he grabbed her handbag.

'Hey,' said Dave.

'Ah doon't like surprises. Let's see who we've ... Ah. Deary, deary me.' He pulled a plastic bag full of uncut diamonds out of Margaret's handbag.

Dave stood blinking, hurt.

'Sorry, Angus. They looked valuable, and well, I did tell you I was a liar. I suppose I'm also a thief. Nothing personal.' She fluttered her eyelashes.

'Evidently not,' said Dave, feeling further diminished.

'Whit ye goot gooin' here, Angus?' asked Campbell. 'A doublecross?' He looked over to Karushi then to Dave again.

'Why would I travel all this way before I did it, if that's what I was going to do?'

Campbell passed the plastic bag of stones to Karushi, who had his briefcase open on the table.

'Gentlemen,' said Margaret, edging towards the stairs. 'You've said nothing yet that in any way implicates anyone. So, I know nothing and I'd rather not know anything.'

'It's no' up to ye to "rather" anything,' said Campbell, continuing to block her.

Dave said, magnanimously under the circumstances, 'Come on. No harm, no foul. You've got the stones.'

'We'll see aboot that.' Campbell looked towards the table. 'Karushi?'

The Indian had an eyeglass to his eye, examining the stones. He scratched one with a metal prod.

Dave thought he heard a thump outside. Maybe dripping water. Margaret seemed to have heard it too.

Campbell was watching the Indian. 'Well?'

'Mostly shit,' he said in his thick London accent. He flicked a smaller rock away. It shimmered. 'This one's gem quality. The rest are industrial. And no pinks as requested.'

Dave nodded knowingly.

'Speak fookin' English,' growled Campbell.

'Geologically, these are them. A lot of fuckin' fuss for not too much. But it's what the Gov ordered.' He shrugged, good soldier.

Another thump. Then a loud voice outside. It was a woman, yelling in Dutch.

Campbell looked up.

In spite of her rather tight skirt, Margaret launched a sudden but seemingly precise kick, karate style, into Campbell's knee.

He fell to the floor, groaning. She picked up her handbag and stepped smoothly up over him onto the steps. He grabbed her ankle before she could go further, but Dave launched himself across the room onto Campbell's shoulder. Margaret scampered up the steps.

Dave heard her say, 'I owe you one, Angus.' He didn't have time to reply, because something hit him on the head.

*

Dave woke but didn't open his eyes. He could hear Campbell talking.

'Och, naw, Mr Dewar. He was as surprised as anyone. No' t'first lad to be ripped aff by his dick.' Dave could feel the slight movement of water under the barge. He was shivering.

A voice talked through a phone like the echo of an angry bee. Dave opened one eye. Campbell was on a mobile. 'Ye wahnt ah tae dae 'im and bring t'stones?'

Dave tried to see if there was anything he might use as a weapon.

'Oh aye.' Campbell clicked off the phone and turned to Karushi. 'Change of plans. We're tae bring 'im tae Glasgow. Have ye got t'condoms?'

Dave sat up. 'Whoa there. Now I know this is Amsterdam, but ...'

'Doon't flatter yirself, Angus. Get dressed. What did ye think ye were goonae dae wi' that wee thing?'

'It's cold.'

As Dave got dressed, Karushi funnelled batches of the tiny stones into each condom.

'Hope ye've an appetite,' said Campbell pulling a bottle of scotch from the briefcase. He filled a tumbler and pushed it across the table towards Dave.

'Good news, Angus,' said Karushi. 'We thought we'd have to do this.'

Dave took a gulp of the whisky. 'So how much money, again?'

'Twenty thousand.'

Dave eyed the growing pile of condoms.

'And we won't kill you.'

*

Dave stood uneasily near the departure gate in Schiphol. His legs were rubbery, partly from all the whisky he'd drunk, but also from the strange sensations the lumps in his stomach were causing.

Karushi pushed a cheap backpack under his arm. 'The hotel address is in the bag.'

Campbell patted him on the shoulder. 'Ye wait there until we come. Naw wee love affairs.'

Dave nodded. He was pushed towards the departure gate. He walked very carefully.

He sat very still on the plane. He didn't try to make new friends.

He asked the taxi driver in Edinburgh to go round corners as slowly as he could.

He stood against the wall of the charmless white and magenta room of the Jurys Inn trying to work with rather than against the movements inside his body. There was a faint smell of vinegar somewhere in the room. The condoms of rough diamonds continued their slow progress like obese worms heading south. The whisky had worn off.

The battered telephone shrilled centimetres from his ear.

The vigorous Australian voice at the other end said, 'Ken, it's Bruce. A quick call while you're alone. Mal's still in hospital in the Netherlands, but he'll be here soon. Okay?'

'Okay,' said Dave.

'I'm still with you, mate.'

'Mate.'

'Here they come.'

Bruce rang off. Dave had no idea who Bruce was or why he had called or who Mal was, but he'd sounded Australian and that was comforting so many kilometres from home.

The hotel room door opened and the Glaswegian Campbell and London-Indian Karushi walked in to find Dave holding the phone.

'For fook's sake, whit's going on noo?'

'Room service. I ... more whisky?'

Campbell studied him, but Dave closed his eyes, still standing.

'Naw, ye already have a full toommy. It's time to retrieve oor packages.'

'I've got a bit of bad news about that. I'm not ready.'

There was a pause. Dave heard the telephone dialling.

'We're here, but we have a wee hold-up. The stupid bastard's constipated.'

Dave could hear the other side of the conversation. Another Scottish voice. 'Noo matter. T'woman in Holland bothers me. Bring him tae Perth. Ah'll meet ye at Scone Castle.'

'Scone Castle!' exclaimed Campbell.

'Aye. I want ye tae take t'train up. Look tae see if ye're being followed. There's something no' right here.'

Karushi fed Dave Indian takeaway on the train up to Perth. There were lots of lentils. 'To get things moving, like.'

An ancient castle crouched atop an outcrop above Stirling. It had clung there for centuries, a piece of historic tenacity that Dave found alarming. Each bump and roll of the train brought aftertastes of the Indian food. Dave sweated. Dave winced. Dave tried not to think about anything, especially when the train entered tunnels.

On another day Dave might have been quite interested to discover that there was another place called Perth in the world. He might have relished the ancient stone wall the taxi drove through and the ivy-covered battlements and lush grounds of Scone Castle. But today he had more immediate concerns. There were tourist buses in the car park and a line of old people winding towards four portable loos not quite hidden behind a screen of bushes. They were frail people easily pushed aside by a driven younger man.

'I gotta go,' said Dave.

'No' yet,' said Campbell.

They led Dave, who walked with a stoop, towards a small church on a small hill in front of the castle.

A ruddy man in his mid-fifties sat on a worn sandstone block. 'Angus, or should ah say Ken,' he said in the thick Scottish accent Dave had heard on random telephones across the globe. The man stood and raised his arms to encompass all that they could see. 'Welcome tae centre of Scotland, laddie. Home tae oor true government for at least thirteen hundred years.'

'Uh, huh.'

'Ah'm James Dewar and this hill is Boot Hill because t'lords of every kingdom would regularly arrive here and empty their boots of dirt. Dirt from their own dear lands tae swear fealty tae their king. And over centuries they made this hill.'

'Yup,' said Dave, when Dewar paused.

'And noo ye've brought a little of yir own land here, and ah need ye tae empty yir boots, so tae speak.'

'Gladly.' Dave looked hopefully towards the tourist line at the toilets down the hill.

'This stone is a copy.' Dewar was pointing to the sandstone block he'd been sitting on. 'T'Stone of Scone is where oor kings were made, but fookin' Edward ripped it off. Held it, and Scotland, tae ransom in fookin' Westminster Abbey.'

'Ah, about emptying my, ah, boots.'

'Oi. Ah huvnae finished. Ye see t'Scots heard Edward was a coomin', so ye think they let him get t'real stone?' Dewar tapped the side of his nose and grinned like an insane person. 'It's somewhere, but no' in Westminster and no' in Edinburgh.' He tapped his nose again, leering at Dave. 'T'Scottish huv nivver given up on oor fight wi' England.'

'Good for you.'

Dewar looked at Dave with clear disappointment. He looked at Campbell and Karushi and then back at Dave. 'Ah wis led tae believe Australians are noo friend tae English.'

'Um, well, you know. I think we got a lot of it out of our system when we made *Breaker Morant* and started winning at the cricket. And we didn't let them get the real Rolf Harris.'

Dewar looked confused.

Dave said, 'I'm more a mercenary than a revolutionary. Sorry.'

Dewar threw his hands up in disgust. 'Aye.' He said to Karushi, 'Over t'graveyard.'

Dave turned and started trotting down the hill, like a hobbled prisoner, towards where Dewar had pointed. On consideration, he'd take the graveyard. Two young hikers who had been taking photographs of the chapel scrambled back away from them.

Karushi caught up with Dave and directed him under an arch and around into the old much-breached wall of the cemetery. He handed Dave a plastic shopping bag and pointed to some particularly high moss-covered headstones.

'You're kidding.'

'Hurry up before the tourists come.'

'No peeking.'

Karushi turned away.

Dave got behind the largest headstone and took down his pants and felt a surge of relief. But then the relief was replaced by pain, the pain of attempting to squeeze particularly large, non-viscous ...

'Aye, thankyou, Ken. You don't need to explain this part in quite so much detail,' said Colley.

'We have photographs,' said Bruce.

'I thought I heard a camera shutter.'

'I had to give the camera to Bruce ... I mean Sergeant Roberts, ma'am. I couldn't ...'

'Focus?' offered Dave. 'Have you ever fallen off your push bike and used your knees as the primary means of slowing? Well the inside of my arse felt a bit like that.'

'Internally abraded,' offered Van Shooten.

'Quite. Move on please, Ken.'

Dave and Karushi headed back, Karushi holding the plastic bag out in front of him, as far as his arm would allow.

'Did you hear cameras?' asked Karushi.

'Nothing but.'

Dewar and Campbell met them on the path near the entrance to the castle. When Karushi handed over the bag Dewar exclaimed, 'Ye could huv washed it.'

'Where?' Karushi wiped his hands on the stone block.

Dave, who felt bruised and abused but otherwise better, said, 'Well, I've done my bit. More stones for Scotland and all that. Go the revolution. Now will that be cheque or cash?'

Dewar looked around in alarm. 'No' here, man. Go wi' t'lads. There's a hire car in t'car park.'

'What, I can poop here, but not get paid?'

'Go wi' Campbell, Ken.' Dewar turned away, holding the bag out to his side, downwind from his nose.

*

Dave was pushed to a tiny jellybean of a hire car, a bright blue Ford Ka. Campbell looked at the key to the car in disgust.

Karushi said, 'Coulda got us a man's car.'

'Ah hope naw one sees us in this thing,' said Campbell unlocking the driver's door. 'In t'back, Angus.'

'Look, I'm sure you fellas need to get on with things. So, here's fine.

It doesn't have to be exactly twenty thousand pounds. A tip for your troubles is only fair.'

'Shut up,' said Campbell pulling back his jacket to reveal the gun Dave had always suspected he had.

'How about this. You keep everything and I'll chalk it up to experience.'

'Get in the back.'

*

They drove. They didn't talk. Campbell put on the radio. ABBA. Dave's luck was turning from very bad to worse. Karushi changed the station. Bono. Cruel and unusual. Campbell turned the radio off. They passed a sign. Birnam Wood.

'Like in Macbeth?' asked Dave.

'No idea,' said Karushi.

They turned down a narrow road and passed four quaint houses before it ended at a walking track leading into the wood. Ancient trees and leaf-covered ground sloped down towards the railway track.

Campell and Karushi got out. Campbell pushed forward the driver's seat so Dave could squeeze past.

'I'll stay here.'

'Act like a man.'

'As opposed to acting like a body you mean?'

'Ah wahnt tae talk tae ye, man. Dewar wis clear. Find oot aboot t'woman in Amsterdam before ye pay this wee dick. But if ye like, ah can drag ye oot and shoot ye.'

Dave didn't like the way that oot and shoot rhymed so well.

Campbell signalled with the gun and Dave climbed out. They skittered down the slope towards the railway tracks.

'The woman in Amsterdam. Convince me ye wirnae working on this taegither.'

'I think I've pretty much established I'm a poor judge of character. And impulsive – compulsively.'

The leaves crunched as they walked. Perhaps there was too much crunching for three sets of feet. Moss covered the rocks and fallen branches.

Dave tried to think of something that might delay his death so that he could buy some time to think of something that might save his life.

'This'll dae,' said Campbell.

'Wait,' said Dave. He reached for his own arse, hoping to save it. 'I think I've still got another package.'

Campbell looked to Karushi, who shrugged.

'Ye dinae count them?' accused Campbell.

'No, I didn't watch them come out. I didn't count them and I didn't wash them. I forgot my scales too and I didn't weigh them.'

'I didn't count them either,' said Dave.

Karushi produced a knife.

'Don't move. Police,' called a familiar male Australian voice.

Dave turned to see two backpackers walking towards them through the trees; a pretty young woman and a tall young man with a familiar tanned face.

'Yes, you, Bruce, but I didn't know that then.'

'But you've known it since the airport in Perth.'

'Nope.'

'I told you,' said Mal. 'No idea, not from the start.'

'Gentlemen, nearly there. Ken, please.'

'Certainly, Inspector.'

The girl backpacker said, 'Come along then. Put your weapons down.' She was blonde with slender long pale legs. She pulled a wallet from her pocket and flashed a badge. 'PC Rowntree.'

The male backpacker grinned at the forest like a new party guest.

'The Bill?' said Karushi.

'Fook,' said Campbell.

They both dropped their weapons.

The police kept coming forward, trying not to slip on the loose leaves as they edged down the slope.

PC Rowntree said, 'Graeme Campbell and Rafi Karushi, you're under arrest.'

'Graeme?'

'Oi, whit's wrong wi' it?'

'I just didn't know your name, like.' Karushi smiled and bent to pick up his knife.

Dave looked back toward the police, noticing the same thing Karushi must have.

Karushi said, 'They don't have guns, Graeme.'

As Campbell bent for his gun, Dave moved behind the nearest tree.

Campbell said, 'Ye doon't have guns, ye bloody idiots.'

'I'm giving you a chance here, Campbell,' said Rowntree.

'And ah'm taking that chance.' Campbell took aim.

The Aussie cop stepped in front of Rowntree protectively. Rowntree said, 'Hey,' and slapped at his back.

Dave came around the other side of the tree and screamed, 'Ahhhhhhh!'

Campbell turned as Dave whacked down on his arm with the lump of tree branch he'd found. He dropped the gun and Karushi bent for it, but the Aussie policeman leapt into the Indian's back and Dave brought the branch down again on Campbell's arm.

'Nice work, Ken,' said that familiar voice.

Before Dave could ask him who the hell he was, Rowntree stepped forward and said, 'You three are under arrest.'

'Me too?' said Dave.

*

Dave was led into an interview room, already full of a number of familiar if unnamed faces. A short woman with fierce eyes and an important police uniform seemed to be in charge. 'Ken,' she said in a soft Scottish accent. 'It is grand to finally meet you.' She indicated the only chair on the door side of the table. 'I am Inspector Colley.'

Dave sat, beaming at them. 'And nice to see everybody too. Can I save you some time? I confess. I'm an illegal alien and I accept I will be deported.'

'Ha, yes. I believe you know Detective Sergeant Malcolm Kemp.'

She pointed to the big red-faced bloke from Perth who'd also appeared in the brothel. He had a black eye and didn't smile.

'Detective Sergeant Roberts.' She indicated the tanned Aussie who'd winked at him in Perth airport and who'd recently rescued him dressed as a hiker in the woods.

'You're a legend, Ken,' he said. 'Dead set. Call me Bruce.'

'And this is our PC Rowntree, seconded from Nottingham.'

She had changed from her hiking clothes into a police uniform. She nodded, rosy-cheeked and clear-eyed.

'Hang on,' said Dave, recalling recent events, 'Why have I been arrested? I saved their lives.'

'Well,' said Bruce, 'I'd like to think the saving was mutual.'

'Yes. Each other's lives, as things evolved,' said Rowntree.

'I understand, Ken, that you have been working with Sergeants Kemp and Roberts since Australia.'

There was a cough. It was from the tall thin man that Dave had seen in Schiphol airport. He was wearing a different, but beautifully fitted, suit.

'And this is our Dutch friend, Brigadier Van Shooten, who, in the spirit of a united Europe, is also along for the ride it appears.'

Van Shooten grimaced, but stood and offered his hand. 'Amsterdam,' he said.

'Ah, of course,' said Dave, wise yet circumspect. He felt like he'd stumbled into the official surrender ceremony at the end of a war. What was most confusing was that he seemed to be the victor.

Van Shooten said, 'Any Serbians yet? Montenegro mentioned?'

'And now you're in Scotland, Ken, and I inherit ye,' interrupted Colley with a glare.

'And like I said, I surrender. You can toss me, like an old caber, out of your very fine country.'

Colley smiled again. It was a polite smile, acknowledging but not enjoying an attempted joke. 'No, we have some more work for ye.' She was still smiling, still without humour.

'You're still on the team, Ken,' said Bruce.

'The pay's nonexistent, the working conditions are lousy, and I'm absolutely unsuited to it. I'm going to retire.'

'You're being modest,' said Van Shooten. 'I have seen you operate. Very good.' The Dutchman gave a precise little nod.

Colley cut across him again. 'The original charge against ye is still pending, I believe.'

'It's still that same deal, Ken,' said Mal, still studying Dave.

'Original charge?'

'The diamond theft from Argyle.'

'Ah ha. It's probably time I cleared up a few things. I'm not Ken.'

Dave looked around at the room full of police. Colley was smiling her waiting smile. They were all waiting it seemed for a punchline.

'I found these stones in the middle of the desert in Australia. Your Ken was dead. A car accident. There was a little tree. I'm a telecom worker. Dave Kelly. Innocent victim of mistaken identity. Um, well ... the rest has kind of just happened, really.'

There was a moment's silence, then Bruce leant forward. 'But Ken, your slick moves at Perth airport, the quick change in the brothel.'

'Your evasions of two separate surveillance teams!' It was Shooten.

'Scone Castle. The woods?' Rowntree.

It appeared to Dave that they thought he was a master spy of Bourne proportions instead of an alternately very lucky and unlucky son of a bitch.

All except Mal, perhaps. He leaned back and said, 'How about a few corroborating details then, old son.' He'd lost a tooth in the tumble down the brothel stairs.

Colley leaned forward, 'Please, from the beginning, Ken.'

'Dave. Dave Kelly.'

*

Deidre gave another little yelp and shuddered. Dave sighed long. He rolled from her, groaning as his injured elbow pushed into the mattress.

'Ye're a noisy lover, Angus,' said Deidre in a pleasingly dreamy voice.

'Likewise.'

They both snuggled naked under the thick doona in the morning chill. Deidre's bed was in the corner of Deidre's one-room stone hut on the edge of a lake on one of the islands of the Outer Hebrides. There was a kitchen table and a sink and a wood stove. Everything except the big flat-screen television seemed from 1830 or thereabouts.

'How are yir aches and pains?' she asked.

Dave felt his face. There were swellings, cuts and abrasions; mementos from Deidre's two suitors, as Dave suddenly recalled.

'So, who's winning then?' said Dave. 'Harris from Lewis, or Lewis from Harris?'

She thought about this before she said, 'It's no' so much them winnin', as me gettin' tired and startin' tae lose. Maybe ah jus' wan' a bit o' fun before men and life happen tae me. It's grey country oot there,' she said, pointing sadly at the tiny window over the sink. 'When ta sun shines, stand in it.'

'Ah, where I come from, we say it's a brown land. When it rains, drink it.'

'Ye're full o' it, Angus.'

'I'm not. I'm a truth teller. Cross my heart.'

'How the hell did ye manage to talk yir way intae ma bed?'

*

Dave met Deidre on a hilltop in the drizzling rain on a road on the Isle of Lewis off the west coast of Scotland.

He had left Ullapool on the car ferry at twilight. Ullapool was a picture postcard of white terraces overlooking the harbour. There were lochs amidst mountains. Fishing boats bobbed. Tourists wandered. Daytripping couples stood about in romantic fug.

Dave had managed to get a little sleep on the ferry but still had a nagging twinge some way along his intestines.

The ferry reached Stornoway at dawn. Stornoway was not cute like Ullapool. It was a working port with industry and bigger shops and lots of businesses all owned by the MacLeods. Even the castle looked pragmatic.

Dave went into an eatery called the Coffee Pot.

A cook was pushing plates of breakfast to a dockworker. When the cook looked up, Dave said, 'Toasted bacon and egg sandwich?'

The cook stepped back, eyeing Dave suspiciously.

The cook said, 'We don't dae toasted sandwiches.'

'Oh. Bacon and eggs with toast thanks.'

'No.'

Dave looked bewildered. He was bewildered. He looked up at the bacon and eggs on the menu and back to the cook, who held her ground.

Dave said, 'You've run out?'

'We don't dae toast.'

Dave missed Amsterdam. He hadn't asked for toast there, but he thought they'd offer it. In fact, was pretty sure they'd offer to toast just about anything.

'It's a custom.'

    'Well, I guessed that.'

    'Ye were in Amsterdam?'

    'That's another story.'

Dave looked around the cafe to see if there was any evidence of toast on other plates. About half the patrons held their hands away from their plates so he could see they had no toast. But the others crouched forward, holding their hands in front, hiding their eating business. Clearly the patrons were listening to every word.

Dave was still trying to work out why they wouldn't do toast. Whether it was religious, or perhaps a political act of defiance against the English, or whether the toaster was broken.

Finally he asked, 'What would you eat with bacon and eggs?'

'A bap ye sumph.' She flicked a smile over Dave's shoulder at the other customers.

'Sounds good to me. Bacon, eggs and a bap ye sumph, thanks.'

'A bap is a breakfast roll.'

    'Yes. I found one on my plate.'

    'A sumph is a dunderhead.'

    'Ah, I thought it might be something like that. I understood the tone.'

Dave made no new friends while he ate breakfast. He made no new friends as he wandered Stornoway. He found MacLeod's Tote Betting Shop and watched stocky horses finish a steeplechase.

'What do you fancy in the next?' Dave said to the only man in the place.

'Not mine to do that,' he said, skittling back behind the counter.

'What's your favourite number?' asked Dave.

'Doon't have one,' he said.

Dave took out fifty pounds and laid it on the counter. He said, 'Want to cut cards?'

'Ye're no' fae round here, are ye?'

Dave shook his head. 'Is there a horse number twenty-two in the next race?'

'Nae.'

'Oh. I had a lucky feeling about that. Hmm. Okay. Eleven?'

'Aye.'

'Fifty pounds on eleven to win.'

'To win!'

'Yes.'

The man wrote out a chit, eyeing Dave.

Dave asked, 'Do you have a telephone directory?'

The man studied Dave, seeming to try to gauge what unspeakable kind of frivolity Dave might make with it, but finally gave the barest of shrugs before getting the directory from under the counter. It was slim.

Dave looked up Dewar.

'Dewar!'

'Yes, Dewar. I told you that when we met.'

'Ye still haven't said why?'

'I'm getting to it.'

'Going ta long way for fook's sake.'

'Will you let me finish?'

There were a few Dewars, but not many. Dewar, James. Ardvourlie Castle, Loch Seaforth, Isle of Harris. Well, as easy as that. Except that Dave was on the Isle of Lewis.

'Oi, yir race is on.'

Dave looked up at the relevant television and the horses running. He looked back down to his chit and then up to find horse number eleven. It was five back on the outside and looking strong. He looked down at his stomach then his chest. His breathing was relaxed, his heart sleeping. The horse, his horse, was making its move. It was third then even first then maybe second. It would lose by a nose. Dave monitored his internals. No rush. No hit. Nothing.

The teller grinned with three top teeth. 'Ye knew. Dinae ye?'

Dave shrugged, seeing him count out a couple of hundred pounds.

'Ye're the grumpiest winner ah huv seen.'

'Can I hire a boat to go to Harris Island?'

'Aye, at MacLeod's. Be easier tae drive.'

'From Lewis to Harris?'

'Aye. Tis only twenty mile by road.'

'So, because I'm a bit slow on new concepts, I can drive from the island of Lewis to the island of Harris?'

'Aye. If ye can get a car.'

'Which ye couldna.'

'Only the bike.'

'Lot of hills.'

'In my country we have water between islands. It's what makes them islands.'

'Ta Isle of Lewis and Harris is surrounded by water and is off ta coast of Scotland. It's an island.'

'But not two. Just one, with two names.'

'Aye, ye sumph.'

The Isle of Lewis, part of the island of Lewis and Harris, contained few obviously particular geophysical features. There were no trees. There were many rolling hills of bog and rock. There was lots of water: lakes and puddles and rain. Sometimes the rain fell hard and blew sideways and hit Dave's skin like cold, sharp stones. When the rain eased, it stopped falling and just hung in the air, generally rather than specifically wet.

Dave pedalled, his bright red and blue coat sodden and heavy. He had not been able to hire a car and had to buy his bicycle outright for a ridiculous sum from a lounging young MacLeod. The young MacLeod had given Dave a particularly disrespectful grin which made Dave wonder if he actually owned the bike. He now believed the look of ridicule to be about Dave's intention to ride.

Dave rode into the wind between five modern houses sitting amidst ruined stone crofts, constituting another tiny village. Black-faced sheep wandered the road. He caught sight of distant lochs as the hills grew steeper.

An hour after setting out Dave had to stop pedalling and push the bike to the top of a very steep hill. He turned to see a jeep coming up the hill. A battered jeep. He looked up at the next hill and could see many hills beyond. He stepped out into the middle of the road and waved down the jeep.

'Who's this eejit ridin' in the rain? He's in ta road aboot to be run doon.'
'You stopped.'
'Aye. An' lucky for ye.'
'Very lucky indeed.'

The jeep pulled up next to Dave. The window wound down to reveal a tangle-haired beauty. Her hair was red and her eyes green. She had a light sprinkling of tiny freckles on her high cheekbones. Dave had fallen in love.

'Ye have nae shame.'

'Are ye lost?' she asked.
    'No. But I want a lift. It's wet and cold and I'm knackered.'
    'Ye should be, for all ta sense that's in yir head.'
    Dave gave his sheepish, winning, little boy grin.

'Ta what?'

Dave smiled and she looked him up and down. *'S fheàrr a bhith dhìth a chinn na a bhith a dhìth an fhasain,'* she said.
    Dave said, 'In my country that means, yes, hop in.'
    'It is better tae be without yir head than tae be without style,' she translated.
    'Um, hmm. Good saying. Meaning I have some?'

'Ye gave that cheeky smile again.'

'You had mud smudges on your cheek. I didn't want to say anything about it at the time.'

'Dave Kelly,' said Dave huddling into his heavy wet jacket, as she jerked through the gears of the jeep.

'From Australia, where they goo oot in ta rain with nae protection.'

'Only rains at night there,' said Dave, deadpan, so she turned in confusion before she saw he was joking.

'Ah'm only away tae Baile Ailein.'

Dave took out the damp tourist map he'd bought on the ferry. 'Baile Ailein is Balallan, right?'

'Aye, in yir English map, aye.'

'How many hills between Balallan and Ardvourlie?'

'Why are ye away there?'

Dave thought he heard a trace of suspicion. 'See the sights. I want to see where the island of Harris meets the island of Lewis without water in between.'

'Ye're wearing a lot of ta water in between. It's a fair ride, but Ardvourlie is before ta beinn. Beinn Dearg.'

The countryside got prettier, the flat bog giving way to more grass and lochs and tumbledown crofts as they drove south. Passing cars tooted horns and she waved as she explained that the newer, plainly rendered houses were part of an island renewal in the 1960s.

'I'm Dave, by the way.'

'Ye said.'

'But you never said your name.'

'Aye.'

'Oh. Aye. Ye Scoots rrrr a coony loot.'

'Aye. We huv tae be. Because mostly people come and take things from us.'

'You got me. I was going to take your name. I was going to use it instead of Dave.'

She smiled.

'Did not.'

'Did.'

She smiled, but then pulled up at a junction that pointed to Leumrab-hagh.

'Ah'm away doon there.'

'And I'm away up there?'

'Aye, so ye say.'

'Thanks for the lift. I think the rain's passed.'

She shook her head at his obvious sumph-dom.

Dave got his bike out of the back and came back to her window.

'If ye're really sightseeing, there's nowhere to stay doon Ardvourlie. Ye doon't want tae try ta bealach. There's a hotel up here.' She pointed down the road she was about to turn into, where Dave could see a bigger building.

Dave gave her a smile and said, 'In my country we have a saying too. You're a bloody lifesaver.'

'Why are ye gooin' to Ardvourlie?'

'A guy owes me money.'

'If it's Dewar, ye won't get it.'

*

And that was that, Dave thought. He mounted his bike again, feeling a short spasm of pain in his abdomen. He pedalled, looking at the approaching mountains with the faintest of hearts. But then he came into the tiny settlement of Ardvourlie, in the shadow of the mountains. There was a loch called Seaforth on his map and a lone fishing boat headed in or out, sending slow glistening ripples in its late afternoon wake. There were sheep and small farms and finally a large country house, improbably signed Ardvourlie Castle.

Dave got off his bike and collapsed on the side of the road near an abandoned two-room schoolhouse. He fished in his pocket for Dewar's address. He looked up as a hire car went past. Lucky bastard, he thought, before he recognised the driver when she stopped at the junction.

Dave leaned back into the roadside fernery, not wanting Margaret to see him. The Margaret who he'd sat next to on the plane. The Margaret who'd left him naked and about to be truncheoned on the barge in Amsterdam. She looked up and down the road for cars and then drove through the gate and down the long driveway towards a hunting lodge that backed onto the loch.

'Who?'

    'Margaret St James.'

    'Who left ye naked?'

    'Yes. Well, another story. Not like now, with you. Warm and naked and not about to be truncheoned.'

    'Hmm.'

It was getting late and colder. Dave needed a plan. He decided to cycle back to the hotel the Lewis girl had pointed out. It was like coming home. There was a pool table, a dartboard and joke signs about being drunk. The big back window offered a view of the backs of small farms or houses. The pub went silent as Dave entered. They were sitting at tables in pairs and fours.

'You were there at a table in the corner, nursing a whisky.'

    'Aye.'

Dave ordered, 'Two whiskies.'

    The barman said, 'That's a bit like orderin' two beers in an Aussie pub, mate.' He pointed to the row upon row of different whisky bottles. 'It disnae narrow it doon much.'

    'Sounds like a man who's been in an Australian pub.'

    'Aye. Ah was there fir a few years.'

    'And you're back.'

    'Och aye. Everyone cooms back.'

    'Two of whatever she's drinking.'

    The publican grew solemn. He began to pour the two whiskies. He spoke to the orange brown liquid in the glasses. 'Ye might want tae be a wee bit careful when ye're in another rooster's yard.'

    Dave put money on the bar. 'Careful is my middle name. Cheers.' He took the whiskies over and sat.

    She looked at him like her luck had changed.

'Ha.'

'Ouch. Careful, I'm tender.'

'She looked at him like a stray cat, turnin' up tae be fed again.'

'So,' she said.

'Aye,' he said and took a sip.

The other patrons were shaking their heads at Dave. An old lady waggled her finger.

'Ye dinae get yir money,' she said.

'No. A very long ride for not much. So, he's not a popular local identity, huh?'

'He's no' local. He came here some years ago and started buyin' up bits of croft and cheatin' us, and trickin' stupid souse heads out of their land.'

She seemed bitter, Dave thought, from personal experience. 'Yeah, well I'm not a big fan myself.'

'Oh aye, but then doon't stand in ta fire.'

'Meaning my own fault right. See, I'm getting the hang of all these wise sayings.'

She looked towards the door suddenly but then back to Dave. Dave became aware that the pub had gone silent. He looked towards the door to see a big sandy-haired man in fishing clothes. The finger-waggling old lady was looking from the fisherman to Dave and back as at an imminent collision.

Dave said, 'This'd be the rooster yard reference.'

Deidre looked at Dave then to the publican where the fisherman was getting a drink. She said, 'If that means ah'm a brood hen, then aye.'

He came to their table and Dave realised he was much bigger than he'd looked over in the doorway. He said, 'Deidre.'

'Deidre!' said Dave. 'Deidre, I'm delighted to meet you.'

Deidre said, 'David Kelly from Australia, this be Lewis MacDonald from Harris.'

Dave stood and offered his hand. 'Must be confusing.'

Lewis engulfed Dave's hand with his own and squeezed. 'What would that be?'

'Lewis from Harris.'

'That's a good one,' he said, looking at Dave like warm beer.

Deidre spoke urgently then angrily in Gaelic.

Lewis spoke calmly back also in Gaelic.

Dave said, 'Uluru, Dwellingup, Balgas.' Dave smiled.

Lewis said, 'Ah doon't like ye, Ken.'

'Ken?' asked Deidre.

The publican said loudly, 'Harris MacLeod, ye're banned from here on Thursdays.'

Dave turned to see another giant fisherman in the doorway. This one had red hair.

The other patrons got up from their chairs and delicately lifted their drinks, moving back to the walls.

The publican brought up half a pool cue from under the bar.

Harris smiled towards Deidre's table. 'Well look at this fookin' get together. And ah wisnae invited.'

Lewis turned, flexing his biceps and fingers.

'Ye'll both be banned noo. Where's oor deal?' yelled the barman.

Dave turned to Deidre. 'Either you're very popular, or Lewis here isn't.'

'Ye'll no' be so smart with nae front teeth,' said Lewis, and Dave turned to make sure he was talking to Harris MacLeod.

'So, it's kind of a farmyard full of roosters and only one hen, then?'

Deidre scowled at him but then laughed out loud.

Harris MacLeod stepped forward. 'And who's this wee tiddler then?'

Lewis MacDonald said, 'Ye can wait yir turn. He's my'on first.'

'And who says ah'll wait. He can fish his own waters.'

Dave felt a surge of adrenalin. He said, 'They're talking about me, aren't they. Gentlemen, I know animal imagery. I come from the land of the kangaroo. Why don't you both hop off?'

MacDonald swung his first punch from his stomach coming up towards Dave's jaw. Dave saw the blur of it and swayed back but was still caught on the underside of his chin and crashed back into his chair. Deidre yelled, 'Ye stupid fookin' eejit. I'm talkin' here.' MacDonald looked down at him and MacLeod swung at MacDonald catching him on the side of the head. Dave heard yelling. There was wood breaking and glass smashing and a ringing in his head. He got up to see Deidre whacking the big redhead about the chest and arms with a whisky bottle. It was strong glass. Lewis MacDonald turned from fending off the barman to see Dave swaying by the table. He launched himself and they both crashed back into the wall. Lewis said, 'Ken, I'm yir contact. For the Dewar business.' 'Oh,' said Dave. 'Right, good. I need lots of help there.' 'Och, noo ye stay away from Deidre.' The publican yelled, 'Ye bucks rrr banned. Both of ye. An' ye, Deidre, ye're banned too. Ye're all banned.' Deidre nodded but she was behind Lewis raising the bottle to dong him. Dave never saw if she landed it because Lewis raised his fist and smashed it into Dave's face.

*

'And here I fell,' said Dave as he slid his head under the doona cover to find Deidre's wondrous breasts once more.

'Oh, aye, what ta cat dragged in,' she said with perhaps less than total enthusiasm. She patted his head then grabbed him by the back of the neck to haul him up to face her again. 'Wha's this Dewar business?'

'A story you might not believe.'

Deidre rolled out from under him and he watched her walk, white and naked, to her clothes. She pulled on a thick jumper and then hoisted her pants too quickly over her perfect firm white arse. She caught him looking and smiled. She said, 'Ah doon't believe anythin' ye say. No' a word.'

'Aye, there you go.'

Deidre went over to the sink and put on the kettle.

Dave sat up and felt a sudden pain he was beginning to recognise. 'Toilet?'

'Oot back.' She kept her back to him as he dressed.

'*That's the end of that then.*'

'*Maybe it was just the beginning.*'

'*You are so full of it, Dave.*'

'*Well, full of something, Terry. Coming to that. The point of this phone call.*'

Dave came out of Deidre's stone cabin and found his way behind. The farmhouse was made of stones with no obvious use of cement. It had two chimneys and an orange corrugated roof.

There was a lean-to shed with one stone wall and corrugated iron barely covering rusted bits of metal and the history of subsistence agriculture. Dave also noticed a collection of more modern, rusted radio bits and pieces amongst encrusted chook poo.

There were a couple of shaggy trees and a few shaggy sheep. The farm fell away steeply, a couple of paddocks going down to the edge of the loch. There was a small island not far out with a couple of low bent trees crouching away from the wind.

The toilet seemed a more modern addition of probably not much more than a hundred years.

Contrary to the beliefs of others, Dave was not full of shit. Not that morning. There was one laggardly condom filled with the diamond gravel. Dave supposed as he strained and wheezed that the previous night's fighting and fucking had finally dislodged it from a bend or cul-de-sac of his internal river.

He went over to a rocky creek that wound down one side of the farm and washed the thing in the freezing water.

Deidre came out with two mugs of strong tea. One of the chimneys was smoking.

'Ye'll be wantin' breakfast?' she asked.

'I could try, but I'm not sure food agrees with me.' Dave straightened, and watched Deidre quickly look away from the shape in his hands.

'One last link to the recent past,' he said. He pushed the condom into his pocket and took the mug of tea, putting both hands around it to draw some heat. 'Would you believe me if I told you that Dewar owes me money for diamond smuggling?'

'Ahh,' she said, turning to look across her farm. 'Ah,' she said again, like she'd just sat in a bath or seen an apple fall. Ah, like ah ha. 'An' Lewis?'

'Lewis?'

'Lewis from Harris. He said he was yir contact. Before ah brained him.'

'Apparently. So, you do believe me?'

She looked across her farm again then back to Dave. She shrugged, closed and watching him.

Dave took a sip of his tea. 'In my country, we have this big empty place called the outback. Apparently, it's not empty. It's chock-full of minerals.'

Dave told her about the car crash and the betting and his useless mate named Terry. Then he told her parts of some adventures in Amsterdam and Scone Castle. At times she smiled. She also looked stony-faced, mostly when he got to explaining his arrest.

*

The police from three or four countries left Dave with PC Rowntree and argued in the next room.

Colley said, 'Do ye believe him?'

Mal said, 'I've never believed him. Just following the diamonds.'

'Which still could be heading for the Pink Panthers,' said Van Shooten.

Colley said, 'My people are following Dewar. He's away back to Harris.'

'Then why are we wasting time here?' asked Van Shooten. 'If this is an international smuggling ring, we need to uncover it.'

'But the diamonds didn't go to Belgium. He met no one from Montenegro,' said Mal.

'That Ken let us see,' said Bruce. 'In the brothel. After the brothel. In the woods.'

'Dewar doesn't have any criminal convictions. Merely associations,' said Colley.

'Fine,' said Van Shooten. 'Then call Interpol. Call Europol. Give all our work over to them.'

There was a simmering silence. It was at this point that Rowntree must have realised that she was not the only one interested in the conversation in the next room. She got up from the interview table and closed the door.

'It was just getting interesting,' said Dave.

Rowntree said nothing. She folded her long stockinged legs back under the table.

Dave said, 'That's why it was so easy to get through all the airports. They let me.'

'They thought you were working for them, Ken,' she said, censorious, like a schoolteacher. Like a policeman. Dave forgot about her legs.

When the other police came back in, Dave said, 'On the barge, there was splashing and arguing.'

Van Shooten looked embarrassed.

Bruce said, 'A police diver was trying to get a look. A lady on the next barge didn't like him knocking over her pot plants.'

'Ah. Okay. Quite handy, when it happened, by the way.'

'Good,' said Van Shooten, 'because we want you to keep going after the diamonds.'

'No, I'm done. Quit while you're ahead. That's what I always say.'

'Harris is a wee place,' said Colley, 'and we think ye are the only one who can get close to him.'

'Folks. People. He told the two fellas you currently have in the holding cell to bump me off.'

'We don't believe he'll do it though, not on home soil. Not himself.'

Dave looked around at his brand new friends, a poker table full of unreadable eyes. 'You don't believe I'm Dave Kelly?'

Colley coughed, then looked to Mal. He looked like a beaten-up boxer who didn't know when to throw in the towel. He nodded to the inspector.

Colley said, 'Let us suppose as a kind of hypothetical that ye aren't Ken, and ye didn't steal the original diamonds. Let us, therefore, consider the more recent charges.'

'More recent?'

Van Shooten said, 'Diamond smuggling into Holland. We will do anything to protect the diamond trade.'

Mal said, 'Diamond theft. And smuggling out of Australia. Interference at the scene of an accident.'

Colley said, 'Fraud. Perverting the course of justice. The assault on poor old Campbell.'

Rowntree said, 'Desecration of a national shrine.'

They turned to her, askance.

'The cemetery,' she said. 'We have photographic evidence.'

'Extreme close-ups,' added Bruce, almost apologetically.

'Yes, we don't take kindly to illegal immigrants relieving themselves on our heritage.'

'Littering and exposure at the very least,' added Van Shooten.

'You're in the shit, Ken.'

'Dave.'

Mal said, 'Yeah. Ken had immunity while he helped us. You on the other hand don't even have that.'

*

'Ye're working for ta police?' said Deidre in disgust.

'Well, not so much working for, as parallel with, perhaps. Or, trying to run ahead of, you know like in the running of the bulls.'

Deidre looked at him again as if he was the stuff bulls left behind.

'Hard to believe, I know,' said Dave.

'Och, no. Ah believe ye. It all makes sense, noo. Ta diamonds anyway.' She turned and started to walk purposefully up along the creek.

Dave followed.

'This fence up here is where ma wee croft now ends. Ma hoose and just enough fir a few wee sheep.'

They reached the top of the rise where a newish fence stretched the other side of the creek.

'But it were once up over yonder knock.' She pointed to a small hill. Then she pointed at the stream and then a mountain. 'From ault tae yon ben.'

'Dewar?'

'He convinced ma da that ta geology was diamonds, and they had a deal. Da got some worthless shares and Dewar got ta land. An' there were nae diamonds, but Dewar noo has ta farm. Like Jack and ta beanstalk, only nae beanstalk.'

'The one girl you finally get into bed is the key to the whole thing?'

'I'm telling it as it happened, Terry.'

'You are riding a bike in the rain in the middle of Scotland and the one girl who comes along ...'

'It's a small island, Terry, even if it has two names. It's like Perth. Not many degrees of separation.'

'Ah'll show ye a thing,' said Deidre scampering expertly across a line of rocks before stepping up to a larger boulder and over to the other side of the fence.

Dave followed, aware of his wounds from Lewis MacDonald's fists again.

They crossed a particularly rocky field up near the road, where a yellow drilling rig sat rusting. Larger rocks jutted, as the field started to turn into the mountains not far off.

Deidre crouched where the core holes had been drilled. 'They took samples for a week, and naught.'

Dave looked at the mud in one of the drill holes. There was lichen regrowing.

'How long ago?'

'Four year, aboot.'

Dave looked over the ancient rocky ground wondering what the north of WA would look like if you added a million years of rain.

'For fook's sake!' exclaimed Deidre.

Dave turned to see a newish-looking jeep pull up on the road. Lewis MacDonald stepped out.

'Oh-oh,' said Dave turning his empty tea mug as a weapon.

'Bloody men!' said Deidre.

'Men!?'

Lewis called from the roadway fence. 'Ah'm no'here tae start, Deidre. Ye've hurt me, but ah forgive ye.'

'Ah dinae want yir forgiveness, Lewis. Ah want ye to piss aff.'

'Ah'm here for this Ken. We've business.'

'Whether ye bash him or no', it makes nae difference to us.'

'Ahh, it'd make a difference to me,' offered Dave.

'Are ye working for ta police noo, are ye, Lewis?'

'What's he bin sayin'? What ye bin sayin'? Ah can explain that, Deidre.'

'Tell those who care.' Deidre snatched Dave's mug and started down the hill.

'Wait,' yelled Dave. He turned back to Lewis. 'Be right back.' Then he went after Deidre. 'Hey, look I know all these men seem to be doing you not much good, but maybe there's one that can make it up to you.'

Dave brought out the condom.

She looked up, murderous.

'No. It's got the stones in it. Will you look after it? Till I get back?'

She looked doubtful.

'Might be worth something. We'll see.'

She took the condom.

Dave said, 'I couldn't help noticing those electronic bits in your shed.'

*

Dave clambered into Lewis's jeep with his hands full of slightly rusted electronics.

'Ye spent the night?' Lewis looked from him to the farmhouse.

'To tell you the truth, with all that whisky and the concussion and all, I'm not sure of anything right now.'

Lewis looked doubtful, but then examined Dave's bruised and cut face and gave a satisfied grunt, before crashing the jeep into gear and lurching off.

After a kilometre in silence, Dave said, 'So, to Dewar's?'

'Aye.'

'And then?'

'Ye're supposed tae be the expert.'

They drove in silence until they neared Ardvourlie when Lewis said, 'So what's that then?'

Dave looked at his electronics. 'There's an old school across from his house. And a phone line still attached. I thought I'd try to listen in to see what's what.'

'Ye soom kind o' super undercover cop, aren't ye?'

'Me?'

'Aw fookin' bastards.'

Dave let that sit for a while. As they came down the last hill into the settlement, he said, 'Given that, and everything, then why are you helping? Not that I want to change your mind.'

'Ye've got me by the balls, aye. Ye bring my auld smugglin' charge up every time ye need soomthin'.'

'Ahh. Well, not me. I'm not a cop. They've got me by the same balls.

Well, not exactly the same balls. Mine.'

Lewis pulled up near the school and studied Dave again.

Dave didn't really care if he believed him or not. 'These places still have shared lines. Shouldn't be too hard. Can I borrow a pair of pliers?'

He tramped across the thick soggy grass to the shuttered little school. The paint was faded, the wood beginning to weather. He stepped carefully over a broken board on the veranda and found a door with a broken lock.

Inside were two classrooms with the remains of a couple of smashed desks, a scattering of multiple-choice maths papers. Someone had spray-painted FUK YE in yellow paint on the blackboard, which also had a couple of good-sized dents in it. The graffiti was an indictment of many kinds.

He found the office, furnitureless and dark because of the boards across the windows. Under the window was the telephone outlet. He stripped out a little plastic to expose the copper wires, and connected up one of the telco jacks to the socket in the wall, winding the exposed wiring around an old RCU jack. He plugged that into the little speaker he'd found in Deidre's shed.

Then he listened to a series of very uninteresting conversations and quite a few monologues of which he understood very little until finally someone said, 'Lord Fotheringham's residence.'

'Aye. Lord Fotheringham. Tell him it's Dewar.'

'Very good sir.'

There was a fairly long pause before a voice clearly close to the English throne said, 'I assume there is a problem.'

'There might be. Someone may have followed t'diamonds. A lassie.'

There was another pause. The sound of breathing. 'Where is she now?'

'Locked in t'cellar.'

'How did she get in?'

'She was posing as a sightseeing widow.'

'I see.'

'Noo, ye dinae. I was suspicious from t'start. T'mystery woman from Amsterdam. T'burglar monitors shoo her searching last night. Ah confronted her in t'study.'

'I'm sure you did, old boy. But now what?'

'Ah've goot local help. To lend a hand with t'heavy work.'

'She's confessed?'

'Not yet.'

There was another pause and the Englishman's voice came in more softly, 'Need I remind you, Mr Dewar, if any word of this leaks out – any word at all, the whole share strategy will collapse.'

'Doon't worry. Ah'll no' waste these years of work.'

Click.

'Hoi!' Lewis was at the school office door. ''Arris MacLeod's truck went intae Dewar's.'

'Well, I'm glad the local help is him and not you. We better get in there.'

They drove past the entrance to Dewar's lodge and down to the loch, then along a track, parking near an upturned boat and some drying nets. Lewis led Dave past a stone outbuilding and up worn stone steps. He tried the kitchen door and it opened.

Lewis laid one of his big paws on Dave's shoulder. 'Ye noo I huvnae finished wi' ye. After this business o'er here.'

'Oh, fair enough. Goes without saying, I suppose.'

As soon as they entered the kitchen, they heard shouting below.

It was Margaret, but speaking in a broad rural Aussie accent. 'James, I know I'm a bit of a stickybeak, but can't we work this out?'

'Who sent ye?' It was Dewar.

'James, you seemed nicer on the ferry. You invited me! Geez, you take no for an answer bloody badly.'

'Careful Harris, she's got a kick on her, I hear.'

'Aye.'

Then came the sound of smashing glass. Wet breaking glass.

'What are ye doin'?' yelled Dewar.

'Defending me bloody honour, ya drongo.'

Smash. Smash.

'No' t'reds? Cheryl, doon't throw t'reds.'

'Then let me go.'

Dave edged down the steps towards the open cellar door. There were broken bottles everywhere and a din coming from inside. Dave looked back, but Lewis had gone.

He peered into the wine cellar.

Harris, bleeding from a gash on his forehead, held out a Scottish shield as he edged towards Margaret. She took a dusty bottle from the wine rack behind her.

'I've got the Grange!' she called, losing her Aussie country accent.

'Noooo,' yelled Dewar in agony.

But Harris kept coming and Margaret launched the wine at him. He deflected it with the shield and then rushed her, pinning her back against the back wall of the cellar.

'Ye'll pay fir this, lassie,' said Dewar.

'Hey,' said Dave, stepping into the room. 'You should let her go.'

Dewar turned, looking like he was seeing a ghost. That's when Dave noticed he held a pistol.

Margaret called, 'Angus, nice timing. You look like you've been in a fight.'

'Ye are working taegither! Ah knew.'

Lewis stepped into the room holding a shotgun. 'That how ye huv tae get a lass is it, Harris?'

'That's my shotgun,' said Dewar.

'Aye, and loaded.'

Dewar dropped his pistol. 'This isn't yir affair, Lewis MacDonald.'

'Aye. It is.'

Harris suddenly swung around, pulling Margaret between himself and the shotgun. He pushed the shield up under her throat.

'T'balance has shifted wouldn't ye say,' said Dewar.

Lewis wavered.

Margaret said, 'I think if you shot Dewar, Mr MacDonald, then we could all go home. No power balances to worry about at all.'

'Whoa, lassie. Noo, let's be calm, laddie.'

Dave said, 'I only came for what you owe me, Dewar. Twenty thousand pounds wasn't it? Campbell and Karushi forgot to give it to me.'

'Campbell!' yelled Harris.

Lewis hissed at him, 'Ye work with Campbells, dae ye?'

Harris yelled, 'Nae. Never.' He dropped the shield and stepped away from Margaret pointing a finger at Dewar, 'Ye'd work wi' a Campbell?'

'Noo, Harris, it were work on t'mainland.'

'A man has 'is honour, Mr Dewar.' Harris strode out, seeming to clutch his honour to his stomach as he went.

Lewis said, 'Aye. Dogs an' Campbells.'

'I broke his arm,' offered Dave helpfully.

Lewis passed him the shotgun. 'Ye're good, Ken.' He started to go, but turned back. 'An' stay away from Deidre.'

Margaret stepped forward and picked up Dewar's pistol. 'Well, that's all worked out well.'

Dave swung the shotgun towards her.

'Angus! Or is it Dave? Ken? After all we've nearly been through.'

Dave tried to glare at her, but it was hard because she grimaced and grinned and mock-winced and seemed to have a pretty good repertoire of naughty girl smiles. But Dave kept the shotgun aimed and she finally relented and put the pistol on the wine rack.

Dave said, 'Mr Dewar. I only want my money.'

Dewar looked at Dave and the shotgun and seemed to calculate before saying, 'Ye're a man after me own heart, Ken.'

Dave stepped back and let Dewar pass, crunching broken glass as they went up the stairs and through a dark-wooded hall covered in shields and tartan. There were guns and short swords and a couple of large antlered deer heads.

Dave kept the shotgun aimed at Dewar's back as he followed him into a study. Dewar went behind a big desk and pulled back a large picture of a young Scotsman standing before a castle to reveal a wall safe. Dewar fiddled with the combination.

Dave said, 'As far as I'm concerned, once I get my money, the diamonds are yours, and I don't care what or why and I've forgotten who.'

The safe clicked open. There was a clear plastic package holding the stones. All of them except the package Dave had given Deidre. Dewar moved them to get to a pile of bank notes.

Margaret said, 'On the other hand, I don't care about the money. I want the diamonds.'

Dave turned.

Margaret stood in the doorway, pointing Dewar's pistol at him.

'But ... I mean, I just rescued you. Twice!'

'And I owe you one. Just not this one. Put the shotgun down on that chair there, before we all get hurt.'

'Who t'fook are ye?' said Dewar.

'Yeah!' said Dave. 'Who the fook are you?'

Margaret indicated for Dewar to step back and went around the desk to the safe. 'Julie Lansky. I'm an insurance investigator. It's not always this exciting but I do get to meet such interesting people.'

'Ah knew ye weren't Cheryl,' said Dewar.

'I kind of liked you as Margaret,' said Dave.

'Now now, boys, we can't have people taking diamonds that don't belong to them, can we – even if certain arrangements seem to have been made on high.' Margaret loaded the stones into her coat pocket.

Dewar sat down behind his desk, as she backed away, still holding the pistol on them. 'Ah'm fooked,' he said. 'Completely fooked.'

'James, you should be fucked. You were going to do very nasty things to me. And to Angus here too, I believe.'

'Dave.'

'I want to thank you for your help on this. All the best.'

'You've broken my heart, um ... Julie.'

Julie put on a mock-sorry face and then ran out of the room and clattered across the stone hall and out the front door.

'Ah'm pure fooked,' said Dewar again, staring out the window as the hire car skidded up the drive.

Dave sat down in a chair near the door. He felt empty. Flat. He wondered if this is what footballers felt, when the siren went and they'd lost the grand final by a point. They'd lie on the grass and stare at the sky. What did they find up there? There was a grand final Dave had seen which ended in a draw. All back next week for another go. There was a coach who cried.

'Ah'm so fooked.'

'Which is where, of course, you come back into it.'

'I see.'

'Maaate.'

'Yes? Mate.'

'You know a bit about shares don't you?'

'Are you back in Australia, Dave?'

'Sitting in a lovely overpriced hotel in St Georges Terrace looking at many cranes building lots of new mining edifices, as we speak.'

Dave ate a room service steak sandwich while Terry sat on the bed looking at the stack of English pounds. There were three mobile phones sitting on the table.

'Beetroot, that's the key to a great steak sandwich,' said Dave.

'It's slightly short of nineteen thousand pounds,' said Terry. 'That'll pay a few debts.'

Dave smiled a tomato-saucy smile. 'Well, I never thought of it like that. I was thinking more double or nothing.'

*

Dave stood at the kitchen table of Deidre's tumbledown farmhouse in Lewis off the coast of Scotland. The condom lay split open, its modest gravelly stones scattered.

Deidre brought a pile of papers from a cupboard drawer, picking bills away from the shares. 'Here they are.'

'Can ah coom in,' called Dewar plaintively from the door.

'Ye set foot in this croft and ah'll kill ye,' said Deidre, not for the first time.

'The shares. Your dad's shares and Dewar's. That's what it's all about,' said Dave. 'Why else would you smuggle poor-grade industrial diamonds halfway across the world. Salting.'

'Salt?'

'No' salt!' called Dewar.

'Hey, who's telling this?' called Dave.

'Well, git on wi' it,' said Dewar.

'The plan was to crush up a bit of this stuff in the hole so you send it in with the core samples.'

'But they'd do other tests,' said Deidre.

'Yeah, that's what was confusing me too. They'd find out soon enough. But they don't want to mine it. They want to make a quick hit on the shares.'

'No' so quick, as it turns oot,' mumbled Dewar.

Deidre blinked. 'Wha'?'

Dewar called, 'When word leaks oot, like. Rumours.'

Deidre smiled. 'Ah, rumours. Yes. And ye uncovered all this?' Deidre opened her arms and put them around Dave and hugged him. She whispered, 'Thank ye. Noo he'll goo tae jail.' She kissed Dave and Dave kissed her back, feeling her body pushing against him and he looked over her shoulder to the bed.

Dewar was now sitting on it. 'Tell her aboot t'better plan.'

Deidre turned, wild. 'Oot.'

He stood, hands up, placating. 'We kin all come ootae this, Deidre MacDonald. A profit.'

She stopped being wild. 'A profit?'

'Tidy. Yir da's dream.'

'If this goes right,' said Dave, 'we leave Lord Fotheringham holding the bag, escape the police of at least three countries and make a largish profit on the side.'

Deidre looked from Dave to Dewar, both smiling.

'How can it be so easy?'

'It won't be,' said Dewar. 'Lewis will have tae help us get him oot of t'country, by boot.'

'And I'll have to give the police something ... to distract them while we set it up,' said Dave, feeling the beginnings of a new rush.

Deidre said, 'Ye're a wee punter aren't ye?'

'I haven't had so much fun since I lost my first house in a card game.'

'And so, I was the distraction for the police.'

'Sorry about that.'

'It took a great deal of explaining, you know.'

'I knew you'd be good at that.'

'And chastising. I was chastised in a number of countries and at many levels.'

'Sorry. Was there spanking?'

Dave made the phone call from the Isle of Skye while he waited to board a fast freighter heading towards Fremantle. Lewis had taken him in his fishing boat, happy to see the back of Dave Kelly.

'I only just managed to get away myself, Inspector Colley.'

'But ye saw her take the diamonds.'

'Absolutely. She either has them or knows who now has them.'

There was more talking in the background of a hotel in Ullapool where the police had set up their headquarters.

'Is this the woman who was in Amsterdam?' said Colley when she got back on the line.

'Yes. The one on the barge.'

'We have video, apparently.'

'She may be going by the name of Julie Lansky. She uses aliases, apparently.'

'You're such a hypocrite.'

'Oh, aye.'

'What about Dewar?' said Colley into the phone.

'I think he was a go-between. Like Ken. And me. Caught up in it.'

'That makes no sense, Ken. Campbell and Karushi were ordered to kill you in the forest.'

'Did I say that? I might have misunderstood. My stomach was playing up. Anyway, I heard her say Montenegro. There aren't panthers there, are there?'

'Very good work. We'll clear this up when we debrief you, Ken.'

'Well yes, of course, Inspector. I'm near Edinburgh now. Shall I drop in?' Dave disconnected the phone. He turned to head up the gangway stairs and to sail as far away from the police as possible.

'Ship. Hmm. Very slow.'

'Twenty-eight days. A lot of sleep. And a lot of cards.'

'Don't tell me you won.'

'We only played for matchsticks.'

'And back in Scotland they had time to salt the mine.'

'Yes.'

'And set the other things up.'

'A lot of it had been set up already. But timing is everything ... apparently.'

Dave offered Terry the last chip on his plate.

Terry shook his head and looked back at the pile of money. 'What you want to do is totally illegal.'

'Compared to diamond smuggling and nearly getting murdered in a forest, a bit of share plumping seems kind of mild. Isn't that what the big end of town always does?'

'They don't get caught. I mean converting this many pounds into Australian dollars could be tricky enough.'

'Naw, you're right. You don't have to do this, mate.' Dave went to the hotel window and tried to find sky above the bigger buildings around his hotel.

Terry said, 'Only, without someone who knows a bit about shares, none of it will work.'

'Well there's that. It's all betting though isn't it? Instead of Wandering Lark, it's Kershader Mining. To win.'

'You never win, Dave. You know that, don't you?'

'I'm on a roll. Ride it all the way, I reckon.'

*

Terry introduced Dave to his broker Ed via telephone then headed to the stock exchange. Dave's plan centred on deniability, for everyone involved. So Ed, in Sydney, didn't know Dave. And Terry was not logging onto computer accounts, as he pointed out he could do, but watching the televisions in the stock exchange foyer. The television screens were there so that old folks could watch their superannuation funds dwindling without bothering the big players who were busy inside watching Greece plunder their funds.

Dave had three new mobiles lined up on the table in the hotel room. He'd put labels of gaffer tape on each one. *Terry, Ed, Deidre.* He'd opened a Stella from the bar fridge.

The Terry line rang. When Dave picked it up, Terry said, 'Kershader isn't on our board yet, but it won't be until it starts to do something. Now, dangle the first bit of bait. Not all of it.'

'Yep, I got ya. It's the opposite of laying off bets around different tracks.'

Dave picked up the Deidre mobile. 'You still there, my lovely?'

'Aye, Dave.'

'Missing you already. Um. One two three, go.'

Dave rang Ed on the Ed phone. 'Account 432 here. I want you to use half the money in that account to buy shares in Kershader Mining. Scottish company. Um, London Stock Exchange.'

There was clicking and keyboard tapping on the other end. Finally Ed came back on the line. 'That's a lot of shares, Mr MacFergus.'

'Good. I reckon it's going to do something.'

'What have you heard?'

'Not allowed to say if I have, am I?'

Dave clicked Ed off and picked up the Terry phone. 'What's happening, brother?'

'Too soon mate and what you put in is too little to start anything. Has the Scottish end started?'

'Yep, and we've bought about fifty thousand shares, I'd say.'

'Yeah, well the whole thing depends on your Fotheringham getting on this, you know. Millions need to play. Not just the local villagers.'

'That's Dewar's job.'

Dave heard noise from the Deidre phone. 'Is anything happenin' yet?'

'Hello darlin'. Not yet, but Terry says it's like fishing. Gotta wait till the fish notices the bait. Your folks buying?'

'In dribs and drabs, although Dewar has more.'

'Keep by the phone, Deidre. When we go to dump it all, I don't want your neighbours being left hanging.'

'Ah'll look after them.'

'We're up,' called Terry. 'We've made the Commodities screen. Trading on the ASX and London.'

'What we worth?'

'Up from twenty cents to thirty-three.'

'Doesn't sound like much,' said Dave.

'Do the maths. The company has to be trading at about a million before they'd list them, you know. Anyway, it means Fotheringham is on, but he's just dangling his own bait. We got to wriggle a bit in the water. Buy.'

Dave dialled the Ed phone and picked up Deidre's at the same time.

'Hey girl. Hey?' There was noise and shooshing at the other end. 'Not alone?'

'In the pub.'

'Okay. Buy buy buy. I always wanted to say that.'

'Everything.'

'Throw everything at it so he panics into buying them cheap.'

'Hello?' said Ed.

'Account 432. Please spend all the rest of my money on Kershader Mining.'

'Hey, it's going up fast. You do know something.'

'Buy please at whatever price it is. Bye.'

Dave clicked off.

'Terry?'

'It's moving up but not fast. It's at forty-one cents. Maybe you should sell. That's double now.'

'Hold your nerve, mate.'

'Forty-three. Big jump. Sell, mate. It'll lose momentum.'

'A bit more, Terry.'

'Dave, fucking sell, now.'

'Forty-five cents?'

'It's forty-five cents. Sell the fucking shares.'

Dave buttoned off Terry.

Dave called Ed. 'Account 432.'

'Yes, Mr MacFergus.'

Dave picked up the Deidre phone and he yelled into both phones, 'Sell. Sell everything.'

Dave buttoned off Ed. He said, 'You hear me, Deidre?'

'Oh, aye my love.'

Dave buttoned off Deidre. He danced to the hotel bar fridge. There was whisky. 'It's after drinking time in Scotland.'

One of the mobile phones was ringing. Dave went over. He picked up Terry.

'Dave, I told you to sell!'

'I have.'

'The price is still rising.'

'Doesn't matter to us, does it?'

'Well, if everyone jumped off, then the price would fall suddenly and Fotheringham would get caught. That was your plan, wasn't it?'

Dave rang Ed. 'Ed, it's um, whatever the MacFergus account is. Sold?'

'Tidy morning's work, Mr MacFergus. One hundred and eight thousand dollars. You would have made much more if you'd stayed in. I'm filling out the CHESS now.'

'Ta.'

Dave rang Deidre. 'Deidre, I said sell. Did you hear me say sell, now before it drops?'

'Ah'll get her,' said Dewar.

There was cheering and glass clinking.

'Dave,' she said, like a cancer doctor.

'What?'

'Well, the way it was was this. Lord Fotheringham explained that we could make a lot more money if we dinae dump him in it.'

'Oh,' said Dave.

'Dave?'

'But, I set this whole thing up so you could get your revenge on him. For your dad. And, you know – get the English.'

'And we thank ye for it. The names Dave Kelly and Ken mean a lo' in this wee croft. But Dave, we had a wee choice. A lot of revenge an' a wee bit o' money. Or lots of money. It's 2010 for fook's sake, no' 1746.'

'Ah.'

'If ta sun shines, ye stand in it, Dave. Ah'll never forget ye, y'know. Got tae goo, we're aw sellin' when it hits fifty p.'

Click.

Dave sat in the empty hotel room wondering why he felt like he'd lost again.

'Poor Dave.'

'Yes, the universe's victim.'

'I think you're a victimless crime.'

CHESS stood for Clearing House Electronic Sub-Register System, Terry had explained when Dave wanted to collect his money.

Terry said, 'I mean the diamond salting will be discovered. You could ring your police mates and give them a tip. Teach that girl a lesson.'

'Not the first girl to break my heart, Terrence. Naw. Let the chips fall, I reckon. I might keep a bit of a low profile, police-wise. Stay in my own backyard.'

'And stop shitting in your own nest?'

The three-day wait to see if anything dodgy had transpired before the stock exchange released the funds made Dave sweat. The sweating could have been caused by Terry's un-air-conditioned garage where Dave camped. Dave could not afford to be seen anywhere around town. Dave could not go into Terry's house because he had been persona non grata with Judy, Terry's wife, ever since Sally, Dave's wife, had left him some five years before, which seemed unfair to Dave, seeing as Judy and Sally and most of Dave's own family thought that was the best thing for Sally and the kids – by a long shot.

Dave made only one phone call.

'Brigadier, it's Dave. Um, Ken, Angus MacFergus.'

'Ah, yes.'

'I couldn't get Inspector Colley.'

'No. Bit of a demotion there.' Van Shooten's voice dripped with prideful satisfaction.

'Or Bruce.'

'Has decided to stay in Britain. Love apparently.'

'Is grand, I hear.'

'Malcolm is back in Australia. I have his number. Soon to be Senior Sergeant, I believe. Where are you?'

'Um, well, if you recall things were very free flowing and I had to run. To save my own life.'

'Yes. Rather a debacle from the Scottish end. But your tip concerning the Australian woman proved partly correct. An insurance investigator.'

'Fancy that. Not the criminal mastermind at all?'

'Nothing to do with the Pink Panther jewel thieves, but she blew the entire operation.'

'She's very beautiful.'

'Well, yes. That is rather beside the point isn't it?'

'You didn't say that, Dave.'

'I did. I've said it to many people, each time I tried to explain you.'

'Hmm. Okay, but what did you say after that?'

Dave said to the phone, 'So, Brigadier, am I in the clear?'

'The gems have been returned. A storm in a teacup, as the English say. Don't come back to the Netherlands, Mr Kelly.'

Click.

Dave watched cricket, a game designed to be watched by someone hiding in a garage for many days. Australia weren't any good anymore, but it was much more fun now that they were no longer invincible. Although Dave did miss Warnie. He emptied Terry's old beer fridge. He fixed Judy's old vacuum cleaner and tidied up Terry's tool wall and repaired a number of very large plastic water-shooting mega-pistols for Terry's kids.

Finally, Terry brought a briefcase full of Australian dollars. Dave counted out eight thousand and pushed it across the workbench at Terry.

'What's this?'

'Consultancy fee, mate. Um, and for the beer. Look, hasn't even made a dent in the pile. Hey, I can buy back my half of the office furniture.'

'I thought you knew. That job's not there anymore.'

'Oh. Well, never liked it anyway.' Before Terry could say no to the money, not that he necessarily would have, given the considerable grief Dave had given him over the years, Dave walked out of the garage and down the drive to look for a taxi.

*

Daryl and Tiny were in the outer office playing games on their iPhones when Dave walked in.

'You,' said Daryl, jumping up.

'Whoa boys. I'm cashed up. Mungo!'

Tiny patted him on the shoulder. 'Good on yer, Dave.'

Mungo looked angry until Dave opened the briefcase. He looked even less angry as Dave counted out twenty thousand dollars. 'Here's the vig,' he said.

Dave counted out more, watching Mungo watch the pile. 'I'm stopping at thirty thousand,' said Dave.

Mungo nodded. 'Your line of credit is back open, Dave.'

'We'll see, Mungo. It seems I've lost the passion.'

*

Dave went around to his ex-wife's house and met Kevin, her jockey husband, out on the median strip. Sally and a variety of court orders forbade Dave to come within thirty metres of the house.

'When your horse comes in, Dave, it comes in,' he said in his thin jockey voice, watching Dave count out fifty thousand dollars.

'These are all the back payments and a few future ones, Kev.'

'I can see that, Dave.'

'I'd like to start seeing the kids, Kevin.'

Kevin studied Dave before he nodded a promise. 'I'll talk to her.'

Dave closed the briefcase.

*

And carried it into the Cash Converters.

Trish Fong left a couple eyeing diamond rings and came to him. 'Dave, where have you been? I've missed you.'

'All over the world, Trish.'

'Yeah, right. You haven't been in jail have you?'

'I have.'

'Ha, yeah right. Please tell me you haven't got more diamonds in that briefcase.'

'I'm not selling, Trish. I'm buying. How much for all my stuff back?'

Dave shouted goodbye for the tenth time to Trish's favourite removalists as they both headed off with an extra beer each.

He turned and looked at his flat, full of stuff, electronic, electrical, white and furnishing. He'd even picked up a new flat screen and a lava lamp and a neon light that could flash: *OPEN*.

He opened his fridge and surveyed the food and beer he owned. He took a Heineken and upended the briefcase. It was empty. He went through his pockets and counted out sixty-four dollars and silver.

There was a knock on the door. Dave took a knee-jerk reaction step towards the bedroom window before relaxing. He laughed. 'I don't owe anyone anything.'

'It was me.'
    'Yes.'

Margaret stood outside the door. She seemed as surprised as Dave felt.

'So, you really do work for Telstra.'

'Ah, not anymore apparently.'

'Aren't you going to ask me in?'

'Sure Julie, Margaret, Cheryl.' Dave stepped back.

She came in. 'Thankyou Angus, Ken, Dave.'

'I've got beer,' he said.

She went into the kitchen, straight to the fridge and got herself a Stella. She said something in excited Spanish as she opened the beer. Then, in English, 'You put me in a spot in Amsterdam.'

'I can explain that.'

'I look forward to it.'

'I needed a little time.'

She shrugged and took the best chair in the room, rocking back so her skirt rose up rather nicely to her knees. 'The clients got most of their diamonds back. That was the job.'

'Everyone is happy. How did you find me?'

'I actually wasn't looking for you. Well, not international amazing super spy, you. I have another case. It appears that one of our clients lost a diamond bracelet. Last seen near a cheeky Telstra worker. He was in her apartment, placing bets and proposing rough sex.'

'Oh. I'm sure he wasn't proposing it be rough. He's very gentle.'

'Hmm.'

'Actually, there's a bit of a story about that.'

'I'm so looking forward to hearing it. And getting the bracelet back.'

'You see, Dave was in the middle of nowhere, only it wasn't nowhere. It was the outback. Dave Kelly was in the outback because of the lady. Your lady.'

'Are you going to tell me this story talking about yourself in the third person?'

'Yes. It seems more objective that way. Don't you think?'

Julie sipped her beer.

Hoping to survive another night, Dave told the story, from somewhere in the middle.

RANDOM MALICE

By the pricking of my thumbs
– Second Witch, *Macbeth*

The roulette wheel is spinning. The ball rolls fast against the wheel.

Amis watches Teddy.

Teddy watches the ball. Teddy sweats. His ruddy face glistens. He looks down at his large pile of chips, all on black. Teddy licks his lips. Not anticipation. Amis knows. It is fear. Everything is on black. Everything he doesn't own. And the ball keeps running round the edge of the large wheel making that endless pillatiky rolling sound. Teddy closes his eyes. Bows his head.

Amis coughs to disguise his laugh. Teddy is praying. Amis looks at the ball. It's starting to slow, tired, ready to drop. Amis hears a whimper. Across the room. Amidst all those people. Teddy is begging the ball.

Pop, the ball drops. Clicketty click, it hops and jumps and stops dead. Red. Teddy stares at the ball. Standing in a time-stopped blank buzz as the chips are raked and the winning bets are paid.

Amis is tempted ... Amis is always tempted ... to pass behind Teddy and to say, 'Bad luck' and be gone before Teddy can turn. But he might see him. Might recognise. It's too soon for that.

Teddy gets into his BMW in the underground car park. The BMW is leased. About to be repossessed. On the back seat are bits and pieces from Teddy's office. A framed business certificate. Boxes of papers. A calculator. A briefcase. A stack of business papers on the front passenger seat has spilt to the floor. Amis's favourite object, of the flotsam of Teddy's washed up life, is a plastic Charlie Brown toy with *Best Boss* on the little plaque.

A passing brakelight makes things glow red. Teddy rests his forehead on the steering wheel. He's crying.

It occurs to him to show himself now. 'Happening by. Are you okay?' He steps out from the concrete pillar.

Teddy turns. Grabs something from beside him. A gun barrel. Amis stops. Should he dive? But Teddy puts the barrel under his own chin. Boom. The roof of the BMW erupts with a spray of goop. The car fills with red mist. A car alarm starts wailing. Teddy's brain matter drips down from the low concrete roof.

Amis grinds his teeth, tasting the metal of an old filling. Where did the gun come from?

Daniel woke, a hand clamped over his mouth.

'Don't move,' said Helen.

The clock radio showed 5.28.

'Don't move,' said Helen again. 'Until I tell you. Then move a lot.'

She took her hand away and Daniel turned. She looked stern. She ordered, 'Take off your pants.'

Daniel was about to say, 'What's gotten into you,' but Helen said, 'If you talk – you'll die.'

Daniel took off his boxers. The radio came on with the 5.30 news.

'If you touch that clock, I'll kill you.'

He kissed her. She was naked already. She pushed him onto his back. She grabbed him in the way that made him instantly hard. She climbed onto him, around him. She was already wet. He reached up and gently squeezed her nipples. She purred. She moved. He moved.

*

She lay in bed watching him as he came out of the walk-in robe and took his watch from the bedside table. She smiled, still getting a thrill out of seeing him in a suit. Very dashing. Very successful.

He saw her watching and came around the bed and bent to kiss her. A quick peck.

'Love 'em and leave me, huh?' she said.

He grinned, still smug from getting lucky. 'I'm that kind of man. And late!' He pointed an accusing finger, but didn't mean it. Much. 'Although the wake-up call did have a lot going for it.'

He headed downstairs.

Helen called, 'Don't forget the wedding rehearsal!'

No reply. He would forget. She'd phone him later. She lay in the warm musky smell of their lovemaking, allowing herself to inventory the parts of her body that were still warm, still tingling. Another news started on the radio. Six-thirty. Time to get the kids up. Christmas soon! 'My god,' she said to the ceiling.

Bradley was standing by his car looking at the river when Daniel drove up in his ute.

A Hearth & Home truck was already by the fence. It was a good time for the river and a good time to look at the outside of the hotel, the sun catching it low, making a feature of the upstairs verandas.

'Mr Bradley,' called Daniel. He noticed the bank man didn't have his tie on and he pulled at his own, rolling it and shoving it into his shirt pocket. 'You should see the river from the second floor. Beautiful.'

'Mr Longo.'

They shook hands.

'Come on in. Looks like some of the lads from the workshop are here.'

Daniel led him through the gate in the building site fence and up towards the old hotel. The yard was strewn with piles of bricks and stacks of white-ant-chewed wood.

'We've redone all the foundations. Re-concreted under and new limestone.'

Bradley took care where he put his shiny shoes.

'Built in 1897, it was offered to the governor of the time. He declined the gift. Now there's a story. Anyway it became a hotel in the 1920s. And it was used as the *Australia II* training camp in the '80s.'

'Yes, yes. And your father acquired it after that and began to restore it.'

'Yes,' said Daniel, losing his smile. He led Bradley into the huge room at the front which had once been the main bar.

A new rosette quivered in the air as it was winched up towards the centre of the ceiling five metres above.

Daniel yelled to the ceiling. 'How ya going you blokes? Heavy enough?'

'Gidday boss,' came a strained voice. It was Hua, one of the more experienced men from the factory.

Daniel said, more quietly, 'That's a Hearth & Home reproduction. Special cast for this one.'

Bradley looked to the dusty windows overlooking the river. The walls had plaster missing in great chunks.

Daniel said, 'We've sorted the structural problems. Now it's onto the more obvious signs of the restoration. The sexy stuff.' Daniel went over to where a long dropsheet hung on a wall and lifted it to expose an ornate jarrah fireplace surround. He stroked the wood, watching Bradley in one of the inset mirrors.

Bradley looked up at the rosette warily as it gave another big hop and clunked to the ceiling.

'They'll bolt it in now. Also tie it off. We've replastered all the ceilings. Do the walls before we get onto the floorboards.'

Bradley looked at Daniel like he had dust in his eye. He folded his arms. 'You realise, Mr Longo, the bank doesn't buy real estate. Well, not individual lots.'

'I'm not selling it.'

Nadif, one of the apprentices, came through an upstairs door and hurried down the stairs. He saw Daniel and blurted, 'I forgot the bolt.'

'Well, hurry mate,' called Daniel.

Bradley said, 'Ahh, while I am the Loans Officer, we use valuers – professionals – to ascertain collateral. It's really nothing to do with me.'

Daniel said, 'I don't want another loan, Mr Bradley. I am not my father.' Daniel closed the distance between them. 'I wanted you to see.'

'I don't understand.'

'Nadif!' called Hua from in the ceiling.

Daniel repeated the call. 'Nadif! Hua wants you.' He said to Bradley, 'I don't want it to just be a file number.' Daniel opened his arms to the fireplace, windows, soon to be replastered walls. 'I want you to see what we're building here. Get a feel for it. See what it is going to be.'

'Watch out,' called Hua, agonised.

Bradley looked up.

Daniel too. It was coming at him, the whine of wire playing out getting faster. Daniel dived, his arms out in front of him. There was a crash of splintering wood and shattering plaster.

He heard Hua yell, 'Is everyone all right?'

He heard Nadif say, 'Oh fuck,' with no trace of Somalian accent at all.

Rosemarie's mother attacked the keys of the organ with concentrated anger. Helen thought it sounded most like 'Candle in the Wind'.

Russell, a kind of trendy young minister in jeans and a t-shirt, stood up the front with Brian and Rosemarie. He read quickly. 'For better for worse, for richer for poorer, in sickness and health.'

Frances squirmed on Helen's lap in a front pew, her eyes fixed on the full-sized nativity scene that had been created near the pulpit. Helen had promised she could touch the baby Jesus when the grown-ups had finished practising.

Russell said, 'To love, cherish and obey, until death us do part.'

Rosemarie nudged Brian and Brian said, 'Ah, Russell?'

He looked at the couple with a dopey smile.

Rosemarie said, 'That's the wrong one, Russell.'

'Oh, yes. Quite right, Rosemarie. The new one.'

'Yeah,' said Brian. 'No obeying apparently.' He looked around at Helen, raising his eyebrows. Rosemarie elbowed him again.

Russell seemed flustered. 'Well, looks like I need these rehearsals as much as anyone. Let me see. To love and to cherish, until death us do part. According to God's holy law.'

They were a good couple. Brian, Daniel's business partner, had been going out with Rosemarie since high school. They fitted. Like Brian and Daniel. Good team. Helen checked up the aisle. Rosemarie's father sat in a pew. Her girlfriends milled. But no best man. His mobile was switched off.

Rosemarie's mother finally found a particularly cruel combination of false notes and slammed her hands down on the keyboards in defeat. 'You'll have to get someone else. I can't do it.' She was near tears.

Rosemarie went over to reassure her, her father joining the pep talk.

'Now?' said Frances, very patient for a four year old.

'Yes. But don't pull anything off.'

Brian came over.

'Sorry Brian.'

'You don't have to be sorry, Helen. Say the word and I'll call the whole thing off for you. There's still time.'

Brian always pretended to flirt with Helen, but she sometimes wondered about the pretend.

'I don't know why he missed the rehearsal. He's usually so ...'

'Reliable? Yeah, well he had a meeting at the old ruin this morning.'

'Perhaps if you held your wedding there or at the factory ... you might be able to get him.'

Brian gave her a raised eyebrow and Helen felt embarrassed, the nagging wife.

He smiled. 'If you want, I'll send him home early. Tell him he can't play with me today.'

'He'd just sulk. And Hearth & Home and maybe half of Europe would come crashing to a halt.'

'That's not a joke.' Brian looked towards the organ, where everyone including the minister now consoled the distraught organist. 'Maybe she can do "Jingle Bells".' He headed over.

Helen looked to Frances. She was standing before the stable scene, bending to look at the baby in the manger, nearly but not quite touching. They needed to be off, to get something for dinner and pick Samuel up from school.

*

Daniel turned the ute into his street, driving one-handed. The Christmas light decoration thing was definitely getting competitive. The twenty-house cul-de-sac was starting to look like Las Vegas. The old guy at the top had his whole house festooned in pinks and greens with a neon Santa coming out of his false chimney. It animated up and out, only to disappear and repeat the process. It was the only chimney in the street of air-conditioned double-storey brick and tiles.

Daniel turned into his driveway and coasted towards the garage. His house was modern too. As Brian admonished, it was not a good advertisement for Hearth & Home Restorations, rather advertising the 'bulldoze and concrete pour'. But Helen wanted 'things that just worked' and they'd signed the mortgage when Frances was crawling, and watched interest rates climb steadily and house prices fall.

Daniel felt his shoulder again. They'd eventually strapped his arm at the hospital, once the car accidents and day drunks had been patched. He'd dodged the masonry but twisted his shoulder in the fall. Bradley had been particularly concerned about the dust stains on his own trousers.

The dining room table was set for two. He heard bath noises upstairs and was on his way up when he glanced into the lounge. In a wooden tub in the front bay window was a leafless twig and taped to it, in Samuel's best seven-year-old handwriting: *Xmas Tree*. He smiled, wondering if he should close the curtains and hide his shame from the neighbours. Another thing on his not done to-do list.

Helen was in the spare room upstairs. The bed was made and she was clearing out one side of the built-in robe.

'Hi.'

She kept her back to him. 'You missed the rehearsal.'

'So, I'm sleeping in here?'

She turned, ready to be mad, but saw his arm.

'A house fell on me.'

'Why didn't you call?'

'The phone copped the brunt. And I didn't want to lose my place in line. I was the first non-bleeding conscious person they saw.' He looked at the bed wondering if he really was sleeping in the spare room.

'Rosemarie's staying over after the wedding shower. It's here. Or have you forgotten that too?'

It was going to be one of those nights. He said, 'My shoulder came out of the socket. Doctor shoved it back in.' It had hurt like hell. 'Might be ligament damage.'

He went to the bathroom and found Samuel in his pyjamas playing with Frances who was in the bath. A complicated line of dolls, tea sets and plastic soldiers was set up around the edge of the bath.

'Hey team!'

'Dad!' they said together in an incandescent blaze of love that wiped out everything else in his head.

'You're home!' said Frances.

'What happened to your arm?' asked Sam.

'Accident. I wasn't careful.'

'Wow.'

Frances said, 'Did you fall over?' She seemed to like the idea that he could fall over too.

'Uhuh.'

Sam said, 'Are we still going shopping tomorrow?'

'Tomorrow? Umm.' Daniel turned to see Helen now hovering in the hall, still on his case. He turned back to the kids. 'I promised, so yes.'

Helen came in. Said, 'Glad I don't have to twist your arm.' But she was smiling. She kissed his cheek and Daniel remembered 5.28 and he smiled too.

*

The store has set up the Wiis and Xboxes and PlayStations and connected them to big flat screens so all the kids and their parents can drool over the graphics on their way to Santa's Cave. Trent is doing a pretty good job of tasting the games. He darts in to grab the throttle of a pathetic kid and takes a few turns, shooting shit. Sharp on the computer front for a ten year old.

Amis had to insist. Sharon had tried to invoke the restraining order, her emotions still confused. They'd get way more confused when she found out Teddy wasn't coming a courting anymore. Amis had burned his file using Teddy's gold cigarette lighter. A momento. He wished he'd taken the Peanuts World's Best Boss toy though. Cheap plastic mass-produced emotion, like Edward Borthwick. RIP. No suspicious circumstances. Sharon would come around.

Amis focuses. Mums are yelling, 'Hey!' at Trent. A chubby man steps in Trent's way. 'No. You go and play on another game.'

Trent starts to go, but it's a feint. He rolls around the back of the fat man and takes the toggle from the girl again. She squawks. The man grabs Trent's hand. 'You mustn't touch.'

'Don't touch my kid,' says Amis.

Chubby, with glasses and a possum-faced beard, blinking at Amis, a shit-eating grin starting.

'Get your hands off my kid.'

He lets go of Trent. Trent pushes the girl out of the way and takes over. The possum man has a striped Rivers shirt, longish shorts, loafers with no socks. Official leisure wear. Mid-level public servant for the Water Board. Brings the oranges to T-ball.

Amis raises his voice. 'Don't you ever touch my kid.'

Shoppers stop. Mothers shield their litters. A man in a Penguin shirt watches, not hiding it.

Possum says, 'He was spoiling Nancy's game.'

Amis smiles. Fun maybe. He copies Possum's whiney voice. 'He was spoiling Nancy's game. You look like a bit of a Nancy to me.' Amis moves forward. Gets in front of his face.

He blinks, looks down, backs away. 'I ... look, I don't want any trouble.'

Shame, thinks Amis. Says quietly, 'Run along now.'

Possum looks around. Realises everyone thinks he's a pussy. But he can't meet Amis's eyes. He shuffles, grabs the girl's hand and walks away, internalising another failure to feed his cancer or heart condition.

Amis says, 'There you go, Trent. Don't say I never do anything for you.' Trent plays.

Amis turns. The Penguin t-shirt is standing next to his kids at the next console, looking. His left arm is in a sling.

'What you looking at?'

The man looks back. No blinking here. He lets the look linger before turning to watch his boy playing.

The little girl says, 'What's wrong with that man, Daddy?'

'Very grumpy, darling.'

Doesn't try to lower his voice. Worker's hands. Fit. The girl's in Osh Kosh. The boy's wearing a Quicksilver brand surf t-shirt. World their oyster. Penguin watching the kid's game, not a care in the world. Amis now forgotten, a glitch, wrong channel, tuned back out.

Amis says, 'Hey, Trent, let's play *this* game.'

Penguin says, 'When we finish.' Still not turning. Physically strong maybe. Cashed-up bogan? But no suntan.

Amis says, 'Looks like you got one of your wings clipped.'

Now he turns. 'We're just here to find Christmas presents. All right?' Not afraid. But not wanting it.

'Excuse me. But you see, I'm just here.' Amis brings one hand up in front of him to illustrate his point. 'And you're just here, too.' He brings up the other hand. He touches his fingertips together. Then apart and together more forcefully. 'We're both just here. And there isn't room for both in the one spot. All right?'

Penguin nods. Can see the inevitable. He turns away and takes the girl's arm and pushes her gently to the other side of the boy, who's stopped playing now and is watching the men. He comes back to Amis. He changes his stance, spreading his feet, balancing his legs. When he's set he says, 'Fuck off.' Smiling. Broken arm and all.

Amis smiles back. He says, 'Come on Trent, we got things to do.'

*

Daniel packed Christmas presents into the back of the station wagon.

Frances said, 'Isn't Father Christmas coming?'

'Yes, poppet. He's coming.' Daniel flicked a look at Sam, who was smiling doubtfully. Helen had explained that his primary school teacher had blabbed to the class two weeks ago, bless her literal twenty-two-year-old heart, and now Sam was a grown-up and sworn to keep the secret from his sister.

Frances persisted. 'But why are *we* buying the presents?'

Daniel bought himself time by closing the back of the car and opening Frances' door. Maybe if Daniel had had a more normal father, he'd be ready for this kind of question. He'd have folklore to grab from. 'Well, Father Christmas ... gives his special presents to good boys and girls. That's right, isn't it?' He put her seatbelt on. Tweaked her chin.

'I know,' she said, unswayed. She was a stubborn thing.

'And mums and dads give more. Because we love you.' He looked over to Sam to see how he was doing. Sam nodded.

Daniel closed the passenger door and got in the front, starting the car.

'How does Father Christmas know we've already got a talking doll?'

Daniel started backing. 'Well ...'

A big blue Land Cruiser lurched into his path and stopped. Daniel hit his own brakes. 'Give me a break.' He looked at the kids and made a smile. 'I didn't see him. Going too fast for parking lots.'

Daniel waited for the car to move. It didn't. He couldn't see any nearby parking spots they might be waiting for. Daniel beeped his horn, two short peeps, nothing pushy. It still didn't go.

Sam said, 'Mum says you have to be patient when you're shopping.'

Frances looked at him, soaking in his wisdom. She nodded, but said, 'I don't want two talking dolls.'

Daniel opened his door. The Land Cruiser had tinted windows so he couldn't see the driver. He got out and went to tap on the window, but as he got to the back it suddenly drove off, squealing up the ramp and onto the street.

*

Helen carried most of the boxes from the spare room as she followed Daniel towards the garage. His briefcase was balanced on the box he carried under his good arm. He'd changed for work as soon as he'd brought the kids home.

Helen explained to Frances, 'He reads the letter you sent to tell him with the list of what you want. But, I think the elves tell him if you get things. Usually, you don't see and it's all a surprise.' Daniel had made a bit of a hash of the present buying.

Haggis dropped his tennis ball at Daniel's feet, nearly tripping him. He yelled, 'Get out of it, dog.' Christmas shopping hadn't improved his mood. 'How come we have to have the wedding shower here?'

'He wants you to throw the ball,' said Frances, bending to throw it. Haggis grabbed it before she could, wanting Daniel to do the throwing.

'There isn't enough room at Rosemarie's flat. They're your friends, Daniel.'

'Inconvenient time for a wedding, so close to Christmas.'

'Well I guess they thought it would be romantic.'

If he heard her irony, he didn't show it. He nudged the handle of the side garage door expertly with his elbow and backed himself through it, holding it open with his good shoulder. 'No Haggis. Stay.'

Helen stepped over the dog with her boxes, hearing the automatic garage doors grinding up. Summer light wound up the bench like a fast-forward sunrise.

Daniel had noticed the drop cloth that hid what the kids had been making. He put the box he'd been carrying next to it, still peering at the thing that didn't belong in his shed. He started to reach for the cloth.

'No,' she said.

'Huh?'

'Santa's little helpers.'

He still didn't get it.

'A surprise. For you. For Christmas.' It was like talking to her deaf grandfather.

'Oh.'

He looked at it suspiciously.

She put her boxes on the bench. She'd wait for him to go before stacking everything up on one of the shelves.

He threw his briefcase in through the open window of the ute and fished his keys out of his pocket.

'The Christmas tree.'

'Right. On my way home. Biggest one I can find.'

Samuel was crying. Helen looked out to the driveway where Sam was holding his bike.

Daniel said, 'Don't play in the driveway, Sam!'

'He's hurt,' said Helen, pushing past and going out to Samuel. His knees were skinned and bleeding.

'The chain came off.'

'Poor man. It's okay.' Helen bent to take a look at his knees.

'Don't cry mate. Laugh it off.' Daniel stood nearby.

Helen bit her lip. Watched Samuel nodding bravely, taking big breaths and trying to make his face smile to please his father.

Daniel patted him on the shoulder bringing a real smile. 'I gotta go to work, matey, but I'll fix the chain as soon as I get home, okay?'

'Yes.'

Daniel grabbed the bike one-handed and lifted it off the driveway.

'We'll put some ointment on in a minute,' said Helen, not hugging him yet. She and Samuel stepped onto the grass as Daniel backed out and down the driveway. She waited for him to look so she could wave but he didn't.

Driving a battered ute. Hearth & Home: Restorations. A tradie. Amis puts the registration number into his Blackberry. Big two-storey McMansion in a cul-de-sac. Upwardly mobile? Rich parents? Light-blue picket fence. The house an invented colour – sage? Amongst the aubergines and terracottas all with little balconies to view each other. Lots of Christmas fruit and power bills. High crime rates, cul-de-sacs. Unsolved burglaries. No passing traffic.

Amis turns the car around at the end of the cul-de-sac so he can follow The Penguin.

Trent is playing on his new Nintendo.

Amis calls one of his contacts in Motor Vehicles. 'June, it's Amis. I've got a ute. Might be abandoned. I need the name and address of the owner.'

*

Daniel parked around the back in the yard. Inside the workshop, trays of rosettes and cornices were drying on the concrete floor. Men were pouring into other moulds. Sanders and saws were spinning next door where the carpenters were doing delicate woodwork etching period designs into recycled jarrah.

Daniel reached the metal stairs to go up to the offices when someone called him.

'Mr Longo.'

Daniel turned. It was Nadif.

'Mr Longo ... I am so sorry. It was my fault. I forgot the fixing bolt and I was so busy getting it, I forgot I left Hua holding all the weight.'

Daniel saw Hua and another older worker, Yusof, moving up with grins. They'd wound the apprentice up. You could do that in the old days, but this kid was from a war zone.

Daniel said, 'Don't worry about it.'

'You not sacking me?'

Daniel saw the men smiling behind the boy. 'No, we'll give you another chance. But there's a rule.'

'A rule?'

'Yeah, no killing the boss.' The men laughed.

Nadif looked stricken, and Daniel patted him on the shoulder. 'It was an accident, mate. Do what Hua tells you and we'll be good.'

The men laughed and Nadif tried to smile.

Daniel headed up the stairs. He was lucky to have Nadif. Apprentices were hard to keep with all the work up north. Maybe they did kill their bosses in Somalia.

Brian used to joke about the united nations of Hearth & Home. 'You're sponsoring these boats, aren't you?' They'd started off mostly white, if you count Italians as white, but over the years the newcomers who were brilliant, patient craftsmen were the ones who stayed. They had families and they were thankful for the work, but Daniel knew they shared the pride of appreciated skill.

Chantel was waiting at the top of the stairs, forcing Daniel to look down so he wouldn't look up her short skirt as he came to the top.

'Oww, Daniel. Does it hurt?'

'Only when I laugh.'

Chantel said, 'You poor thing.'

'I gotta learn to duck.'

Daniel headed to his office. Brian was at his door but watching Chantel wiggling back to reception. 'You poor thing,' he said, aping Chantel.

'I am poor. In every way.' Daniel tossed his briefcase on his desk. Looked at the computer-generated sign: *We Love Sheridan* that Brian had sticky taped to the wall. Sheridan was the big job. Daniel's eyes drifted over to the old black and white photograph of his own hotel, in its heyday, blu-tacked underneath. He sat down, realising Brian had followed him in. 'Oh, and thanks for your concern.'

'Hey, I meant it. And I don't even want to get into your pants.'

'My pants are spoken for.'

Brian sat on the couch. 'Hua told me what happened. That old pub will kill you one day.'

Daniel must have grimaced because Brian spoke again, quickly. 'Sorry mate. Joke. I wasn't thinking.'

Daniel picked at a pile of envelopes on his desk.

Brian said, 'Miller's went into receivership yesterday.'

'What?' Daniel looked at him but he just kept nodding. Brian would have crunched the numbers. Would want to talk strategy. Shit. 'Where's our boom, dude?'

Brian made his old joke. 'If only the Chinese were interested in quality tuck pointing.'

They went out to the Sheridan city site to make sure things were ready for the show-and-tell, using one of the refurbished rooms to shave and change into their corporate suits. Sheridan wasn't a Chinese company. It had once been Scottish and was now Japanese and expanding quickly into Australian hospitality.

Brian waited until they were on their way down to greet Osaka before he whispered, 'We should hit them for an advance.'

'Are we in that much trouble?'

'Miller's owed us a lot. Even if we do get forty percent of what they owed us, it'll be months, maybe years before we see it.'

Daniel whispered, 'We already got the first instalment. They'll think we're hicks.' Then he beamed, 'Mr Osaka. Delighted to see you again.'

The Sheridan bigwigs were admiring the new wallpaper in the lobby by the lifts.

'Beautiful,' said Johnson, the American.

Brian, all smiles, said, 'The pastel colours you've chosen are very warm, very charming.'

McClusky was the bean counter. 'And this hotel will be completed?'

Daniel said, 'Ready for painting in one week, and the final fretwork.'

'You can have your staff back in within a fortnight,' chimed in Brian.

Nods all round except Osaka, who picked at invisible dust on a door jam.

McClusky asked, 'And Rockingham?'

'On schedule. Daniel?'

'On schedule, as agreed.' They were looking at his arm. Daniel said, 'Fortunately, I oversee the work now and no longer need to be quite so hands-on.'

'Thankfully, this means Daniel will be sparing us his golfing talents this visit.' Brian to the rescue again.

Smiles. Daniel happy to wear it. He was an angry golfer.

Osaka whispered to Johnson who said, 'Mr Osaka asks after your family hotel.'

Daniel smiled. He couldn't help bowing ever so slightly to Osaka. He said, 'Very slowly. A labour of love.'

Osaka nodded wisely. He said something else in Japanese.

McClusky said, 'Sheridan's offer still stands.'

Osaka had made a number of offers to buy the old hotel. Daniel was having trouble finding polite ways to say no. He could feel Brian's restlessness as everyone waited on Daniel's response. Daniel smiled and said, 'Mr Osaka and I have the same tastes.'

Osaka smiled for the first time. He bowed. The bigwigs went into the nearest room to inspect the refit.

Brian whispered, 'They love us.'

'And we love Sheridan.'

Daniel stood at the deli counter waiting for his change. He was in his favourite overalls, nicely plastered and paint-impregnated. The chicken roll and drink were in his sling, like a carry bag.

The owner said, 'Home, mate?'

'Nah. Do another run tonight maybe.'

'Business must be good.'

'I wish.'

Daniel took his dinner back to his ute and headed back to the workshop. He'd let the guys go at knock-off time, not knowing if they could cover overtime under the present circumstances. Brian was at dinner with the Sheridan mob and other contractors and hoteliers. Daniel figured he could turn out the moulds to finish drying overnight and get another load on before he headed off.

When he got to the side door, it was already unlocked. He twisted the handle a couple of times trying to remember if he had locked it before he left for dinner. He was tired. It was possible.

He put the Coke and roll on a bench and touched the nearest plaster. It seemed firm. When he straightened he noticed a blue glow from one of the upstairs offices. Someone had left a computer on. He grabbed the roll and wound down the foil and munched on it as he went up the steep stairs. His office was empty but his computer was on. He turned on his office light and went in, reaching for the mouse to close things down. It was parked on the Sheridan page. He scrolled down. It wasn't just Sheridan. It was Brian's overview of all their current accounts.

Daniel turned towards Brian's office but the lights weren't on and all Daniel could see was a reflection of himself in the glass divider. 'Brian?'

Daniel looked the other way. Reception was dark. He closed his computer and grabbed a heavy metal T square from the drawing desk. He turned out his office light.

'Brian?'

He went to the top of the stairs. The workshop floor was still down to a third lighting where he had left it when he went for food. Upstairs was darker but seemed empty.

He heard movement and looked down. A figure was running to the door.

'Hey!'

They scrambled for the handle.

Daniel threw the T square. It spun like a boomerang and boomed loudly on the large metal wall before clattering onto the empty concrete floor.

They had the door open and were gone.

Daniel clambered down the metal steps, slowed by his bad arm, and ran out into the darkness. He stopped, just outside the door, scanning the yard. Like other factories, they had high security lights aimed at doors and gates but with lots of darkness in between. He heard an engine start. He saw the car up at the road. A four-wheel drive. It went past the gate. Blue.

Daniel headed for the ute, but dropped his keys, managing to kick them under as they fell. The blue car was long gone.

*

Helen woke alone but with a feeling someone was downstairs. Daniel's clock showed 2.14.

She put on her dressing-gown and went along the hall, the night-light a dull blue. Frances was asleep, her night-light on too. Sam was in bed, his covers fallen to the floor. The air conditioning was on, but the night was warm and his curtains moved slightly. He liked his window open. She went in and folded his doona at the end and pulled the sheet over him. He didn't stir. He slept with a smile of perfect beauty and Helen wanted to stroke his face, but heard noise downstairs.

A light was on. It was Daniel's home office. Helen went halfway down the stairs. 'Daniel?'

She could hear his voice.

'And I woke you?' He listened. 'You had to get up to get the phone anyway. Sorry. No, his mobile was off. Sorry. It'll wait till morning. Goodnight Rosemarie.' Daniel sat in his leather chair holding the telephone. He was dressed in his filthy overalls. He had his work boots on, in the house.

He saw her in the doorway and put the phone down. 'I woke you too.'

She sat in the chair inside the door. 'Big order on?'

'Oh, you know,' he said standing.

'No, I don't know. I got the sack from Hearth & Home when I got pregnant.'

'You didn't get the sack. You got promoted. I better get some sleep.' He went to the door but she stayed sitting, seeing if he needed to or would share.

'Come on, mate. It's late,' he said, patting her on the shoulder as he went out.

She followed him up, aware in spite of herself that he was leaving dusty boot tracks on the carpet of the stairs.

He sat on the end of the bed unlacing his boots expertly with one hand.

'Mate!' she said.

He looked up, blinking.

'Well matey, I'll catch you tomorrow, mate.' She hung her dressing-gown on the hook behind the door.

'What?'

'Mate is what you call someone who hands you a hammer. Mate is the name of someone in a bottle shop.'

'Ahh. Darling.'

'And don't bring your work boots into the house.' She picked them up off the floor and took them into the ensuite.

He had moved over to his side of the bed when she came back. He was struggling to get out of his overalls with his back to her.

'Is there trouble at work?'

'What makes you say that?'

'You don't usually give Brian nighty-night calls at two a.m.'

'His mobile was off. Otherwise I wouldn't have woken Rosemarie.'

Helen considered his non sequitur.

He seemed to realise it because he said, 'Nothing. Usual stuff. Deadlines. Banks.'

'Now that wasn't so hard was it?'

He didn't turn around. He kept working on his overalls, managing to get them down.

'Is that all?'

'Sure. Just late and tired. That's all.' He turned and smiled. Yes, tiredly.

She climbed into bed and said, 'Well thanks, mate.'

He'd gone into the ensuite. She wondered why she hadn't helped him with his overalls.

*

They met at the bank where Bradley had called them to a mysterious meeting. Daniel told Brian what had happened at the factory the previous night as they waited amongst the customers.

'Did you phone the cops?'

'I tried to phone you, sheriff.'

'I died with my boots on. By the way, Rosemarie is pissed at you.'

'There's no way you could have left our accounts up on the computer?'

'Not on your computer. Our accounts would make pretty slim viewing. Was anything missing?'

'Not that I could see. Have to check when we get back from this.'

Bradley shook hands but without a smile. When they settled across Bradley's paperless black desk he said, 'So, there's nothing you'd like to tell me.'

Brian said, 'Could you give us a clue?'

Bradley ignored him, looking pointedly at Daniel. 'Did you think my seeing your old hotel would mitigate things?'

Daniel asked, 'Mitigate?'

Bradley looked at his computer screen with a frown.

Brian said, 'What?'

'Mr Longo, are you still under the terms of bankruptcy provisions?'

Daniel didn't understand. Perhaps it was his lack of sleep.

The banker repeated the question, 'Are you an undisclosed bankrupt?'

Bankrupt? Daniel turned the word again.

Brian said, 'Mr Bradley, as Mr Longo's accountant for ten years and business partner for six, I can assure you that Daniel has never filed for nor been declared bankrupt.'

Daniel found his voice. 'What's going on?'

Bradley was nodding to Brian. 'I'll go through the credit rating details. Institute searches in the bankruptcy declarations. It may be a computer error.'

'You bet it's an error,' said Daniel, getting angry now.

Brian put a hand on his arm. Asked the banker, 'Our line of credit, Jeff?'

'On hold. Not withdrawn, mind you.'

'But effectively frozen?'

'My hands are tied. Until we can sort this out.'

'I've always paid my bills. Always,' said Daniel in Brian's car.

'I know Danny. Shit. Could it have been your father?'

'What! How?'

'No, I mean was he ever bankrupt? You know so they've confused the info with the same surname.'

'No,' said Daniel quietly. The truth was he didn't know.

'It could explain the glitch is all.'

'Have I ever let you down?'

'No man. That's not what I'm saying.'

'I'm sure.'

'Shit!' said Brian at the next lights, banging on the steering wheel.

Daniel gathered all the men from the workshop. They knew something was up. Daniel's mouth was dry. 'The half-pay should only continue until we get the second payment through from Sheridan. Or if the bank fixes up their fuck-up.'

He looked around to find an encouraging face or even one that was not grim. Only young Nadif looked hopeful. Everyone else started looking at their feet, probably doing sums in their heads.

'Look, I won't let you guys down, okay?'

Brian was in his office working the phone. 'Ron, it's not alarm bell time! I only want it taken out to ninety days. We've got a big one on. You know the big outfits take their time in paying their end.'

Brian looked at Daniel, grimacing as he tried not to scare one of their main suppliers.

Daniel visited. He wished Merry Christmas and dropped off wine and whisky and hampers that they probably couldn't afford but didn't share the offered beers. He showed a couple of the bigger joints the figures concerning Sheridan, as an act of good faith, he said, but only because the Miller's problem had spooked folks.

Daniel had got to Sheridan's Rockingham site before knock-off time. He drove home late, making the lists in his head, of what Rockingham would need to start, of the next stage of the city, of what could be done at the factory to generate short-term cash.

When he turned into his street, he nearly hit a car. It was a stupid place to park so close to the corner but he had started to relax too soon, in sight of home. He looked in the rear-view mirror, annoyed, but realised the car was familiar. It was a blue Land Cruiser. Like the one at the factory and maybe somewhere else too.

Daniel turned into his driveway. The bedroom lights were off. It was after ten. He put the ute in reverse and backed out, his headlights sweeping the little picket fence that separated his driveway from the one next door and then picking up the blue Land Cruiser, still parked at the entrance to Daniel's street. Daniel drove back towards it, suddenly turning his headlights to high beam to see the number plate. It lurched forward and drove past, heading into the dead end.

Daniel slammed on his brakes but he smiled as he did a three-point turn at the entrance to his street. He could see the Land Cruiser at the other end, its headlights now on sweeping at the bottom of a semicircle of Christmas lights. It was trapped in the dead-end street.

'Got you now, you fucker.' Daniel drove slowly down the centre of the street towards the Land Cruiser as it came back towards him. But the other car wasn't slowing. It sped up and moved to the middle of the road. Then high beams came on, dazzling Daniel. He turned his steering wheel instinctively away and to the right and hit the brakes. He saw grass and a birdbath in the next door neighbour's front yard. He veered left and smashed through the side picket fence and into his own front yard before the ute stopped.

*

Helen watched the neighbours and the police. They'd finally turned off the flashing blue light so that the Christmas reds and greens and whites could glow brightest again. Haggis had refused to stop barking until Helen locked him in the laundry.

Daniel was standing near the shattered pickets adjoining the Hoseys talking to the young policeman. 'It was the same one.'

'But you didn't report this … burglary?'

'I am now.' Daniel was talking loudly.

The policeman seemed sceptical. 'Nothing was taken?'

'I don't know. Computers … information. You know, who can tell.'

An even younger policewoman came back from the Hoseys next door. 'They didn't see anything. Heard the bang.' The Hoseys were a retired couple. They stood in their driveway, looking concerned. When Helen had waved they'd looked embarrassed. Everyone was in shorts and nighties. Everyone in the street had been in bed when the bang had brought them all.

Daniel said, 'I'm not making it up.'

The policeman nodded to the policewoman. They must be barely twenty years old. She went back to the paddy-wagon.

Daniel said, 'Why would I give you the licence number?'

Sam and Frances hugged into Helen's legs.

A group of neighbours stood in a group out in the street but short of Daniel and Helen's property line, like their boundary was forbidden.

The policewoman brought back a breathalyser bag and held it for Daniel. She'd put on a white rubber glove.

'I haven't been drinking.'

'You breathe long and steady into this until I tell you to stop, Mr Longo.'

'I don't drink. Never.'

He glanced at Helen and she nodded back to him. She willed him not to fight them. Blow and get it over with. He looked from her to the clumps of neighbours.

'We can do this here or at the station, sir.'

Daniel took the end of the thing and blew into it with his eyes closed.

Frances said, 'Are they giving him a drink, mummy?'

The policeman looked over and smiled.

The policewoman took the device and looked at the reading.

The neighbours craned.

'Thank you, sir. That does clear up that aspect.'

'You want to tell them I gave a clear reading?' Daniel pointed at the neighbours.

The young policeman seemed to consider it, but instead said, 'You might want to consider not driving while your arm is like that, sir.'

Daniel had explained to the police how his hurt arm was unrelated to the accident. Daniel had talked about a burglary at the factory. About a blue Land Cruiser stalking him.

'Good night, sir.' They were leaving.

Daniel stood panting and glaring out at the Christmassy houses but before he could embarrass himself anymore, he turned on his heel and stormed across the lawn towards Helen and the kids. But he wasn't coming to them. He went past as though they were shrubs and headed for the door.

'Daniel!'

Frances said, 'Daddy squashed the fence.'

'Daniel.'

He finally stopped.

She pointed at the ute, parked rather neatly, if sideways, on their front lawn. The police sat in their police car at the end of the drive talking into their radio, filing their report. She said, 'You going to get it towed home?'

*

Amis pours Glenfiddich. Gulps. Feels it warm him. He breathes deeply, calm. He turns on his computer. Looks at the empty glass in his hand. He hurls it against the far empty wall. It bounces and slides along the carpet and clatters into a chair.

Amis pokes the keyboard. *Longo*. He pulls up the details he already has. The easy ones and the business files he copied. A useful list, but not complete.

Amis looks to the glass, unbroken near the table. He goes to the glass. He looks down at it. He smiles at the metaphor. He sees himself, as though from above, looking down at the glass appreciating the irony.

*

Daniel said, 'If you'd accept a cheque, I could make it more.'

Riley looked again at the scrap of paper Daniel had given him. It had the Land Cruiser's licence number on it. He looked across at his computer screen. Riley was a fat private investigator. D-fence Investigations was on the end upstairs in an anonymous, partly vacated suburban complex. He wore jeans, an untucked checked shirt and a mocking smile. 'I think, in the light of everything you've told me, that would be most unwise, Mr Longo.'

'No, my credit is good. Very good.'

Riley grunted.

'What?' asked Daniel.

'*You* ring them. I rang them. That's what they're there for.'

'It was good. How ...'

'You don't pay your bills. Traders, banks, governments report you.'

'I pay my bills. It's a mistake.'

'More than one it seems.'

'On the phone?'

'Yes.'

'You can wreck someone's life on the phone.'

'You have to know who to phone. You have to know what you're talking about.'

'Could *you* do it? Could *you* make this happen out of nothing?'

Riley grunted again. Yes, he could do it. Daniel knew he was a cop once. It was on the D-fence's website.

Daniel looked at the back of Riley's computer screen.

Riley said, 'It's skittish times, Mr Longo. Everyone is afraid. Afraid they'll go down too. Debt is the new bubonic plague.'

'I need the name,' pleaded Daniel. '*I'll* track them down. *I'll* find out who's targeting us. What stupid industrial espionage thing is going on. I just need the name.'

'And I have it. Just pay me in cash.'

Daniel stood to go, but didn't. The man wasn't his friend. It was business. He had no secretary. Bits of electronics lay heaped on the filing cabinet. A registration of business certificate was on the wall. Another frame held a press clipping of a case that Riley must have solved. He was no more and no less than Daniel had been ten years ago, scratching along working for himself. Daniel said, 'Look, all you've done is make a couple of phone calls. A mate in the cops or something.'

'But you have to have the mate in the right place. You have to know who to call and what to ask for. And they have to be looked after.'

'I'll give you three hundred. For the name and address. Any other stuff I need after that, we'll negotiate.'

'I'm not a greengrocer.' He pointed to his computer screen. 'This isn't spoiling fruit.'

'But hold on a minute. That's exactly what it is. You've already made your phone calls. It's a worthless name and address, unless I pay for it.'

Riley looked hurt but Daniel could see him thinking over the point.

Daniel took out his wallet and opened it towards him. 'All I could scrape together is three hundred.'

Homely Chase seems deserted apart from the postman on his scooter. Homely Chase. There were no Roads in the whole suburb. Nothing so dreary as a Street. One Avenue and two Drives but the rest was an intricate swirl of dead ends called Court, Grove, Rise, Vista, Place and Chase.

Daniel hasn't fixed his fence. Not very Italian of him. A pleasing gap in the dinky picket fence adjoining the next front yard. Missed the birdbath. That looks Italian. Couple of lions and he'd be sure.

The postman comes back. Only a few letters and Christmas cards. Vans did the heavy lifting of online Christmas shopping. Amis lifts his clipboard. Raises a pen for show. All lowly official and belonging and forgotten. Amis waits until the postman leaves the street before he gets out of the car. Stretches his back. Long year making thankless house calls. He wanders to the nearest house, four up from Daniel's. Makes a show of looking at his clipboard. Mimes seeing the broken fence. Ah ha. I see. He wanders along the curb. No paths. No paths in these dead ends. If you're going to chase in Homely Chase you better have your own wheels. And an escape plan.

No tradies. No minions cleaning their pools, edging their lawns, improving their plumbing. No one watering. No curtains ruffling. No cars in drives. The residents are all out for the day, Christmas shopping or working to pay for their third toilet.

Amis pushes a blank envelope into Daniel's letterbox, feigns forgetting something, goes around and gets the letters out of the letterbox, searches for his envelope so he can correct it. Helen. Wife of? Christmas cards. Danilo. From Melbourne. Power bill.

A dog barks. An odd grinding noise. Amis turns to see a street sweeper enter the cul-de-sac. A clean Homely Chase is a happy chase. It grinds slowly towards then around Amis's hire car. Missed a spot.

The dog is barking too much. Amis looks at the house. Wonders if Helen and the kids are home. Decides he'll knock. He pockets the power bill and the letter to Danilo and heads for the front door.

*

Daniel pulled into a bus stop to check his phone. He'd turned it off before meeting Riley. He'd missed a lot of calls, mostly from Brian. He hit Brian's number.

'Daniel. Where are you?'

'On a lead, mate. The security system guys there?'

'Well, about that ... Yes. And gone. Can we afford that?'

'Have to.'

'Have I authorised it?'

'Brian, no time. Has Chantel given you the new computer passwords?'

'Eventually. What's going on?'

'Maybe don't share them with the guys downstairs for now. I don't know yet who or how big this is.'

There was silence on the other end. Daniel thought he might have lost the signal. 'Brian?'

'Daniel?' He sounded pissed.

'As I say, I think the next step is who. So we go on the offensive. Take it up to them. I've made a list. Could be competitors, disgruntled debtors, even Sheridan. Maybe they want to get out of the contract or collect the insurance. Maybe Osaka is really after my hotel.'

'So many enemies.'

'Yeah. Who knows. Anyway, I think the cops'll be useless.'

'About that. Chantel said they've called a couple of times.'

'I reported the burglary. And my car bingle.'

'Uhuh?'

'Anyway, the cops will plod along filling out paperwork. We need answers fast.'

'I wouldn't mind a few myself.'

'I'm telling you.'

'Dan, when we formed this partnership, remember our agreement? Rule one – you aren't to keep everything to yourself.'

'I'm telling you.'

Silence.

Daniel said, 'Anyway, I'm onto something I think. I'll get back to you, as soon as I know. Like I'm doing.'

Silence.

Daniel buttoned off. That's all he needed, having to stroke Brian as well.

His phone started chiming again. He clicked it off and headed out into traffic to the address Riley had given him.

*

Amis stood at the medium height fence that ran from the house to the garage. The dog wagged its tail. 'How you doing pooch? Good dog.'

Washing on the line. Mum, Dad and two kids all right. Here is the underwear. A cricket bat next to the totem tennis. Practising alone. One of those ridiculous round trampolines with a big net around it. No falling now. Good insurance prospects. A child's pushbike leans against the garage wall, its chain dangling. No helmet. Tsk tsk.

The dog drops a chewed ball by the gate. 'They lock you in, did they?' A latch over that side of the gate. Not locked. Amis watches the dog. Ears up, tail wagging. 'Good dog.' Amis opens the gate. He kicks the tennis ball and the dog runs after it into the wide garden bed. Thick belt of shrubs along the fence. No security lighting. A security door at the back. Another to the laundry.

The dog drops the ball at Amis's feet. He picks it up and feigns a throw. The dog races off in the direction of the throw but stops in the middle of the yard, confused. Amis smiles. The dull grind of the street sweeper is the only sound in the suburb.

Amis goes back to the driveway and looks at the garage doors. Remote control. Easy. The dog has followed him out. Amis still has the ball in his hand. He throws it down the drive, high so it bounces. The dog chases and times a jump, catching it three-quarters down. Amis can see the street sweeper past the front edge of the house. It's coming back down the cul-de-sac. It is three houses away and coming towards Daniel's house. The dog drops the ball at Amis's feet. Amis lifts it for a throw. The dog runs halfway down the drive. Amis mocks a throw but only half. The dog edges further back, winding up for a spring, getting excited, ready for the throw. Amis edges forward. The dog edges back. It's coiling, hardly containing its joy. The street sweeper is at the front of Daniel's house now. Amis gets ready to throw high. He thinks of Teddy and realises why. The anticipation is always spoiled by the fulfilment because that's the end.

*

Helen sat with her sister Leonie on the grass near the small pool so they could watch Frances doing her swimming lessons. Leonie's kids were in the main pool. So was Samuel, doing level 6.

The planning of Christmas lunch which was at Leonie's this year had filled most of their time. Helen had steered her end to mentioning the pressures of the wedding and the shower. She'd tried to deflect her sister from 'the fence incident' even though it was the first thing Frances yelled to her cousins. 'Daddy crashed his car.' Helen had joked, 'When they do it, it's not called a crash.' She didn't say she had waited in bed with her own questions. But he hadn't come up. His home computer was still warm in the morning, but when she tried to see what he'd been doing, she couldn't get in. He'd changed the password.

'So, Daniel's okay?' Leonie was looking at her intently.

'I think so.' Helen looked away to Frances, off a little from her group.

'It's a shame Daniel can't come to see them swim,' said Leonie.

Leonie had her radar up, Helen thought. She nodded but kept watching the pool.

'It's *great* Daniel can't come?' asked Leonie.

Helen would like to tell, to explain or ask, but it seemed disloyal.

Leonie said, 'It's a shame you ever met the no-good son of a bitch. Let's beat him to death with champagne bottles.'

Helen laughed. 'Why champagne bottles?'

'They've got really heavy bases. Haven't you noticed? I've always thought they'd be good for bashing someone.'

'You're an evil person. I think I told Mum that.'

'Often. So?'

'Frances starts kindy next year. Samuel's got school. Daniel works twelve hours a day and he's part of the secret society of the Cosa Nostra.' She shrugged, feeling foolish.

Leonie shrugged too, giving just a touch of her patronising 'poor you' look.

'I look around our street. During the day there's no one there. The postman's motorbike is a highlight. I ... I'm going to turn into the woman with the huge spotless house – the heart and soul of the school canteen.'

'No you won't. You're not her.'

'I'm getting there.'

'Helen, save dolphins or defend a forest or ... Get a job, girl. It's time.'

Helen said, 'His father.'

Leonie nodded seriously. She knew Daniel's father had committed suicide. That he'd hung himself one night at the old hotel. It was a couple of years before Helen had met Daniel, but she'd had to share with someone when Daniel told her the secret and she'd told Leonie.

'He's nothing like his father, Helen. I'm sure of that.'

'He's so determined to be – not like that. He won't relax. He ... There's stuff. Anyway, it's cool. All good. Just bumpy before Christmas and all.' She shrugged but made a more convincing smile.

Leonie hugged her and Helen was relieved to be able to hide her face. She knew it would be a betrayal to explain that she could put up with everything except that Daniel wouldn't talk to her anymore. She'd lost her best friend and she found it lonely. She couldn't say that to her sister because she'd only then said it to herself and she hoped it wasn't true.

*

It was a run-down weatherboard with a battered surf ski lying on the lawn next to the blue Land Cruiser.

Daniel took off the sling and left it in this car. The bandage on his shoulder didn't allow much movement, but he didn't want to look too wounded.

He knocked on the door avoiding the cracked glass panel. He knocked again, rattling the glass until the door was opened by a weedy young man with stubble and a sleeve of green and red tattoos. Music belted out. The Steve Miller Band.

Daniel stepped back and opened his arms. 'Well?'

The man squinted.

Daniel could smell dope.

He said, 'Here I am.'

The man stood in board shorts and a Bintang singlet, blinking.

Daniel said, 'You want to tell me what this is all about.'

'Do I know you?' he asked with a strong Kiwi accent.

'I don't know. Do I know you?'

Daniel tried to fold his arms in a demanding way but the bandage got in the way and the Kiwi shook his head and started to turn away.

Daniel stepped in and pushed him up against the wall inside the door, his good hand on his throat. 'Why are you doing this? Who do you work for?'

'I don't know what you're talking about.' He looked scared. He looked truthful.

'I've seen your car. At my factory. Outside my fucking house.'

'I only just bought it. I swear, bro.'

Daniel eased back.

Another voice said, 'What the fuck, eh?'

Daniel turned to see a big Maori coming out of the kitchen. He turned back to the Kiwi. 'Where from?'

Before he could answer, Daniel was punched in the side of his face. It knocked him to the floor.

The Kiwi was saying, 'I dunno. Never saw him before, eh.'

The Maori was looking down. He had rugby shorts on. He seemed to be deciding whether to punt Daniel.

Daniel felt his cheek. It didn't feel broken. He said, 'Who'd you buy the car from?'

'It's not stolen,' said the Maori.

'Who?'

'Fuck you,' said the Maori shaping up, loosely.

Daniel started to get up but had to struggle as he could only use one arm. He got onto his knees. Knew he was an easy target. He looked at them both and let them see that he knew it.

The Kiwi said, 'Who cares. Custom Motors, Skip. Tell 'em we sent you, eh.'

*

There was a white car parked on the street a few doors up from the house. Helen took note because it was uncommon in Homely Chase. She wondered if it had anything to do with Daniel.

Frances said, 'Mum, why's Haggis sleeping on the road?'

Helen saw the shape and turned into their driveway, clicking open the garage doors. The side gate was open.

'What? Where's Haggis?' said Samuel. He had been reading.

'On the road,' said Frances.

Helen didn't let them go out the front. She hustled them through the yard door of the garage and into the house.

Samuel ran through the kitchen and into the lounge room.

Helen yelled, 'Sam!'

'I'm seeing out the window.'

Frances stood at the door to the hall, unwilling to follow her brother past this threshhold, but knowing something pretty big was happening.

Helen put the kids' towels on the bench and said, 'Go get *Bananas in Pyjamas* from your room, darling, and I'll get us lunch.'

Helen waited for her to go up the stairs before dialing Daniel. His mobile was off. She called the factory.

'Hearth & Home.'

'Chantel. Can I talk to Daniel?'

'On his mobile, Mrs Longo. How's getting the shower going?' Bright and bubbly and not a care in the world.

'What? Oh. Lot to do.' Helen needed Daniel to take care of this while she distracted the kids.

Chantel said, 'Is Dan going ... um, is Mr Longo going to a bucks' night?'

'I suppose so. Thanks Chantel.'

The girl wore very short skirts and had a barely disguised infatuation for Daniel. Helen was never worried, but it did get wearing, pretending not to notice.

Helen tried Daniel's mobile again. It was still off. She went to the lounge. Samuel stood in the bay window where the Christmas tree needed to go.

'Samuel, I need you to be brave.'

'I am.' He said it matter of factly. He was.

'Look after your sister and don't come out, okay?'

'What are you going to do?'

Helen didn't answer. She got a jumbo garbage bag and took it out the front. She was sure she'd latched the gate. Blood came from Haggis's nose and from one ear. She bent to touch him. She prodded his side. It felt harder than usual. He was dead. She needed a shovel to slide him in so she didn't have to touch him again.

'Your dog?' A man was coming along the road.

'Yes. I thought our gate was locked.'

'Damn shame. For the kids.'

Helen looked at him and he indicated the house. She turned to see Samuel and Frances in the window. She motioned for them to go.

'You want a hand?'

'Oh, no, I can manage.'

He bent, ignoring her. 'No problem. It's this sort of job we men come in handy for. Come on fella.' He hefted Haggis, a little roughly by the hind legs and swung him upside down towards the garbage bag. Helen looked away, as she felt Haggis's weight in the bag. Then he took it.

'Where do you want him?' He had the garbage bag held out in both hands.

He had a suit on but no tie. A close-cropped beard. He gave an apologetic smile. 'Sorry. That sounded callous. My son has a dog, you see. Feel like I know this one. I was making house calls, when I saw you come out.' He pointed to the white car parked down the street.

She nodded and led him towards the back. She'd need to bury Haggis perhaps, for the kids.

'Round the back?'

'Thank you, Mr ...?'

'Armstrong. Charles Armstrong.'

'My maiden name was Armstrong.'

'What a coincidence. Maybe we're long-lost cousins.'

She stopped at the gate, to let him through first. He smiled oddly, but when Helen looked closely, he turned to look down the drive. 'Looks like you need a new side fence.'

*

Daniel took his briefcase into the sales yard trying to look jaunty and uninjured as he walked.

A salesman stepped up with a bright, 'Looking for anything in particular, sir?'

'Window-shopping, mate.' Daniel took a couple more steps, but called back, 'But if I see something I like ...?'

'Pete. I'm Peter. I'll see you right.'

Daniel nodded and wandered into the office. He stood near the counter as an older woman put down the phone. 'Can I help you?'

'Pete sent me in.'

She nodded, neutral.

Daniel said, 'I bought a blue Land Cruiser this morning.'

She began to shake her head, sensing a complaint. 'You'd have to see the salesperson ...'

'No, nothing like that. Great car.' Daniel smiled. 'I found a whole pile of fishing lures and tackle in the spare wheel well. Thought I'd drop them back to the previous owner. Ask how she handles off-road.'

Daniel smiled.

The lady nodded, hitting computer buttons. 'This morning? It might not be entered yet. I always have to chase them up to do the computer things.'

Daniel watched her find the car and get happy. But she had second thoughts. She looked up and stared at the swelling on Daniel's cheek. She took in the bandaged arm. She said, 'I better check with the sales manager. I'm sure he'll say it's fine, but ...' She shrugged, but wasn't really apologising for playing it safe.

Daniel nodded. Sure. Not a worry.

The lady went towards the back offices and Daniel stepped around the counter to look at the name and address on the PDF copy of the sales document.

*

Mr Amstrong had his coat off but wasn't sweating in spite of the spade work. He patted the mound under the jacaranda tree and stood to look at Samuel then Frances and finally to Helen before clasping his hands in front of him and bowing his head.

'Dear God, take Haggis into heaven. Let him run around in green fields, where there aren't any cars.'

Samuel nodded but Frances stared at the man distrustfully.

He said, with no hint of a patronising tone, 'Look after Haggis, because he is the best dog in the world and we will miss him. Amen.'

'Amen,' said Samuel, solemnly.

'Thank you, Mr Armstrong. You've been very kind.'

'I know what it's like to lose a ... If you don't mind, Helen, I should wash up and get back to work.'

'Oh, yes. This way.'

The kids stayed by the grave as Helen led him towards the house. It was clear he'd lost someone and it seemed recent by the way he'd shaken the thought off.

'What do you do, for a living, Mr Armstrong?'

'Please, Helen, call me Charles.'

She nodded. She must have told him her name earlier. 'In through here.' She pointed to the laundry.

'I sell insurance and superannuation.' He must have seen her look because he laughed and added, 'It's all right, Helen. I'll spare you any sales pitches today.' He started washing his hands and Helen turned away to think about lunch. She should try Daniel again. The kids were heading in.

He called something but Helen couldn't quite hear it so she went back to the laundry door. 'Could I have a glass of water please?' He'd left the toilet door open. He was urinating.

Helen suppressed a gasp and backed into the kitchen. She went to the fridge and opened it towards the kids. 'Okay, so ... who's hungry?'

'Beautiful,' he said and Helen swung around. She felt uncomfortable, suddenly.

Armstrong was looking up the hall and around the kitchen. He said, 'You have a beautiful home. You must be proud.'

Proud? Helen put a plate of polony and salad on the table. Helen remembered the water and got a glass from the cupboard. He was between her and the ice water slot in the fridge. 'Thank you, Mr Armstrong, for all your help.'

He smiled, but moved towards the dining table where Samuel had sat. 'You folks having a party?' He looked at the glasses and plates Helen had stacked, ready.

'It's called a shower,' said Samuel.

'A friend of Daniel's, my husband's work partner.' Helen was surprised at all the information she'd volunteered. Perhaps she felt he needed reminding that she was married. She poured the water.

'These are good.'

He lifted the pages of sketches she'd been doing for the old hotel. Furnishings and ideas for colours.

Samuel started picking at the food on his plate. Frances stood by the back door, neither in nor out. She was glaring at the man.

Helen wanted him out too now, unsure why. She took him the water, looking for polite words which would send him away.

'You're very talented. Ah, thanks.' He looked at her, too long, but suddenly said, 'I better get back to work. Sorry. I so miss the feel of a happy family.' He picked up his clipboard from the bench. He'd been carrying it earlier. He must have put it down. He was going.

'Oh, could you do me a favour?'

'What?'

He opened up the clipboard. 'My supervisor. He sometimes checks that I'm seeing clients. A bit like those call centres where they say it might be recorded. I get signatures to confirm I've been.'

He pulled out a silver pen. He was advancing on her again. 'I've been here, you see. A small white lie that I've been trying to sell you insurance?'

'Is it really necessary?' She found herself backed against the counter.

'I can really try to sell you. Big house. Worth insuring.' He winked. Smiled. 'Here and I'm out of your hair.'

She took his pen and signed the thing.

He looked up at Frances and said, 'Boo.'

She didn't see the joke.

Helen tried to give him back the file.

He said, 'Oh, um, sorry. Can you date it?'

*

It was a brick and tile with heavy security screens, automatic lights in the drive and out the front. Daniel knocked again. He thought he could hear a television inside.

'Who is it?' A woman's voice, very timid.

'Ah, is Amis home?'

Silence.

Daniel added, 'I'm a friend of his.'

'He doesn't live here.'

It could be true. Daniel said, 'You couldn't give me his address, could you?'

Silence again from the lady in the house. Only the indistinct mumble and periodic ping of a television game show.

Daniel said, 'An address.'

Silence.

'Then I'll leave.'

She said, 'Tell Amis the restraining order means he can't send other people either. Okay?'

Shit, thought Daniel. This guy was scary. He said, 'He didn't send me. Mrs Blyte? My name's Daniel Longo. Has he said anything – about me?'

'Tell Amis I didn't say anything.'

'I don't know where he is, Mrs Blyte.' Daniel looked at the door. It was solid wood with a deadlock. The place was a fortress.

The voice came again, 'I'm going to call the police now.'

*

Timing. Timing is always important. Timing and props. Bags with airline tags. Wait for the cleaners. Everyone gone home but one young conch working too hard.

Sims marched him to filing, Amis filling his head so he has no chance to think. 'The beauty of insurance, son, is that the secrets must be told. Every one put down and kept on file, for only us to see. Financial. Accidents. Health. Family histories. Every asset and every liability must be written down in the file. Why?'

'They have to,' Sims had said. Good dog.

Amis looks up from the files. He's Hartley, from Sydney. See the bags. 'They have to write it down or we won't pay should the worst of the worst happen. They have to volunteer their secrets.'

Sims nods. He wants to finish his other work. He wants to go to the pub. Possibly a young wife.

Amis chooses to bore him an appropriate amount. 'But you have to be able to read them, Sims, or there's really no point is there?'

'Ah, no. Mr Hartley?'

Amis sighs. Long-suffering. Patient senior of the firm. 'Look at the Longo file again. His father's death.'

Amis points.

Sims reads, 'No suspicious circumstances.'

'Which means?'

'Suicide.'

'Now down here buried in family medical history.'

Sims flails, but is a trier. 'His father had nervous breakdowns?'

'So this fellow Danilo's father was as mad as a cut snake and he offed himself, and we insure the son to the hilt. Does he sound like a particularly good risk to you, Sims?'

'Ah, no sir.'

'No. He's trying to push up his fire cover. An old property waiting to be "an insurance job".'

'Oh,' says Sims battling to show intelligent interest.

Amis throws him a bone. 'Who's your IC?'

'Ah, Mr Chang.' Confusion. 'Shouldn't you know?' forming somewhere in his brain, sluggishly.

Amis gets up. 'I have to head back to Sydney, now. Take this to Chang. I want *you* to make sure this file is gone over with a fine toothcomb. You got that?'

'Yes, Mr Hartley.' Smiles. Maybe a feather. Maybe an inside track.

Amis up. Grabbing his bags, other fish to fry. 'These files are a gift son. If people are going to give us their secrets, we don't want to waste them.' Pat on the shoulder.

*

Helen sat at the kitchen table working on the drawings for the old hotel, a CD of Amy Winehouse playing. She was obviously feeling maudlin. If she got onto Carol King, or a third glass of wine, she'd be singing out loud. She had waited for Daniel but had finally eaten her dinner.

The kids had not settled well. They'd both demanded to go out one more time to talk to Haggis before bed. Frances referred to the Grumpy Man and it had taken time to winkle out that she meant the slightly off-putting insurance salesman. Helen had explained about the formal tone of funerals, but Frances set her jaw in the way she had and that was that.

The doorbell chimed and it made her jump. It was late. Maybe it was Mr Hosey from next door, wondering about the fence.

It was Brian, in sports gear.

'Hello. What are you doing here?'

Brian wandered into the house, looking into Daniel's study and into the lounge room.

Helen shut the front door and followed Brian as he went into the kitchen. He had always made himself at home in the new house. She wondered if this was about the wedding.

Brian stood at the counter.

Helen said, 'Tea?'

'Daniel?'

'Well, I won't ask you the same thing.' She put the kettle on.

Brian saw the drawings and went over to the table. 'Rockingham?'

'Oh, no. I'm fiddling with ideas for the hotel.'

Brian looked aghast. He said, 'You're not dumping Hearth & Home to get into the old hotel are you?'

'What!' She went to the drawings. 'No. These aren't for Daniel. They're for me. A little hobby, like watercolours or studying literature at university.'

He didn't smile, possibly didn't get the joke. He lifted drawings, suspiciously.

Helen said, 'Brian, are you on your way to or from a sport?'

'Indoor cricket. Not going.'

'Good.' Helen headed to the lounge room, calling, 'You can get sweaty and help me move these things.'

She had moved what she could to the walls but didn't want to drag the sofas on the carpet. She went to an end of one of the three-seaters. One of the things she'd found out about men and boys, there was no difference, was that if you wanted them to talk about what was bothering them, you had to give them a physical activity.

Brian went to the other end of the couch.

'To your left. Against the wall.'

They moved the couch.

Brian looked at the stick that the kids had labelled *Xmas Tree*. He said, 'Nice Christmas twig.'

'We're going through a minimalist period.'

They moved the other couch and Brian sat on it, but still wasn't ready to share.

She went to the cupboard. Someone had given Daniel a bottle of scotch for Christmas not knowing he never drank. She waved it and Brian nodded. She went to the kitchen for glasses and ice. Another thing she'd discovered about most men apart from Daniel was that liquor loosened lips. It occurred to her that she might already be tipsy.

She went back into the lounge room and gave Brian one of the drinks. She sat next to him and said, 'So what makes you think Daniel would dump Hearth & Home – the most important thing in his whole life?'

'No, you're right. Pure panic. It's this emergency meeting with Sheridan tomorrow.'

Helen nodded as though she knew things.

'And with everything else that's going on, and now him disappearing all day.'

Helen had not been able to get him either. She'd assumed he was with Brian. She felt she should make an excuse, but had too little to go on.

Brian said, 'Helen, what's this about an offensive? Who does he suspect? For that matter, what does he suspect?'

Helen had assumed Brian knew what this was about.

Brian seemed to misinterpret her silence for reticence. He sat forward, imploring. 'I know he saw the suppliers yesterday, but what's he doing today? He didn't go and see Sheridan did he? Tell me he didn't do that?'

'I think it might be time to make things clear, Brian. I don't have the faintest idea what you're talking about. Not a single word.'

Brian blinked at her, his mouth hanging open.

It hurt, Brian's assumption that Daniel would tell her, his incomprehension that Daniel hadn't. Daniel told her nothing. Brian was still looking aghast. She smiled, hoping she seemed lighthearted, but looking at his face she suspected it came off as trying to seem brave which meant her smile made her look pathetic.

Daniel had no plan. He'd waited in his car for Blyte to appear. Lights went on and off in the house and finally stayed off. It was after midnight when he gave up. He supposed he could scrounge up another few hundred dollars and go back to D-fence with the name and address. It still didn't answer who might be employing Blyte.

Daniel registered the YMCA Christmas tree stall after he'd driven past it on his way home and U-turned across the highway. It had been set up in the car park of a library. Sports fields lay empty behind. The trees were padlocked behind a temporary wire mesh fence, ready for the next day. It was long closed.

Daniel sat in the car park and gulped down the dregs of some Red Bull. He tossed the empty can into the back of his ute and grabbed a crow bar and wrenched open the lock.

*

Helen woke to scraping noises. She was on the couch in the lounge room. Haggis was scratching at the back fence. She heard it again but woke more fully. There was no Haggis. It was a day to the shower, then the wedding and Christmas. She had the start of a headache.

The lights were still on in the kitchen and she couldn't see outside. She heard a thump at the back door.

'Who's there?' she called.

There was a whooshing scrape and then a bump at the back door.

Helen looked to the rack of knives on the counter.

A key went into the back door.

'Daniel?'

The door swung open and Daniel stumbled in backwards, dragging a large pine tree.

'I got it,' he said proudly, dragging it like a fish he'd hunted and brought back to the cave. He tugged it and hauled it two-handed through the doorway so the branches spread, knocking the kitchen table back, chairs clattering. Some of her sketches spilled from where Brian had left them. 'I got it,' he said again, dragging it towards the lounge room.

He left a trail of pine leaves in his wake. Helen managed to get past him before the tree reached the vase in the hall. She grabbed it up as the tree swept past, knocking over the stand.

Helen listened upstairs but the kids hadn't stirred. The scraping stopped and Helen went in, still carrying the vase of gerberas.

Daniel stood panting as he looked at the Christmas tree covering the whole floor of the lounge. It must have been three or four metres tall.

'The biggest one they had.'

His arms and face were covered in little red pricks from the pine needles. He had a huge bruise on his cheek. It was blue and puffy.

He saw her looking and said, 'Oh. In the wars again. The good news is that my shoulder feels pretty good.'

Helen put the vase on the table and found her drink on the floor under pine branches. The ice had melted but it tasted sweet.

He looked at the couches and to her drink. 'What's going on?'

'Exactly,' she said. 'What's going on?' Brian had told her about the bank and the suppliers and the credit ratings and the burglary and she'd told Brian about the fence and the blue Land Cruiser.

He picked a sheet of paper from a branch of the tree. It was crushed and torn at the edge. 'What's this?'

One of her sketches. 'Nothing. Embroidery. No, the first tree decoration.'

'Have you been drinking?'

He looked over to the mantel where Brian's glass was. His eyes kept darting around the room as though finally registering all the changes to the furniture.

'Brian was here,' she said.

He blinked as he looked down at the tree.

She wanted to go to him and hug him but the tree filled the floor between them. She stepped as far as she could though. 'Dan, I had no idea about all you've been going through. It's awful.'

'Can we talk about it in the morning?'

'It's one a.m. or something so it is morning, technically.'

He looked at her, confused.

'I'm sorry. That sounded bitchy. I waited up so we could talk.'

'I just need to sort it out. Come up with a plan.'

'Maybe I can help.'

'No, I'll fix it.'

'I'm worried.'

'Don't.'

'Will you tell me what's happening?'

She'd gone out of focus for him again, she could tell. He looked into the far distance and she couldn't tell what he was seeing. He looked bewildered. Still without seeing her, he said, 'It's okay, Helen. All good. I need to do the tree.'

'Well, messages. You've got a meeting with Sheridan tomorrow. You need to see one of the suppliers again. The dog is dead. And buried by a passing stranger. Samuel has passed his next level at swimming. Oh, and Brian wants me to convince you to stop being paranoid.' She stopped herself from saying, I didn't know Brian even knew about your father. Instead she said, 'There. Do I do that as well as Chantel?' She left the lounge room. She closed the back door and looked at the wreckage of the kitchen. Fuck it. She'd do it in the morning. Maybe she wouldn't do it, ever. Maybe she'd go on holidays.

He didn't say anything.

He didn't come up and say sorry. He didn't come up at all.

Daniel needed sleep but couldn't go to bed because Helen would be waiting for him and he didn't have any answers for her. He couldn't say don't worry anymore because he didn't know what the problem was and so he couldn't fix it. He needed sleep because he needed to meet with Sheridan in the morning. And find out which supplier had cold feet again. And to raise cash to find Amis Blyte.

He pushed the base of the tree's stump into the tub he'd placed in the window a few days before. Weeks? He went to the other end and he tried to hoist up the tree. The needles stung. He had to close his eyes. He grabbed at the outer branches but they twisted and broke. He had to slide his hands deep into the thing to find stronger wood. He pushed, resting most of the thing on his good shoulder. It scraped and dug as he pushed it up. He got halfway when it spun and twisted off his shoulder bouncing off the couch and back onto the floor.

He stood panting. It had sounded like rice spilling. He wiped his face and found bits of blood on his hands. He bent and grabbed a branch and dragged at it but it simply slid towards his feet. He went to the thinner end again and pushed it up. He lifted and turned so his back was into the tree. He backed it up towards the corner and into the bay window. It started to slide. He turned with it and tried to catch it but his shoulder pulled again, hurt. A branch flicked his eyes. He wrestled. Pushed himself at it. His boot stepped onto one of the lower branches. It toppled at him. He slipped back and fell, the pine tree coming with him.

Daniel lay on the floor under the stupid Christmas tree. It wasn't actually a tree, he thought. Not a baby pine tree like in the cartoons. It was more likely a branch of a larger tree. It wasn't even that heavy. But unwieldy. He laughed, under the tree, vaguely aware of an ironic, symbolic thing here. It would not beat him. He sobbed. Twice, before he reminded himself it was only a Christmas tree that needed putting up.

Daniel opened his eyes. Frances was in her pyjamas holding her Banana doll. She was looking down at him through a tree, studying him from on high.

Daniel said, 'What time is it?'

'Christmas time.'

He smiled. Fair enough. He slithered out from under the tree. He hadn't gotten it up.

Frances said, 'Haggis got deaded.'

Daniel got up and patted her on the shoulder.

She said, 'The Grumpy Man did it.'

Daniel looked at his watch. Sheridan. 'Shit. The meeting!'

He had no time to shower, but changed into clean clothes. He grabbed his battery razor and his briefcase and headed for the door. 'I'm off,' he yelled to the laundry where the machine was on.

He threw his briefcase into the ute and zapped the roller door. He started the car and his razor at the same time, running it over his chin as he put the car in reverse. He headed out and looked in the rear-view mirror. Bike. He slammed on the brakes but heard the crunch.

A cry? Daniel turned the motor off and ran to the back of the ute, seeing the broken front wheel under and Sam laying on the grass. Sam turned, scared.

Daniel's feet were stuck to the driveway.

Sam looked from the bike to his father.

'For Christ's sake, Sam. How many bloody times have I told you not to play in the driveway?'

'I'm sorry.'

Daniel stepped towards him, his anger rising with the relief.

Helen ran from the back, reaching Sam first. She dived down to him, hugging him up to her. 'Are you okay?'

'I was fixing it.' He started crying.

The two of them were locked together in a hug, Sam bawling.

Daniel said, 'I didn't see him.'

Frances was at the back gate but wouldn't leave the backyard. She just looked.

Hosey from next door was craning around the gap in the fence.

Daniel grabbed the bike and dragged it from under the ute. 'I've got this meeting, but I'll come straight back, okay. I'll fix this.'

Helen turned and looked at him. She wasn't angry. It was another thing. Her look was strange.

Daniel said, 'I'll come straight back from the meeting and I'll explain everything, Helen. That's a promise. Okay. I'll sort the bike out, matey. I ... That's a promise.'

The look Helen had was spooky. Daniel didn't know what it meant.

'The meeting,' said Daniel and he got into his car.

*

The meeting was on an office floor Sheridan had hired for their visit. By the time Daniel found his way to the conference room, Brian had clearly been at it for a while. Charts were on boards and papers were spread before Osaka, McClusky, Johnson and a woman in a power suit.

They looked up at him, annoyance and smiles turning into narrowed eyes that Daniel tried to avoid. 'I'm sorry I'm late. I ...'

'I've explained you were needed on site, Daniel,' Brian said, curtly.

Daniel settled in one of the high-backed leather chairs and

concentrated on not rolling the thing back and forwards.

Brian said, 'Well, gentlemen, I hope that brings you up to date. The city site is virtually complete. Rockingham to get fully under way on January second.'

Silence. Daniel thought the information was to catch him up. They'd moved up the Rockingham date by a week. He nodded again. Still the silence. Everyone was looking at him. He felt his chin, where he'd missed a bit during his driving shave. Little scabs from the Christmas tree. Maybe he should explain the humour of it all. Instead, he nodded again.

Brian said, 'Any questions?'

McClusky looked to Osaka who nodded and McClusky said, 'Is Hearth & Home filing for bankruptcy?'

'That's a damn lie,' said Daniel. He was standing. Brian was tugging at his arm. Daniel shook him off. 'We are not bankrupt. Nor have we ever been. The bank has it wrong.'

Daniel turned to get Brian's support but he was looking at the table. He looked back to Osaka, who wasn't looking back either. He turned to McClusky. 'Who told you that?'

They didn't say anything.

Daniel said, 'Was it Amis Blyte? See, I know the name. I'm on the trail of whoever is setting us up and I'll put a stop to it. And that's a promise.'

Brian started gathering up his papers.

'Did he phone you? All I need is a contact number. Anything you can give me.'

McClusky turned to look at Osaka. He would not look at Daniel. He looked sad.

Daniel said, 'It's not true,' perhaps too quietly.

Only Johnson stayed for a handshake. The others left with curt nods.

In the underground car park Daniel tried to hit Brian with ideas but he didn't respond. 'I'll go see the bank, Brian. I'll go over Bradley's head. Threaten to sue the bastards if they don't reverse their decision. I'll get them to put out something to Osaka. Big apology, so we don't even miss a beat. You don't think it was Osaka that sent Blyte?'

'So we can't finish their hotels for them and cost them thousands of dollars?'

'I'll go back up and offer the old hotel. See if that was it?'

'It's over, Daniel.'

Daniel staggered before following Brian to his car. 'You can't give up like that, mate. We have to save the business.'

'It's gone. I have a wedding tomorrow. Then it's Christmas Eve and then Christmas. On Boxing Day I'll beg Rosemarie to let me watch the cricket even though I will technically be on my honeymoon. When I come back, I'll get a job.'

'You can't quit.'

'It's quit, Daniel. The bank. The economy. Sheridan. And you.'

'You shouldn't have worried Helen with all this.'

Brian shook his head. He got into his car and drove away.

Two weeks before, Daniel had a thriving business, a happy family and a friend's wedding. It seemed impossible that it could go so quickly to nothing. He wondered whether Brian might have done something desperate in order to pick up Hearth & Home for a bargain price. Or maybe make quick money. Was there more to him visiting Helen? Was there a deal in the room upstairs before he'd arrived?

Daniel was metres away from his ute when the four uniformed police stepped out from their hiding places. Two had their tasers drawn. One said, 'Danilo Longo?'

They took him to a hospital in a paddy-wagon that smelled of disinfectant. Orderlies in t-shirts and black pants stood alert, like athletes waiting for the whistle to blow. A nurse took papers at reception.

Daniel kept trying to reason with them. 'If I'm not under arrest, you've got no right to hold me.'

'We do, Danilo. Under section thirty of the Mental Health Act.'

'Mental health?'

A young Indian orderly, not much older than the apprentice Nadif, said, 'It's okay man, it's just some tests.'

'Just go with Aziz, Mr Longo.'

The orderlies stepped forward which made Daniel back away.

'You can't grab someone off the streets, no matter what section you've got.'

'Calm down,' said the older orderly.

'No one's taking me anywhere.'

They reached for him and he slapped their hands away. 'Wait a minute.' A cop hit him from the side and another pushed him. They grabbed his wrist and twisted it in a way that forced Daniel face down onto the dirty lino floor. Daniel tried to wriggle out from under the cops.

One of them said in his ear. 'You quieten down now. We don't grab people from the street for no reason. Your wife signed you in here. And she's bloody right, if you ask me.'

*

Teddy had friends. The crematorium is full. Amis stands at the back. Sharon and Trent sit near the front. There's Teddy. Teddy's box anyway, with a framed photo of the man, smiling confidently. On the conveyor belt ready for the fire. No open casket for this one.

An old minister, portly, balding. Church of England collar, possibly dandruff flecked. 'A man does not take his own life. The vicissitudes of life can wear slowly. We are frail. People can break. Although I knew Teddy only slightly, it seems to me that he was broken.' Dandruff takes a theatrical breath. Bows his head.

A little nativity scene by the door. Little doll wise men with little toy camels. They have farm yard animal toys gathered round the tiny baby in the manger. Wee wee baby toy things.

Sharon's head is bowed.

Dandruff starts up again. 'Some of us do seem stronger than others. But we are all weak. None of us is strong enough. On our own.'

Amis turns Teddy's gold lighter in his pocket. Thinks he might have to go back to Hearth & Home. Get a keepsake from Danny boy.

'On our own, we may try, but we fail. God knew this. God knows our frailty. The trials life puts before us. That's why He sent His son.'

Time to go. The advertisements have started. Teddy's brother looks at his notes. Ready for Edward Borthwick's life story. The organist plays 'Abide with Me'. Amis rests his hand on the nativity scene. Plucks the baby Jesus from the manger like a grape.

Taking down Daniel's business had been easy. Easier than Teddy's. Young bull ripe for cutting from the herd. But the coup de grâce was the committal. The signed letter from Helen, fearful wife of. His father was the gift. The spark of the idea. The JP in his pyjamas. Amis in weak-arse home-knitted jumper, earnest and sleepless, 'She doesn't want to be seen to betray him in his fragile state. My brother has been under strain. Has done things. Our father committed ... committed – ended his own life. We merely want him to be looked at by the doctors. It's an emergency, your Honour.' That smug look. 'I'm not a judge.' Too right, you're not.

The paperweight? He recalls a paperweight in Daniel's office shaped like a fireplace. A wonky amateur thing full of cute. One of the wife's drawings? Yes. A Helen sketch. Amis smiles at that thought. Would Danilo ever trust her again?

They are coming out of the crematorium. Not many dark suits. Mostly office clothes. Kids in their dancing gear. Amis waits amidst the roses and low hedges lining the walks, brass plates on the ground next to every plant.

'Dad!' Trent smiles. Good boy.

Sharon stops on the path, her arms folding, her hands scratching at the other arm in her nervous way.

Amis forward. Hand on her shoulder, feeling her collarbone. 'My thoughts are with you in your time of need. Anything I can do?'

She doesn't look at him. She knows.

Amis turns to Trent. Flicks a casino chip up in the air. Trent catches it. Turns it, not understanding what it is or where it came from.

Amis whispers to Sharon, 'You make me hornier than hell when I see you dressed in black, Shaz.'

Trent. 'Another man came to our house, Dad.'

'Another man?'

'No, I didn't, Amis. I didn't.' She's looking at him now.

Trent. 'He was looking for you. He wanted your address.'

'I didn't tell him anything. I didn't even open the door.'

Amis knows she's telling the truth. He puts his arm around her shoulders. She quakes ever so slightly. 'Who was it, Shaz?'

'I don't know. We didn't open the door. Trent, tell him.'

Trent smiles. She's stupid. He says, 'His name was Daniel.'

'When?'

'Yesterday.'

'Amis, you're hurting.'

He's squeezing her. He loosens his grip. Daniel. He opens his free arm to Trent who steps in, unsure. Amis hugs them both to him, letting them feel his strength.

Daniel underestimated. Loose ends now. 'It was my fault. I got too cute. He won't bother you again.' He steps back. 'I got to take a raincheck on our reunion.'

*

He parks up the street in the white Statesman and waits for them to come home from swimming lessons. The thing is on the back seat. Perhaps Helen will wear the loose dress again. Bright African colours. A kind of billowing thing that makes you think about what's under there. Maybe a cheesecloth thing that lets you see the smudge of the bikinis.

The Volvo comes late.

Amis walks up the drive unseen and stands to the side of the garage door, cradling the thing.

Helen in mother mode. 'If you don't start knuckling under, Mister, you are going to spend the holidays in your bedroom.'

Rustling plastic bags. Silence. Good boy.

'Why did we have to put things back?' The little spitfire. Amis's favourite.

'Because we didn't have enough money.' Helen.

'Cos our credit cards bounced.' The boy, bitter?

Amis steps around.

Helen has bags of shopping. She turns and drops a bag, spilling packets of chips and cheeses.

'Sorry, Helen. Didn't mean to scare you.' Big smile. He holds up the thing and it wriggles.

Helen bends to pick up the bags. Thigh-hugging skirt. Loose blouse with buttons undone.

'Let me help you with those.' He hugs the wriggling puppy to his chest one-handed and bends to pick up food items. Party food.

Samuel stands at a plaster-of-Paris object on the bench. He's watching the dog. Frances glares, still in the car. Helen is flustered, trying to gather things. Her knees point at him from her skirt. Amis puts a plastic container of pate into Helen's bag and catches sight of flesh above her bra. She looks up catching him look away. She's standing. The tight skirt is better than the loose dress. She's embarrassed.

Amis up too. 'I suppose you're wondering what I'm doing here.'

'I do assume you don't wander the neighbourhood doing good deeds, Mr, ah ... Armstrong.' Getting it back together. Taking charge.

He holds up the puppy. 'I couldn't get Haggis out of my mind. So, unless Daniel has already got another puppy.' He holds the thing up.

Sam comes forward. Amis tosses the puppy half a metre. The boy frantically catches it.

Amis is already looking at Helen. He's downcast. 'I've overstepped the mark.'

On the back foot again, she says, 'We'll have to ask Dad.'

'Quite right too.'

The little girl with big eyes. Amis reaches into his coat pocket and pulls it out. A cheap plastic marionette. He gets the strings untangled and makes it jiggle. It is fun, the broken dance. He holds it out towards her. She wants it. But she won't take it. She knows about the gingerbread house.

'Mr Armstrong, this is really too much. We can't.'

Shut up, Helen, I'm working here. He turns to her. Smiles. 'With my kids, I know, you can't give one without the other getting something too.'

'We really can't.' Closed. Her defences are up. Suspicious now. No one's this nice.

Nice boring answers, Amis. Always walk to the door carrying your plausibles. 'Confession. My neighbours were giving puppies away. And I would like you to let me try to sell you a very good insurance deal. I did do the spade work. Sorry. Poor joke.' But it wasn't. It was rather good.

She smiles.

Amis looks down at the marionette, hanging limp. The little one is watching it.

Helen says, 'This is the most complicated sales pitch I've ever seen.'

'I'm a complicated fellow.' He smiles the truth at her. He gives her Amis. It surprises her.

The marionette is snatched from Amis's hand. She's taken it. Amis is almost disappointed. Thought maybe she was a tougher diamond.

'Friends?' he says, demanding his blood price.

She doesn't smile. She shakes her head. No. I'll take your present but I won't like you.

Pure uncomplicated amorality. And hair smelling like apples.

Helen asks Amis to help with the Christmas tree. It lies in the centre of their loungeroom as if chopped there. Three days until Christmas and no tree.

Amis takes charge. Like the dad. Sam, bricks. Frances, keep the puppy safe. Helen, you take that side. They lift, easy does it. The crown bends at the ceiling.

Helen pants. 'Put in the bricks.' A branch twists at her chest, pushing back more blouse.

Sam races in to plop bricks into the bucket surrounding the base of the tree.

Amis is jovial. 'You are making me work for this. Any wood needs chopping? Painting? Any other thing needs attention?' He makes sure he isn't looking at her. No lascivious smile to give away the innuendo. He feels her check though. He says, 'And on the other side, Sam – to balance it.'

He heads for the bricks. Stops to scraggle the puppy's ears. Eager beaver, dying to help.

Helen smiles at the boy, bursting with maternals. She turns to catch Amis watching. He doesn't avoid it. He wants the Daniel gossip. To feed on the crisis and feed it too. 'It must be very difficult. Having to hold this shower, right now.'

'What do you mean?' She's gone hard again.

Amis swerves. 'So close to Christmas.'

She relaxes slightly. But she's not panicked. Not like Amis expected.

She says, 'Samuel, before we collapse here.'

Is she tough or doesn't she know where he is. He watches her. 'Shame Daniel can't be here.'

She looks back, shaking her head. Not getting it.

Amis says, 'So I can lay things out for both of you. Given your success in life, you might want to consider Life Assurance too.'

The boy puts the last brick in. It feels like enough. She lets go of the tree. 'He's very busy, Mr Armstrong.'

The boy takes the puppy. 'I'll show you outside.'

The girl jumps to follow but turns back and says, 'Don't you hurt Mummy.'

'Frances!' Mum aghast.

Apples runs off.

Helen is stuck in the corner of the fake bay window, trying to push branches. Amis steps to cut off her movement. Says, 'Let me help,' as he pulls branches aside, and starts to move back.

She steps forward and Amis moves back into her path. 'Oh.'

They stop. Sweat on her chest. Full breasts, panting slightly. Tiny beads of blood where the pine needles have jabbed her chest. Just a little prick.

'Sorry.' Amis steps back.

'Thank you.'

'My pleasure.'

She is only half out. She hasn't stepped away. Amis looks at her face. Her lips. Quite close and stopped for him. Then she steps through and goes to the centre of the room. She takes a deep breath with her back to him and then turns, bright and innocent, and looks back at the tree. But she's flushed.

Amis risks. He says, 'I hope he takes care of you, Helen.'

'He does.' She answers too quickly.

He meets her gaze. It's all sympathy, calling the lie a lie.

'He does.' Weak. And she doesn't even know where he is. 'Look, I won't stay.' He steps to her and lays his hand on her shoulder, his thumb touching where her pectoral starts to become breast. The tiniest innocent squeeze and he's past her and in the hall. 'Can I leave you my card?'

'Yes.' She hasn't come out. She's getting herself together.

He lays one of his fake business cards on the dresser by the front door. 'I am going to sell you some insurance one day, Mrs Longo.'

He opens the front door and turns back. He looks down the hall where he can see all the way out to the children playing in the garden with the puppy. He could live here.

*

The doctors didn't believe Daniel. With three of them working in a tag team Daniel had also begun to doubt.

'In what way are they persecuting you?'

Daniel was on his side of the interview desk. 'Not persecuting. Except for Blyte. The bank, Sheridan, Brian ...' Daniel didn't even want to consider the next person on the list. Found he couldn't say her name, so he skipped it. 'I think that's more ... a loss of faith.'

'And Amis Blyte?' asked the kindly lady doctor or psychiatrist or whatever they were. None of them wore white coats. They looked more like high school teachers. State school teachers, nearing retirement. When Daniel didn't reply, she repeated it. 'Why is he persecuting you, Danilo?'

Daniel looked away again, shaking his head. Every time they called him Danilo, he knew he wasn't among friends. He smiled. He needed to get out of here. He said, 'Maybe he's not.'

'And you haven't met him?' said the skinny one. He reminded Daniel of his first metalwork teacher.

Daniel said, 'Maybe he doesn't exist.'

They had moved on quickly from do you know what day it is, which he'd done reasonably badly at: 'Very close to Christmas.' And who is the current prime minister of Australia. 'Julia. Her husband used to be a hairdresser.' When he asked if they could steer away from Geography as it wasn't his best subject, they'd asked more specific questions about why he thought he was here and he had tried to calmly list the pressure he was under and the actions he'd taken that might make it look to outsiders (and his wife) as though he were crazed. He was sane enough to give the answers that would get him out.

The third doctor, whom Daniel was having trouble placing in his imaginary teacher common room, asked, 'Have you ever conjured up, in your own mind, what he might look like?'

As opposed to conjuring it up in someone else's mind?

She went on. 'Does he look anything at all like your father?'

'No.'

'No, he doesn't look like him?'

'This is not about that. No.'

They nodded at the last doctor. She'd impressed them. The man on the end looked at his watch.

The kindly one, maybe home ec. or drama, said, 'Let's have another discussion later, Danilo.'

'I'd like to talk more about your father next time,' said number three, the deputy principal perhaps. 'Would you think about that?'

Daniel nodded. He didn't want to think about that. He thought he should have answered yes. The unseen Blyte looks like my dead father. They might have been pleased and let him go. You're damaged, son, but like the rest of us. Go and pay a psychologist and talk about it for a few hours every week.

An orderly led Daniel along a corridor. There were shifts of orderlies with lots of keys.

Daniel had trouble walking. They'd taken his shoelaces and his tie and belt. He had to hold up his pants with his good hand and shuffle along the corridor like one of the zombies out of *One Flew Over the Cuckoo's Nest*.

They got to one of the heavy doors with the big glass viewing panels. It was like a medium-sized hospital ward with beds and men lying and milling about.

The orderly said, 'Listen, you're not gunna hurt yourself anymore, are you?' He was looking at Daniel's various wounds. He'd picked up a few extra scrapes from the police that morning.

'No. I'd rather not.'

'I can get the nurse to give you something. And I can put you by yourself or with the other blokes in the ward.'

Daniel shrugged. He wondered whether they'd already given him something that made him feel flat. He had a headache.

The orderly unlocked the door and the men looked up mostly with a vague hope which turned to disappointment when they saw it was another inmate. The orderly said, 'You want, I can make a call for you. Only cost you ten bucks.'

'No, I think I'm all talked out.'

It was nothing like *One Flew Over*. It was more like a late night at casualty. As an experienced inmate explained many of them had voluntarily come in for assessment, sometimes prompted by parents or partners and sometimes when they recognised the signs that the Black Dog was taking over and they needed their medication upped.

Daniel thought he might be starting to relate to that. He sensed the bottom of the well and not knowing where to find the light. Action had kept such thoughts away. Daniel was an emotional shark. He needed to keep moving, not brooding. He'd picked that trick up from his dad.

A youth with bandaged arms lay on the bed next to him. He'd admired Daniel's injuries and asked, 'What did you do?' Daniel had to think a while before he said, 'I'm a businessman.'

A television was on in the little day room.

Most of them went elsewhere to eat. They had plastic knives but real forks. Daniel turned the fork, considering that more damage could be done with that than the usual butter knife. Dinner was a roast, possibly pork and vegetables boiled to tastelessness, followed by damp apple pie with cold custard.

Daniel tried to sleep. He dozed, aware when the television was turned off. A nurse came around giving out medicines at one point. Daniel asked for aspirin. They turned the lights down to one third.

Daniel woke to see an old man sitting in a chair by his bed. He was in an old suit. He was watching Daniel. He said, 'Catatonia.'

Daniel said, 'Sleeping.'

'Cat a got ya tongia.'

Daniel stayed lying down. He closed his eyes. He said, 'When I was young we used to visit my father in a place like this. Heathcote.'

'They had no right closing that place down. Free tobacco in the old days.'

'I remember the beds. And a goldfish pond. In the grounds.'

'Way back we used to make lamps. They'd give us these coloured bits of plastic and we'd weave them around old flagon bottles. Empty unfortunately. Put on a lampshade and hook up a light globe. Therapy. If you weren't mad when you started you were when you'd done a few lamps.'

Daniel wondered whether the old man was really there. He looked nothing like Daniel's father who was younger and never wore a suit. Danilo's mother had divorced Danilo's father and moved herself and the kids back to Melbourne where her family were. And she'd met someone else and they'd had a good life and lost contact with his father until he sent a letter when Danilo was fifteen. 'Coming good. Getting rich.' And when he turned seventeen Daniel returned and re-met his father as Daniel and was apprenticed and ...

Daniel said, 'Is it so bad, being mad?'

He was surprised when the old man answered. 'What makes you think I would know? No. I'm pullin' your leg. I'm usually all right until I get on the grog and I forget to take my meds. It's like being on one of them hypnotist's shows.' He clicked his fingers. 'You wake up and you can only tell by the looks on everyone's faces that you've been a chicken or Elvis or maybe wanked off in public. Only you can't remember.'

Daniel smiled.

But the old man lost his humour. 'Other times. Most of the time, I just feel sad. I feel unhappy and so lonely.' He started weeping.

Daniel sat up. He looked for someone to call. There were mumbles and the faint smell of farts but no one to call. 'Hey, it's okay.'

The old man started sniffling.

Daniel leaned over and patted him on the shoulder.

The old man said, 'I've got a bit of a hard on. I don't suppose you'd give us a tug.'

Daniel took his hand away. 'No. No thanks.'

'I'd tug you.'

'No mate. Go to bed.'

He got out of his chair with difficulty, but he picked it up and dragged it to the other side of the next bed where the young bloke was sleeping and he sat staring at him.

Daniel thought he probably shouldn't sleep.

But he must have because he woke with a start. An orderly with a beard was shaking him.

'Come on. Time to go.'

'Now?'

'Change of plan. You're needed at home.'

Daniel sat up. 'What?'

The orderly headed back to the door.

Daniel went after him holding his pants up and only realising in the corridor that he'd left his shoes by his bed.

'What?'

'Trouble with your kids apparently.'

'What? What's happened?'

'They didn't tell me.'

They'd reached another door at a deserted nurses' station. The door wasn't locked. 'Here,' said the orderly fishing in his pocket and bringing out a ten- and twenty-dollar bill. 'For taxi fare. You gotta hurry.'

'Okay. Thanks.'

'Is your wife seeing someone?'

'What?'

Daniel turned to the orderly but he was already heading back towards the ward. Daniel grabbed the top of his pants and raced along the corridor and out the front door of the hospital in his socks.

*

The shower, once called a hens' night, was in full swing. Rosemarie had insisted on margaritas and things had started to get sloppy. Those of Rosemarie's friends who were already married yelled tips concerning married life over a '80s music compile that included Cyndi Lauper and Madonna.

Helen's sister Leonie had left her kids with her husband Ian and come over to help. She'd commented that the music probably meant this was quite a feminist gathering really. 'Was there a golden era of faux feminist pop, do you think?' asked Helen, tipsy herself.

'Right from the start, share the chores.'

'Right,' said Rosemarie.

'You're not his servant.'

'Check. Lazy bastard.'

'And get a joint cheque account.'

'But his wage goes into it. Not yours.'

'Yeah. Keep some money. Men don't understand how much cosmetics cost.'

'Or handbags.'

'Right,' said Rosemarie. 'Get a handbag.'

Cheers.

'Where's the stripper, Helen!'

'Yeah. Beefcake!'

They started slow hand clapping.

'I didn't order a stripper,' Helen whispered to Leonie.

'I think we better get a couple more drinks into us, or it'll be a long night.'

Everyone suddenly went quiet, looking to the lounge door.

Helen turned to see Daniel. He was bruised and dishevelled. He was panting.

'Yeah. Get it off.'

'What's happened?' he yelled at Helen. He looked manic. He didn't have his shoes on. 'Where are the kids?'

'Get it off!'

Helen went to him. 'Daniel, what are you doing here?'

'What's happened? What's happened to the kids?'

'Daniel, they're upstairs asleep. What are you talking about?'

He didn't answer her. He turned and ran up the stairs, holding his pants up.

Helen turned to the women who'd gone quiet. She couldn't think of anything to say.

Leonie said, 'Wow, Rosie, Brian must be having a doozy of a bucks' night.'

Helen followed Daniel up. He was moving from Samuel's room to Frances's. They were both asleep. He stood in the centre of the room touching her mobile made of stars. Helen went to him and laid her hand on his shoulder, but he recoiled as though stung. He looked at her in a kind of fury but went into their bedroom. The telephone was ringing.

'Daniel?'

He didn't answer her. He picked up the landline in the bedroom and listened. 'What's this about?' He listened again, looking at the wall and not her. 'On my way.'

'Who was that?'

Daniel went into the robes and got a pair of shoes and a belt. His shirt was crinkled and dirty. His pants the same.

'What's going on?'

'Blyte. He's real.' The same venom.

'I never said he wasn't. I never got the chance to say he was or wasn't.'

'I'm taking the Volvo.' He left the room.

'Where's your car?'

He'd gone. Helen hurried down the stairs, where Leonie was waiting.

'Can you watch the kids?' Helen gestured to the lounge too.

'Are you sure you don't want to stay?' Leonie was worried. She was giving Helen permission. Permission to hide from whatever Daniel was going through.

Helen squeezed her sister's shoulder but followed Daniel. He hadn't even taken the keys. They were on the kitchen bench by the back door.

He came back out of the garage, patting his pockets and looking bewildered again. 'I forgot the keys.'

She dangled them and he reached and she took them back.

'I'll drive.'

He nodded.

When she got in and started the car, she waited.

He finally said, 'He said he was at the factory.'

She snorted. She couldn't help it. But he didn't react. They drove in a cold silence.

*

A glass smashes on the workshop floor of Hearth & Home.

He stands on the upper walkway above, looking out at the alarm which is clanging loudly. Daniel's business partner. Not wearing any pants.

'Something old, something new, something borrowed something blue.' He's swaying as he gives his speech as though to some crowd on the workshop floor. 'Ladies and gentlemen, I give you the groom. Unemployed and for better or for worse ... in sickness ...'

A young girl comes out of the office, doing up her blouse. She shouts, 'This place is freezing at night.'

He turns and rests back against the railing. 'It's a cold, cold world, Chantel. I obviously never asked you to work late before.' He's smug. He's fucked the office girl.

She scowls at him. 'You gunna turn that thing off?' It's not love.

The alarm system wasn't here before. Another surprise for Amis.

No-pants turns and looks down again. He nods to the ground, his nods slow and drunk. He nearly falls at the top of the stairs, grabs the railing, in time, staggers down. Hairy, skinny white legs. He goes to the new console by the back, studying it blearily. Red lights flicker.

She comes down the stairs. Great legs. She's got her bag.

Brian is his name. Yes. Accountant. Getting married. Tsk tsk. Brian picks up a mallet and starts smashing at the console. It bends easily. Aluminium. It cracks. Brian smashes through to the electronics. He smashes again. The alarm stops.

He turns to the girl. 'Yes.'

'What?'

'I can turn the thing off.'

'Can you smell petrol?'

'Anything else I can do for you, Chantel?'

'A job would be good.'

'I need one of those myself. How about great references?' He leers.

'Yeah, right.'

He turns to kiss her, but she's on her way to the door. Amis lets her go.

Brian No-Pants sees the thing on the floor. He still doesn't seem to notice the wet petrol everywhere. He picks up the tiny plastic thing. Out of the nativity scene and out of the church, it's not a baby Jesus.

Brian calls to the open door, 'Hey, we made a baby.' He giggles. He looks at the steep metal stairs that lead back up to his office. He climbs.

Amis turns the gold cigarette lighter. It's warm. He's had it in his hand all this time.

'What did Blyte say?'

'He heard I was looking for him. He said he'd explain at the factory in fifteen minutes.'

'Is that what's happened to our credit cards?'

'What?'

'They've been stopped.'

He scowled out the window. He shrugged.

She tried again. 'How was Brian's bucks' night?'

He snorted. He shook his head. He glared at her. She had to drive and couldn't keep returning his angry looks.

Finally Daniel said, 'I lived with my father. I know how it goes.'

'Okay. Yes. It must have been awful.'

'It was. And it wasn't. But I'm not like that. I've seen it and I know.'

'I know that.' She reached to pat his thigh like she used to when they drove but he flinched away.

They were only a couple of streets from the factory when he said, 'I'm not mad.'

'I know. What?'

'Then why did you have me committed?'

'What?' Helen pulled off the road. 'Daniel, when did I do this thing to you?' He wasn't listening. He was looking the other way. 'Dan, I have never ...'

'He's burnt the factory.'

Helen looked. They could see the red glow and fire engines.

'We have to get out of here,' he said.

'No, we have to go down and see what's happened.'

He opened his door. He got out, but leaned back to say, 'They'll think it was me.'

'It's your factory. Why?'

'I have no fucking idea. None.' He was open and honest and afraid in a way she had never ever seen. He looked like he might cry and Helen wanted to get out of the car and hug him. But she said, 'Wait here. I'll go and see. Will you wait here?'

He wasn't sure.

'Please, wait.'

He nodded.

Helen had to explain her connection, to talk her way into the yard past a policeman. There was an ambulance and two fire trucks pouring water uselessly. The heat was turbulent with a seething kind of wind. The metal walls were clenching.

Helen saw someone on a stretcher being fed oxygen from a bottle. She hurried over. It was Brian. His face was shiny. They'd smeared cream on. 'Brian!' she called. His eyelids flickered but didn't open.

'You know this man?' A policeman in a tie.

'Yes. Brian Harwood. He and my husband own this factory.'

'Mrs Longo?'

'Yes?'

'Have you seen your husband? Tonight?'

She shook her head. It was a reflex.

'As you can see, this is no time for misguided loyalty, Mrs Longo. You could be in danger. So is he.'

'But he didn't do this.'

'He's not in the hospital, if that's what you think. He killed an orderly and escaped this evening.'

The detective watched her face. Helen could feel him studying her. She didn't hide what she was feeling which was shock, confusion and nausea. He signalled towards a uniformed policeman. 'I'm going to send a car to park outside your house, okay?'

Helen nodded. She looked to the factory as warnings were shouted and the firemen stepped back. The roof buckled and metal screamed as it fell in.

She said to the detective, 'How long's the fire been going?'

'Half an hour we think. A lot of chemicals, so whoosh.' He seemed a little excited by it and caught her watching. 'We're searching the area now.'

Helen nodded, looking at her feet and not where she'd left Daniel.

*

He'd had to lie down in a dry drainage ditch amongst the broken glass and stiff dead grass when the police car came past. Its powerful spotlight swept the wire of the fence behind. A chopper with another searchlight was on the other side of the industrial park. If they used the infrared cameras they had, he'd be found easily amidst the treeless bitumen, security lighting and unclimbable fences.

Daniel went along the ditch until he was at the darkest point between two streetlights and crossed the road to a shared business complex where they had a short brick wall built around their postboxes. He lay behind it in the darkness watching the progress of the chopper.

Car headlights came up from the direction of Hearth & Home and Daniel hid until he saw it pause and caught the shape of the Volvo under a streetlight. He stepped out, so she could see him. If she'd told anyone, he was a goner anyway.

Daniel opened the passenger door but Helen said, 'You should probably get in the back.' When he did, she drove off, fast.

'Have they got it under control?'

She said, 'You should probably lie down. They're looking for you.'

'Me?'

'Brian's been hurt.'

'What was he doing there?'

'I don't know. They're taking him to hospital.'

Brian? 'Maybe Blyte is after Brian too.'

'Why?'

Daniel didn't say anything. He was no closer to knowing. Blyte had phoned him but only to come see his work. Daniel still didn't know why. He thought he'd reached his limit, the end of his capacity to fight back. He'd like to find Blyte so he could surrender to him.

'Why were you in a hospital,' Helen asked.

'Because you had me committed.'

'So it was a mental hospital.'

'No, it was a veterinary clinic.'

'And you escaped.'

'No. They let me out.'

'There was no fight.'

'No.' Daniel sat up. 'They said there was something wrong at home, with the kids. They let me go.'

'Was there an orderly, um up a ladder or knocked over by a door?'

'No. They woke me up. He gave me taxi fare.'

'But not your shoes.' She was asking strange questions, not quite believing his answers.

'What?'

'You couldn't have lit the fire, anyway. You were too far away. Near home.'

'Stop the car.'

She considered it.

'Stop the car now.'

She pulled over in a side street. She said, 'You did get a phone call. I heard it ring.'

'Fuck you,' said Daniel and got out onto the verge and started walking. It was a tree-lined street of Californian bungalows, with white pickets and roses. Most of the house lights and Christmas lights were out for the night.

The Volvo drove next to him for a few paces, and then accelerated slamming the rear passenger door he'd left open. Helen stopped the car a house ahead and got out and came around to the path.

Daniel stopped.

She called, 'I needed to figure it out, for myself.'

A dog started barking.

He stepped up to her, 'Figure out what?'

'I know none of this. I need to know what's going on.'

She didn't even trust him. Believed he could do such things. 'Forget it.'

She moved her right foot out, squaring her legs.

Daniel thought it looked odd.

She pulled back her arm, like she was stretching her shoulder. Then she punched him. It caught Daniel full on the chin. It wasn't hard. It didn't have force. But Daniel found himself on his bum on the footpath.

She stood over him, flexing her fingers like they hurt. She looked at him accusingly and she said, 'Owww. That hurt.'

'Yeah. Sorry. You punched me.'

'Yeah, I did. Ha. Good.'

Daniel stayed sitting on the ground. He said, evenly, 'I shouldn't need to prove to you I'm not a madman.'

'Why's that?'

'Helen, you know me. You know me better than that.'

'But I don't, Daniel.'

He looked up at her. She meant it. She wasn't asking. He didn't know where to start with her confusion. He did everything for her. Everything for her and the kids. Gave them everything.

She must have seen something, forgiven him something because she said, 'Get in the car. And tell me from the beginning.'

'There is no beginning. That's the problem.' Daniel got up. He'd tell her. He'd tell her all that he could think of. He needed to tell.

*

The police car was parked outside the house when Helen arrived. A couple of cars remained on the front lawn. Helen parked in the garage, her headlights catching the drop sheet that the kids had draped over their work in progress, a wonderfully misshapen eagle that they were making for Daniel for Christmas. It had refused to take shape until Samuel had come up with the idea of putting metal spikes onto the tray, so they could build its legs and its outstretched wings.

She went back out the front and asked the police if there was anything she could get them but they had takeaway coffee and the police radio on.

Inside, the party was over. Rosemarie was asleep on the couch with a leather jockstrap on her head. Someone had written on her forehead in texta. *Property of Rock Machine MC*. Helen hoped it was not permanent marker.

Leonie came in from the kitchen. 'Bumpy night.'

Helen nodded.

'Kids are good. Other girls have caught taxis, pretty soon after the police car arrived.'

'Can you look after the kids tomorrow?'

Leonie nodded.

Helen went on. 'You're going to hear strange things. Maybe in the newspapers. None of it is true.'

Leonie's lips went tight like they had always done when she was angry and trying not to show it.

'Helen! Great party.' Rosemarie was pointing at Helen from the couch. Helen squeezed her sister's hand but went to the couch to give the bad news. Rosemarie was very drunk. 'I gotta say this, as a friend. Your husband has fucked up my husband's business, but you, you're all right by me.'

'There's been a fire. At the factory. Brian has been hurt.'

'What? No.'

'I'll take you to the hospital.'

Rosemarie started keening. It was a shrill, piercing howl that wouldn't stop. Helen tried to hug her but she kept screaming in her ear.

*

The half-moon tumbled in the river like a discarded piece of paper. It lit the debris and building materials in front of the old hotel and made oddly shaped shadows that reached towards Daniel as he stood at the front door, looking out. The neighbourhood kids had long considered the place haunted, even before the mad Italian had offed himself inside.

Daniel closed the door and bolted it. He could still see because the moonlight was everywhere through the front windows, not blue like in the movies, but a dull white. He went up the stairs. He went to the spot on the first landing that overlooked the bar area where he knew the wood was scored by a rope burn. It could have been anything really. The whole place had dings and scratches and lumps and wounds. But Daniel knew what the mark was.

He'd lied to Helen when he'd said he knew what his father was like. He didn't. He knew he needed company, that he could not be too alone, but he had seemed fine just before the end. No fierce-eyed screaming at postmen, all of whom young Danilo's father had considered spies or cuckolds. Nothing like the afternoon he'd chased, cornered and tried to strangle the cat after it had scratched him. There had been no displays, no outward symptoms or cries for help.

He smoked like a chimney, of course. Pieta Longo had given up the grog, when Daniel came back. Drank black tea all day. And he had mantras and pride. 'We're building this, Danilo. We're building this thing. That is all that matters.' Daniel's father taught him the trades, enough to get by on. He got him an apprenticeship as a plasterer. He'd ensured that Daniel got an electrician's ticket too. And he gave him advice. 'A man looks after his family. Not like me, Danilo. You are strong.' Call me Daniel from now on. 'A man is strong, for everyone. Respected. Looked to.' It was possibly old village stuff, Daniel now thought, or what Pieta had failed to do, but Daniel loved his father and he had not had his father for so many years and the truths and tips Pieta handed him were like a pat on the head and a kiss on the cheek. Daniel had hungered for them. And also the easy company of other men working without much talk, just odd swearwords or the occasional complaint about the radio station.

Daniel had gone to Bali with a couple of workmates. His father had insisted. His father had never told him about the debts. Nor about the worry. Nor that he had started drinking again. Daniel didn't know him at all.

And now there was Blyte and now all of it was gone. Daniel grabbed the balustrade and yelled into the empty bar. 'You prick. You fucking prick. You fucking, fucking, fucking prick.'

Daniel slept on a pile of drop sheets upstairs woken only occasionally by the scampering of river rats on the warm December night. The sunlight surrounded him early so he started working.

He found the replacement rosette out in the yard and dragged it onto a trolley, pushing it into the bar room. He found the cable Hua and Nadif had been using and rigged a pulley leading to the upstairs balustrade. He went up into the manhole and crawled his way along the roof cavity and dropped a weighted line down through the hole for the electric light. He went back down to the floor and tied a stronger wire to the string and went back up again and dragged wire up through the ceiling attaching it to a hoist. It was an easy job for two workers, but not an impossible one for Daniel alone. His shoulder felt pretty good. He worked slowly, hoisting the rosette up a metre at a time until it clunked into position up on the ceiling.

Then he tied the cable off right next to where his father had once tied his rope.

After breakfast the kids went with Aunty Leonie to her house so they could go to swimming lessons from there. Maybe they'd have lunch with their cousins. No, they couldn't take the puppy.

Helen drove to the address Daniel had given her. The house had no garden at all. It was like a prison.

The woman who looked at Helen through the security screen was small and ungroomed. Her eyes were dull. She might be medicated.

Helen said, 'I'm looking for Amis Blyte.'

'He doesn't live here.' He used to. It was clear. A bad past.

'Could you tell me where I can find him?'

She shook her head fearfully. 'No.' She started to close the door.

Helen said, 'Please, Mrs Blyte. He's doing something to my husband.'

The door paused halfway.

Helen said, 'I don't know what or why but I need to find out. I need your help to try to stop it. Please.'

She was looking at Helen with sympathy but her head was shaking.

'So I can speak to him.'

'Don't do that. Don't.' She opened the security door and Helen followed her into the lounge room.

A sullen fat boy sat on the couch playing a computer game. He looked up at Helen as though she was a passing fly.

Mrs Blyte said, 'I told him, if Amis was after him, there's nothing he could do.'

Helen looked at the trembling mouse of a woman. It was inconceivable, but she had to ask. 'Are you and Daniel, were you ... seeing each other?'

The woman looked agog.

'Is that it? The reason.'

'No.' She looked at the boy as she said, 'A very kind man took me to coffee twice. And he died. I know it was Amis. I know.'

'But why would ... Why is Amis after my husband's business?'

She flicked her eyes to the boy again, but tossed her head away from him in a tiny act of defiance. 'He's probably not. Amis likes doing things to people.'

'But why choose Daniel. Why do it to us?'

'Run. Get your husband and go. Go anywhere. Go.' The woman was terrified. Terrified for Helen.

It made Helen whisper, 'Why don't you?'

She smiled like a twisted grimace. She shook her head.

Helen saw the framed photograph on a dresser in the corner. She went closer. The woman and the boy and ...

'Amis insists.'

Helen felt her stomach lurch.

'If I take it down, Trent tells him.'

Helen thought she might be sick.

*

Amis has a radio on but hears no news reports about a mad pyromaniac. He looks at the Daniel file on his computer. An insurance enquiry about the factory might legitimately be made to police.

The telephone rings. Not Amis's mobile. The landline that Amis uses when he's not being Amis. He picks it up, says simply, 'Yes?'

'Mr Armstrong?'

Ha. 'Helen! What a wonderful surprise.'

'Look, I know this is out of the blue, but ah, you said if I ever needed to talk.'

'It would be my pleasure, Helen. How's that puppy doing?'

'Good. This isn't a social call, Mr Armstrong.'

'Yes, Helen.'

'It's my husband. He's got into all kinds of trouble. And I don't know what to do. Who to talk to.'

Amis notices his left hand is squeezing him, kneading his erection.

'Can we meet?' she asks, scared and breathless.

*

Helen watched Armstrong who was really Amis Blyte come down the steps of the flats. He got into a white car and drove out towards the park she'd mentioned on the other side of the city. She'd used the card he'd left her for the phone call and the real address from his ex-wife Sharon Blyte to find him.

She grabbed the multigrip from the car seat and went up to Amis's flat. She placed the open mouth of the tool around the doorhandle as Daniel had once shown her. These kinds of locks were weak, but it was all in the timing. She gave it a sudden wrench but it slipped. She tried again, but didn't have the strength to make the trick work.

The kitchen window was next to the door. It had flywire but no security screen. She pushed at the aluminium but the window was locked. Helen looked around the courtyard of flats. Amis's car had been the only one in the car park. She lifted the multigrip and hit it against the window near the handle. The glass cracked and when she hit it again it smashed and fell, half the window collapsing inside onto the sink. She took down the now slashed flywire, reaching in to unhook the lock. She slid the window open before hoisting herself up and into the sill, her knee getting caught in her skirt as she tried to scramble in. Some burglar.

The flat was barely furnished. On a table in the lounge room was a computer. There was half a bottle of scotch and a glass, and on a manila folder, Daniel's paperweight. It was the misshapen clay stove they'd bought in Tasmania. She turned on the computer and opened the manila folder. She found a hairclip. It was one of Frances's, a colourful mermaid. The file was full of personal and business details, facts and figures; bank statements and insurance summaries; a recent letter from Daniel's mother. Helen found the committal form with her signature.

She found another page full of doodles and writing. She noticed her name. *Helen.* It was circled a lot of times.

She closed the file and turned to the computer. It was password protected. Reflected in the screen she could see Amis standing inside the room. She turned.

He smiled. 'Saw your Volvo round the corner. It did seem unlikely. You've got too many friends.'

She edged back until she was against the table. She reached behind her, trying to clasp the paperweight.

He said, 'Daniel has perseverance, but you have guile. Much more dangerous than brute force, I think.'

He stepped forward and she flinched which only seemed to make him smile as he snatched the file from her hand. 'Is Daniel here?'

Helen thought quickly. She might be able to escape if he thought Daniel was in the bedroom.

'No he's not. You're not a good liar, Helen.'

He took out a gold lighter and set fire to the file holding it up under the flame. 'Don't you two do anything together?'

'Your wife will be talking to the police about now.'

He dropped the flaming file into the metal rubbish bin. 'I don't think so. She's tried that before. The police are wonderfully logical. They like reasons. Nice little breadcrumb trails that they can follow. She's cried wolf too many times before.'

He came towards her again and she stepped back into the middle of the room.

'Helen, you're breaking my heart, girl.' He typed in a password and called up a folder. He deleted it.

Helen drifted towards the passage ready to make a run for it.

'How are Sam and Frances?'

She stopped. 'They're safe.'

He had the paperweight. He was turning it. 'You sure?'

She was less sure now than she had been. He could know about Leonie. And swimming lessons and all kinds of things that weren't a secret. She wasn't sure. He had Frances's hairclip.

The computer had deleted the file. Smoke rose from the rubbish bin. He moved towards her.

She said, 'Why are you doing this?'

He grabbed her arm above the elbow.

She tried to shake him off but he held tighter until it hurt.

'Sharon has delicate arms, like a bird. Yours are stronger. You're like a filly. A strong young filly, not yet broken in.'

He made her drive him to the old hotel in her car. Helen couldn't think what else to do. If he did have the children she needed to buy time. She hoped Daniel would know what to do – something spectacular that would rescue them both from this evil man.

'The photograph behind his desk,' he said when they pulled up. 'It's his?'

'And the bank's.'

'But it's not listed in any of the assets, the business or Daniel's.'

'It's in my name.'

Amis seemed to get angry at that. It was a loose end she supposed. Maybe he'd make more mistakes.

He took her by the arm again and aimed her at the gate. 'So it couldn't be taken if the business collapsed. Of course.'

They walked slowly through piles of wood and bricks and empty pallets, Helen waiting for Daniel to spring out and save her.

Blyte held Helen still at the open door and peered over her shoulder. He whispered, 'No shouting now. Even though it is a bar.' He was becoming playful, excited perhaps. He pushed her inside and they both looked. Under the stairs, in a cupboard. Behind the bar.

She put her handbag down and said, 'Why are you doing this?'

He didn't answer. He pushed her towards the stairs. A rope was tied to a railing above them. It went all the way up into the ceiling.

'Why?' she asked again.

He adopted a bad Kennedy accent. 'They ask why and I ask why not?'

They started up the stairs.

Daniel saw Helen's car parked outside the gate. He had bought an iced coffee and an egg-burger, but he hoped she'd brought good food. Maybe news. He wanted to tell her he'd discovered some things inside himself that he'd try to work on.

At the top of the first flight of stairs were doors to rooms along one side of a corridor. Blyte pushed her towards the first door.

'Why Daniel?'

He shrugged as he opened the first door and looked in. He pushed her towards the second. He said, 'A smile? The sweep of hair over an ear. The sparkle in the eye during an unguarded moment. A chance meeting – blossomed into so much more.'

He was mad. He was half-playing at being a James Bond villain with all the funny lines. Or was it Hannibal Lecter? But not all play.

He was looking at her. He said, 'I like what you're seeing, Helen. You'll have to tell me sometime.'

He pushed her to the next door. Nudged her to open it. They were all empty. Half had missing floorboards, a couple of windows were gone.

Blyte pushed her to the steep narrow stairs at the end. She thought she could kick down easily and knock him down, but he started up later. He said, 'I'm watching those shoes Helen, but mostly I'm watching above the shoes. Way above the shoes.'

Daniel got to the door and was about to call to Helen when he heard the car. He turned to see a police paddy-wagon pulling up next to the Volvo at the gate.

He dropped the food and ran into the hotel.

Helen pushed off at the top of the narrow stairs and ran. She called Daniel's name as she ran along the corridor of the third floor towards the larger stairs, but halfway ahead the floorboards were gone. She could hear Blyte behind and she swerved into the first door to her right. More floorboards were missing, but she balanced on the good ones and tottered towards the open window going to the outside balcony. He pushed her from behind and she fell against the wall and down to the floor where something stabbed and tore at her leg.

Helen's handbag was on the bar. Daniel scanned the room picking up two sets of footprints in the dust heading towards the stairs. He grabbed a chisel from a pile of tools.

She'd torn her skirt when she'd fallen and a nail had torn her thigh. She brought her hand up looking at the blood.

Blyte was panting as he stood above her.

Helen scrambled up quickly, her back against the wall.

'I think we're finally alone, don't you.'

She looked towards the door and he stepped back in the way. He waited for her to look at him again before he said, 'They'll blame Danilo. Free pass.'

He was going to hurt her, kill her, but she couldn't think of what to say to a sociopath. Or was it psychopath? She couldn't recall the difference.

'People need the world to make sense. Need logical causes for everything. That way, if they're good little vegemites they've got a chance. If there's no why, no reason, there's nothing they can do to protect themselves.'

He was feeling expansive. Perhaps he was gloating, or maybe it was his egotistical form of foreplay. Along the wall was the sash-window with no glass.

'Ever read the story in the Bible about Job? Its message is that, no matter how many trials you are put through, if you keep your faith, you will be rewarded. Is that what you believe, Helen?'

She didn't answer. She moved a step along the wall as though settling her weight. She thought, keep talking you motherfucker. She watched him, vaguely aware that it was the first time in her life she had even imagined the word motherfucker.

'The devil gets God to do these awful things.' He did the accents. 'Who's ya best man, God? Bet ya ya can't torture him to death.' Jack Nicholson? 'Oh, yeah. Just watch. Gdah. Gdah.' Goofy. 'I love that story.'

'And which one do you think you are?' Helen took a defiant step towards him as she spoke, but she also took a step towards the other end of the room. There were mostly full boards that way, one small jump. She felt blood dribbling down her leg but wouldn't look.

'I'm sure not Job. I'll tell you why I do it, Helen. It makes me hornier than hell.' He started to undo his shirt.

If she could get him to undo his pants, she could run, maybe. She put her hands on her hips, even more defiant, taking another half step, slightly back. She said, 'I think you like to hear yourself. I think you're a legend in your own lunchtime.'

He winced. Didn't like it. But then he smiled again. 'Tell you what, if you're really really nice to me, maybe I'll let you go.' He was lying. Not even trying to hide it.

Helen wasn't close enough to the window yet.

Then Daniel called out. 'Helen?'

He wasn't in the doorway but Blyte turned towards it and stepped back.

Helen ran for the sash-window screaming, 'Daniel!'

Daniel heard her. She was above, on the third floor.

Helen ran along the veranda, dodging more holes on her way to the door at the end. It was locked. She turned.

Blyte was walking, unhurried, watching where he put his feet.

Helen stepped to the edge, and onto a rotten board. Her foot went through and she tried to turn to see Blyte, but her foot became stuck under another floorboard.

Blyte kept coming. 'This place is a deathtrap really.'

'Hey, you there!'

Helen looked down to see a policeman in the yard below.

She yelled, 'Help me. He's crazy.'

Blyte stepped away from the edge of the veranda.

The policeman yelled, 'Now Mr Longo, there's no need for anything silly. We want to talk.'

Helen yelled, at the top of her voice, 'Amis Blyte. It's not Daniel. It's Amis Blyte.'

He was gone.

Daniel could hear Helen's voice yelling on the other side of the door to the top veranda. He tried the handle but it was stuck again. He bumped his good shoulder into it and it swung out. Helen stood there. Her foot was stuck and she had blood all over her skirt.

Down the steps. Button the shirt. A baby cop waiting. 'It's all right, Mr Longo. No problems. Your wife's sister sent us. To make sure you're all right.' His hand reaching back. Taser? Gun?

Amis looks frightened. 'He's upstairs. He's got a weapon.' Keeps on down the stairs.

The cop isn't sure. He backs away from Amis. Draws his pistol.

Amis says, 'He's got the woman. His wife.' Amis needs the gun.

Sees the bits of wood in the centre of the room. Broken floorboards. 'I think he's going to hurt her.'

The cop looks up suddenly, aiming his gun.

Daniel's voice. 'Amis Blyte.'

Amis grabs the piece of wood and cracks it down onto the young idiot's head.

Daniel yelled again, 'Amis.'

The man swung around after hitting the policeman and Daniel recognised him. He was the orderly in the hospital. He smiled and said, 'Danny. Am I glad to see you. You're just in time.' He looked down at the groaning cop.

Daniel had the chisel by his side as he stood in the middle of the upstairs landing.

Blyte raised the wood again over the policeman.

Daniel hit down on the rope with the chisel. It frayed but held. He stabbed at it again and the rosette hurtled down for the second time crashing onto Blyte.

*

Helen sat on a milk crate in the corner while one of the ambos put a butterfly bandage on her cut leg. They thought she'd need a couple of stitches.

Helen had already called Leonie. Until her sister had assured her, Helen's greatest fear was Blyte's threat about the kids. They were fine. In fact Leonie was concerned about betraying Daniel by sending the police to the old pub. It had probably saved their lives.

After that, Helen just felt empty. She watched the ambos take away the hurt policeman on a stretcher. Then Blyte's body was loaded onto another gurney.

The detective from the factory fire questioned Daniel. 'Who is this?'

'Amis Blyte,' said Daniel.

'What's the story?'

Daniel clouded, searched the room, blinked.

Helen called, 'There isn't one.'

'No. Why'd he go after you people?'

Helen said, 'No reason.'

He looked from Amis to Helen, doubtful. He looked to Daniel. 'But that makes no sense.'

'No, it doesn't, does it,' said Daniel.

*

They held the wedding ceremony by Brian's hospital bed the day before Christmas. Brian was weak but tried to be upbeat. Rosemarie was dressed in her beautiful white wedding gown.

The minister said, 'To have and to hold.'

Brian said, 'But not too tightly.'

Daniel had the ring. Brian had forgiven him once he heard that Blyte was real.

The minister said, 'From this day forth; for better or worse; for richer for poorer.'

Brian intoned, 'Poorer.'

Daniel looked back to find Helen with the kids. He smiled but she looked away again. She'd been distant since the hotel.

The minister said, 'In sickness and ...'

'That's me,' said Brian.

And the minister said, 'Brian, you're not taking this seriously.'

Rosemarie said, 'He will.'

Brian said, 'I do, I do.'

It was a strange wedding, as though they had washed up on shore after a shipwreck.

*

Frances was having trouble settling. She lay on her back in bed with the sheet pulled up to her nose but her eyes shone with the expectation. 'Can I see him?'

Helen said, 'You can listen for his reindeer landing on our roof.'

'He'll wait till you're asleep,' said Daniel.

He edged past Helen and kissed Frances. 'I love you.' She nodded, closing her eyes. Of course.

He turned to smile at Helen, but she had already turned away, heading to Sam's room.

Sam was pretending to be asleep. The puppy's face poked out from under his sheet. They'd named the dog Nemo which of course they'd had to explain to Daniel was a famous fish. 'Fish?' he'd said. The kids loved it when he didn't know things.

*

Helen went down to do the presents. It had been a pretty crazy lead-up to Christmas, she thought and smiled at the mundane understatement. And it wasn't over.

The tree twinkled. Daniel had finally put up a couple of the Christmas decorations. It was a big tree. They'd put presents under the tree, the ones Frances had seen Daniel buy. 'See, these are those presents, but he'll bring more.' The white tip of an eagle's wing poked out of the wrapping paper. The kids had not had time to paint the bird's feathers. In truth, Helen had not had time to help them. They'd promise Daddy to paint them later, on Boxing Day.

Daniel came into the room and sat on the couch trying to catch her eye. Helen went past him and got the bags of presents where she'd hidden them in the pantry. When she came back, Daniel got one of the kids' stockings and held it open for her to put presents in.

He said, 'He's gone now, Helen.'

She took the full stocking and put it under the tree. But it wasn't over.

When she turned back, he had the next stocking open and ready.

Helen stayed by the tree. She was still angry with him. The targeting was not the point, she realised. It was a thing they'd gotten through but now they were back where they started. Only now their old niggling problems were laid bare. She said, 'When there's a war, you need warriors.'

He nodded but with his half a shrug.

'But, when there's not ... the warriors and hunters – have to learn to be something else.'

He sat on the couch trying to think it through. He looked up finally and said, 'What?'

He made her smile. She said, 'I'm still trying to work that out.'

The voice came from outside the room. 'It was the night before Christmas.' Amis Blyte.

'Mummy!' Frances.

Daniel reached the door first.

'He came in my window.'

Daniel strode towards the stairs. 'Let her go.'

Blyte raised the knife.

Daniel froze.

Blyte smiled and said, 'All was quiet in the house. No one was stirring, not even a mouse.'

Daniel said, 'Let them go. Let them go, and I'll do what you want.'

Frances was annoyed but not frightened. Blyte had her by the elbow in the way he'd held Helen at the old hotel.

Blyte said, 'Helen. Go into the kitchen and turn on the gas. I want you both to know that you can save yourselves at any time. Just run out the door.'

Helen started for the kitchen.

Frances called, 'Mum!'

'I'm coming back, bloss.'

Blyte said, 'She's coming back. She always comes back.'

Daniel said, 'Let the kids go. Please, let the kids go.'

'Please. I like that. Maybe I will Danilo. Danny boy. Maybe I won't.'

Helen went to her bag. Her mobile was missing. She picked up the landline. It was dead.

'Go into the lounge room and turn on the heater gas,' Blyte ordered Daniel.

Helen turned the stove gas on, as she'd been ordered, then looked to the knife rack. One of the knives was missing, the one he held near Frances's throat.

She heard him talking to Daniel, 'Now pull out that rubber pipe. Pull harder.'

Gas hissed like a dying sigh.

Frances called, 'Daddy!'

Helen ran into the hall nearly colliding with Daniel as he came from the lounge.

Frances and Blyte were gone.

Helen yelled, 'I'm coming Frances. I'm coming.' She looked at the kitchen knife in her hand then to Daniel, but he was running out the front door.

Past Little Bloss's bedroom to the boy's room. Empty? Maybe not. Later. To the Royal Chamber. Little Bloss squirms.

'Frances. Stop that now.' She stops. Good girl. He pushes her to the other side of the bed.

Plans for this bed. Amis lifts Helen's nightgown from on top of the bed. He feels the material, slippery like an excited woman. He brings Teddy's lighter out. Click. Whoosh.

'Do you like fire?'

She won't answer, but she's already fixated with the way the nightgown drips molten flames onto the bedspread.

'I do,' says Amis. 'Fire is pretty.' He drops the burning gown before the flames reach his hands.

Pushes her to the wall and opens the walk-in. Lots of pretty dresses. That African thing with the colours. Amis back to feed them to the fire. Helen is in the doorway, panting again. Angry. Good.

'Hope you got fire cover, little lady.'

It pisses her off when he gets referential like the Joker in *Batman*. Her eyes go distant, her lips tight, just for an instant. Ha.

He pushes the girl back to stop her running to her mother and feeds the dresses to the fire. It's a sluggish flame. Needs to catch the varnish and glue of the bed. Around twenty-seven seconds according to a video. 'The modern home is so full of chemicals and plastics that the ignition point is quite low, the fuel load very high.'

The fire alarm in the hall starts a shrill beeping squawk. The smoke has raced along the ceiling searching for air vents.

Helen hovers. She's wearing shorts, showing lots of smooth tanned leg. There's a bandage high on her inner thigh.

'How's your leg?'

The lights go out. Everything. Amis can see though by the blue-green glow of nylon burning. Daniel with another plan. The Eveready Bunny tat-tatting his little drum.

The fire alarm keeps squawling. Batteries, see.

'Mummy, I'm frightened.' Finally.

'We can't stop the fire now. Let her go.' Finally, they are scared. Helen's hair is flat. It's lost its usual bounce and lustre.

'Can't do that, Helen. I need her.' He waves the carving knife in the air so it catches the firelight. The smoke is getting acrid. Thick black stuff. He pushes the girl in front of him. Gestures for Helen to back up.

Amis needs the boy too. Calls up the hall, 'Daniel, I've still got Frances. No jumping out.'

They shuffle along to the boy's room. It is dark. He'd like the boy too. With the boy and the girl, he can ask Daniel to kill himself and watch Helen watch.

'Sharon is talking to the police, Helen.' Reproach.

He pushes the girl into the boy's room. He lights a kite suspended from the ceiling. It becomes yellow light like a flare. Lots of paper and books. He lights a drawing on the wall and it races up to a noticeboard, licking the ceiling. More paper on the boy's desk. His window is open, the wind puffing curtains. He might have gotten out but he's allowed lots of good oxygen to feed the fire. A curtain catches. A green snake writhes up, to turn orange at the ceiling where it escapes into the air-conditioning vent.

'Light to work by.'

'Samuel!' Helen, afraid.

Another fire alarm starts beeping on the stairs. Out of synch. One squawks and the other beeps. The house is alarmed. The house feels the fire flooding through its ceilings, taking short cuts to the wood and paint.

Amis calls, 'Sam, dude. Fire, fire.' It is big and yellow on the desk.

The puppy yaps. A teeny bark from the cupboard. Good dog.

She bites his hand. The girl bites sharp and he lets go. Amis turns with his knife to stab her. He could get her leg. But Helen steps towards him. He has to look at her. She's got a knife too. Small. The girl scrambles.

Amis could still get them. Step up stabbing into Helen's belly, deep and then down on the little one's back. But he has the boy.

He grabs the cupboard handle again. 'Sam, join the party!'

He opens the door. A big blur. Pain in his nose, eyes watering.

Daniel stepped out of the cupboard as soon as he'd punched Blyte. The man stood stunned but not clear against the yellow and orange fire burning on the other side of the room. Daniel bent to grab Sam's cricket bat.

Blyte stabbed him, in the side.

It was sharp brief pain like ice. He turned back to see Helen step in and swing down into Blyte's back.

Daniel yelled, 'Sam, get out.'

Helen plucked her arm back and he saw she had a knife. Blyte began to turn towards her.

Daniel brought the cricket bat down on his collarbone. He heard it crack, but Blyte still stood. Black smoke filled the top of the bedroom pushing down towards them.

Sam was out from under the bed. Blyte had seen him.

Helen stepped to Blyte again stabbing him in the side.

Daniel yelled, 'Helen, get the kids out.'

'Nemo!' yelled Sam, trying to push past Blyte, but the man reached out towards Sam's arm.

Daniel swung up with the cricket bat connecting with Blyte's jaw and he finally went down.

Samuel fell on top of him and then crawled to the cupboard where he found the puppy. Frances stood aghast by the door. Fire alarms were screeching all through the house. Something exploded wetly in the master bedroom. Glass things were cracking.

'Helen, let's go!'

Daniel pushed Sam out and he grabbed up Frances and ran for the stairs. The main bedroom had caught in the roof and embers were already falling in the upstairs hall. Greenish flames were running along the edges of the carpet. Black smoke nudged aside the grey. Daniel had turned off the gas as well as the power, but the house was flaring and whooshing and feeding on itself. It growled.

He ran with Frances, Samuel running with the puppy. Sam opened the front door, bringing a sore gasp of cool air. Then they felt the heat surge behind them, the fire suddenly hotter with the new oxygen source. People were on the lawn, more neighbours coming. Someone had a garden hose but didn't seem to know where to point it.

Daniel took big gulps of clean air.

Sam said, 'Mum! Where's Mum?'

Daniel looked behind. Helen wasn't there.

He got her on one of her kicks. Grabbed her leg and pinned it to his stomach. Ha ha.

Smoke not bad on the floor. Cool. She gags. He'd pull her down. His right arm aches. No power. Pull her down and not let go and they can drown in the fire. Spit the blood out to breathe. He feels a blow. His face numb now. She'd got him with something.

He wriggles his fingers. She isn't there. Another hit. Ha. Doesn't hurt. Like the boarding school. Ha ha, don't hurt. He'll have to hurt Sharon. But not too much. Bring her back. To order. Whack. Trent knows. Rebuild the family. Dull thuds somewhere. Maybe he will die. No. Just rest.

She had the cricket bat and she pounded down on Blyte's body making blood. She needed him gone. She needed to be sure. She was coughing, choking up a salivary lava, but she wouldn't stop until she had made certain that he would not come near her children again. She raised the cricket bat, but couldn't bring it down.

Daniel had the bat. He tossed it onto Samuel's burning bed, bright yellow-white through the thick smoke. He took her hand and pulled at her, as though they were heading out towards a dance floor.

Her clothes were smouldering. In the hall, the flames were running all the way up the walls to the ceiling and flaring out like orange island flowers. Daniel led her gently, her legs wobbly. Her hair smoked. The fire alarm over the stairs gurgled into silence and she looked up to see it melted white amidst orange. There were little dots of blue flame in the lounge and some green on a picture frame. The heat was burning her eyebrows. It was somehow watery. He pulled her down the stairs. It was like they were on a boat, going to the ball. He pushed her out into the cold air that tore into her lungs and made her double up and cough until she vomited.

She fell amongst people on the cool damp grass. Frances and Samuel found her. She lay on the glass looking back at their house. She was in a lifeboat, the ship on fire. The Christmas tree caught and whooshed white in the window, popping each little glass pane, cascading sparks. Helen giggled. They'd done it. They had the best Christmas display in the street.

ACKNOWLEDGEMENTS

The author wishes to acknowledge the following sources: 'A Young Girl's Confession' from Marcel Proust, *Pleasures and Regrets*, 1896; *Sunsest Blvd*, written by Charles Brackett, Billy Wilder and D.M. Marshman Jr, 1950; the online quotes in 'For the Birds' epigraph have been morphed from www.onestopclick.com/tag/56/business-connectivity/United Kingdom and gettingafreewebsite.com/the-g1-blueprint; Wayne Swan in www.bncc.com.au/2012/newsletter/wayneswan2012; opening image in 'Small Claims' comes from 'Old Drive-in Theatre in McCamey, Texas' by Clinton Steeds, Flickr Yahoo (www.flickr.com/photos/cwsteeds/4974191705/lightbox).

Ross Hutchens and I have worked on many stories together since back in the day, including 'Small Claims', 'For the Birds' and 'Random Malice'. Story conferencing can occur in front of a basketball hoop.

Sue Taylor and I have worked on many television shows and feature ideas together including 'For the Birds', 'The Ring-In' and 'Double or Nothing'. Story conferencing can occur in restaurants serving very bad food in a variety of countries.

It does not take many glasses of wine to unlock screenwriters' scurrilous stories about the producers with whom they've worked. On the other hand ... without Ross and Sue, I don't believe these stories would have been written. Their interest, encouragement and criticism have been absolutely essential. Their friendship is dear. Any faults of course with the finished stories lie entirely with – the director.

Georgia Richter has toiled once again with great wisdom, sensitivity and patience. I do hope I have not broken her in the process as she is too important to WA writers. Thanks to the rest of the team at Fremantle Press, especially Claire Miller, Clive Newman and Naama Amram.

Michelle Johnston has read all of this. She has read the worst first drafts and read them in the worst circumstance – under my unwavering critical gaze monitoring any reaction with seismic sensitivity. For your unflagging valour, thank you, babe.

The stories that make up this collection have had a variety of inputs. There has been encouragement, criticism and suggestion from producers, government agencies and broadcasters. Money has changed hands and lights have been turned to green. A lot of care and work and belief has been invested.

'Small Claims' (nee 'Just Desserts'): Ross Hutchens and I received script development funding from the Australian Film Commission for a number of drafts. I also received valuable feedback from SBS as part of a production funding initiative and further development assistance from ScreenWest with a valuable script edit from Victor Gentile. I'd also like to thank Rebecca Anderton for some timely advice. This project had a public reading at what is now PICA. I'd like to thank the actors who worked with me along the way, especially Paula and Marcus.

'Random Malice': Ross and I received script development funding from the Western Australian Film Council and ScreenWest over a number of drafts. Ken Kelso script edited a draft.

'The Ring-In' (nee 'Random Variations'): ScreenWest invested in a number of drafts of this project. Sue Taylor first worked with me on this story, with script editing by Ian David. It was later picked up by Ian Booth and I worked with Carlo Burelli as prospective director and another script edit by Ken Kelso. Cheers, Ken.

'Double or Nothing' (nee 'Crossed Lines' and 'The Scottish Play'): won a script-pitching contest and was picked up by Sue Taylor and Ross Tinney and developed with Sandy Ross at Scottish Television. I was working with Sue at the time on the television series *Minty*. I'd also like to thank Murray Oliver for his script feedback and Steve McCall for his crucial 'canny' notes on Scottish pronunciation and spelling for the prose story.

'For the Birds': I'm not sure anything official ever happened with this, but I worked on it with Ross and Sue. I have some notes from Margaret Kelly at ScreenWest but I can't find a contract or any record of money changing hands. I wrote a number of drafts and do remember some lunches but come to think of it, I paid for my own food. Those bastards!

I would like to acknowledge the essential investments made by ScreenWest in the development of these stories. The Western Australian Film Council and ScreenWest have nurtured many projects and screen practitioners through Western Australia and continue to do so.

I would also like to acknowledge and thank Lotterywest for their superb and continuing contribution to the arts in Western Australia.

I'd further like to thank the script assessors at AFC, WAFC and ScreenWest for their feedback and service to writers, in particular Margaret Kelly and Victor Gentile, and to the WA chapter of the Australian Writers' Guild. Cheers Alan. I'd also like to thank Gwenda Marsh for teaching me to write for television and for making so much of it absolutely magical.

First published 2013 by
FREMANTLE PRESS
25 Quarry Street, Fremantle 6160
(PO Box 158, North Fremantle 6159)
Western Australia
www.fremantlepress.com.au

Also available as an ebook.

Consultant editor: Georgia Richter
Cover design: Ally Crimp
Cover photograph: 108178784 (RF) Cinema, Vetta Collection; photographer: Ferran Traite Soler
Printer: Everbest Printing Company, China

National Library of Australia
Cataloguing-in-Publication entry

Elliott, Ron, 1958–
Now showing / Ron Elliott
ISBN: 9781922089243 (pbk)

Fremantle Press is supported by the State Government through the Department of Culture and the Arts. Publication of this title was assisted by the Commonwealth Government through the Australia Council, its arts funding and advisory body.